TERMINATION OF SPECIES

Andrew Burt

ReAnimus Press

Breathing Life into Great Books

ReAnimus Press
1100 Johnson Road #16-143
Golden, CO 80402
www.ReAnimus.com

ISBN-13: 9780967298481 (Paperback)
9780967298498 (Hardback)

First edition: October, 2023

2309151244
10 9 8 7 6 5 4 3 2 1

For Laura

ACKNOWLEDGMENTS

I'd like to thank Ken Roberts, of the Northern Colorado Writers' Workshop, for the germ of the idea of the race, which arose during after-workshop convivialities; as well as for the concept of the epic nonfiction book he was working on, which he will recognize in morphed form herein, now having taking on Biblical proportions.

Thanks to all those who've read drafts and given feedback, in particular David Brin for his excellent comments; the good folks in the NCWW and Critters.org, notably C.S. Miller, Jen Cole, and especially Brandon Hatch for his extensive comments; and to the gang who've found themselves (willingly) Tuckerized in the following pages to benefit the Critters fund drive.

And as always, to Laura, with much love, for her unwavering support.

TERMINATION OF SPECIES

ANDREW BURT

We will now discuss in a little more detail the struggle for existence.

— Charles Darwin, *The Origin of Species*

CHAPTER 1

Looking back, perhaps love had been in the chill night air. Before Weston even met *her*, for some reason he couldn't explain, he played bishop to c4. Careful, safe, calculated, and not Weston's kind of game at all. And he had to credit that damn bastard Orring for meeting her.

That night, with Weston's legs dangling unbeknownst over the precipice of eternal love, his anonymous opponent responded with a tentative pawn on the queen's rook side. *Hm, Pawnking Cole. So you claim in real life you're a 3000+ Grandmaster – surely not old Kasymov. What do you think you're up to? Scared?* Something nagged Weston; maybe the rook. Foreshadows of his own heart being captured? Weston concentrated with his gut as he walked through the cold Denver night with purposeful speed. Knight to b5 threatening the rook? Maybe? His own queen was overworked, but he would have two passed pawns in the end game. Pawnking would have no clear play, and a material disadvantage. Make him squirm. What would Kasymov do? Slash and burn, go for the queen. But Weston was impatient, and it wasn't clear yet how to play Attila on this chess board. Weston shivered, picking his path along the ice-caked sidewalk; the chill air dried out his eyes as it seeped beneath the seal of his spex and he made every blink with a rasping pain. He blinked rapidfire moves in four other online games, weak master-level players all, decimating them, stalling himself for time. But deep down, he hated overanalyzing. It was as if his gut knew he would soon meet *her*. What the hell. Knight to b5.

That Denver night was quiet and calm; Weston saw only a dozen moonlit shadows on the 17 crosstown as it hummed by, dank vapors wisping from the sewer grates, only a handful of shoppers in Gil's itty-bitty Kwk-y-mrt, so quick it has no vowels, as Gil said. New York (where Weston was born, and lived in fits and spurts) may long have been the town that never slept—but Weston never thought that of Denver (where he'd lived at ages three, seven, eleven, and an eternal two years now since he'd clicked the big three-oh). Weston wished for the Denver nights of his childhood—graveyard silent—and reveled in those rare reprises, such as when it was frozen and foggy and miserably cold like tonight. Nobody to push and jostle you and maybe rip your spex off again. Respite from the physical world so you could get some shit done. Like pick up an order at Gil's for old Mrs. Nussbaum... if he played his cards right.

Weston tightened his parka and sat on the metal bench outside Gil's little market on 3rd Avenue, scuffing away the dusting of snow with a mittened hand. "Amigo," he said, tipping his spex at the other resident of the bench, a triple-sweater-and-half-ski-masked fellow sucking a wino-tube that vanished under the layers of grimy brown cardigans. The wino's limp arms lay sprawled, wrists up. An ad for Old DoubleBarrel beer flashed on the digital rouge on his forehead, bright herky-jerky SpringRoll dancers against neon backgrounds. The brash, tinny music was irritating, as designed. Probably the guy's Market ratings were so negative he couldn't get any joblets, with just enough disability pay to cover his spexfeed but could only wait for enough passersby to blink on his ads to silence the damn noise, so the wino could shuffle into Gil's to buy another refill slug for his tube. The man's spex were crackled with age marks and fastened around back with a chain-link of twisty-ties. Cheap African clothes, incompatible with his spex, the fibers blinking out of sync. Under the wino's d-rouge Weston could see his skin was covered with pustules from using the rouge for so many years. He jerked his head, either in returned greeting or from chronic Net Jag. Disgusting.

Weston tapped his foot furiously and concentrated on the games in his spex.

When playing chess, which was most of the time, Weston looked much like a young Humphrey Bogart, his eyebrows lifted in cocky calculation, cigarette dangling. Chess was his refuge since discovering it when he was eight. It moved portably, since his homes matched the spiral of his mother's wages—and spirit—from grand and glamorous to small and dumpy. But always there was chess. At nine he could beat anyone in person, and by twelve he harbored dreams of chess championships, of beating Garry Kasymov, the greatest to ever play the game. Weston's play was inspired and intuitive. Perhaps too much so. With their constant avoidance of landlords and collection agency stinkbots, and lack of a mentor, Weston never studied chess theory, relying solely on raw talent. Knowing, all the while, that talent without study was insufficient. He played anonymously to hide his shame. He pressed on like Icarus to see how high he could soar with talent and fearing the day he would find out. So far, with a global monetary structure pointed more like a thumb-tack than a pyramid, chess garnered him a few paltry meal-money dollars betting online, a buck or two to help his sister, and many glorious victories against lesser grandmasters. But not yet enough to earn him the courage to reveal himself, courage to say, I, Weston Foard, am no longer anonymous, I have arrived, play me.

That was always a wistful *someday*.

Weston took in a deep frozen breath. Just past four a.m. according to his spex. Ads for lotteries and ratings doctors scrolled by at a lazy two seconds apiece in his own spex, blinding colors clashing when superimposed on the wino's ads. He checked his Market cap. Feh. Down a hair from when he got up. At least Weston wouldn't stoop to wearing ad makeup.

Finished with his exhausting, smelly hour's stint in a suit of armor as a bouncer at the Microboozer and his stomach growling so loud he couldn't think, he'd stopped by Gil's to grab a couple milkboxes of Wheatios for himself. But there was no such thing as a free breakfast. Learn to count the cards, his dad had said; so Weston studied his neighbors in his South Denver walkup: Half an hour, if he toughed it out, and the old widow Nussbaum who lived below him would up-blink an order for anchovies, light rye, and dry cat food to the Market that he could piggyback on and scrape a few bucks for the delivery. Unless that bastard Orring Lepri aced him again. But hah! — Not if he sat here. Weston could sweeten his bid. *Mrs. Nussbaum*, he could say, *on that bid #27A8HH6F6 — I'm standing outside Gil's right now, you'll save five minutes...* Weston smiled. Winning was great. Rook to d7.

But half an hour! Weston adjusted his spex' polarity so he could just barely see the light snow flakes falling, tipped his head back against the waves of icy, arctic death emanating from the brick waiting to take anyone to the hereafter who tarried too long. He wondered dreamily where old Kasymov was out there, the three-time comeback Champ, whom Weston would love to beat, and wished he would someday be good enough to beat, and on account of whose half-century of Goliath-like stature in the chess world Weston chose as his own anonymous online moniker, David. Gameboard visions of mate dancing in his head, Weston set to finishing up his quota of iron ore dumping in West Virginia. A couple of the roboloaders collided while he was distracted with the cold and the chess, but he could explain that. Dog ran through or something. Job didn't pay shit anyway. He waldoed the steamshovel to clean up the mess one had spilled tipping over and blocking the second. He uprighted the loader, and set both back on their paths while waiting for his opponent to retreat to protect his king.

Damn, it was cold out here if you sat still. The snot in his nose was ice. -10C, said his spex. Old Gil was heartless; his five buck a minute "floor charge" kept buzzflies like him waiting outside. So, the lesson was clear: Don't sit still. Death awaits. Weston bopped back up and jogged in place, batting his mittened hands together.

God how he hated exercising. But death claimed his father young, three grandparents, over half his great-grandparents: all heart disease. Bad deal at the gene table. He visualized himself tubed-up in a hospital bed, seeping away like them. Weston's doctors—back when he was a kid and his mother could afford such—told him bluntly: Exercise or Die. He hated every minute of it, but empty black death—a lot scarier.

Gotta kick those Goddamned genes's ass, he thought. *Hate those genes*. Run, run. He jogged till he could hardly breathe. He bent over double, hands on hips. His muscles never developed much despite the endless work. It was always a struggle. It felt like a struggle against death. Ugh! What next? Can't stand still. *Where's that order, Mrs. Nussbaum? Come on!* He dreaded more exertion. But, the alternative—

Off with the mittens. Above the warm glowing window filled with ads was a little half-brick-wide ledge where they'd dug in the steel bars. Weston tippy-toed and gripped the ledge by his fingertips, pulled himself upwards with a whoof. Down; up; down. *Going. To. Beat. Those. Genes.* Genes were a damn good player. Damnit, he was going to live to old age. *Can't. Give. In.* Chin ups were—how'd the slogan go?—were good for the Body, that was good for the Soul, and that was good for the Market. Up down up; that, and if he kept his spex on the job, Weston could forget the cold. Ha! His opponent was probing Weston's pawn structure, didn't see the noose tightening. Queen to g3.

When he finished hosing down the roboloaders (they hosed each other down, but Weston liked to think he was essential; at least, in between chess moves), half and hour plus five, and Mrs. Nussbaum's order for anchovies and cat food still hadn't materialized on the Market—that's when he realized the Market was chewing him up and spitting him out, just like the old stock market ate his mother. Well, his father too, in a different way, but being a "professional" gambler the old man pretty much chewed himself up before he died; different sort of market. Same result.

Weston paused, looked at his hands, trembling white from the cold and blotchy red from the exertion; long thin fingers, his wiry body the gristle the market spit out. At thirty-two, he looked like Humphrey Bogart at fifty, sans cigarette. The Market did that. It had to be fed, constantly, a vast hungry beast the size of a planet, eating people like Wheatios and spitting out a tangle of bone and cartilage. Just as it ground up his mother, when "the market" meant only stocks, bonds, securities; when they spoke of "the market" in lower case. Libby Foard had been a stock broker. MBA from NYU. Harvard Law Review. Made the big times at Goldman Sachs. Three bedroom penthouse on the Upper East Side. Oak parquet floors made from planks of sunken galleons. Honduran mahogany cabinets and Cararra marble, both kitchen and bath. Power lunches at Sardis; on the company. Solid gold berets in her golden hair like tiaras. Laughing all day, rosy cheeked, never stressed, smug even, because she'd already made a killing in pre-session trading in the morning, before the market opened for the peons.

It took Weston years to understand her downfall, how the market gnawed her face to a gaunt skeleton, then crunched her bones until she was so thin and frail like a barren wintry tree she couldn't look anyone in the eye. Now Weston saw it in the mirror every morning. Couldn't run from it. Cursed, like her. Mother and son, neither of them were *quick*. Facts needed to simmer. Stacked daintily like building a house of cards. Fill a slot there; then *pop*—the right decision— buy Microsoft at 82.10, Intel at 107—techs were in for an up day; dump Pfizer, bad news from Brazil. 24/7 trading killed that. No time to think, and she'd withered.

Now the Market was everything, soup to nuts and the kitchen sink. Literally. Want hand soap, buck a bar? Too late, sold. Think fast. Don't think. Gimmenow order, two bucks. React, react, react. The quick or the dead, pick one.

As if it was listening to his thoughts, his personal carbon scrubber went *pling!*, announcing it built another microdiamond from CO_2 scrubbed from the air. Great, waited just until he'd left, or he could have turned it in for some cred for breakfast.

Weston almost bagged it right then. To hell with Mrs. Nussbaum. He'd take a stand, show you he didn't need the Market. Maybe join that big netless commune in Antarctica. But damn—he needed the money.

It wouldn't be giving in if he hung around another five. Outsmarting the Market was never *giving in*. Besides, Pawnking just said, "back in five." Must be sweating.

He jogged in place for five on the brittle concrete. Checked his watch. Come on, Mrs. Nussbaum. He barely lost a prime gig as a river guide when the terrorist group de jour blew a dam upstream and the gig was canceled; fucking Cyberistas. Luddite green ecoterrorists using technology to try to blow civilization back to the middle ages. What was so fucking great about the middle ages? Another five jumping rope until he was nearly hyperventilating. Still no order. No Pawnking. Damn these slackers. Another five of pushups?

Nuh-uh. No, fuck it, enough's enough and he spat frozen spit as if the Market cared. Pawnking inched a pawn forward. Shit, he wasn't supposed to do that. Weston punched his own arm; he shouldn't have waited, he should have been snug and warm by now, then this idiot wouldn't have moved his pawn. Damn it, of course he'd been giving in. Right now it felt like a cardinal sin: Don't wait for the Market to come to you, go after the Market. He should never have thought he could wait for Old Mrs. Nussbaum to place an order. Hell, what if she'd packed it in last night? Fool. Wait and you're bait. Tenacity was all well and good, and though Weston would never admit it, he was nothing if not fearlessly tenacious, with jaws of a pit bull—from his mother's side—and he hated to let go a "sure thing." One lover called him that, a pit bull, but one who leaped about wildly biting after every shadow that moved. To his mind he wasn't undisciplined; rather, he always credited his success with balancing that persistence with knowing when to cut and run—his father's side. So what if he cut and ran more often than some people liked? The decision computed in an instant: Tenacity was overrated. Just grab your damn Wheatios and snooze/lose/fuck you, world. This ain't your grandparents' millennium.

Weston spat again, stamped the snow off his feet entering Gil's, thought open the fridger, grabbed a couple Wheatios packets, snatched the anchovies and cat food anyway, waved his old school cashcard while he eye-dragged the slider bar to the customary 'excellent' rating for the store's portfolio, tipped his imaginary hat to old Gil sitting on a barstool grunting around with a farm of joysticks on his lap like they used to swing construction cranes, and hustled homeward. Calm and quiet, who needed that? Don't get soft; what was he thinking? Kid stuff. On the way he snapped off the Spoonio, pulled the milk ripcord, munched his breakfast steaming in the cold, nudged his own pawn forward one, and turned up the gain on his top Market prospects with a double-blink.

It was one of those Sunday five a.m.'s when the Market was especially buzzing. Excellent. Action was the best medicine. What were the AI curators offering as his best bets? Tour guide needed to trawl a bunch of Chinese tourists around the wreck of the Titanicus in the Marianas Trench; paid 150 flat, 7.5 docent rating required. Read bedtime stories to a pair of twins in Johannesburg, reading rating 10+ needed, funny voice rating 3+, sexoffender rating of zero point zero, paid two per second until the kids were in theta sleep. Balloon payment for filtering network intrusion reports to try to trace the Cyberistas; real identity verification required. Weed whacking a castle in Scotland with a robotrimmer. A billion job-ops a second, 24/7. Weston's filtered, prioritized selections usually slowed down mid-weekend, not just because he was sometimes old-fashioned and liked to think Saturday and Sunday were special somehow, but because a lot of other folks were foolish old sentimentalists too. There was always a bit of Monday pre-rush, but there was more buzz today than usual. Something going down but who knew what. Somebody knew. The Market knows all. But not Weston, bottom of the food chain. Weston saw the crushing pyramid of unfairness above him. Ah, well. And in his Don't-I-Wish queue, backup vocalist for Cher®'s Calcutta concert tonight, five percent of net, suborbital to pick up ASAP. Cher®, obfuscatedly related to a 20th century singer (who knew how?), looking ancient as the hills yet hot and still a hit. Weston marveled at that kind of talent. Only in chess did he have the remotest possibility of such fame, but there's no money there, unless you could beat Kasymov. Maybe in ten years, if the old guy hung around; or maybe if the old guy kicked it.

Weston thought twice about bidding on the Marianas deal as he yanked open the warped gunmetal door to his complex on the fourth heave. A few straggling mother-of-pearl digipaint flecks plinked off his hair. Long before he'd moved in someone dented the hell out of the door trying to find the digipaint's controller and finally smashed it, no doubt pissed off at some ad it displayed. The landlord never repainted. People thought Weston was just living in squalor like any decent struggling artist. He couldn't explain to the silent ones that no, he wasn't much of an artist, but he wasn't ashamed of facing deprivation to help his sister. Winnie had been injured not long after his mother died, vegetative after being hit by a drunk driver. Her vivacious spark snuffed by a selfish jerk, back before self-driving cars began saving so many lives. He sent all he could to make her life comfortable and fund in his small way research into repairing her smashed brain. From his own perspective, he was doing very well. And someday he'd beat Kasymov, and that would be that. Marianas was crappy pay, but he liked the jobs where he'd meet interesting people. At least it wasn't an in-person, like the skanky-suited bouncer job. In-person sucked, since everybody who was anybody went VirtuPersonal, and Weston liked to collect people. Not the dregs who hung out with other real people, *interesting* people. That was from his father's side: Know the players at the table. Then at night if he couldn't sleep Weston could slip on his spex and replay them, read their faces, looking for clues. Why hadn't the Norwegian tipped him after the ten minute White House tour? Did he need to tune a rule in his Humphrey Bogart-atar, turn down the corners of the mouth, not smile so much for Scandinavians? Crinkle the eyes more for Thai women? He especially liked using his Bogart image for VPs. He'd constructed the avatar's image to confuse; any customer who overlaid his Bogart in their spex with an image of the real Bogart would see so many differences they often asked, "Is this what you really look like IP, are you really related to Humphrey Bogart?" Especially the women. He never lied, yet never confessed that though unrelated, he actually looked *more* like Bogart than the avatar, albeit without the frequent puffy red Spexeye and yeah, he needed a hair cut. He just winked. Rook takes pawn.

But in the end, he only toyed with the Marianas gig, let the time expire, even though it had been a generous thirty seconds — they must have been desperate, and might have bumped the pay if he'd bid it higher. Truth was, he was tired, and that was real. Pawnking finally moved.

Weston resigned. That ought to piss off anyone placing side bets on his game. Eighteen moves ahead Weston could see that he was the sure winner, but it would probably take Pawnking a painful half hour to realize he'd lost. A nice long twenty minute nap would do him wonders. Weston sent Pawnking a list of the inevitable moves, just so he could stew on it and know he'd been beaten by a master so grand he didn't even need to score it as a victory. Too bad Pawnking wasn't Kasymov; there was beauty in those moves. Yet deep down Weston knew Kasymov hadn't the faintest clue to his existence, a patzer, a dilettante with no official player rating, just bouncing about the anonymous net chess lounges. But someday... someday...

Punching his code into the stairwell — the waveby reader hadn't worked for years — he yawned in weary anticipation of a nap. He took the stairs three at a time, the spare Wheatios packet sloshing in his parka. But he paused at the landing below his. It wouldn't take but a moment to pay an in-person to old Mrs. Nussbaum. Score a delivery for lunch, maybe. That would go a long way toward paying for dinner.

He poked his head into the hallway and back out with the quickness of a sewing machine needle. Empty. He squared his shoulders and pushed confidently into the corridor redolent of stale cooking oils.

Mrs. Nussbaum's door opened before Weston could ring. Her wrinkled face filled his vision, spexless, wearing her crummy old contacts, which wouldn't have a tenth the power of a pair of spex. Weston felt sorry for her.

"Oh, hello, Mr. Foard. So nice to see you."

"Good morning, Mrs. Nussbaum. I thought you might be ordering your usual today, so I picked it up just in case."

She looked back over her shoulder. "Oh, that's so kind of you, but my order's already been filled. Perhaps another time. Not tomorrow, though, or the day after. My daily pension deposit doesn't go far." She looked back over her shoulder again.

Weston handed her the anchovies, bread, cat food and patted her wrinkly hand. "You keep these, then," he said. "For a rainy day."

Christ. Suddenly Orring was coming out of her door, laughing.

"Thanks for the tip, Mrs. N., you're too kind! No, no, my pleasure. You take care now." He gave a small bow as her door closed, then nearly bumped into Weston, but not close enough to ruffle his golden pinpoint oxford dress shirt. He pulled back in such a natural way it made Weston look like the oaf who'd cause the near collision. "Well, hey, Weston. Wrong floor for you, isn't it? Not looking for me, were you?" Orring's raised chin made even a simple question an insult.

Damn that fucking arrogant asshole, he must have scored a long term deal with Mrs. Nussbaum when Weston wasn't watching. "Don't pee your spex, Orring. Just going to offer Mrs. Nussbaum a cheaper rate on her deliveries." Not that that would injure Orring. Not that he even could underprice him. Orring would probably bid for payment in jellybeans to spite someone like Weston. God, he might even bid it as charity. Then con her for triple what Weston would have, and she'd be glad to pay it. The devil was like that. Word was he earned a Ph.D. in computational molecular biology, a generalist in the field of high-frequency radio-elastic protein-protein switching matrices, as if that was a field wide enough to be a generalist in, though chances were he was so specialized he couldn't even explain the birds and the bees. Word was, he just slummed it on these local IP jobs because he liked the constant rush of winning a bid. Those big ol' science orders on the Market were usually for a couple entire weeks of work at a time. Though ten, fifteen years older than Weston, and balding with a trim blond beard gone to graying that made him look past fifty, Orring obviously adapted to the hurly-burly 24/7 instant economy like a ten year old. His spex fairly crackled with a dozen simultaneous transactions. Yet Weston could feel Orring's probing eyes on him through the spex, eyes so alert and merciless they actually *had* turned his own mother in for petty tax evasion. Twice. Weston believed firmly that you are what you make yourself; here was a fellow who'd made himself evil.

"Well, knock yourself out with Mrs. Nussbaum. I saved her life; told her to avoid the NetBetics insulin pump—last week Cyberistas killed half the people using 'em. Like the new suit she insisted on buying me? GoogieSoft-Armani. Any color, pattern, and texture you want. Feel the fibers." Orring rubbed the silky fabric of the sleeve seductively between his fingers.

"Careful your cuffs don't brush the ground, Orring. I hear those GoogieSofts don't clean shit up like you'd think."

Orring said something, no doubt a lethal barb, and perhaps patted Weston on the shoulder as he went by. Another power trip; the power guy walks away first.

Weston didn't notice.

His dreams suddenly came true.

He didn't even notice Garry Kasymov's agent was pinging, a crusty old man, urgent realtime audio-video requested, subject "GK requests match, ten million, winner take all." All he could hear were harps and the smell of flowers.

Weston's heart stopped—but not for that reason: Across the hall, she—*that* she—an angel in golden hair and hazel eyes—floated from her door as if carried aloft by coachmen, to the trash chute, deposited a dainty bag of trash, smiled—*smiled*—at him oh so briefly, and wafted like a celestial princess back into her Elysian palace. He'd never seen her before, had no idea of her netaddress, name, shoe size, anything. Just that she was the most heavenly creature on earth or above. Her door clicked shut, a click with the musical beauty of a symphony's last note.

When Weston's heart returned to beating he heard it pounding like a train running doubletime. He couldn't understand what just happened. His first thought *hadn't* been how he could leverage his ratings with a merger, as, he thought, his lizard-brain genes should have mandated; no, his first thought was that he wanted to spend the rest of his life with her. He didn't know her at all—what on earth possessed him to think something like that?

CHAPTER 2

Father Chris Giordano surveyed the street performers from the open air café along La Ramblas. Human statues, frozen until animated when a passersby blinked them a small sum: A silver mermaid caught by—or catching?—a silver fisherman; a museum caveman; a tree; a Roman emperor in marble; a winged angel in bronze. A group of children in white wearing floaterfeet zipped playfully around the human statues, as if little angels. Lovers at tables under white umbrellas sipped from giant, shared glasses of Sangria. Through shared spex views publicly transmitted by those around it, Chris could see workers atop the bee-hive curves of Gaudi's Sagrada Familia cathedral, held aloft on pillars supported by turtles, ministered to by blocky stone people. He could see inside up through the tree-like columns blocking the stained glass like a forest, and the raised, austere altar where a service was being conducted. Gazing the other way with his spex at maximum magnification, Chris could see with his own eyes, at the far end of the street, Christopher Columbus towering above the tourists by the bustling docks, pointing the way to the new world.

There was important work to be done here. God had called him to Barcelona.

And Cardinal Canini called him to Rome. Chris sighed and blinked an acknowledgment to the cardinal's office that he would be there soonest. Now what roadblock did the cardinal have in mind for Chris and Project Job? No matter. If God wanted Chris to continue to find the modern day Jobs, then Chris would find the way.

He removed his spex and continued to listen to the woman sitting beside him at the café table. The sun warmed his hands as they lay flat on the table. Chris guiltily ignored the accumulated list of confession requests from the Market. He hoped it hadn't looked too rude or arrogant to don his spex in the middle of her story; the spexless were understandably sensitive about such things. He needed these untouchables to open up and tell their stories, not clam up.

"Used to have a pair of Chanel," she said with a nod to his spex, her Spanish accent identifying her as probably born in the upper class, and fallen on hard times—exactly the kind of candidate Chris was looking for. "I keep thinking I should blink in to the library. To look for my daughter, you know? But all the good databases are pay."

Chris would liked to have shared his spex, but he'd learned the hard way not to interfere with those whom God chose for affliction. But God couldn't fault Chris for sharing a small appetizer. "Here, Carmen Elena, some tapas. The chicken ones are good—good protein. How did you lose those spex?" he asked, nonchalantly. That was a key question. He couldn't outright say he was looking for what, in his mind, were the most exemplary of all people on the earth; but if she were being tested by God, this is probably where it would spill out.

She didn't touch the tapas. "The spex? Oh, they were the last to go. I'd lost everything else first. No one would even steal them for fear of the RodeTanden. I woke up one morning, not far from here. It was raining, and I'd been delirious with the RodeTanden. I was weak. Wet. Lying against a bakery. I went to blink up a weather forecast, since the rain was running into my eyes. Then I realized, through my fever, that the rain was running into my eyes *because* I had no spex. It was nothing. I'd lost the service months before. I'd only kept wearing them to shade the sun and because it kept people from looking away from me when I walked down the sidewalk. But now with my flesh falling off from RodeTanden, it doesn't matter, si?"

Chris nodded with sadness. He involuntarily glanced down at his own spex, lying on the table, which were recording Carmen's tale for later. He noted that she made no pretense to cover up the scabs and open sores from RodeTanden. "RodeTanden, that's one of the new plagues from the Amazon Accident, isn't it? How did you catch it?"

The waiter brought them their coffees. Chris began to order sangrias, but she stopped him; coffee. The waiter curled his lip at Chris's choice of guest, but Chris just smiled and thanked him loudly.

"Si, from the dying of the rainforest, the Amazon Efflorescence—La Floración. So many new sicknesses. How? Oh, the usual way. Untested fish. When you're on the street and there's a perfectly good fish that gets tossed into the recycle bin behind a restaurant, you don't start looking around for a test swab." She smiled, showing her blood-red teeth from the RodeTanden.

"So this was after you lost your financial situation?"

"Of course. You don't think I'd ever have eaten untested fish before? No, no. I hardly ate fish, but what we did eat was from our own private farm on the estate."

That was typical in Chris's candidates, the loss of fortune before loss of health. It followed the biblical pattern.

"What did you do before? I don't recognize your name."

"Were you here five years ago?" she asked.

"No. I'm rarely in one place very long. I've been around the earth two or three times in the last five years."

"Good for you. The scandal here was... a brief flame. My father and uncle owned one of the largest wineries in Spain. I ran the charitable foundation branch of the business, teaching nutritional literacy. After they and my husband were killed when their suborbital burned up, it was discovered that the books had been fixed and someone was adding engineered flavanols into the wine. The climate, you see. The grapes lost their charm so they had been secretly repairing them. To taste like they used to, like people remembered. They had to hide the costs of these repairs. All to bring joy to people, to make the wine taste how it was supposed to. How is that a crime? The company was ruined. I was implicated, as the only living relative. I fought to save the foundation. I wanted it split off from the rest, but the naysayers thought I was doing this for personal gain. So I said I would resign if they left the foundation alone. I did—but they shut everything down. Everything was lost. It was as if an evil settled on my family. I was sick to see the foundation closed. I thought we had done some good for society."

Chris nodded, unconsciously checking for the green dot of the food chemical composition correctness sniffer in his spex. "Here, please, I can't possibly eat all this." He placed a tapas on her plate as he ate one himself, the rich ham and olive taste filling his mouth.

"You must have been very angry. Did the Church help in your solace?" Another key question. Most of the time it elicited comments about how they became furious with God and would have nothing to do with the church. Job got upset, but he never cursed God. Complaints, even wishing God would leave them alone, which was fine; but not abandoning the Lord. He knew from Father Abascal that she was devout now, but if she had some period of renouncing God, that was that. Though they may have nonetheless been good people, ones who ever renounced God were not the ones Project Job sought.

She finished the tapas and Chris put another on her plate. He dared not feed her a complete meal; one candidate, Dirk in Copenhagen, had been hit by an autobus after a meal with Chris. It may have been coincidence, but Chris sided with caution after that. If they were truly modern day Jobs, then they would not be offended at his lack of hospitality.

Carmen left the smoked ham croquette on her plate to answer him. "Si, the Church. I went to my church after Diego, Papa, and Tio Fernando were killed. Father Carrion seemed to think we all sinned, and I was only welcome in the bread line once a month. I explained I was sure it was not Papa's or their fault. I never trusted the accountant, and anyone could have put in the flavanols. He all but kicked me out of the parish."

"Ah. And that was when you were mad at God?"

"'Happy is the man whom God correcteth,' Father," she quoted. "I was never mad at God." She shrugged. "He has a plan. I found Father Abascal instead."

Quoting Job—a sign! And Father Abascal had spoken highly of Carmen Elena. Word had made it back to Chris; many were sympathetic to his project and sent him tips. "I wish I could help you, Carmen Elena, but I have nothing to offer, only to take. You have given me plenty, for which I can't repay you but with that tapas."

"De nada, it is nothing. It is a shame I cannot find my daughter, Alma, but that too must be God's will."

Chris frowned. That almost sounded greedy, fishing for reciprocation, and not characteristic of the Jobs of the world. He imagined her daughter having been kidnapped off the street. Or worse. Nonetheless, to Chris's stubborn mind, an "ideal" Project Job candidate, afflicted at God's will, would not ask for help, even for a lost child. He shrugged. "I regret I can't help." He looked self-consciously at his spex—but he dared not. "I'll tell you what. If I run across word of her in my travels, I will send to Father Abascal. What happened to her?"

"Alma, she's with God now. She was killed in the earthquake four years ago. Terrible; so many people died. The spexless shelter collapsed on us. I was put in hospital. They were not keeping close track of where they buried some people—who cared, they were only spexless. Perhaps there is some database that records it; I spend what money comes my way on searching. I just want to put some flowers on her grave."

Chris put his hand on her arm. This was, unfortunately, an unexpected bonus: It was typically hard to find Job members again since they were almost all spexless; yet Carmen had a link he could use. "If I find anything, I will let you know. Stay in touch with Father Abascal."

She maintained her positive attitude even in the face of catastrophic desolation. That beatific smile. Chris had no doubt Carmen was a Job.

He had a line on another candidate Job in Peru, but first he must deal with Cardinal Canini and his ominous demand to return to Rome.

CHAPTER 3

K's agent had called, Kasymov's agent, God's agent, Weston's dream instantiated — and all Weston wanted to do was think about a girl. They would play a match, sure, sure, fine, whatever —

She lived below him and two doors down; a knight's jump away. Weston's thoughts drifted to her every time he moved his knight in a game. Chess was designed all wrong. It shouldn't be about protecting the King, but about the King and Queen as powerful pieces protecting a new piece, the Princess. In fairy tales, men always fought for the princess, not for their king.

—but my *God*, he was going to play *Kasymov*. And human against human, not Advanced Chess, no help from software or teams, mano-a-mano, him against the greatest ever, just two brains battling it out. He couldn't think about a girl, not now. Focus, Weston, he told himself. Practice. Prepare.

Pawn takes Black's knight. What would Kasymov do? Weston quickly intoned a voice-over for a Grand Conquistador car ad — self-drive so quiet and smooth you feel you're in the clouds — imagining as he did so that the Black knight he'd just captured was her suitor, and he'd paved the way for himself. *Her* suitor. He didn't even know her name. He riffled through a stack of Kasymov's games in his spex. The answer was in there; what Kasymov would do if he, Weston, just captured his knight. At least he knew Kasymov's name, he wasn't some anonymized grandmaster; his games were an open book. Kasymov would set up a trap to open up his queen side, maybe make a play for his rook. Five moves ahead, there it was. He'd done much the same in Kasymov vs. Stoneham ten years ago. An insistent red flashing reminded him that an ore roboloader was stuck.

Weston sighed and unstuck the sprawled creature. What was *she* doing right now, he wondered? Watching and old flattie film on her spex—no, she would be more old-fashioned, watching it on a roll-down wall screen. Something romantic. Casablanca. Fine. Nine moves ahead, Weston would have Kasymov's queen for a bishop, and Kasymov would resign.

He checked his move against the cruddy public Kasymov simulator. Allegedly the simulator was a fusion of an old chess AI with an illegal memcopy made of Kasymov during a brief hospital stay. Weston shivered at the thought someone would steal a memcopy; it made him think of Kasymov as dead. At any rate, Kasymov was very much alive and the simulator seemed to predict the same results when fed Kasymov's earlier games.

Arrgh! It was a trap. Eighteen moves ahead, Kasymov's sacrificed queen led to mate. Concentrate! he told himself. You can beat this guy, you can! You're good enough. Just need to study more. Unless he was right and it was the simulator that was wrong. He sighed; if only he could remove his doubts by getting access to GoogieSoft's MS. GRAY simulator, 99% accurate in prediction (too bad the GoogieSoft team who wrote MS. GRAY didn't know what to *do* with the accurate prediction, but, hey, their loss).

Weston was certain, in his own mind, that he could beat Garry Kasymov, the greatest to ever play the game. Kasymov almost lost that distinction to the machines, after a long series of lost and drawn matches. But by the time the bickering stopped and rules for software participation in tournament play were finalized to allow humans and machines equal resources—books, advisors, any resources a player, a *team* really, wanted to provide—by then, Kasymov had found his confidence. "At first they played so strange, so alien," he said of software chess systems. "Finally I realized I didn't need to understand *them*. My own play was good enough." And he'd never lost a title match since. At 78, he seemed even stronger than when he'd already been labeled the best ever, better than Carlsen, Kasparov, Capabanca, Lasker, Fischer, Alekhine. He'd become, in fact, so assured that his backers now matched huge sums of money to anyone would could beat him. Ten million, his agent had offered Weston. Weston knew he was the one. He could topple The King.

But damnit, only if he could study. His Market filter was flashing high priority jobs at him like a burst gun. Big pay! Easy work! Help a Nigerian retrieve money he'd invested 200 years ago with Bank of England that he could now access because of a time machine—now there was a classic. And every time his eyes roamed over a knight on one of his chess boards, he thought of *her*—her playful eyes, the knowing smile that said she knew just what he was thinking, that they were tuned to the same wavelength, the way she tossed her hair back that said she brooked no nonsense from people.

No! Not now. He didn't have time for romance; not even plain sex. If only Kasymov's agent hadn't... but this was what he'd waited years for. Damn that Kasymov—he was the master of psychological play. He probably *knew* Weston was distracted. Perhaps he'd even arranged for her—No, that was lunacy.

He was so tormented Weston physically wrenched at his hair where it protruded around his spex. Must study! Ten million—he'd be set comfortably for life. All the good he could do for Winnie! But only if he won. Zip if he lost. Disgrace. Number two was the biggest loser.

He stared at the knight. Forced himself to see a knight, not her apartment, a knight's jump away, himself knocking on the door, a bottle of wine in his arm, a fire crackling, cinnamon-scented candles—

Arrgh! He couldn't concentrate. And the damn roboloader was stuck again, and the voice-over people demanded a line *right now* for a live spot, and they'd never give him another line again and would report him as a Cyberista if he didn't blink his ass over right now. He was going to have to quit those jobs.

That was it. He marched down the beaten concrete steps and knocked boldly right smack on her door. He bit the inside of his cheek. A group of teenage kids in ad-painted balloon pants giggled by. Their rainbow hair dragged on the ground, crackling with static-powered audio of an old baseball game. "Buy some Joe, Joe?" one of the girls asked, and they all erupted into hand-over-mouth laughter. Inside joke? Or were they laughing at him? This was crazy. He shouldn't have come. But her eyes... her eyes...

Holy Christmas, her *eyes!*—she hadn't been wearing spex! He quickly whipped his off and shoved them into his baggy pocket, tried to rub out the red creases on his forehead that never went away. He'd imagined her so intimately he hadn't realized she wore no spex. What if she was some kind of retro-weirdo, only went out with spexless guys... Or was a recovering Jaggie; maybe this was even a half-way house—

She opened the door. An angelic vision. With pink spex on. "Oh, hi," she said, pausing briefly as if to match up his face. "You're the guy who delivers for Mrs. Nussbaum sometimes, aren't you?"

Weston felt sheepish without his spex, twisted his hands in his pockets, but decided against the embarrassed move of putting them on. "Uh..." Shit, he couldn't think of what to say. All his rehearsed lines vanished, light years away on a display in his spex. Knocked on the wrong door, oops? No, would make him look stupid. I live above you and heard a noise? But she'd find out that was a lie; he lived a knight's jump away.

While he gyrated she pocketed her spex and deftly slipped on a lightweight green sweater that brought out the little flecks of green in her hazel eyes. She tucked the sweater into her black racing sweatpants. "Yeah, you're Orring's friend, right?" she asked.

Orring's *friend*? She couldn't know how deeply that was an ax-blow to his heart. But it shook him from his confusion. Play like Kasymov. Bold. Slashing. Attacking. "Hi—I'm Weston Foard from upstairs, and I thought maybe you were new to the building. I was just going down to Little Jakarta to get some Sambal Ikan Bilis, and I know this is forward, but I was wondering—"

She giggled. "I bet you blink that line at all the new girls in the building, don't you? Just kidding, it sounds great. I'm Jasmina Simonis. I was going for a run anyway." She cocked her head, a daring smile on her face. "Think you can keep up?"

Jasmina. An angel named Jasmina. He'd said "Sure, uh, you bet," and she'd jogged past him before he realized what he'd committed to: Twenty kilometers in freezing temperatures over snow and ice. Running. In these lame-ass sneakers. His mind cried, "Uh... wait..." but Jasmina was already at the end of the hall, the door creaking open. Okay, Weston—fish or cut bait? Was she worth it?

He sucked up his breath and jogged after her.

CHAPTER 4

Chris arrived in Rome tired. The oppressive gray clouds above only made him wearier. The train ride was long, with frequent stops, too bouncy to sleep well. With fewer people practicing Catholicism than ever, only cardinals could expect a hop on a suborbital and not even all bishops managed a jet.

Cardinal Guiseppe Canini kept Chris waiting on the hard backless bench outside his office in the Vatican. Already over an hour, despite the scheduled appointment time. Several times Chris saw the cardinal through his door. The cardinal saw Chris as well, and flashed his pious smile.

Another cardinal left his office, Canini shaking his hand vigorously. Chris overheard him speak to his secretary; the cardinal had no other appointments today. The cardinal nodded, and ambled back into his office. Chris straightened, mentally preparing to go in.

It was nonetheless another hour before the secretary looked up at Chris, almost looking above Chris's head, though it was hard to tell through the frosted spex. "His Eminence will see you now." He ushered Chris in.

The cardinal was mixing a drink at a hidden bar beside his work table. The cardinal was a large, round man, and oofed into his comfortable ergo-chair when he sat. His skin was fleshy soft, almost puffy.

"Sit, my boy, sit."

My boy. The cardinal was younger than Chris, fifty to Chris's fifty-one. With the cardinal sitting at his table, the only seat was the sparse rigid chair in front of it. The cardinal followed Chris's eyes to the alcove with the luxurious leather couches and delicious danishes sitting on the end tables. Canini's spex were nearly translucent, so you could see his blue eyes as they stared hard at you.

"Tell me, Christian Agnostikos. Do you feel an affinity to the people you study? Do you feel you are like Job, yourself?"

Chris hated it when the cardinal used his full name. It was a cruelty his mother had visited on him, choosing Agnostikos, "agnostic," "not knowing," as his middle name. His Italian father chose "Chris," planning for it to be short for "Cristoforo," but his mother erupted in a Greek fury and said if his father wished him named for Christ, she would name him for Agnosticism; and his father changed his mind, that therefore his first name should be Christian, and with a slamming of doors, Chris was named. Having a repudiation of religion as his middle name made him the butt of jokes in school and seminary; but for better or worse, it made him more inquisitive. There were many things he did not know.

He did not fancy himself a Job. Though if he was, Cardinal Canini was certainly an instrument of his torment.

"I am terribly blessed, Your Eminence. To be able to do the Lord's bidding, with the Holy Father's blessing... I can think of no greater reward." He scowled inwardly as the cardinal briefly raised his eyebrows. He didn't mean to rub it in that Pope Paul VII himself approved the Job Project. Okay, yes he did mean to rub it in. Forgive me Father; tomorrow.

"Hmm. I'm conferencing in Monsignor di Fuoco, from the budget office—"

Chris's spex blipped with a holo conference request. He blinked ok and Msgr. di Fuoco appeared, tight-faced, wispy hair, thick dark goatee, nodding in acknowledgment. Chris's heart raced.

"Welcome, Monsignor. Monsignor di Fuoco is helping the Holy Father prioritize all our affairs; determine where best to allocate our limited resources. Monsignor?"

"Gratzi, Your Eminence. So: how many of these 'perfect people' have you found, Father Giordano?"

"With another yesterday, twenty-seven, Monsignor." He felt blindsided. He knew the Holy Father was very ill, very weak. Not seen in public for weeks now. He'd have to be careful here. He opened his palms to surreptitiously wipe them on his trousers. A crow cawed on a nearby windowsill.

Msgr. di Fuoco spoke. "In all the world, in all the excursions the Church has paid for you in the last ten years, you've only found twenty-seven? People you can't even document as existing, yes? Why should we not doubt the veracity of this mission of yours? Even the Holy Father may weary of this. At last report you didn't even have a *title* for this purported book of yours. Why do we continue this charade, Father?"

"I'm happy to report I do have a title, your Eminence. *Modern Jobs: Lessons for Humanity.* As the title indicates, the purpose of Project Job is not to *do* anything with these poor people, Monsignor. You know that. It is to document their lives so that we all may learn from them. To study what it is in them that they withstand the blistering attacks of evil and yet do not repudiate God. Surely if we can learn from them the source of their, almost, yes, 'perfection' as you call it, we can all glorify God better ourselves. Greatness doesn't lie in winning battles or elections. *These* are the greatest humans on earth. We must study them to better ourselves, or we are not doing all we can to praise God." He sensed they were not pleased. "I will also be authoring a book of their lives, that Christians and non-Christians alike may improve their own lives and come to find Christ. These people are nothing short of miraculous, Eminence, Monsignor. They are almost direct proof of God's existence." This last he knew was pure spin; he couldn't say that he simply had a *feeling* that something big was coming and that these people were somehow crucial. He couldn't say he himself was unsure of God's existence any more, only that these modern Jobs were critical to humankind's very survival. None of which heresy could he speak. He spread his hands in a shrug. "People can't help but be inspired."

"Yes. No doubt. But it is time you began writing that book, I think. I am appointing Monsignor di Fuoco your Ordinary. You will take up residency in Convitto San Tommaso. If God means for you to find more of these Jobs, they will come to you. We also need a list of your Jobs and their whereabouts. The authorities believe some are terrorists and we have pledged our cooperation."

Chris interrupted, "I can't break my vow of privacy with them. These are good people, not terrorists. To round them up would be—" he wanted to say 'a sin' but thought better of telling a cardinal what was and wasn't a sin. "It could destroy what little is left of their lives, as well as undermine the entire purpose of the book, to show the best of humanity. I—"

"Prepare that list as your first task in Convitto San Tommaso. That will be all. Go with God."

And like that, Project Job was decapitated.

Chris began to leave, then stopped at the door. He opened his mouth to voice further objection... then left. He would have to find a way to continue. He didn't know how he knew, but humanity depended on this.

CHAPTER 5

Martin Sandoval watched a reddish crab snatch a morsel and scuttle up the beach past his lounge chair. "A hundred million years ago, my friend, one of your ancestors might have eaten one of my ancestors." With his toes he absently piled sand on top of a sand-ad, feeling the grains tickle his toes. The little robot inexorably wriggled out of the pile and displayed another ad, now for Cokesi, now for a local snorkel and airshoot rental outfit. Martin smiled with the warm sun and dumped more sand on the little adbot.

He adjusted his spex and continued reading a paper from the conference that was the reason the university paid his way to be here, physically on site, in Grand Cayman. He didn't look a gift horse in the mouth for such luxury. Most mid-level faculty were expected to spex in to conferences, not to mention knock off a steady stream of joblets on the Market to supplement their income. Freedom from joblets for a week was one of the biggest perks of on-site attendance, though most attendees would still grab some low hanging fruit. Martin left his news collector filter powered up; some grad student's joblet was to sift through the flood of feeds curating for anything interesting, prioritizing any user ratings. He even turned down his newsalert threshold to crisis-only. Martin could relax like he rarely did.

"Pay me back with a big, fat grant," the department chair said, with a frown, but a kindly twinkle in her droopy eye. There was an unstated assumption that if your department could afford to send faculty on-site then they had money; therefore, they were worthy of more.

Around the reading field in his spex he could see the little white clouds drifting by in a sky so blue he longed to dive into it, distracting him from the article. Water dripped off his barrel chest from his recent swim in the emerald waters, cooling him pleasantly in the breeze. Palm trees rustled. Martin smiled and briefly closed his eyes. He could sleep forever on the sand.

Something cold splashed on him. "Oops!" Jerald Kovacic said. "Here's a rum punch for you. They were two-fer at the bar." He handed Martin a large, bright yellow glass with a pineapple chunk perched on it, then sat down on the adjacent lounge chair. "To the IEEE Conference on Dependable Biocomputing!"

"May we return next year! Cheers!" Martin raised his glass. "Jerry, did you see the paper from I. St. Thomas on *Evolved Algorithms for Fault Tolerance and Fault Prediction?* It's very interesting. You might be able to use it in your neural interface work. Autons that diagnose their own errors and repair them. Do you know this I. St. Thomas from NYU?"

"Never heard of him."

Martin blinked up a search on I. St. Thomas.

"There's very little on him on the mesh. I even put out a thirty second joblet for any human private investigators to nibble on to supply a background check, but no action on that either. Even his sheet at NYU is practically bare."

Jerry forwarded a blinker from his own spex search to Martin's spex. "Classified stuff, you can bet. Big money, good to meet. And you're in luck, look, he's here at the conference. Supposed to be presenting on Thursday."

"And we are here to network, eh? I wonder who funds him. It sounds like a BARPA thing." He blinked up a search on recent funding areas from the biodefense funding tracker agent. "Here—" he spexed over a packet—"See, they were looking for automated enemy warfighter prediction and prevention. Perhaps you could propose a joint project on using NEWT to speed up his system or something. If he has BARPA money, Lizabet could be very happy."

The lounge chair beeped and popped up a pinger in Martin's spex space, an angry red star in his view, pulsating rapidly. It demanded another fifty dollars for an hour. "Oh-oh, time for me to go." Martin jumped up before the chair started to give him shocks. "The chair says I must pay or be thrown in prison for a very long time. I'll burn if I stay longer, and Lizabet will be most unhappy if my expense report only lists lounge chairs!" He wrapped his towel around him, deciding against another swim, and removed his spex to wipe the sand off with his towel. "See you for dinner?"

"Yeah. That Italian place."

"No, no, Jerry, that looked dumpy. We're in the Caribbean, we should have seafood! I want some swordfish. How about that place a little north of here. You know, we passed it—"

"Lizabet would shit a cow if she saw that on the expense sheet."

"Oh, c'mon, I can take care of it from my NSF grant. My treat. I'll make reservations. I'll see you at the hotel, seven o'clock?" Martin asked as he turned to go.

"Seven it is. But you have a friend."

Martin turned to see what Jerry was pointing at. A filament from the chair attached itself to Martin's towel, like a strand of sticky white chewing gum. Martin pulled the towel away, but the strand only thinned, wouldn't break. "Amazing strength," Martin commented.

"Oh, for the good old days where it was a human attendant you could persuade out of things."

"Or bribe."

Martin reminisced how ubiquitous cameras had been installed to prevent police abuses and corruption, but in the end caused the unintended consequence of scaring them to prosecute every observable indiscretion, no matter how small. The behavior of no longer overlooking small infractions for fear of being seen and scolded for it permeated into the commercial world too. No more turning a blind eye to pedaling your bike a bit above the speed limit. Nobody seemed able to do the rational thing and quit labeling those activities as forbidden; everyone just grumbled at the absurdity of treating every little thing as a capital offense. There was no slack afforded from too much observation. Too much money to be made in Enforcement. Martin knew in his heart he wouldn't likely get away without paying the ridiculous fee for the chair. But he hoped.

After several seconds another strand shot out from the chair and attached to Martin's leg. Martin rolled his eyes, then reached down with his prosthetic arm to his leg and pinched the strand so hard it broke with an audible snap.

"Nice trick," Jerry said.

"Couldn't do that if I got a cloned arm, now could I?" It was a point of pretend feud between them. Jerry's young son was a clone, and Jerry made it clear he preferred the "all natural" approach to things.

"Feh, can't trust tech," he ribbed Martin back. "It Murphy's on you when you most need it."

Now broken, the goo on his leg turned to dust. Martin toweled off his leg and prosthetic fingers, which looked as human as his other hand. He put on his spex, which by now he could hear beeping madly. "I can't believe this. This chair is broken. It says I'm still sitting in it and haven't paid. I know I'm heavy," he laughed, "but really, my friend, I'm not sitting on you. I know this because the sand is scalding my feet! Ow! Ow!"

He tossed the towel on the chair and hurried up the beach, posting the holo of his chair encounter for his meshlife friends to watch, enjoying the chuckles they posted back (almost, he thought, faster than they could have watched it). The beeping the chair had initiated was getting uncomfortably loud now, so he took off his spex and ambled ahead carrying them.

As he reached the cool Bermuda grass of the hotel's gardens he heard his spex change tone to a grating buzz as they received automated legal approval to exceed the low volume Martin had set. An elderly woman turned to look at him and fell off her floaty chair with an *oof!* Martin helped her back on.

Other guests in swimsuits looked at him, annoyed at the scofflaw sound. He smiled, gestured at the spex and shrugged a what-can-you-do? At least he could feign that his red color was sun burn and not embarrassment. But he couldn't hide that he was spexless. He brought them to his face to put back on, the lesser of the two evils, but it was too loud. Damn, should have brought a spare in the beach bag.

"It's a broken lounge chair," he said to a group of curious teenagers playing in the pool; "it's after me, run, run!" he laughed. He tossed their bathysball back to them that had popped out before he approached.

The buzzing was getting quite noticeable now as he neared the door to the palm-treed lobby.

"Oh, for heaven's sake." He walked back to the pool and dunked the spex in the water. He'd dealt with broken self-pay units like the lounge chair before. He was convinced sometimes they were programmed to act broken to extort more money from customers not wanting a hassle. The lounge chair would stalk him, he knew, even after he bought a new pair of spex—these were just cheap spex he'd purchased from the hotel room's Wal-mini-mart to wear to the beach—but hopefully the chair wouldn't have very good algorithms for linking the single-use identity he used for the purchase to any of his other identities.

The spex stopped buzzing with a pop. He tossed them into the used towel bin. Martin went to his room down the hall, humming with the steel drum music coming in from the patio.

He nearly bumped into his hotel room door, which wouldn't auto open without spex. He twisted the manual door knob, more out of irritation than any expectation it would unlock. "Occupant thumbprint detected" appeared in digital ink on the door at eye level. After a pause, "Account overdrawn" appeared with a grating buzz, then "Please enter new credit account or report to registration in the front lobby."

"Uh! Why can't I do that right here? There's nobody in the lobby either, probably just another touch panel." But the door wasn't voice aware, it appeared. Martin paused. He'd supplied a one-time credit account with just enough funds in it to cover his stay. He'd be capitulating, letting the lounge chair win, if he supplied another account. Besides which, he lacked the spex to create another one-time account, and he'd be damned if he'd enter his master account code into a public door pad. Who knew where this door had been.

He retrieved the dead spex from the towel bin—thank heavens the pool attendy bot hadn't emptied it—and returned to the lobby. "I want to report these spex are defective," he said to the clerk-o-mat. The lobby was arched with live palm trees with water fountains tinkling peacefully between them. On the presumption that guests at a four star hotel were of a quality that they would always have spex and wouldn't need to speak directly to an AI, the kiosk for the spexless was off in a dark corner, behind a pink cinder block half-height wall. The kiosk was a thin cylinder that came up to Martin's belt, finished in mahogany with a pad of digital paper on top. At least it wasn't a reusable pad; God only knew what germs you picked up from those. Of course, at a *five* star hotel you got a real human at a registration desk who could take care of these idiocies, Martin mused.

"Hello?" he asked he AI. "Hello? These spex of yours don't work," he said, waving the inert glasses, "and your lounge chair was chasing me when I was no longer sitting on it. I should get a refund for my room rate, don't you think? Hello? Or a free dinner."

"Please identify yourself," the kiosk said; rather rudely, Martin thought. A box appeared on the flat surface for Martin with an icon of a thumb being pressed.

"Oh, how quaint," Martin said. He pressed his thumb in the indicated box. "Do you even *have* a voice interface, my little friend?"

"Voice activation affirmative," the unit said, with what sounded like a snooty air. "Mr. Martin Luis Sandoval," it continued, not even accenting his middle name according to his preferences. "Please enter an account ID to cover the overcharge. Say 'charges' to review your charges."

"But I haven't overcharged anything! Your lounge chair is broken, I tell you. I did not sit on it past the time I paid for."

"Say 'charges' to review your charges or enter a charge code, or say 'exit' to exit back to the previous menu."

Martin hung his head. The level of complexity of this AI was possibly not even enough to qualify as an AI. He wondered if this was deliberate on the hotel's part. He was sure it would be entirely intelligent when it came to *taking* his money.

He thumped the pedestal and turned to leave—bumping into a man in a bathing suit, well-tanned with close cropped black hair graying at the temples, above his Giorgio spex.

"Really, do watch where you're going," said the man curtly, in a British accent.

"Sorry, I'm just in an argument with a lounge chair. It's nothing, but the principle of the matter. Only this AI is too much 'A' and not enough 'I'!"

But the man was walking off. "Bloody spexless," Martin heard him swear under his breath.

"I—!" Martin threw up his hands; the man was gone. Martin saw a sheet of e-paper on the tiled floor. The man must have dropped it in their collision. Martin scooped it up. He glimpsed "Itinerary for Irwin—" before the page blanked except for "Incorrect DNA Detected" in large, blinking red print. 'Irwin', that was a name that began with 'I'. He could perhaps be the mysterious I. St. Thomas, the man with the article he'd thought so highly of. Martin frowned. Fate might just be like that. If so, so much for the prospect of Jerry and him working with this fellow on his neural interface research. He knew the type, far too conceited, the kind who would never discuss projects in progress even if the patents were already filed. Would probably want a Non-Disclosure Agreement just to shake his highness's hand. His talk would probably be boring too, all smoke and no fire.

Dejected, Martin set off down the corridor looking for a housekeepy. He'd heard if you reached *just so* into the robot's cart you could grab an unimprinted pair of spex. He wandered down the empty halls, occasionally passing a guest, "Good afternoon," and on down the green carpet patterned with bird-of-paradise flowers he went, searching for a housekeepy.

He could as easily have asked to borrow a pair of spex from a guest, especially the stunning brunette whose hat he retrieved for her when the gust from the outside door blew it off, and who might have felt generous enough to let him do a quick payment blink from his account to the hotel, or he could go bother Jerry—but that was giving in. Martin wanted to set this right, and Quest Mode was now engaged. There was also the matter of testing the veracity of his information about housekeepies. A bit of hacking always raised his spirits.

Around a corner, up ahead—there. Martin saw a housekeepy come toward him and stop at a guest door. He could hear it announcing "Housekeepy!" (though surely it knew the room was empty), then the door clicked loose and the housekeepy rolled ahead, nudging the door open with the red felt piping that girded its boxey torso top and bottom. Martin jogged to reach the room before the door shut behind it. He sidled in.

"Housekeepy," the robot said in its tinny canned Caribbean-accented voice to the empty room. Empty but for Martin.

The housekeepy lurched forward toward the bed. It apparently spotted the bedspread piled on the floor, as it went toward it and began grabbing fabric with outstretched waldoes.

Martin watched for a minute as it balled up the bedspread and dragged it to an open space on the floor. Martin had never really watched a housekeepy before; he hardly traveled and was more likely in a bar than in his hotel room when a housekeepy was around.

A waldo removed the "change sheets, please" placard on the bed, scanned it briefly with a camera stalk, then (as Martin always suspected) began making the bed up with the sheets that were already on it. He should share his video of this charade, he thought; he might score a few ratings points and give people some laughs. He instinctively checked his Market cap. Not bad, not bad at all.

Martin compared the housekeepy's waldo with his own prosthetic arm. Primitive in comparison. His was vastly superior to the housekeepy's primitive waldo, even if he did have to talk his arm's AI into doing certain things. Like now.

While the housekeepy was taking delicate pains to ensure it shortsheeted the bed (ha! thought so!), Martin leaned over the unit and reached up under the cowling. It began blubbering "Housekeepy! Housekeepy!" as he approached and "Make up room later? Say 'yes'." He bumped a shelf inside—and felt a sharp electric shock.

"Damn!" He hoped the shock didn't damage his arm. Diagnostics still showed green. He kept feeling around for where the spex might be kept inside. He chided himself for not waiting until it cleaned the bathroom, when it theoretically would have opened up. Or, maybe not; the bathrooms weren't as clean as one might expect. But it was too late to quit now: As he found a pair of spex, the housekeepy shrilled "Alert! Alert! Tampering detected! Police notified!" And then: "Room secured."

"Oh crap. You turncoat!" He swore at the housekeepy. Martin raced to the door.

Locked.

He donned the spex and quickly blinked up his master credit account, fumbling it the first two times. The housekeepy kept screeching "Alert! Police notified!" and waved its silver waldoes defensively, even though Martin was off by the door.

"Jerry! Thank God! Here's my location. Please get over here quick. Get me out before I get arrested!"

CHAPTER 6

The plans for the match were finalized. Starting in two weeks, six games in six days, no more than three minutes apiece. Ten a.m. Denver time, nine p.m. in Baku. Each would wear special spex that locked out everything but the game. The games would be displayed as ten second blips between ads, so Weston was encouraged to introduce a cliffhanging move each ten seconds. Only having two weeks to prepare unsettled Weston, but Kasymov's agent made it clear that that was how long it took to build the optimal audience; longer and people's short attention spans wavered. The rest suited Weston. Kasymov no doubt thought the short game time would constrict Weston — and no doubt the scans to ensure he had no neurohancers — but he played by instinct, not studious concentration or perf enhancement; he smiled slyly. Weston would be on display at the Mexxon Four Seasons casino downtown, in a fishbowl, literally a bell-shaped glass booth, where his every move — pawn or pick of his nose — would be holographed and played in spex around the world. The bell was also EM impervious and laser-tunneled to keep the Cyberistas out, since they'd nearly killed Kasymov's last opponent. Death was good ratings, but not in chess. Kasymov, meanwhile, would be secluded in his villa on the Caspian Sea in Baku, fresh caviar and a valet a finger-snap away. Weston and the audience would see of the chess god only what Kasymov wished. If he scowled, it was a calculated scowl. Weston knew that. Yet his scowl could freeze butter in an Atlanta summer. His furrowing gray brow scared the feathers off chickens.

Weston pinned a fierce clip of Kasymov in the upper right corner of his spexspace. Kasymov looked down on him like Big Brother, reproaching him for not studying when he wasn't studying, for not studying hard enough when he was, for making wrong moves and for ever daring to play the Master. Weston studied his face for clues; his every move was written on that face.

And Weston found that when Jasmina was near him during the next couple days, when they were sitting quietly, she practicing Quantum Meditation or attending to whatever it was she did, and he knee-deep in chess (when he wasn't sending her a barrage of love notes), her mere presence cleared his mind and allowed him to focus more deeply than ever before; a chess fugue. She tried to teach him the rudiments of QM, but its bullhokey of seeing, nay, *being*, in multiple states at once didn't work for him; he had his own methods: And he consistently beat the net's Kasymov simulator. While he still didn't know how he could prepare in time and if the simulator was any good, it felt... *right*. He felt suffused with good fortune that so long as Jasmina stood by him in the tournament, he would win.

Some melodious sound was clambering for his attention. He searched his spexspace, but could see no alerts. A warm, sunny, contralto sound.

Jasmina! Oh shit. Cold guilt coursed through his veins. What had she said? He replayed the last few seconds of audio his spex recorded. "Are you asleep?" she'd asked tenderly. She straightened a lock of his pillow-mussed hair and bit into an apple. "Want a bite?"

"Think I dozed off for a second." He looked around the room, glad his spex hid his panicked glances. Bits of shiny antique motors decorated the room, which was generally static—the digipainted walls fixed in a yellow and gold floral pattern that morphed so slowly Weston wasn't even sure it *did* change, except where she'd penned out boxes for family pictures and a window; even that showed only a conventional exterior shot of the actual outside view. They'd been simul-linking a holo together of Three Men and a Clone, but it had ended minutes ago. He'd have to blink up a summary so he wouldn't look like he'd missed the ending.

"What's this?" Jasmina asked curiously—they'd linked spex, and she'd been rummaging around his spex, as he had hers.

"Oh. That. That's an old memcopy of my mother. I can't get up the nerve to delete it. You can play with it if you want, but it's not her. It's disgusting. It's like a gruesome death mask made of plaster. They say they're interactive, but it's so... *wrong*... that it gives me the creeps to open it. I tried replaying some static memories of when I was kid, you know, see things from her standpoint, but it was so warpy I couldn't take it. I don't know why I don't just delete it."

"I'm sorry." She rested her head on his shoulder for a while and they lay silently. "Listen," she said after a while. "There's... I know it sounds cliché, but something I have to tell you." She straightened her skirt. "I should have told you a couple days ago, but I didn't know if, you know, it mattered. If you'd still even respect me in the morning."

Weston took off his spex and placed them on the bed. He looked up into her warm hazel eyes, then sat up. "I *definitely* respect you in the morning. Just don't ask me for a run." His legs were still tight from the day before yesterday's; and last night. "So, what, you're a neo-communist? A retro post-modernist? A Cyberista going to poison my water supply? You've got a crazy aunt locked in the closet? At least she's quiet."

She pushed his side playfully, her hand warm against his chest. "No! Nothing like that." She looked at him searchingly. "Well nothing *exactly* like that. Look: I... I'll tell you straight up: I don't do joblets. I work in a building. I'm an auto mechanic. All day long." She said nothing, watching for his reaction.

How did he feel? *Revulsion*, certainly, for anyone so unemployable they had to do the same job all day long, and a manual labor job at that, better done by bots. *Let down*; her reality was even grittier than he'd feared. *Ashamed*; that he'd fallen for someone so dysfunctional, ashamed at himself for not somehow seeing it. He involuntarily looked at her fingernails.

"Yes, we use soap," she said, holding up her immaculate smooth nails for inspection. He could see the hurt in her eyes.

He took her hands and felt their smoothness. "That's not what I... It doesn't matter to me," he said, but he could see in her downcast eyes that he hadn't been fast enough, and his words hadn't rung true. She rose from the bed, went to the closet and began dressing. If this hadn't been her apartment, she no doubt would have said, "I'd better go," and left. But this was more awkward. The burden was on Weston; she couldn't offer him an easy solution. How much did he care for her? He knew he should follow the standard Market dogma, cut and run, but he felt like he couldn't here, not with *her*. Snooze/lose, he knew it in his mind, but his heart said wait.

He had to buy time, to think. "So, do you work with robots? I thought maglevs were all repaired by robots." That was it—show interest in her work.

"Not maglevs. Automobiles. Remember those? Gasoline? Internal combustion engines? You're not *that* young."

"*Cars?* No, I—" It wasn't that he'd forgotten. It had taken working hundreds of piddly jobs to save up for his first one at fifteen. But he'd climbed out of the social muck implied by driving a *car* some ten ancient years ago, when he'd sold that junker Impala that was as old as he was. He toyed with his spex on the bed, spinning them around. "Look, I'll help you get some real jobs. We'll build your ratings back up." He waved his hand. "There are rating doctors..."

Fists on hips, she shot back, "This isn't about ratings. I *like* being a mechanic." She finished putting on a purple track suit. It was so old, he noticed, it bore no interactive ads, only fixed logos. So old-fashioned it made her look sleek. "I'm going for a run. You don't have to be here when I get back." And she was gone.

CHAPTER 7

C hris strolled the noisy streets of Rome. His father had been a tour guide in Rome and little Chris often tagged along, or ran errands for his mother, who worked in a store selling tourist trinkets; little Chris would run the streets to suppliers to get more boxes of baubles. He thought best when he walked, so he walked until he became tired, found some café for dinner, then rode the Metro back to the dank apartment Cardinal Canini had him assigned to write his book. In truth he did little but sleep there, and that only when he felt exhausted enough to tolerate the rock hard bed whose only evidence of having springs were the ones that poked him. He didn't have the stomach to compile the list he had been ordered to provide; it made him physically nauseous to contemplate it, to chart a path between his love for his Jobs, whom he could never rat out to authorities who wouldn't understand, balanced against his vows to follow the will of God and his superiors who interpreted it. He played for time with Monsignor di Fuoco by saying he was tracking down the whereabouts of the Jobs, and trying to verify identities, which, he explained, he had not himself had any need to do. What was a name to him but a handy moniker to call them by? So far this was working and forestalling his nausea, but he knew it wouldn't work for long.

So he wrote his book. He dictated his book subvocally as he walked, narrating inside his head as if he were telling their stories, remembering all he could about each of the Jobs he had met. He did the work himself, without AI assistance, hoping for further reprieve.

It was bright and sunny today, warm enough for short sleeves, and his walk took him around to the beautiful park space in the Villa Borghese, through the Piazza del Popolo, along the Tiber river where he picked up a shaved ice at a cart by a bridge, sitting on the ancient stone walls to eat it with the tiny plastic spoon, finally meandering here to the Piazza Navona. Tired, he sat on a marble bench by the *Fontana di Nettuno*. He watched the fountain play, and watched the few winter tourists watching the fountain. In the middle of the fountain Neptune battled a sea serpent coiling around his legs. Chris tried to blank the thought of himself as Neptune and Cardinal Canini as the serpent. That was unfair; Canini was a man of God, whom Chris shouldn't question or liken to a serpent, the symbol of Satan.

In the middle of the square tinkled another of the piazza's three fountains, Bernini's Fontana dei Quattro Fiumi, the Four Rivers. Chris's spex reminded him that despite the rivalry between the famous artist and Borromini, who built the Sant'Agnese in Agone church here, the rumor was false that Bernini designed his fountain's sculpture so the faces of the personified Rivers covered their face or looked away from the church instead of at it, as was customary. The dates of construction dispelled the delightful rumor, as the fountain had been built first. Perhaps, Chris thought idly, Bernini knew there would be a church there, and shared the same doubts about the Church as Christian Agnostikos himself had right now. Perhaps Bernini's sculpted face looked not away from a rival artist, but God himself.

Canini's pest, Monsignor di Fuoco, had badgered him for the day's notes on his book. It wouldn't be so bad if only Canini's motives were pious ones. Canini was trying to waste Chris's time to derail Project Job, not to enhance it. Doubly grating was that Chris slowed himself down to avoid naming names. Canini was too clever. Why should the Church be so hurtful?

Chris constantly analyzed his own doubt, or his *Doubt* as he thought of it, with a red capital D. It wasn't God's existence he doubted. He couldn't remain a priest, he'd long ago decided, if that was the root of his problem. There was, absolutely, to Chris's mind, an entity with all the powers ascribed to the God of the Bible and a Jesus Christ who was the son of God and sacrificed himself for mankind's benefit. It was mankind that he doubted; mankind's capacity to ever be worthy of God's love, to ever rise from the cesspit of evil it thrived in. There were some good individuals, to be sure, but when grouped together in collections, in organizations, they seemed never able to escape evil. It was the Church, with a capital C, that came to symbolize all that he had lost faith in. Was the Church simply one of the false prophets the Bible warned against? This was the central distillation of his Doubt. As Victor Hugo put it, "Religions pass away, but God remains." Could he remain a priest in light of that Doubt?

There were, to be sure, many good works the Church accomplished. But they seemed the exception to him, to have come to be despite the Church, not because of it; unwanted accidents of goodness. This whole matter here of shutting down Project Job, that was a perfect example. He needed to find the rest of the Jobs, didn't they understand that? And what was wrong with them, demanding he turn in these, the best of all people, not protecting the weak? Politics had no place in the Church. Well, that was naive. Humans were human.

But it ran deeper than that. Chris had in the past blindly assumed that whatever direction the Church took, whatever the Holy Father said, was without flaw, the direct communication from God passed on as if the pope were Moses. That was idealistic, he knew that, but yet, wasn't that fundamentally what they *really* meant when they admitted, yes, the pope and cardinals on down, they were human and fallible, But— It was that "but" that caused the problem. They might make errors, but never having admitted any large ones, the implication was that the large scale history of the Church was one of coming very close to implementing the direct word of God. The Holy Father was, while, of course not "a god," in the sense that a Roman emperor declared himself to be a god, yet the pope was certainly venerated in much the same way as one of Caesar's brood.

Chris *ugh*'d in disgust. What was it about Project Job that should cause it to even gain the notice of this Canini, let alone make him want to destroy it? The Jobs were the very best of mankind, evidence of man's perfectibility and capacity to be worthy of God's love and forgiveness. If their goodness could somehow be magnified, collected as a group, it could rise above the failure of all other of man's collectives.

Chris had made it clear he'd veritably found evidence of God's existence. Shouldn't Canini jump for joy? There was still a need for faith; it wasn't as if he'd found direct physical evidence of God's existence, which might eliminate the need for the willing leap of faith on which everything was based. Sure, if there were actual, incontrovertible *proof* of God, then a lot of non-believers would get the crap scared out of them and join the church; but it would be a false piety. But Chris wasn't demonstrating that; only narrowing the belief gap, which in the days of declining attendance should be welcomed. Who could want to turn away an increase in true believers?

Chris sighed. He should start back; it was too early yet for dinner and the digipaint ads on the buildings were particularly annoying here.

As Chris rose, a young boy came over, perhaps six, with neat blond hair and big brown eyes behind his training spex. "Buon giorno," the boy said politely in Italian that Chris thought marked him as from the north, perhaps Venice; "Hello. Are you the priest?"

"Of this church? No, son, I'm not." He looked around; no adults seemed to be paying him any attention. There was just the tourist chatter, no sound of worried parents looking for a child. "Where are your momma and papa?"

"No, are you the priest El Cyb told me to talk to?"

The blood drained from Chris's face. El Cyb: a terrorist. One of the Cyberistas, each of whom hid behind the annoying anonymity of calling themselves El Cyb as individuals. For some reason this woman kept initiating contact with Chris. She was not one of the Jobs—and he never mentioned her to Canini so that couldn't be the reason they wanted the list of Jobs—unless they were spying on him and misunderstanding. What did he have to do with terrorists? Nothing that he wanted, certainly. But there was one thing of which he could be sure each time she contacted him: Inevitably something bad was about to happen. Then she would spar in spexspace with him later about forgiveness. Chris regretted and barely would admit to himself that he enjoyed the intellectual banter, or that he hoped he could save her soul. But she was certainly no Job. Death followed her like a piper.

Chris looked around rapidly. Nothing abnormal; the Piazza Navona was full of the routine knots of tourists and locals and irritating adbots. He knelt on the cobblestones in front of the boy and grasped his arms gently. "What did El Cyb say?"

"She said," and the boy looked up and squinted like he was trying to remember, "she said, 'get out of here, there's a gas...a gas...'"

Chris very much doubted it was a buildup of hydrogen gas from some resident's fuel cell charger. Or might they still pipe in natural gas? He didn't doubt something was about to explode.

"What else did she say? Tell me everything. Can you replay your spex? This is very important."

"That was all. I think." He twisted in Chris's arms. "She said you'd give me a biscotti." The boy kept looking nervously up at one of the upper level windows of the apartments across the piazza. A number of the shutter-framed windows were open on the bright yellow building down from the church. Chris never knew if El Cyb was nearby when these things happened or not.

Oh my God, Chris thought; he didn't have time for this. He picked up he boy and blinked the "112" emergency service, quickly blinking through the menus to "bomb report/terrorist," blinked on Yes for "near my current coordinates" then "unknown more specific location," winding through the menus for time ("unknown but probably soon"), finally clicking "innocent bystander / not affiliated with terrorist group making bomb threat" before it thanked him for his report.

He must—what? Run? Duck? Warn everyone in the square? Surely there would be gas sensors spread throughout the buildings, so the police would sense a genuine buildup if there was one. His spex hadn't received any alert from the authorities what to do, so presumably nobody else in the vicinity had either. He settled on the latter option.

"Attenzione! Tutto! Evacui la zona! Evacuate the area! There's a—a bomb! Bomba!" He ran around the square. He leaped over adbots. He hoped there would be enough time for people to flee when he warned them. Was it right to tell them to flee, or would they be running from safety into harm's way? His went with his gut. "Run! Bomb!" On a hunch, he pointed to the yellow building the boy kept looking at. "Bomb! Run! Funzionamento! Bomba!" He made shooing motions.

Some of the tourists looked at him askance, as if he were a lunatic. Probably their spex weren't translating him correctly, so he shouted in English, German, and French for good measure. "Bomb! Run! Laufen! Bombe! Courir!" Eyes widened. They fled. He thrust the boy at a burly looking man. "Take him, get out of here!"

Chris ran around the square until he was satisfied people were fleeing. He'd feel really stupid if this were a false alarm—terrorists operated on terror, so some percent of claims were intentionally false. Still no official warning from the authorities in his spex. He started to run after the emptying crowd, when he realized the building itself wasn't necessarily empty.

He ran toward the yellow building yelling "Evacuate! Bomb!" when the world erupted with orange fires of hell as the building exploded outward.

CHAPTER 8

His mother had run out on him, too, after she'd washed up in the stock market. Washed the dishes one night, and left. Weston had gone into an apoplectic frenzy. What don't kill ya makes ya stronger, his father said, and shrugged. Weston had lived.

Weston went into a frenzy now to do the Market proud.

He pounded up to his room, paced about, trying to understand where he'd gone wrong. Someone like her—totally foreign territory. What was it he said to make her so angry? He'd only tried to help. Lacking the inspiration to understand, he'd jogged tight-jawed back to her apartment, which he'd left latched with a LetMeIn. She wasn't there; still probably at "work." But her pink spex were there, on the night table where she'd left them—and left him without a way to contact her. He bounced to the street and zig-zagged through alleys looking for where she might work. Without success. He couldn't concentrate long enough to formulate a coherent spex query to locate her. Every search turned out empty, just maglev dealers, ridesharers, and ads for rehabilitating one's Market ratings. There were no listed auto mechanic shops in jogging vicinity. The constant array of flashy singsong ads and hammer blows of prioritized jobs irritated him to distraction. All he could think to do was stalking the stairwell of their building and the nearby alleys. For hours he dashed between the streets and his and her apartments like a monkey caged. What cruel fate, he despaired, for him to screw up and lose her after the astronomical odds of finding her. He couldn't even concentrate on chess problems, despite Kasymov's dour face—in fact, the last useful stretch of chess contemplation had been this morning before Jasmina woke him, when he'd slid through two full hours of gloriously whipping the pants off the Kasymov simulator. The submerged guilt at not being able to study now gnawed at him like an unrequited hunger; like not knowing if the public Kasymov simulator was any good. Yet she was a Chinese finger trap, this one. She'd caught his heart and the more he struggled to free himself the deeper he dug in. How could have fallen for a spexless loser who worked one job, in person, doing actual labor? But the instant he thought it he knew she wasn't the loser, she was the strong one and he wrong for even thinking otherwise. Oh, Weston my boy, what have you gotten into?

But he was there when she returned. He happened to be in her living room, pacing, forcing himself to see Kasymov's simulated move. Why had the simulator said bishop to a8? Maybe, probably, it was right. He cursed himself and the simulator both for their disagreement. If only he could know; but the MS. GRAY simulator was as off-limits as —

Jasmina walked in her door, paused, studying him. He could see her balance tilting between snide remark to drive him away or deep meaningful question that would force him to delve deeper into himself than he wanted. And in that instant, basking in her confidence that she had not only done nothing wrong, but that her life style was *good*, Weston suddenly saw the very Kasymov-like trap the simulator laid for him, pinning his queen, and how to avoid it, and how to beat the master (or at least the program that maybe acted like him). He blinked over his set of moves, knowing they were the winning moves, and he spoke before she did.

"I don't know how you do it, Jasmina, but somehow you've got this clarity of vision about your life, and the moment you walked in, it flowed through me so completely I... I can't explain it. I saw a whole chess game unfold. I know that doesn't sound right, but chess is to me what old cars are to you. I don't know what I said wrong this morning," he added, "but I want to."

"Old cars aren't the point," she said, sitting on the couch in pre-QM position, and patting the seat for him to join her. Wariness still on her face.

Oh boy, here comes the 'commitment' speech. Weston thought he was fast, but... wow.

He took off his spex out of courtesy; she was still spexless.

"Why do you work so many jobs?" She asked.

Weston almost blurted that this was an odd way to lead into the commitment bit, but caught himself. "Well, same as anybody." Oops, wrong response. "I work hard because you are what you make yourself. I like to think I've beat the Market once in a while and done okay."

"That's not quite what I meant. Sure, you work hard. But why at so many jobs?"

Ah, this was the 'justifying-my-way-of-life' speech. He'd head her off with indisputable facts — "Jas, that's how the Market works. It's provably more efficient with smaller units. I mean, you did take economics in fourth grade, right?" — yes, mainsplainingly knew-it-was-stupid-as-soon-as-he-said-it indisputable facts.

She rolled her eyes only slightly. "But don't you think it'd be great to be like those guys hundreds of years ago, who did one job? Don't you get just a *little* sick of the incessant change? Sometimes?"

He idly fiddled with the wooden pull knob of the drawer in the end table next to the sofa, feeling its smoothness, listening to the squeak of the wood on wood. Like most of her other furniture, it was genuine, old wood particle-board furniture, with drawers that only opened by pulling them rather than thinking them open. She was really one retro chick.

"I — That's not a fair question; everyone gets sick of work *sometime*. Even your medieval farmer. But I bet we get a lot *less* sick of work than they did. The market ensures we do only what we want, so it must minimize boredom." Ha, refute that! But even as he said it, he remembered thinking some time ago, yesterday maybe, that the Market was chewing him up. No; that was just a lapse. You are what you make yourself, and he was happy with his success.

She put her hand on his arm, tenderly. "Weston, I'm glad that works for you. You don't know me very well, so I'll save you the disappointment. I enjoy the one-job thing. I even enjoy the boredom. Gives me time to think about pleasant things, things like spending time with you. I know it's hurt me, and I'm living in this dump, but I'm afraid I don't define myself in terms of the Market."

Oooh, low blow. And it hadn't been the commitment speech. He wished it had, as he was now more confused than ever. "So, what you're saying is, that's it for us? I mean, I can deal — "

"No, no! I don't mean that. I'm more the type to just make a quick painless exit if things aren't working, but that's not it here. I mean, if you can accept me as I am, I really want to get to know you."

Now he felt like a shmuck. He should have been able to tell she wasn't breaking things off. God, why hadn't he seen this coming? It was just like chess. Moves in a relationship. See the board. You shmuck.

He gave her a big squeeze. "Okay, but only if you can give a second chance to this rude oaf that I am."

Jasmina squeezed him back, and went off to get her spex so they could link a holo. When Weston put his spex on to check on the stupid roboloaders and hoping to sneak in a quick chess problem, his spexspace was ablaze with bright red priority messages from Kasymov's agent.

They'd found a bigger market for the tournament than anticipated, which was good news; but to grab it, and to avoid credible threats from the Cyberistas, the tournament had to start sooner.

Tomorrow.

Take it or leave it. Snooze/lose.

CHAPTER 9

"Well, *that's* a fine mess you've got us into," Jerry said, wiping at his hands to remove the solvent the police had applied to ensure his fingers were really *his* fingers for fingerprinting. He rubbed under the ankle bracelet with the xRFID tag that would alert the jailers if he somehow managed to leave the cell; unless he left his foot behind. (Even then, he suspected the bracelet would detect blood and scream.)

Martin lay on the metal bunk in the cell across the corridor, tapping the fingers of his flesh and bone hand on the beige cinderblocks in time to Beethoven's fifth piano concerto. Afraid he would bend open the cell bars, they'd wanted to confiscate his prosthetic arm. They were skeptical when informed it didn't come off without surgery and grilled him for hours while they checked out his story that he'd lost his arm as a child, in a car crash before self-driving cars, when a fool had been texting. He'd upgraded to the most recent arm system just a few years ago. They wanted receipts and medical verification. They settled on putting him in the less comfortable, bomb-proof maximum security cell. He hummed the tune in his head, missing the sound of music coming from his spex. "So, I didn't tell you to bash the door lock with a chair leg. I could have ripped it off its hinges if I'd wanted," he said, gesturing to his arm. "I thought you would hack into it. That would have been a lot less noticeable to the nice policeman when he showed up."

"You owe me dinner for this. The Italian place."

"I can't believe that policeman tried to shake us down for money. I mean, '*restitution*'."

"What did you expect from a little island country? And you're changing the subject. The steak place. Or I'll tell Lizabet only to blink over bail money for me and let you rot until you're an old man."

"We won't need bail money, and I'm already a dirty old man. Did you see that woman at the beach? Besides, Lizabet needs me. Mine is bigger than yours."

"You wish," Jerry said.

"My grant *is* bigger than yours. Over ten percent."

"Now I know why we never let you travel to conferences. If you miss your presentation on Wednesday none of us will ever get to attend in person again, you realize."

"Oh, come now. Simply we'll prove our case, pay nothing, and be out of here in — look, here are the spex now." A slot in each cell wall clicked open, revealing a pair of spex.

"Wear the spex provided for the arraignment process," intoned a Caribbean-accented voice from an invisible speaker in the wall. It repeated the message in French and Spanish. Digipaint above the cubbyhole displayed the message in all three languages in a stern font. The universal translation icon pulsed to show it could say the same thing in 5,000 languages. "Damaging the spex is a felony punishable by up to five years imprisonment," it added.

"I love it when you talk dirty to me," Martin said, putting on the spex. They felt slimey. He hoped it was from some cleaning solvent and not the remnants of the last user.

"Shhh!" Jerry admonished from across the hall.

The spexspace resolved to a courtroom image, with a real person, a woman magistratee, presiding from what appeared to be an imposingly tall bench. A gigantic Cayman Islands flag hung behind her in a room that looked to be of marble and mahogany. Martin wondered what the woman was actually doing in meatspace — playing golf? at home soaking in her bathtub? sunbathing? She looked like a golfer. She was hot, Martin mused. He could imagine long golfer's legs. But tub won out as Martin decided that made the proceedings the least stressful. He tried blinking up a scenery manager to create a view to match his imagination so he could post it to his meshlife friends. "Goats testicles!" he said aloud to Jerry. "Damn spex are locked."

The charges against them displayed in a window: Breaking and entering, theft, destruction of property, invasion of privacy, and unlawful detention of an autonomous productivity device.

"Martin Luis Sandoval, DNA ID 54RG0209F4TQ89Y, do you confirm for the record your identity per the Reformed International Genome Identification Database?"

"Of course."

There was a pause. Then from across the aisle Jerry said "Yes" and suddenly his image joined the conference.

"So," the magistrate said with a scowl, "what was you two boys up to?"

Before Jerry could speak, Martin rushed in with the story he'd planned. "Your honor, this is a terrible misunderstanding," he said, with a grand sweep of his flesh arm. "I was walking by the hotel room when I thought I heard a cry inside. Like a child, 'help!' So I went into the room—you know how kids like to play inside of things, I thought one might have crawled into the housekeepy and become stuck. I was reaching in to be sure, when it attacked me! It tried to electrocute me! Then it locked the door, and I became afraid what it might do. I called my friend, and he was only attempting to rescue me."

"Uh huh. You didn't think to blink that little 'SOS' glyph to call the police."

Jerry started to say something but Martin waved him off from across the jail hallway.

"I... I was... dazed. From the electric shock. The hotel's beach chair already tried to attack me, I—"

"Uh huh. Bail is set for fifty thousand Cayman dollars. Don't be leaving the island, defendants Sandoval or Kovacic. Restitution in lieu of trial is ten thousand Cayman. Trial before me is set for," she looked up at what must have been another window in her spex, "September 23—"

"But this is months away!" Martin protested.

"Trial, at your option, in front of the Honorable Cayman's Automated Judiciary Expertise System, which, you are advised includes enhanced triplicate biometric lie detection deposition, could be scheduled as early as July 4th."

"But this is also months away!" Martin protested again. Not to mention, he thought, an AI system coupled with infallible lie detection would hang him.

"Then you'd best consider the restitution," she said.

The spex went black.

"Return spex to wall storage immediately," intoned the urgent voice.

Martin gave a little faux jump as if to rush, but nonetheless placed the spex in the cubbyhole rapidly. "Well, that went well."

"That went *well?!*" Jerry rolled his eyes. "I don't know you. *A cry, like a child, 'help!'*" he said with a strained laugh. "We seriously need a lawyer to get that trial date moved up. Lizabet won't pay for us to stay down here at these prices, and I'm not dipping into my retirement funds for this."

"Ten thousand *'restitution'!* That's robbery!" Martin said.

"*A cry, like a child, 'help!'* God, we're going to be locked away here for life."

"They can't prove I didn't hear a child."

Jerry tested the strength of the bars. "Those housekeepy's run a video log, to prove they didn't break anything."

"Ah, but they turn off when they smell sufficient human DNA in the room. Privacy."

"You better hope. I'm guessing the privacy shutoff is only if it smells the DNA of a designated guest in the room. Else it would shut off when a burglar was in the room. And that, like you, would be stupid."

Martin shrugged. "Time will tell. Speaking of time, where is that Lizabet with our bail money. Pardon me, 'restitution.'"

"Making us stew."

"Damn, I didn't know how much I missed my spex. How did we live without them?" Martin rubbed his eyes. "I feel so naked."

"You wish you were naked," Jerry said.

"With that hot judge, yes," he said playfully.

A dark gray guardbot floated in with a simulated sinister rumble. It carried two trays of food shaking in front of it. "Stand back from the cell door, mon," it intoned.

Martin stepped back half his foot length, and leaned forward to peer at the guardbot.

"Failure to execute directives will result in a nasty jolt, mon." The guardbot gave off a *zzzzzzt!* sound for added warning.

Martin backed up quickly to his metal bed and the guardbot immediately lurched toward his cell door, just as a metal hatch slid down. The guardbot inserted the tray of food on a shelf fixed to the cold cement wall and backed up as the hatch slid up. It repeated the process for Jerry, who was much more accommodating.

"Bon appetit," Martin said as he dug into his conch stew.

"I could use a Caybrew," Jerry grumbled.

"But otherwise this isn't so bad food, yes?" Martin said.

"So what are we supposed to do now?" Martin asked after dinner. "No spex, so no calling my mama, papa, and sisters in Argentina, no books, feelies, no coasting..." He badly missed his cohorts, the constant joking among his friends and family, the various joblets he had left in process, the constant flow of contact, information, and entertainment. To the ceiling he shouted, "Bored now!"

~~~

By the end of the first day the novelty definitely wore off. By the next day they were ready to kill each other, if only to relieve the boredom; if only they could reach each other.

CHAPTER 10

C hris came to consciousness to the donkey braying of approaching sirens. He couldn't have been out long as a stillness still held sway around him. Those who fled had yet to return (wise, as one never knew if there were multiple bombs). A veil of dust hung in the air.

His body was numb, his head hurt too much to open his eyes, but he realized he was wet. His first thought was that he was bleeding, but when he brought his hand to his face water dripped off his arm. He forced open his eyes and saw a bare-breasted sea-nymph. He'd been blown clear over the plaza to land in Neptune's fountain. His head rested on the edge of the inner fountain, his feet braced against the nymph; another few centimeters and he would have drowned while unconscious.

The yellow building in front of him had very little yellow left except around the edges of the gaping maw. Furniture and rugs dangled with plaster debris from the floors of the apartment building like a tattered old doll house. Neptune's head lay in the water of the outer pool near Chris, knocked off by the hunks of concrete debris that shimmered yellow and white under the water. Adding insult to injury, the stream spitting from the sea monster's mouth landed on poor Neptune's face.

A pigeon sitting on the nymph's head pooped and flew off as the braying polizia floaters arrived and disgorged squads of policebots of all sizes, both unarmed self-controlled ones and remotely-human-controlled armed units. Several ambulance floaters arrived next, two of the human EMTs finally spotting Chris and rushing over. "Signor, padre, ti prego resta ancora, please stay still." The med techs slipped a flexible stretcher fabric into the water below and around him, careful not to jostle him. At a touch the stretcher conformed to his body with gentle pressure. His leg and side hurt like hell nonetheless as they lifted him out of the fountain and set him on a waiting stand; the pain eased as his skin absorbed anesthetics from the stretcher. One tech scissored his shirt and pants open, then ran diagnostic tape up and down his legs, arms, torso, around his neck, over and about his head. One checked readouts on datapads embedded in the stretcher while the other went off to help with other victims in the building.

"Father," the tech said, "You have a broken leg, cracked rib, and a concussion. I can treat those now, or would you prefer to be taken to hospital?" He looked at Chris for an answer. "Ah, you have no spex. I can loan you some if you'd like to check our ratings, or the costs."

Chris's head pounded, but he recognized the logo on the ambulance as a reputable firm, not one of the opportunists who preyed on those with low ratings. The church's insurance would cover this.

"Fine, go ahead."

He drifted off as the anesthetic increased to a pleasant floating sensation. He was dimly aware of the techs working on him, of his body moving around. A snap that might have been his leg being set; but he felt nothing. He imagined the warming feel of the QuickFuse bonding the bone back together.

"State your name," said a voice. Chris swam his eyes open, but only the med techs were standing around him, and they didn't look as though they'd said anything. Chris looked down—a policebot the size of small dog with a flashing light on top extended a microphone boom toward his face. "State your name," it insisted.

Chris gave his information and consented to DNA verification. He couldn't feel the scrape of the policebot against his skin. "Identity confirmed. Father Giordano," it began, "area scans prior to the event indicate you were wearing spex. Do you have them?"

Chris feebly patted his pockets. "No, I don't seem to." He rested his head back and closed his eyes.

"Please look at the sensor," the bot requested with a chime. "You have the right to human-assisted interrogation if you wish."

Chris weighed the options. It would take longer, and right now he just wanted to sleep, but holding his head up to look at the bot was more than he could imagine. "Yes."

"Do you request a live interrogator? Please say, 'Live person.'"

"Live person," he growled.

~~~

"So, Father Giordano, you understand you're not under arrest. At this time. We just have some questions." Chris had been "escorted" to the central polizia station in the Piazza del Collegio Romano.

Chris sat so upright in the chair he felt he was back in school, with Sister Grunhilda ready to rap his knuckles with a ruler. His ribs were sore under the tight corset, and his leg ached where they'd fused the bone.

Detective Mannino was thin, with a small dark goatee that made him look slightly like the devil. He slouched in a chair across the table.

"We've found your spex," he said, and held out what was left of the crushed pair. "We were able to open them with a warrant. However, there was nothing on them beyond what had already been saved by your central server, which did not include the conversation with the boy you mentioned in your call. Why did you not uplink the conversation when you reported the bomb threat? Oh, and before you answer, you have no objections to our running the recording of this interview through PMAA, Post Mortem Accuracy Analysis, do you?"

PMAA—so they were recording not just audio visual, but bioelectric, MRI, and thought scans of him, and would crunch over it afterwards with sophisticated programs to detect any lies. He was indeed a suspect. To refuse PMAA meant they would likely detain him.

"No, of course not. Well—" he added for accuracy's sake, "*yes*, I personally have philosophical qualms about it, but I see the practicality, and I have nothing to hide, so I consent. I will waive right to counsel for now, too."

"Very good. So, your conversation with the boy wasn't uplinked...?"

"The boy! How is he?"

"We haven't seen him. Do you know him?" He stared at Chris to answer the prior question.

Chris inspected the sparse, church-like room, thinking back. "No, I'd never seen him before. And I didn't waste time uplinking the conversation because I felt, at the time, that it was more important for me to warn people in the area."

"Instead of leaving this to the police?"

Chris tried not to grimace. "My prior dealings with reporting such things have not been the most... fruitful."

"You've reported bomb threats before?"

"I'm sure it's all in your database. But, yes. This terrorist, El Cyb, she keeps contacting me. This is the third time."

"And how do you know this 'El Cyb'?" Detective Mannino asked.

Everything still sounded cottony and distant to Chris. "I don't. It's all in the prior reports. We've never met face to face — that I know of. She spexes me. They've tried to trace her connections, but she uses a system to obscure her path. 'MIX SIX SIX Pretzel Routing' she calls it. The first time she contacted me I told her I would have to report any serious crimes unless they were in the secrecy of confession, Detective. We weren't in confession at the time, and she said she didn't care, and explained some technoglop, to convince me how futile it was to trace her; she said I should feel free to report everything. Something about the encrypted data packets are randomly re-encrypted and exchanged with other servers. It's all in the records." Which the police were looking for contradictions of; the thought alone made Chris sweat. What if he accidentally said something that didn't exactly agree?

"Except what she said in confession."

"Yes." And it was damn hard to keep straight which was what.

"You don't know her. But you *might* have met her?"

"I meet a lot of people in my line of work, Detective. Yes." He had, in fact, often wondered the same thing, and tried to match up personalities; to no avail.

"What does she look like?"

"Do you know the new stage play, 'Betty Crocker'? I'm sure it's an avatar."

Det. Mannino smiled. "No doubt. What does she want from you?"

Chris threw up his hands. Bad idea; he winced at his sore ribs. "We talked theology. She wanted absolution. Those conversations are in the record, until I began hearing her confession."

"Any chance we could get copies of her confession?"

Chris sighed. Not there was anything revealing she'd said; she hadn't shown true contrition so there was nothing to absolve her of. Yet. Chris held out hope he could bring her onto the path. But priests had died before breaking such a holy vow. "You know I can't do that, detective."

"Hmph. The conversation with the boy. The bystanders' spex were mysteriously blanked out, as if by an electromagnetic pulse. A nearby peacebot caught some of the conversation, but it's indistinct. What did he say this El Cyb said you would give him?"

Chris threw his head back; he was dog tired. "I honestly don't remember, detective. A biscotti, I think."

"Why would a terrorist say that?"

"I imagine it was to bribe the boy to deliver the message."

"And when did you join the Cyberistas, Father?"

"I'm not one of them!"

"We have to ask you that, for the PMAA. You understand."

Chris sniffed. How repugnant to be called a terrorist. He treasured life. He began to think of his parents—

"What do you know about this group, the Cyberistas?" the detective continued.

"Only what's in news reports. They have some manifesto that says humans and especially our technology are a danger to the limited resources of the earth, that they're upset about extinction of species, frogs, mice, what we've done to the climate, and so on, so they use our technology to try to stop our, well, technology."

"And you agree with them? You are upset about the climate and the frogs, Father?"

"I think it's a shame. I do think they are a problem, clearly. Just look at the huge sea wall around Venice. However, I believe in the ultimate goodness of Man, and that people are good at solving problems. We will find peaceful solutions. We do not need terrorism. Detective. Listen. My parents were killed when terrorists sank the ferry from Naples, do you remember? We do not need terrorism." He wiped at his eyes. He'd long harbored a dream that he could reform the terrorist who killed his parents. He didn't want to admit even to himself that was why he was talking to this El Cyb.

The detective nodded; blinked about in his spex. "That's all for now, Father. If you can wait just a moment for the preliminary PMAA results."

Or, Chris thought wryly, the detective needed to finish off a few sideline joblets. He wondered if you could tell from blink patterns what sort of task someone was doing. Chris rubbed at his face and waited. He wanted nothing more than a hot bath and a long sleep.

"Thank you, Father. You can go, but please don't leave Mesh-enabled areas."

"Roger, Houston, no space travel for me."

"Or visiting certain parts of Africa, floating free states, etc. There's a list you can look at when you get some new spex." He stood to show Chris the door. "And if you hear from any terrorists, *outside of confession*," he added with a sneer, "keep the conversation this time and inform us immediately."

"You'll be the first to know." Chris had a sinking feeling this was a promise he'd fulfill all too soon.

CHAPTER 11

Weston nervously loosened and tightened his plaid bolo tie. Paid bystanders (and those few who actually *wanted* to watch the game in person, like Jasmina and some local chess enthusiasts) crowded around the glass bell. Though standing live in front of the stage, most watched the action in their spex. Weston adjusted his spex, cleared all the irrelevant windows, and for the first time in the years since his mother's funeral, put his market filter on hold so it wouldn't interrupt him. Without his spex flashing and bobbing and clanging, the silence inside the bell was deafening.

Finally, after agonizing minutes, Kasymov's stormcloud-gray visage appeared in his spex. He looked relaxed and confident in a woolen vest, a crackling wood fire behind him, a cup of steaming tea held unwavering in his hand, an ivory and mahogany chess set before him. Kasymov won Black, giving Weston the advantage of the first move. Weston imagined Kasymov's immense mental database of openings. Weston never had studied such, and merely played instinctively. He'd always thought this a benefit, that he wasn't "tainted" by knowing how someone a hundred years ago played after a given move. Besides, there were too many openings to memorize; that wasn't Weston's strength. Seeing Kasymov's formidable face today he wasn't so sure ignoring that side of chess had been a good idea. Kasymov urged Weston onward with an impatient rap of his knuckles in the middle of his board.

Weston looked for Jasmina in the crowd. She was hoping to get time off to come; Weston had even squelched his snide remarks that from such a scummy job any boss ought to be grateful to give the time off. She was just to his right, her face nearly pressed to the glass. She smiled radiantly at him. Weston gave her a "here we go" face and moved. Pawn to e4. Blink the punch-clock.

The pieces flew like knives in a gang fight. Pawns advanced. Knights leaped. Bishops sluiced down diagonals. With so little time on the clock for the entire game and the hard moves coming in the middle game, the opening had to be furious. Weston flew on autopilot, letting his subconscious prune away the useless moves that resulted in poor positions five, ten moves ahead. He played what he dimly thought might have been known was a Ruy Lopez opening, unsure of the name and its exact moves, dimly wishing he hadn't neglected memorizing the classic openings.

On the seventeenth move, Weston knew he was in trouble. He'd declined Kasymov's offer of a pawn on the eighth move, in what theorists knew as the Closed Defense, Marshall Gambit. Weston realized that by not having taken the pawn he left himself in a passive position. Now he'd really blown it. Kasymov opened up key diagonals that he exploited with surgical precision. Weston tried to regain the bishop he'd lost. He suddenly sensed, in his intuitive way, storm clouds surrounded him on all sides. Most of the roads from here led to defeat. He paused, spinning through conscious variations in his head. He bunched up his hair, wishing for redos like he could play in his spex. Six or seven moves down the road he'd either be down two pawns or his pawn structure would be a shambles. Hi imagined Pawnking laughing at him. Weston ground his teeth and forced out everything else.

Weston blundered onward, pigheadedly believing he could put up a fight. Long stretches of seconds ticked off his clock as Weston pressed his eyes with his palms, mimed moves with his hands, rubbed his neck. Kasymov glared at him, angrily, clearly wondering why Weston was wasting his valuable time by not resigning. Weston's shirt was nearly soaked now with sweat born out of furious calculation and despair and fear and self-loathing.

Kasymov slashed through Weston's weakened defenses. He slammed down his Black pieces with such force his board shook. He responded so rapidly his arm was a blur: clock move clock. Weston could all but smell burning rubber. Kasymov's superiority was almost comical and his eyes played a mixture of childish glee and anger and disappointment. Weston had let him down. Kasymov had even said he was scouting the world for a worthy opponent. Weston failed him not only as an opponent, but demonstrated that his exhaustive search amongst the unknown and anonymous players of the world had also been a waste of time.

Then Weston saw it—more precisely, felt it. He jumped his knight three times, sacrificing a rook and a pawn for the gamble.

Kasymov shot his hand out for the next move—then froze. Shock, admiration and contempt washed across his face. Weston didn't know if the contempt was directed at himself for daring to show up the master, or self-recrimination at missing a move in his haste. Like removing a veil, Kasymov's position was instantly revealed as terribly overextended.

Kasymov pressed his lips hard in concentration. He drummed his fingers. A vein throbbed on his reddening forehead. Weston watched Kasymov's clock ticking down, using the time himself to furiously consider where this mess would lead.

Kasymov finally glared at him, as if to ask, "Well?" Weston flushed, his face prickling. Was something obvious? Was Weston supposed to resign? Was he looking foolish in God knew how many million spex? Spot The Fool always had enormous ratings; everyone would blink in to watch a big idiot. But Weston felt sure he could at least play this out for a draw.

He analyzed, seconds ticking away. The sure thing he thought he'd felt—was no longer there. His moves had been stupid, in vain. He saw Kasymov's plays; probably winning. The seconds ticked so loudly he couldn't be sure of anything.

Kasymov stood.

Oh God, Weston thought, please just offer a draw. Stamping away as if Weston had been an idiot for not resigning would crush him. Please offer a draw. Should Weston offer it, or would that only heap on the insults? Was it that obvious Weston had lost?

Then Kasymov forced a smile. "The game is yours. I resign," he said with a curt nod, and faded out.

Weston felt—nothing. Novacaine-dentist-numb. The crowd outside was murmuring so loud he could hear it through the dampening glass. Then he saw Jasmina pounding on the glass, eyes so happy tears edged out.

Then Weston leaped out of his seat. "Woo-hoooo!" he screamed. "I beat Kasymov!"

CHAPTER 12

*P*resently *George and his hatchet made their appearance. "George,"* said his father, *"do you know who killed that beautiful little cherry tree yonder in the garden?"* Chris read; the little boy he was reading to was nearly asleep, from what Chris could see in the EEG monitor window. The church embraced The Market for charitable causes such as this, Chris reading a bedtime fairy tale to a little boy somewhere on the planet. Chris wasn't privy to the amount bid as a donation to the church; he simply accessed a list of prioritized requests that had already been processed by church software for suitability and, secular rumor had it, size of donation. Chris didn't much care for the parents' choice of fairy tale, Weems' fanciful account of an old American politician, but put his best effort into it.

This was a tough question; and George staggered under it for a moment; but quickly recovered himself: and looking at his father, with the sweet face of youth brightened with the inexpressible charm of all-conquering truth, he bravely cried out, "I can't tell a lie, Pa; you know I can't tell a lie. I did cut it with my hatchet." — "Run to my arms, you dearest boy," cried his father in transports, "run to my arms; glad am I, George, that you killed my tree; for you have paid me for it a thousand fold. Such an act of heroism in my son is more worth than a thousand trees, though blossomed with silver, and their fruits of purest gold."

The boy now asleep, Chris silently closed the connection and took a sip of red wine. Ah, a hint of strawberry and perhaps rose petals. Enough wine on an empty stomach and his legs felt woozy from the alcohol and not sore as hell from being blown across the Piazza Navona. He fingered the D.O.C.G. label with the black rooster that marked this bottle as genuine chianti classico from up north in Tuscany, where he'd been born just outside of Florence. This particular bottle came from a vineyard where he'd played as a boy when visiting his father's parents; he knew the family. For that matter, he knew the grapes.

His reverie was broken by Monsignor di Fuoco's head popping into view with a buzz. Chris shook his head to clear the cobwebs. "Your work for the day, please, Father."

The avatar of the monsignor appeared, religiously, twice a day to collect Chris's work. Chris wondered if it was really him or an AI simulation. He decided to test, out of annoyance and boredom.

"Later today would be more convenient, if that would be convenient for you as well," Chris demurred. "I give a sermon in Zimbabwe in five minutes."

"No, Father, now is more convenient."

It was really him. How boring and dedicated. Perhaps evil was as simple as dedication to a dull, wrongheaded cause.

Chris reluctantly sent his corpus.

"This? This is all you've accomplished? You need to work harder, Father. Much harder. I expect significantly more tomorrow." He blinked off.

Chris grunted. Things like this shook his belief in the rightness of the Church, fueled his Doubt. Christ often warned of false prophets. Not that di Fuoco fit the mold; a wolf certainly, but hardly in sheep's clothing. The Church itself, though, was the question. Had it remained true to Christ's teachings? "Ye shall know them by their fruits," indeed, Chris thought.

He poured the rest of the wine bottle into his glass and motioned to the waiter. The Ketaphine was wearing off, his legs starting to ache and the euphoria of the Ketaphine fading. Nice while it lasted. He could see why the junkies went crazy for the Moon Dust they made from it. Too potentially addictive for Chris's taste. Time for more of the other, natural painkiller. "Si, another bottle, per favore. I'm ready for the antipasti; I'll have the Fichi Ripieni con Pecorino."

"Grazie, grazie." The waiter went to fetch the wine and the appetizer of figs wrapped with prosciutto and stuffed with pecorino cheese. It was chilly by the window where Chris sat in the trattoria he'd chosen at random, but he settled himself in for a slow dinner.

He had his manuscript for his book, *Modern Jobs: Lessons for Humanity*, open in one spex window, a list of charitable joblets in another, and a football match between Italy and France in a third. Damn, Italy was losing again. He squinted to browse the list of joblets. A few weddings, a couple funerals, a house blessing, a large number of confessions, including some with the sin listed in the title—"confession, adultery," "impure thoughts of murder, & misc.," "spanked my daughter after I caught her with a dog," "Repaid evil with evil, need help," "Greedy and can't stop rolling in money," "Is hugging a tree in a carnal way a sin? if so, much to confess,"—as if that made it more attractive to a priest to hear the "good ones." People competed in everything, even in seeking redemption.

For that matter, he thought, as he began to give a brief sermon to a Mass being held for people in Zimbabwe (though joined by a handful of others around the globe), they even competed in Mass now: His listeners would judge him on the various attributes of the sermon. Indeed, he had won the gig based on their ratings of his synopsis. He spoke (eloquently, he thought) on finding Christ's immortal love through good deeds on earth.

Two boys whizzed past on their air blades, a gust of wind from their passing blowing at his napkin. Chris looked up. Was one of them the boy from the Piazza Navona who'd warned him of the bomb? At that speed who could tell—they were almost a hundred meters away now down the maglev trail. Crazy kids.

None of the joblet requests were tagged specifically for him, and his rating in the church, as it were, was already in the dog house care of Cardinal Canini, so he pushed the list off to the side and continued subvocally dictating notes on his book. Canini might be of the false-prophet camp, but his pestering did at least get Chris to write up his notes.

Kalvin and Lindsay Bos of Port Elizabeth, South Africa. Both worked for the same nanopharm company. On the day the company announced bankruptcy and let go both Bos's, Lindsay learned she was pregnant. The public health system in East Cape is cash-strapped to the point patients must pay up front for the electricity they use. The Bos's had lost their private insurance through the company. Her pregnancy was not easy, and she was forced into bed rest for much of it. Being unable to work, and with Kalvin unable to find another job of comparable pay, the Bos's lost their home. With mounting medical bills, they moved to public housing. Their Mesh credentials were compromised and additional bills rung up against their retirement savings, which they had been using for medical payments.

The pregnancy was not planned; in fact, both Kalvin and Lindsay had taken preventive measures, he a permanent spermicidal implant and she an implanted egg sterilization system. The odds of a viable pregnancy were over ten million to one against.

So far this is, while sad, not unremarkable. Heartbreaking stories such as this happen to all too many families. What makes the Bos's story unique is what happened after the birth of their child, a girl whom they named Faith. Being unable to afford genetic testing beyond the minimal from the public health system, the Bos's were unaware they were both carriers of the recessive gene for Zellweger's Syndrome. Zellweger's is an outgrowth of the Amazon Accident. It is not, per se, a genetic disease, but a new prion, never seen before the Amazon Accident, causes excruciatingly painful neurological dysfunction in those who carry a certain gene. Because of the neurological nature of the pain, existing pain killers are ineffective.

A rare gene, the odds of two carriers meeting and having a child with the gene are one in 100,000, making this odd happenstance a combined improbability of a trillion to one against.

Faith has survived four years so far, though five is the record with current medical technology. She cries constantly, though she has no apparent higher order mental functioning.

The Bos's faith has been severely tested, though they remain devout Christians. Lindsay said, in her interview, that she felt like a caterpillar on a leaf of a tree in a rain forest — she could see the leaf, but not the tree nor the forest of God's plan, thus it was not for her to question why she was getting rained on. She was certain God would call Faith to Him in His time, perhaps to be an angel. This is an ultimate example not just of belief in God, but faith in God's will. They do, it is true, anticipate release from this burden, and have a burial plot and headstone for Faith already selected. Is this what keeps them going? A promise of mortality? If so, they might be less than perfect exemplars of modern day Jobs, but there is no evidence they harbor any such feelings. It is clear they love their daughter and bear their burden with grace.

Chris paused, and blinked up a search window. He had a gopher to get an update on any of his Jobs, at least to the extent the Mesh had information on them. Once a Job became spexless...

He dragged the Bos's record over to the gopher with a thought, and off it ran. The waiter set his figs down in front of Chris, and he delighted in the taste of one while the waiter uncorked the new bottle of chianti.

As he bit into another of the luscious, cheese-filled figs, his gopher blinked and buzzed at him. Chris paused, the half-eaten fig in mid air — his gopher only buzzed when it found something important.

Lindsay D. Bos, Port Elizabeth, SA — date of death, 14/02. Cause of death: Rhinoceros.

Just three weeks ago! Chris pulled up a more detailed account of her death.

Lindsay Bos, 32, of Port Elizabeth, was killed by a charging rhino yesterday. Bos was on foot filming the rhino by hand after her filmbot broke down. Her husband says the holocording she was making shows the rhino charging her from behind as she walks back toward her safari floater. Her spex sent a distress signal. However, Bos was alone at the time and died of her injuries before assistance arrived. According to her husband, Bos had taken the dangerous job in order to...

Chris put the fig down, removed his spex, and rubbed his eyes. So tragic. He tried to think if he'd had any contact, if he in some way had caused it, as he blamed himself for Dirk's death. But no. This was simply a rhino charging, as they were prone to do. The poor father, Chris thought. Now left to care for Faith alone. After a suitable time he'd have to get in touch with Kalvin and get an update. First, he needed to send his condolences. Chris was never the parish priest type, who dealt well with such things; he'd felt a calling involving deeper searches for truth. He drained his full glass and poured another.

Placing his spex back on, he noticed the charitable joblet queue icon was pink now, signifying a joblet that requested him specifically. Curious, and procrastinating on the condolence letter, he opened the joblet list.

The top joblet was a rare public confession request: "I damaged some property and hurt some people — EC." El Cyb.

CHAPTER 13

"**N**o, I'm still not speaking to you," Jerry said as the taxi floated up to the hotel conference center. "That's the last mess you get me into. My Market cap is all shot to hell." He had briefly checked in using the public spex at the jail, despite the risk of getting pinkeye. He had been grousing about it the whole floater ride. "People think I flaked on all those joblets. Not to mention our *restitution*. That was a month of my income!"

"Jerry, Jerry, no, you know I'm so sorry. I promise I'll repay your half."

The mahogany conference center door refused to open as they approached. "We must smell as bad to the door as I do to myself. And look at you, Jerry, you look like a survivor of a suborbital crash. Maybe not even a survivor."

Jerry grunted. "Not talking to this one, who look even worse. Let's go buy some spex. This wind on my eyes is driving me muddly."

"Hmm." Martin wished he had some spex, so he could poke around some hacker warehouse sites to find a way into the hotel, not to mention he was jonesing to know what his meshlife friends were up to. Being spexless was true deprivation. He scanned the building, feeling the wind on his eyes perturbing as Jerry had said. "Come, there's a side entrance door propped open. We can run past the sniffer."

They managed to sneak into the hotel conference center without raising alarms. Even the waiterbot hadn't objected when Martin straightened a stack of lunch platters about to fall as they hurried past it.

Martin checked his watch. "My session began five minutes ago only. Everything is fine."

He swaggered into his session, ignoring the audience comments under their breath, "Oh God"... "What's that smell!"... "Who let these trash in?"... "I'm calling security." Even those attending only by spex raised eyebrows and eww'd at the uncouth, homeless-looking man powering down the carpet. The carpet flashed his footprints in red.

Martin ignored them with his head high, noticing only the cute redhead sitting on the aisle. He winked at her.

"Hello, everyone!" he boomed from the front, amplifying with his own voice. "Does anyone have a pair of spex I could borrow? Anyone?"

People shifted uneasily in their seats. Martin sensed their disgust with the grotty spexless guy who couldn't possibly be a speaker. He walked the front row of the audience. "C'mon people, or we won't have a lecture..." A young man a few rows back, sporting the red armband and half-bald head of the Ampy's, with an amputated hand replaced by the fad d'jour, a vase of roses, shouted "Ho!" and pitched a pair of spex at Martin's face.

Martin swiped them out of the air and gave a deep bow while flipping the Ampy the bird. "Thankee kind sirrah asshole." The Ampy bit his thumb at Martin in the traditional Ampy response.

Martin made his way up to the podium, trying to log into his spex account as he went. He blinked in to find his ratings a mess, aborted joblets, a half-eaten chess game, now forfeited. Damn, he thought, remembering; I was winning that. He pulled up his presentation.

"Good day, bonjour, boungiorno, guten tag, ni hao, etc. etc." He cleared his throat. "Umm, one more item... I seem to be having some trouble accessing my account. It's not really zero, and I stashed a public copy of my notes we can plink off of, but... hmmm." Snickers from the audience. "Er, is there someone I could proxy from?"

"Ho!" The Ampy blinked Martin proxy access.

"Thankee, sir ass," Martin said quickly, with an appropriate rude gesture.

"De rien, fuckhead," the Ampy replied. As a loud aside, he added with a grin, "It's patched via some poor slub's spex account in the room here." People laughed, though nervously, each probably running off to check if it was their money being siphoned.

"Yes. Here we go." Martin broadcast the first slide of his presentation, a giant brain pulsing atop a spinal cord. The three dimensional brain rotated and zoomed in on the base of the brain, revealing the spinal cord to be a collection of oversized atoms. Further zooming showed the constituent parts of the atoms, the protons and neutrons in the nucleus, zooming into those to reveal quarks, zooming further to show vibrating strings, attached to cartoon violins and cellos, being played by a small, smiling lizard with hundreds of hands. The text faded into to reveal the title of Martin's talk, "New Features of the NEWT Programming Language To Make Programming Quark and Substring Level Computing Devices Even Easier."

Martin fell easily into professor mode, teaching while checking his friends' meshlife updates. "You all know what a pain in the penis it's been to handle multi string algorithms when they begin vibrating on a sympathetic harmonic, yes?" Martin cocked his head, and continued, "I hear the chorus of rhetorical 'yes's. I apologize for that. I never thought people would try to synchronize multistate string computations, which was my lack of foresight I suppose. And it was definitely my laziness that I didn't do anything about it." He grinned; he was getting the audience hooked, and he felt exhilarated. "Well, a billion femto-pricks sneaking past my filters has a way of catching one's attention. Yes." He thought briefly back to when his spexspace had been locked out for days with the flood of tiny devil-faced avatars knocking at this door requesting, "Please, sir, may we have some more multistrings?" He'd relented and blasted a message that he'd add it as a top priority feature in the next release. And here was that release. He could sense a sigh of relief and anticipation from the audience.

His NEWT language was gaining in popularity as a means to quickly smack out efficient code to solve the most difficult problems. He was loving the attention.

"Et viola!" he said as he demonstrated: "Note how NQ-complete problems, like Qoph-null matrix reduction, are now elegantly solved with only a few strands of code."

"Question?" It was from the hot redhead he'd winked at.

"Madame?"

"I use NEWT for creating mental models to predict terrorist behavior under a universe of psychological stress combinations. I'm the first to admit programming isn't my specialty." She bunched up her long red hair in two hands. "I need some way to mimic Zamora's n-dimensional quantum exploders. If you know what I'm talking about."

Martin was in a warm glow. She was gorgeous. What was she saying? Did it matter? Of course it mattered, his logical brain kicked in — if you can persuade her to meet you for drinks for an extended answer, and then a consulting arrangement...

She wasn't broadcasting any ID. Not a problem!

"Well, hrmmm, yes," he said in his deepest voice. "That is somewhat outside the scope of this talk. I could meet you after the session?" He spexed her a private sideband message, "For a drink?"

She smiled, but it was the friendly, "Sorry, you lose, don't spin again" kind.

Martin began to persist, "Mademoiselle *Anonyme*, I'm sure that — " when a gray security dronebot floated in. "Cease activities!" it commanded in a thick accent. "Attention!" It sounded an obnoxiously loud klaxon. It caused Martin's and assumedly everyone else's spexspace to blink rapidly bright red. "Alert! Your attention please!"

Martin sighed. Lord knows what kind of nearly spexless tweaker in Jakarta or Little Rock might control the damn thing. Martin couldn't place the accent and didn't care enough to crank up an analysis filter. Is it here, he wondered, because of my spexless appearance or the stealing of someone's spex account? Or, maybe, he thought hopefully, it's here for someone else.

It floated slowly, menacingly toward Martin. It stopped in front of him.

"Excuse me," Martin said. "Are you human-controlled or AI?"

"You are in violation of Cayman Penal Code section — "

"Damn hard to tell humans from bots anymore," Martin said with a guilty smile to the audience as it droned on. "Especially distinguishing an incompetent AI from an incompetent human." The audience laughed; a little.

"Everyone must remain in this room," the drone said. "There must be restitution."

The audience began slipping out the door; it was clear this session was done for. He was even getting snickers on his meshlife holo feed.

Martin tried to push through the audience to reach the gorgeous woman, and waved to try to attract her attention, but she'd turned her back, and the security bot and the exiting crowd blocked his way. The moment was gone.

"People, do not leave, there must be restitution," the drone said with another klaxon blast, which hastened the crowd's exodus.

Martin tried to juke around the drone. The security bot was surprisingly agile, and successfully blocked his exit. The robot said something garbled in the thick accent (probably human remoted, Martin decided), which ended with "You must make restitution."

"Say what?"

"You must make restitution," the drone repeated.

"Restitution? For what?"

"You must make restitution."

"I don't owe anyone anything. Now leave me alone." The rapid red blinking of his spex field was getting annoying. Since nobody else was coming in the room he guessed it only affected a few meters radius.

"Are there charges? What do you mean, 'restitution'?" Martin could see people milling outside in the corridor, but drifting away. "Jerry! Someone, come help me with this deranged bot!"

In a louder voice the bot said, "Do not leave the scene. You are next," the drone said swiveling its front toward the hall. That nudged the rest of the onlookers away quickly. Only Jerry remained, then he too gave a wave of resignation and left Martin to his fate alone. "Damn these corrupt little islands," he swore under his breath.

"You must make restitution."

"Oh, fuck it. How much this time?"

CHAPTER 14

The euphoria lasted all afternoon and evening. He'd run to the glass and kissed Jasmina through it, he'd dashed into the crowd, jumped around thrashing his arms, hugged, kissed and twirled Jasmina, and they'd rushed off to Duke's Steak House for a lunch of real meat and strong beer, courtesy of a flash loan on his momentary stardom. There'd be hell paying it back if he lost the match, but, that wasn't on the agenda. No unknown had ever beaten Kasymov in the first game of a prize match.

Weston partied like he'd won the whole match. He started soberly gleeful, beaming intelligent eyes, embarrassedly asking repeatedly, "Did I really do it? Pinch me." He ran a group of tourists through an old Italian villa and moved a couple tons of iron ore in the background. By midnight his face was one giddy smile.

"Waiter! 'Nuther round for my friends!" Weston called out with a drunken wave. Weston was dimly aware that he was buying drinks for himself, Jasmina, and a dozen strangers at the bar.

"Weston, honey, do you think maybe you've had enough?" Jasmina asked. "Remember, you have to play Black tomorrow." Jasmina played with her Peachtini, only her third.

"Payback tomorrow?" Weston shook his head. "I'll pay 'em back when I win the ten million. Maybe not even then if I don't feel like it. Never have to pay back anybody if I beat Garry."

"No, *play* the *Black* pieces. You said White has an advantage because it moves first, didn't you? You won with White today, but tomorrow you play Black."

"You're testing me see if I'm drunk, arn'tchoo." People laughed too loud in the background.

"I *know* you're drunk, and that's what I'm worried about."

"Well, I'll tell you. I'm *drunk*."

"I think it's time we put you to bed, soldier." Jasmina rose and tried to lift Weston by the armpits. He scrunched up but didn't rise.

"Wheee!" He looked sad-puppy-eyed. "Jus' one more drink?"

"Okay—*Coffee*." She went to the waiterbot, talked, and returned to her seat.

"Coffee. Learned to drink coffee in a bar. Did I tell you the only place I ever met my dad was in a bar? Ran out on Mom 'fore I was born. Only would see me in a bar. 'Son,' he'd say with a glass in his hand, 'I'm no good for you. That's why I left, you understand, don't you?' Every two, three years we'd meet. Gambling town if one's nearby. Always in a bar. Atlantic City, learned to drink coffee. Thought that would make me look grown up. Was ten. Double bourbon for Dad. Black coffee for me. I thought if he thought I was grown up he'd... he'd... But all he ever did was tell me all about gambling, drifting, working spot jobs, not working, and 'I'm not your role model, kid, you hear me?' With all that free time, and me nearby you'd think he could've... All that free time, you know?"

"Weston, here, drink some coffee." Jasmina held his cup to his lips.

"Taught me chess, y'know. When I was eight. Mom never knew: when I was playing chess I was with Dad."

"So, this is where the mighty Kasymov slayer hangs out!" It was Orring, looking fresh as morning dew in an orange suit.

Something in the back of Weston's mind flashed Danger! Bad man approaching! But the front of his brain interpreted this as a not quite urgent need to empty his bladder, and flattered at the compliment, he waved Orring to sit with them. Orring had already begun to sit.

"Hello, Jasmina," he said in a businesslike way, as if uncomfortable that she was here.

"Orring," Jasmina replied, enough put off by Orring's intrusion that Weston noticed even through his haze; and was surprised at himself for noticing.

"Wait—" Weston waggled his finger at the two of them, "have you—" But he knew enough to cut off the sentence before he embarrassed anyone. He didn't think they'd been lovers, and even if not, it didn't matter. Certainly Jasmina had a past, lots of pasts, surely, for someone as beautiful as she was. He smiled and stared at her stupidly, glad for the here and now. "Nevermind."

Orring paused, his mouth open, forefinger raised expectantly, as if contemplating the best time to pounce. "Weston. That was some mighty amazing play today. And if I may say, knowing your anonymous chess lounge skills, might *lucky* play. Congratulations."

"You know I play as David?" Weston winced about two seconds later. If he didn't, he did now.

"Of course! I try to be an informed neighbor. And as I was saying, that was mighty lucky for you that Kasymov resigned. I checked things out, a grandmaster or two here like PawnKing Cole, a simulator or three there — including, I might add, MS. GRAY — and, my friend, Kasymov must be kicking himself tonight for not seeing pawn to f6."

Weston shrugged. "I beat him. Tha's what matters." A frown was forming at the points of Jasmina's mouth. Too much shop talk. He shrugged again, thinking this communicated "enough, end of conversation" to Orring. It irked him that this patzer had access to MS. GRAY, though.

"Ah, but that's what I'm saying, Weston. What about tomorrow?"

"Whip his ass."

Orring's head see-sawed his doubt. "But what if I said I had a client who offered you a million now, untraceable physical cashcard, and a million at the end, for the rights to your ten million and a say in what games you, ah, play less well at." He waved a cashcard seductively.

Jasmina grunted her disgust and rose. "Wes, I think it's time I go."

Weston rose. "Abs'lutely."

"Think, man. Two million or nothing! Think about Winnie!" Orring's voice trailed after them as they left.

CHAPTER 15

C hris ate the rest of his figs, ordered linguine con vongole for his primi pasta and branzino in cartoccio for his secondi piatti, his main course. He penned a couple personalized greeting card messages for some Baptisms; his ratings were always fairly good on such things. That done, he debated with himself: The breeze was delightful.

The terrorist's confession request was marked public, which was rare, but not unheard of. It meant the confessee had no expectations of privacy; indeed, expected public knowledge. Downing the rest of the glass of wine, he alerted the polizia, initialized the trace and recording spexware they'd given him, and drained two more glasses of the chianti before he was ready to blink on El Cyb's request.

Chris initiated the connection and said a brief prayer to let the confessee know he was there.

What Chris called Betty Crocker's face appeared, unafraid to be seen during her confession. Though she was, of course, veiled completely by the anonymity of the Betty Crocker avatar; Chris might as well have been looking at a blank wall, although this one conveyed facial expressions.

"Forgive me Father, for I have sinned," she said, looking in fact contrite.

"Before we begin, you know I've alerted the authorities and they will trace this connection, as well as monitor it."

She nodded. "I understand. And as you know, they won't be able to trace it." The background behind her was bright, but fuzzy.

"So you say." Chris fidgeted. It wasn't natural to hear a confession in public.

"They won't. The 'MIX SIX SIX Pretzel Routing' software recrypts and reroutes everything that passes through it. They will trace your spex packets to a certain node, and not beyond. They will see all the traffic exiting the node, and know that the data is in there, somewhere, but not where or how, nor from there where it goes. Which node is the first collector changes randomly with each packet, or I wouldn't talk to you. In some cases the data piggyback on other connections, modifying one data bit here, one bit there. Your liberty is protected just as much as mine by the wonderful young idealists who willingly run the software. That's for the benefit of your audience."

Chris sighed. "Please don't treat this lightly."

"I'm not trivializing this, Father."

"Call me skeptical, El Cyb. Starting with this 'El Cyb' nonsense. What's your real name?"

"You'll laugh. Or at least not believe me. El Cyb is the public pseudonym we all use within the Cyberistas for anonymity. My parents actually named me Sibylla. Hoping I would be Oracular, I imagine. My friends call me Sib — and yes, the irony is noted. Even intended, I suppose, given my livelihood. Please, call me Sib."

"Sib. I'm still skeptical of your earnestness. But go ahead."

"Thank you. Father, something I did destroyed a building and hurt some people."

Chris harumphed. "This wouldn't include the building by the church in the Piazza Navona would it? Oh, and those hurt wouldn't perhaps include me?"

"I'm ready to switch to private confession now."

"Really, if you won't treat this seriously —"

"I am!"

With a grunt Chris blinked the "private" icon. "I don't appreciate being a messenger boy for your terrorist group. Not to mention one that tried to kill me."

"I'm sorry, Father. I was sure it wouldn't kill you. We were sure the only other people in the building were bad people anyway." She added sweetly, "Am I forgiven?"

"It doesn't work like that!"

"What do you mean? I thought if one confessed one's sins, they were forgiven." She hung her head.

"You tried to kill me then you expect instant absolution. I'm only human!" He drank a shaky sip of wine. "I have to keep in mind your disposition. You've shown me no contrition. I told you this last time."

She pursed her lips. "Is it not enough that we fight for freedom?"

"What freedom? You're a terrorist."

"'Terrorist,' 'Freedom Fighter' — the label is attached by the victors."

"You imply you fight for a just cause."

"It's a hard struggle against oppression."

"Who are your people? Who is oppressed?"

"That would be telling. Your audience might find me."

"I have no audience now. You requested privacy mode."

"You have an audience."

"Then they have to face God for that, since the sacrament is private." A pit formed briefly in his stomach at the thought that the police would be so bold as to monitor sacred connections. He hoped she was simply wrong. "So. If you believe we are still being monitored, then come tell me in person."

"Would that I could! Father, you are a kind man, but you can't be so naive to think I could visit you and not be..."

Chris sighed and clinked his silverware together. "If I am to determine your contrition, you have to give me something. What are you fighting for? Freeing the Yak farmers of Mongolia?"

"We cannot identify the specific oppression, or we risk discovery, so we fight against all oppression, anywhere."

"If you're contrite, you won't commit any more acts of terr — any more acts that hurt people. You could have killed me; you could have killed those two people in the building, the people in the square. You could have killed the boy."

"The boy. Such a wonderful boy. So innocent. Do you regret not having children, Father?"

"I took a vow of celibacy. All God's children are for me to tend to."

"But your church now allows priests to marry, with special permission, does it not?"

"If God's Will can be shown at play, yes. It was a formality, a step toward Protestant reconciliation. But it's still controversial, and rarely requested."

"Isn't that backward, Father? To encourage the sinners to have children, while the most devout, who give their lives to God, can't have children to pass along what must be some of the best genes?"

"I don't know that one's calling is in one's genes. I do believe it's best to devote oneself entirely to God and not have the... distractions... of an earthly family."

"Sometimes two can be stronger than one. If only things were different, Father. Perhaps we would have fallen in love, gotten married, had children..."

"Do I know you? Who are you, the Great Deceiver, here to tempt me?" They must have met. Perhaps she was one of the Jobs?

"You know I can't tell you anything like that."

"Then let's stick to the subject, if you intend this to be a real confession. I can't absolve you of your sins if you don't show regret about them, not to mention resolve you won't do them again."

"That's a dealbuster?"

A singing troubador ambled over to Chris's table. Chris blinked him a token and waved him away. "That's a dealbuster."

"That doesn't seem fair. People have impure thoughts all the time, yet they get them forgiven, I assume — then have them again. Do they lose the forgiveness from the prior cases?"

"I hardly think sins add up that way in God's eyes. One murder is a mortal sin all by itself. If you were forgiven for that, then you showed genuine contrition. If you do it again, presumably you were still genuine before. If not, then you were false the first time, and that has it's own drawbacks. Look. Sib. We all sin; we can't promise not to sin. Just to *try* not to."

She paused. "I'm okay with that, then. I don't *want* to ever do it again. I'm truly sorry that I've hurt anyone, including you."

Chris narrowed his eyes. "You can't split hairs with God, you know. If you're thinking that 'if only the government would give in to our demands then I wouldn't have to hurt anyone again' — that isn't the right attitude. God knows what's in your heart."

"Hmmmm; I wonder." She looked wistful.

Chris's pasta with clams arrived, steaming. The smell shook him back to reality, and that it was time to bring this sparring session to a close.

"Sib. Okay, look. I get the feeling you're a good kid."

"Who said I was a kid?"

"Good *person*, then," he said around a last mouthful of linguine. "I don't think you've quite got the contrition idea down yet, so you need to work on that. Here, here are some links to articles you should read." He blinked over a set of links he kept on hand, ranging from simple descriptions to meatier reading like St. Thomas Aquinas. "See how far you can get with those; I don't expect you to read them all, but some should resonate with you."

"Okay; I'll look at them. We have a lot of spare time around here. One question, then I'll let you eat your sea bass." The sea bass had only just arrived; their surveillance was frightening. "Could absolution be conditionally tied to my turning myself in?"

Chris's eyes brightened. If he could turn her onto a path of righteousness... "That could go a long way. Will you? I'll help you."

"I don't think I can." Her face hardened. "I've got to go. Thank you," she said, and she clicked off.

Hellfire! Just as she was coming around. Yet somehow he knew this wasn't the last he'd hear from Sib. This wasn't going to be an easy situation, but if he put in the effort, perhaps he could save her soul, and a few other people's lives too.

CHAPTER 16

The next morning was bright and sunny, snow melting in great rivulets. Denver weather was as quickly changing as the Market. Weston had walked like a gawking tourist to pick Jasmina up at work, from where they'd catch a floaterbus to the hotel for the match.

She was elbows deep in a 1953 Corvette's Powerglide automatic transmission. Canute, her boss and Classic Vehicle Restoration's ruddy-faced owner, poked fun at Weston, threatening not to give Jasmina the rest of the morning off. It was Weston's first visit to CVR. Now inside, amid the smell of grease, Weston thought he recognized one of the guys, perhaps from a courier run delivering parts. He tried to check his records, but his business logs were jumbled and incomplete at best; hunger usually outweighing the desire to keep accurate records. Even now half a dozen uncompleted jobs flashed red as he blinked through his Market queue, victims of studying for Kasymov. Tonight, he promised himself, he'd polish off some of the quicker jobs. He grumbled something back to Canute, more upset because of his plummeting ratings than Canute's remark, of which he'd only heard the needling tone of voice.

Weston glanced around the shop. A dozen other mechanics torqued and ratcheted about in knots of twos and threes. "Quite a setup you've got here," Weston commented. He was thinking how he might turn the conversation toward Canute suggesting someone take over Jasmina's work so she could call it quits.

"Yeah, we've got bulk," he said with a nod. "But most are only, what did she say you chess guys call 'em? Patzers. Jasmina's the only expert in the bunch. She puts in the time, learns all the nuances."

"Hmmph."

"You should see how fast she can smooth a block for an MLS gasket down to 10 Ra's. Smooth as a baby's bottom. It's a shame about the Axelrod's, but that's how it goes, I guess. Doesn't really matter for the vintage work, though."

Weston nodded knowingly, though he had no idea what automobile technobabble the man was going on about. He shielded his eyes from the snow reflecting through the windows on the large garage doors, then put on the spex he'd been holding; he wasn't as over his hangover as he'd liked. "I'll sit over here and wait," he said to Canute. "Run through some chess positions." He pulled a thin, adaptive blanket from his pack, sat and tipped his head back against the cinder blocks, what he told Jasmina was his version of a Quantum Meditation pose. He tugged up the blanket that would adjust to Weston's brain waves and warm or cool itself to an optimal cozy body temperature.

Truth was, he was anything but meditative: he'd been madly scrambling to learn about opening books in chess. Over hundreds of years now chess masters had analyzed the first sets of moves in games for their strengths and weaknesses, good and bad variations. He'd always played by instinct, analyzing from first principles, only dimly been aware of the names Ruy Lopez, Sicilian, King's Indian, Caro-Kann, Queen's Gambit Declined. Besides, the computer could always advise what was the best move (though Weston had always thought of the same moves on his own), so there had been no need to learn specific names for patterns. After his hair-breadth win the day before Weston was panicked that his understanding of the fundamentals was seriously lacking. He rapidly blinked through the massive databases of opening game analyses. Experts had analyzed the moves so players could concentrate more readily on other aspects of the game and not have to create each analysis from scratch, but they were expected to learn the material over years, not hours, and not in the midst of critical games. Yet Weston found it increased his confidence, the more he studied, as each of the thousands of openings he read went down rapidly, intuitively. He mentally played each move thinking what he'd do before he read the analyses, and found himself hitting the analytical bullseyes. More than anything he was licking the spoon for any useful tips. But he had a long way to go; each required a pause of thought. He feared somehow Kasymov would know what he was studying and, with his choice by playing White, choose an opening an hour from now that Weston had yet to study.

"Hey, sleepy," a soothing voice said. "You don't want to be late."

Weston noted the lateness of the time in his spex then took them off as they prepared to slush down the sidewalk. He liked best to look at Jasmina's eyes with his own. Somehow time always flew when he was in her company, and flew pleasantly, as if he were dodging terrible accidents and he was grateful to be alive.

"Great, let's go. Did you know this opening book stuff is fascinating? I never realized people had invested so much energy into studying chess. I've always just... played. It's like learning how to read from soup bag labels then deciding to visit this thing called a library."

"That's great!"

But she looked worried as they jostled onto the crowded floaterbus and it surged forward. He could sense her saying, Don't get overconfident, don't disrupt your routine, don't try anything weird.

"You know, though, all I need to win is having you there."

She smiled. "Just don't blame me if you lose!"

"I won't lose. I hope."

"You could try QM," she said, to which he replied with a raspberry against her shoulder. "How do you know until you try it? It's about seeing all the positions possible at once. They mean like for an electron, but if 'all positions' doesn't sound like chess, I don't know what does. I looked up how it gets used in chess: some chess players say there's a kind of 'convergence' to checkmate that shimmers stronger with their best move. You could, I don't know, see all the attacked squares many moves ahead at once."

Weston looked skeptical. "That's kind of how I see it now. You can, uh, show me later." He winked.

~~~

Seated once again in the gray folding chair inside the bell — and thinking he should ask for a more comfortable chair for next time — Kasymov began his attack. He'd blinked into Weston's spex reassured

and cocky, all the lines on his aged face seeming to smile with conde-
scension. Kasymov never lost to others; Kasymov only lost to himself.

He began his white-pieced onslaught with an opening Weston
didn't particularly recognize but timidly mirrored, then concentrated
to remember in his new found ally of studied openings. It was — yes —
the Giuoco Piano opening. The database had warned that Black must
play carefully to emerge ahead, that it led to early fireworks, and
noted as poor a move Weston had contemplated. He thanked the stars
he'd had the foresight to look the opening up, and proceeded to fend
off Kasymov's development. When he came to a crucial decision
whether to make a defensive pawn move that, he foresaw would lead
to a draw, or a dangerous nudge of his bishop that might lead to an
advantage, he went for the gamble.

Kasymov began slashing back, but Weston easily parried and built
his strength. It was as if having the revelation of the opening book
analyses had exploded his abilities to a new level. He danced his
pieces lightly around the board, feeling intuitively that White was
sluggish. By the twenty-fifth move, he felt confident. This was easy.
He began moving his pieces with gusto, bold flourishes, big smiles.
Jasmina smiled back contagiously, but waved him away from paying
attention to her. Weston pressed his attack, seeing Kasymov's face
kink and knot, and kept pressing, pressing, until Kasymov leaped
from his seat and resigned and blinked out in huff.

Weston had done it again! He threw the board into the air with a
wild fountain of pieces. He ran outside the glass bell and twirled Jasmina high in the air. "I'm invincible! Did you see it! I obliterated him!
Playing Black!"

CHAPTER 17

Martin sat on a padded bench outside the conference room where I. St. Thomas was due to give his (or her, he thought with unrealistic hope that it might yet be a 'she' and she might be attractive) presentation. But probably *he*, Martin thought: He had a hunch it was the rude "Irwin—" he'd run into in the hotel lobby. Martin hoped to snag him before he went in. Martin had found that introductions made *before* panels seemed much more rewarding than those made after, when a crush of people might vie for a speaker's attention. Not knowing for sure what this St. Thomas person looked like was of course a handicap, but Martin enjoyed the challenge.

He scanned the loop of images from public video feeds from both the hotels public casts and those forwarded by passersby or sensors people had randomly planted who knows when. Hmm, how about this fellow, he thought, zooming in to his face and querying for name matches. Nope.

He did see the woman from his presentation the other day, the one who'd snubbed his offer of a drink. She was walking fast, determined, swinging her arms forcefully. Anger Walking, the latest fad. Exercise and therapy all in one. Going for a good *grrr*.

Martin smiled and tipped his imaginary hat as she stormed toward him. She passed without slowing, giving him a glare he could feel right through her spex. She marched past, down the corridor with a swoosh. *Whew, spexy!* Martin admired the lines of her long legs in a flowery, blue Caribbean batik sarong until she turned a corner.

Martin settled back to scanning his meshlife and sipped a Red Stripe beer he'd secreted in a water bottle. People started filing into the conference hall like brownian motion of particles near an edge, some people passing by, some falling in. The beer was good.

After a time a man and woman jostled down the way. The man was guiding the woman, one hand on her back, almost propelling her down the hall, his other hand on her arm as if to ensure she didn't bolt away. She was the woman from his talk, the Anger Walking woman. The pressed lips and set of her face said she was still quite angry. The man looked some twenty years her senior, putting him around fifty, Martin estimated. He had a pouch slung over his shoulder, with some sheafs of e-paper crisply held in one pocket. He'd never seen the man before, Martin thought at first. Then his spex flashed his face and displayed a time stamp of Martin's recorded past, with a first frame showing, yes, of course, it was that rude man at the hotel lobby kiosk. Martin zoomed his spex on the e-papers, and sure enough, "Confidential Property of Irwin St. Thomas" was all the fuzzed-out text that was readable.

The couple stopped abruptly. They were arguing in whispers. She pushed his arm away from her. Martin upped the gain on his microphone and squinted to enable lip-reading mode.

"This is my show, Isabelle, and you will not upstage me," he said.

"You don't even know the results. It's my work."

"You're being psychotic. Now be a good lass and take a seat." He began to walk inside without her.

"I'm giving this talk, Irwin. We agreed. If I don't give this talk, I'll publish all my notes. I don't give a crap how many years it sets back my career, it will end yours. This farce ends now. I'm giving this talk."

She pushed past him, strode to the front of the conference room. Before he could say anything, chasing after her, she announced, "Hello, everyone, I'm Isabelle St. Thomas, and this is my husband, Irwin. Welcome to our update on Evolved Algorithms for Fault Tolerance and Fault Prediction."

Martin had followed them into the room and watched as the man gestured for her to continue and took a seat on the aisle a few rows ahead of Martin. Enhancing the room's reflection off her spex, Martin could clearly see a furious scowl on the man's face.

Martin listened, mesmerized by her beauty and her intellect as she gave what felt a masterful talk on a subject he knew absolutely nothing about. Something relating to an approach to rapidly Darwinizing a universe of algorithms (whatever that meant specifically, he could only guess, but didn't bother to hunt down in the flood of other domain slang). He got the impression from the graphics that their work involved gobbling up a ton of algorithms that might not be related to their goal and mixing them using some kind of adapters to make their I/O uniform, then tweaking random algorithms, somehow, to see if the whole soup produced an algorithm that was relevant to their goal. Their "algorithmic goal state," as she called it, another domain slang, seemed to be in the area of fault tolerance, an area Martin knew well, producing something that wouldn't be susceptible to crashes. She kept referencing their "application domain" as predicting terrorist behaviors, an apparent specialty field of her husband.

Martin thought he got it—that they were using software to build AI software to predict terrorist attacks—but he didn't really care. What he knew were three things: One, she was beautiful, inside and out; and as a mostly lizard-brained creature he couldn't stop those feelings. Two, her husband was an ass. He didn't deserve her. Three, she used his NEWT language and could use his help.

What man wouldn't be drawn to the damsel in distress image that conjured up? Even if she seemed fully capable of fixing her own distress.

When the police floater bot and two people in scary, police-officer-looking suits came in, Martin's first thought was, "Oh fuck, now what law did I break," while his second thought was to duck down and crawl out along the seats—his whole row was empty enough for him to contemplate it.

The entourage passed him, however, and stopped before Irwin St. Thomas. One floater bot went to Isabelle, circled around her, and guided her toward her husband and the others with a beeping noise.

Martin had the audio and lip-reading enhancements only suspended and reactivated them with a blink.

"—etective Creque of the UN Cyber Command Investigations Unit. The two of you must come with us," one of the people said, a tall bald woman.

"This is absurd! On what authority? You can't arrest us, we've done nothing," Irwin St. Thomas said, loud enough for everyone to hear.

"Don't make a scene," the other cop said, the short man with the burn scar on half his face, which looked shaped like a rooster, in a Rorschach kind of way.

It must have been serious, Martin thought, for them to send real people.

There must have been some exchange of spex warrants or other credentials, as Irwin St. Thomas blushed despite his tan and guided Isabelle by the arm to follow the police out.

Martin swore. This complicated things. At least they weren't arresting *him* again.

CHAPTER 18

As he walked the streets around the Circus Maximus, now a huge, empty, green field, Chris found himself subconsciously looking for the boy. He didn't know his name, so to his mind he had somehow become The Boy. The odds of actually seeing him were astronomical, Chris realized, but he scanned every child nonetheless.

A tour bus floated up and disgorged its flock. Chris walked through them, smiling. Even though he was more or less a tourist here too, their cackle and the sparklers of their unsolicited spex traffic was annoying and made it hard to dictate. He quickly turned down a random sidestreet.

The morning sun was unusually warm; it would be hot by noon and Chris had forgotten his hat. Chris was adding more detail to the Lindsay Bos chapter. In a background window—background like the thought at the back of his mind—he was fumbling for words to express his sorrow to her husband. He'd blinked through a few sympathy card storelets, but none of the sentiments seemed quite right. If he'd caused her death, somehow, because of a misstep in Project Job, like with Dirk, he at least owed the man heartfelt and non-machine-generated sympathies.

A young girl ran by, parents straggling. Wasn't The Boy. He couldn't understand why he was looking for the boy in the first place. The boy had been doing fine before and Detective Mannino said he was probably doing fine now. Hmph. As if Mannino knew; or cared.

But he was really just stalling what he ought to do—call Kalvin Bos.

He blinked up Kalvin's contact link. Gah. How he hated death. Blink—

"This is Kalvin." Gruff. The guy looked haggard. The bags under his eyes were the same dark of his hair. Chris hadn't noticed before that the man was going gray at the temples. His stubble looked unkempt, not stylish. It looked to be a small apartment. A huge crucifix hung on the wall. Faith wailed in the background.

"Hello, Kalvin, this is Father Giordano. I talked with you and Lindsay a couple years ago. I just heard. I'm so sorry for your loss." Bleah, that sounded empty.

"Yeah. I 'member you. Ever write that book?"

Chris was suspecting Kalvin might be drunk. "I'm working on it now, in fact. I hope you'll find it a fitting memorial to Lindsay." Chris had walked down a lane, now realized it dead ended at a stone wall, and began to backtrack.

"Great. A memorial. I don't need a fucking memorial. My kid needs a mother."

"Kalvin, I'm sorry, this is a bad time. I just wanted to express my condolences."

"Terrific. It's all bad times now. Death pretty much blows, you know? Life not so great sometimes either."

"Have you talked with Fr. Aaronson at your church?"

"Usual blah blah blah. We're heading up country, into the bush. Getting out of here. Too many memories. Too many *memorials*."

"Is that a good idea?" Chris blurted out. "That's off-mesh, isn't it? If Faith needs medical assistance..." Which was, of course, the problem that happened to Lindsay.

"Everybody dies, Father."

Chris wasn't sure he liked the sound of that. It didn't seem wise for him to interfere with a Job—but nothing should prevent him from having a chat with Father Aaronson. Later. Right now—

"Kalvin, there's a favor you could do for me. I know it's crass to ask now, and I was going to call you in a few months, after... but since you're going off-mesh, would it be possible to get a copy of Lindsay's shoot? I'd like a copy for my records."

"Figured you wanted something. Everybody does."

"No, honest, it's not—"

"Yeah, yeah, whatever." Kalvin pressed his lips tight and stared off to the side. He paused for an unnatural length of time; or perhaps it was natural for someone inebriated.

Chris cleared his throat. "I'm sorry I asked. I'll—"

"Hell. I'll send it."

"Thanks, and—"

"Something else you wanted?"

"No." He opened his mouth to explain again he hadn't meant to ask this time, and was thinking how to phrase it—

—When Kalvin nodded and cut the connection.

The video pinged in arrival seconds later. Kalvin must have been watching it recently.

Chris began playing it, seeing superimposed on Rome in front of him the last moments of Lindsay Bos's life, just as if he were standing in the dense thickets near the Sabi river. He felt helpless. She hiked from her floater toward a copse of acacia trees where Chris suspected lurked the fateful rhino. Presumably Lindsay even knew there was a rhino in there and was the reason for her venture; nonetheless Chris wanted to shout in a covert whisper, "Don't go over there! Back up and get out of there!"

But Lindsay found the rhino, a mother with a calf. The mother didn't seem too concerned, as Lindsay kept her distance. "The calf's so young," Lindsay narrated. "It doesn't even have any horns yet. That means it's no more than a month old."

Chris watched with dread as Lindsay circumnavigated the copse, filming from all angles, wishing she'd never have come, expecting her to say something that gave away why the rhino charged. It didn't seem particularly interested in her. Chris assumed somewhere she must try to grab the calf, or something else daring; that was ultimately what the video people paid for.

The video went on; it would need substantial editing to remove the cruft.

Chris realized he'd wandered in a circle back to the Circus Maximus. Now a bunch of kids were playing football down in the bowl, down where the chariots once raced. Unconsciously Chris cut down the grass toward them. As he approached he saw they played with a floater ball over a temporary QWKST maglev field they'd set up. He languidly scanned their faces as Lindsay Bos narrated her rhino shoot then started back to her floater.

Chris was within earshot of the children when Lindsay's spex noted a bass rustling sound. Then—oof—they were filming the air—the trees sideways—the ground. The rhino thundered past. The spex came to rest upside down, showing Lindsay Bos's foot dangling from the top of the frame.

Birds chirped in an otherwise frozen scene. A breeze sighed.

"Attenzione! Watch out!" cried the children in annoyance—Chris had veered right through the kids' field. They were equally inattentive and had kicked a ball right at him. Chris looked up to see the ball on a bee-line for his crotch.

Suddenly alert, he noted he had a good angle on the goal—the goalie had run out to defend at the far side of the penalty box—but that wouldn't be fair. Instead he dived and headered the ball toward the middle of the pack.

He slid, scraping his chin, and bounced up into a defensive stance. He wiped the blood from his chin with the back of his hand, a self-satisfied grin on his face: He still had the instincts.

He stood up, smiled at the kids—none were The Boy—and skirted their field as he walked onward. He sadly shut down the video of Lindsay Bos's foot, idly fingering the packet of candy he carried in his pocket in case he should find The Boy.

Chris headed toward the old Roman Forum and walked among the tourists. Many of them wore ads on their clothes to reduce the price of their tours.

He stood and stared at the Mamertine prison where St. Peter and Paul were allegedly imprisoned.

"She was murdered," a voice said loudly in his ear.

"Shit!" He jumped. He looked around—nobody was particularly near him. He rewound the video on his spex. There were a number of people around, though none bent close to shout in his ear. It must have been a trick of acoustics. Sound bounced funny here.

Who was murdered, he wondered? Probably someone talking about an emperor's wife. They were always offing each other.

He hiked up to the road above the Forum, where he could survey the whole of it laid out before him.

He leaned against a waist high wall and watched tourists trying to land replica coins on top of a row of columns below them. "Lindsay," he thought he heard someone say. He jerked his head toward the source. Hard to tell—just tourists, adults, kids. There was a gelato cart down the sidewalk, and Chris made for it. He could use a little treat. On the way, he could have sworn someone whispered, "rhino charged the headlights." He shook his head; he was just spooking himself.

He stopped, leaned against the wall again, and replayed his spex. Someone had said "rhino," but it was part of a sentence of one stroller-pushing mother talking to another about a rhinovirus. "Charged" was a word from two teenage girls' conversation that just happened to waft his way more loudly on that word. "The head-lights" was said, but in a sentence uttered by a taxi driver complaining to his dispatcher.

Weird that they should be so accentuated. Or maybe his brain was trying to tell him something?

Or God.

Chris did have a strange run-in when he was a child, where, alone in his empty bedroom in an empty house on a quiet day, the word "Paul" had boomed out. It hadn't scared him at the time, but as an adult he'd remembered about it and wondered at the cause. Scientifically, he decided, it must have been some weird channeling of an outside noise. That was before entering seminary. After, he wondered if it might have been God or some such; but couldn't see any reason for it, and reverted back to the scientific explanation. It hadn't happened again, and he'd never thought much about the cause since. Until now.

That had been one word, and while the name of an apostle, he couldn't say it had anything to do with him entering the priesthood. This was curious: whole sentences, relevant ones at that. He played back the suggestive collage of voices: *Lindsay Bos was murdered, because the rhino charged the headlights.*

CHAPTER 19

Weston partied publicly that night in Jasmina's apartment. News of his victories brought him chess groupies, and he danced and toasted for hours in his spex. He visited virtual parties worldwide, small ones in people's homes, rage clubs in spexspace, yellow-liners on highways (who wanted him to join them In Person as they dodged the floaters, those nuts), and he was sure some were gala events for bigwigs, not him, which he'd somehow crashed tagging along another partygoer's spexways. He slid between them like a windblown leaf in fall, sometimes dancing in three or four simultaneously. Jasmina accompanied him at first, reluctantly. She sat on the couch, dancing only virtually, and half-heartedly at that. At some point Weston realized he hadn't seen her in half a dozen party fades. As soon as he finished his flam dance, he double-checked that she was still in the apartment.

"C'mon!" he shouted, though the room itself was of course quiet. "We've been invited to do the double-pole!" Half of his spexspace resolved to the prolonged night of the North pole, the other half the midnight sun of the South. Partiers leaped, spun, and jiggled between the two. With only a handful of settlements at the poles and very limited bandwidth, getting invited to do a fifty-fifty was a rarity, and the chance to virtually span the globe was an honor few could legitimately claim. Apparently they played a lot of chess in the cold.

Weston extended his arms to her. "C'mon! Let's dance it in the real!"

Jasmina unfolded from her QM pose reluctantly, tiredly. "Okay, but, just one round. Maybe I could help you study your openings after that. Maybe show you some QM."

"Study, shmudy!" he shouted clasping her hands and spinning around. "I can beat the old guy easily. I only need a win and a draw to beat him, or three draws, and I play White tomorrow. How can I lose! Dance with me! Wheeeeee!" Around and around, the world became a blur.

"Whoa... dizzy," she said.

He sensed she wasn't interested, and he sped up their spinning, hoping that would get her into it. Maybe now was a good time to spring his surprise gift on her. "Not half as dizzy," he yelled over the virtual din, "as you're going to get when I buy out your servitude contract! Faster, faster!"

She stopped dead. Hands went to hips.

Weston lost his balance when she let go. He tumbled onto the sofa, whiplashing his head. His spex flew off and thudded to the floor. "What'd you do that for?"

"What do you mean, buy out my contract? I don't have any contract."

"Sure you do, with Canute." He rolled his eyes. "Look, it's okay to admit it. Lots of people have them. It's not like it isn't obvious when someone only works one job."

"I'm nobody's wage slave! I work one job because I *like* it. You know what? I used to live in a self-drive camper commune. Why? Not because I was poor. Because I *liked* it."

Weston, even though slightly drunk, could see that if she were his ex named Rosalisa, she'd blast him with double barrels of "where the hell do you get off"s and "besides it's none of your damn business"es. But Jasmina just folded her arms and dipped her head quickly as if to let the anger slide off.

"I appreciate the gesture, Wes, but honest, I'm not bound under any contract. It's part of who I am. Look, you're tired, I'm tired, let's not get into a fight over it. I've got to get up early tomorrow, so I'm going to bed. Come on whenever you're ready."

"Jasmina, wait!" Weston cried, but she retreated to the bedroom.

Weston threw up his hands. He knew he should think this through, and like she'd said, he should study, too. For a long while he tried both. He finally concluded there was no way he could study, her feelings were more important than that; he just felt mopey and guilty and distracted the whole time. Talk about the QM being-in-multiple-states thing; whoo. Yet he couldn't figure her out. Why would some-one *want* to do only one job, and spend so much time at it that you became an expert not only in that, but in tangentially related areas? What was the point? His head began to hurt. He twirled his spex, de-bating whether to check if the double-pole invite was still valid, he could just pop in for a sec to say he did it... then decided that this was really his one shot in life, and he better not blow it. He could talk her out of that abysmal One Job philosophy of hers later, after... Later. He was tired.

Something niggled at him as he prepared for bed. Something Canute had said about how good Jasmina was. What was it he'd said?

As he swished his dentabots he rewound back to his conversation with Canute. He'd been holding the spex in his hands, so there was no video except sideways views of old cars and car repair detritus. He found the audio: "It's a shame about the Axelrod's, but that's how it goes, I guess."

What the heck was an Axelrod? He subvocalized the word into a search box. Axelrod's Syndrome: A degenerative brain disease?! Simi-lar to Alzheimer's and initially confused with it, it had been traced to a virus that had recently made the leap from the Candango mouse to humans after the Amazon Accident. It was particularly common in people who had had the first—and last—wave of implant tech, a magnificent failure resulting in conservatives banning it. Weston wondered if Jasmina had tried implants. He couldn't find any tips to tell; all the articles just kept referring to the same spectacles of people gone berzerk. Feng Zhao's squelch gun massacre. Gruesome. He went back to reading about Axelrods.

Because of the more rapid degeneration of the brain in Axelrod's than in Alzheimer's—death occurred in 90% of patients within five years—and a fear that it might mutate into a more infectious form, victims of Axelrod's often volunteered for the newest treatments for Alzheimer's. The most promising was a highly experimental one, very expensive, millions, if you weren't on their list. Some kind of memcopy that was chemically redownloaded. Ugh, he thought, re-membering his grandmother's creepy, disgusting memcopy. High suicide rate: Victims of Axelrod's typically found modern life difficult, for the increased brain activity of a 24x7 society, especially the use of spex, was not only quite painful, but accelerated the degeneration... CVR—no wonder she... Oh, God: He was losing her.

He was her knight. He'd have to find a way to win the money for her too, not just Winnie.

He shut off his spex and crawled silently into bed beside Jasmina's gently snoring softness.

CHAPTER 20

In a light rain, almost too light to be called rain, Chris sat at a café near the Forum nursing a cappuccino. Despite being the scene of the prior voices, no more had appeared, here or anywhere.

It would take time to locate free image enhancement software. No matter how he played Lindsay Bos's video, he couldn't see any headlights of any floater through the thickets. He had a gopher searching for info whether headlights could even enrage a rhino into charging. Meanwhile, he put his notes in order on another Job.

Jasmina Simonis, age 30, birthdate December 21, born in New Hampshire, USA. Moved around frequently as her father, Peter (Pierre) Simonis, served in US Army as a mechanic. Transferred and demoted often due to drinking problem. Discharged, became race car driver around time Jasmina was ten. Killed in racing accident when she was 15. Mother, Annette, had no education past high school diploma, technologically backwards. Struggled to feed Jasmina and her two siblings (older sister, older brother).

Work profile: Jasmina is a Mechanic; restores antique, petrol-powered cars. Unusual in that she only works one job — no joblets at all. Due to having contracted Axelrod's Syndrome, which leads to an inability to tolerate multiple concurrent brain tasks, causing severe migraines, etc. Disease is degenerative; without a cure she says she will likely die within ten years. Deeply into Quantum Meditation as naturopathic means to control the Axelrod's. "In a good session I can get, I guess, my brain in some kind of, like, infinite levels of reality, and leave my pain behind in some of them. Or maybe it's that I get so calm my brain forgets it has this damn monkey on it's back, and that amnesia lasts a while."

Footnote: QM is a new fad relaxation and concentration technique pain-fully similar (here Chris went back and deleted "painfully," sneering at the fad but knowing he shouldn't make editorial judgments) *to TM —*

Transcendental Meditation — that was a popular fad until — (Chris decided just to link to the Wikitannica article; enough digression). *QM practitioners say they feel like some divine intelligence takes over their bodies and minds while they are in their QM trance state.*

Chris sighed, and just linked to the Wikitannica article on the bizarre stories of people who claimed to have learned foreign languages and solved unsolved math problems while in QM trances. So much poppycock. It was understandable how it would appeal to Job candidates, but he worried it might in some way be an expression of their lack of faith in God — and, thus, potentially disqualifying them from being Jobs. He quirked his mouth. He'd leave her in the book; she was properly footnoted for others to digest.

One marriage, six months, divorced. Video clip: "Oh, he was a gem." She rolls her eyes, smiling. "Harmless enough, but never did a day's work, and I was stupid. You know — I thought I could fix him. I've never been able to earn much — the Axeldrod's, right? — and he took every dime." She rubs her temples. "Then I fell in love with one of his friends after we got divorced. Boy was that a mistake. Oh, then my mother got into some weird negative form of QM — I'd told her about QM, but she got off on some tangent — and had a brain hemorrhage and died. I don't know for a fact it was the antiQM, I guess." She rubs at her eyes, which are spexless.

"I'm a magnet for trouble," she says with a laugh, pushing back her hair.

Religious feelings: "Um. Well, my parents were Catholic, but didn't go to church except maybe three-four times a year. Sometimes I stop into this little church near my apartment on Sundays. (Here he had included a photo of the white wooden church.) Once a month maybe. When it's empty. I sneak in and sneak out."

"Has the Church given you any comfort in coping with your disease?" Chris asked.

"Er, sorry Father, but not really."

"I feel for you. Perhaps it's part of God's plan." Chris had been hoping to detect some behavior to rule in or rule out whether she was a Job. The real Jobs were the hardest to detect; they simply didn't blame God or have a bad thing to say.

"God's plan, huh? Pfffft, who could say? I guess. Pretty inscrutable giving people Axelrod's for the hell of it. I guess I could get into the plan thing; be a Joan d'Arc kind of thing, all sacrificy."

Chris took off his spex and rubbed his own eyes. She was a hard one to classify. Not for her attitude, which was angelic in endurance, but that she was higher level functioning than most Jobs. She had a paying job, albeit only one. She didn't really praise God, but she certainly wasn't complaining about her lot in life.

He noticed his cappuccino was finished and donned his spex to blink an order for another, thinking how he disliked the touristy cafés without a human to work with. A priority call had flashed in: From Sib.

He felt a pang of fear—trouble followed her like Job—or perhaps she caused it, like the Sphinx of Greek myth, a demon of death and arcane wisdom. Yet his heart lifted as well. The other clergy in the dormitory were never interesting conversation.

"Why do you come here so often? To the Forum, I mean," she asked.

"I didn't realize I do."

"Your wanderings end here more than anywhere else."

"Hmm. Frankly it's disconcerting that you know something like that about me. But—" He considered the question. "I suppose it's because it's so old. It's been here two, almost three thousand years... It gives me perspective, I suppose. Sort of like coming to talk to them—not the old Roman emperors, the Just Ordinary Romans. We're not so different after all these centuries."

"What? They lived lives nasty, short, and brutish."

"That's Hobbes—'solitary, poor, nasty, brutish and short.' But not from their perspective. Though we can't argue that; it's solipsism. Anyway, whatever they were, are we so superior? It'd be enjoyable if they were alive to talk to. Short, indeed."

"Everybody dies, Father."

"Yes of course." He sighed. He didn't want to be reminded of Lindsay Bos just now, or what might soon be in store for her daughter. "Nasty, brutish and short may not be far from the mark for any of us." Perhaps, he thought, coming here to the forum made him feel closer to the Biblical Job. He added, "I just mean that our problems of daily life are much like theirs."

"I disagree. Think how much more you command than they did—people today are nearly what their gods were. Though, three thousand years is a blink of an eye for a god, so perhaps the similarity is strained." She laughed. "Don't you wish you were an old Roman god? All that power. All that... *perspective*. Now that would be thrilling."

"An awful lot of responsibility. As a god I would want to use my powers wisely. I doubt I know how to do that. I'm more content seeing the future than creating it."

"How much of the future? Immortality?"

"Hmm. I hadn't really considered it. Immortality would put us on God's level, so that's hubris. We shouldn't want to outlive what time God grants us."

"What if God granted the immortality? Does not Ecclesiastes 3:11 say, 'He has also set eternity in the hearts of men'? Does not Jesus promise eternal life in 1 John 5:13? And assuming scientists are right that the universe must end one way or another, immortality isn't happening unless we can leave this universe. So you'd meet up with God sooner or later. He can wait a little, can't he? A trillion years would be nothing for God. People have always searched for the fountain of youth, no? Didn't God even gave Job a dip in the fountain of youth and restore his youth so he lived twice as long, reflecting the desirability of longer life? People aren't sad that turtles or redwoods live hundreds of years?"

Chris sat back comfortably into the café chair. A good philosophical debate always invigorated him. "Well, that's only one translation of Ecclesiastes. Nor may that be the kind of eternal life Jesus was talking about. But, assuming, for sake of argument, that God granted or otherwise approved this immor—this *extensive longevity*, then by definition He would be signifying that he was willing to 'wait a little,' as you put it. The flaw in your logic is that we're not likely to get a clear signal that He has approved this immortality."

"No? But you, by that I mean the Church, take full advantage of advances in medicine. The pope right now is in a coma and receiving the best medical care possible to keep him alive."

Chris raised an eyebrow. "How do you know the Holy Father is in a coma?"

"I have it on good sources. He's had a stroke and likely is a vegetable. He's on life support. He's undergoing a treatment that may, not so academically, inhibit his aging; possibly for a *very* long time."

"I ask again, how do you know this?" He had feared the rumors were true that the Holy Father was gravely ill. It didn't bode well for Project Job.

"It's confidential, Father. No more can I tell you that than I can tell you where I am. So view it as a hypothesis. You're free to make inquiries of your own to verify it firsthand. Or you can try to disprove it. I'm confident you can't find any evidence to disprove it, since I know it to be true."

"Lack of evidence of a thing doesn't prove it, of course." Chris stroked his chin and decided in favor of another cappuccino. If it was God's will for the pope to be ill or die, then so it was. If it was God's will that Chris not finish Project Job, then so it was. "All right. Let's posit that the Holy Father is in a vegetative coma."

"And receiving a life-prolonging treatment," she added.

"Just so."

"An experimental treatment that may prolong his life indefinitely."

"That's harder to swallow. I've never heard of such a procedure. Church doctrine dating to St. Thomas Aquinas basically hold that ordinary measures to prolong life are reasonable, but excessive means are not." A loud group of tourists sat at the table next to Chris, and commandeered the extra chairs from his table. He thought about moving to a more peaceful venue, but his cappuccino order was in the pipeline. He turned up the echo canceling speakers on his spex, but they were only partially successful. He harumphed; to no effect on the loud gaggle. He went inside, found a human to cancel his order, and headed back into the streets. The food had smelled burnt in the kitchen anyway. "So. Let's assume for sake of argument this life prolonging treatment is reasonable and somehow the Holy Father desired it. So what?"

"'Every intelligent being naturally desires to be forever,'" she quoted Aquinas, spexing over a floating citation to the *Summa Contra Gentiles*. Francis Bacon wrote "whereunto man's nature doth most aspire; which is, immortality." She cleared her throat. "It's called the

'KL' procedure. Not much is known about it. So: 'So what?' So what happens to the Church? It would have no leader for... ever."

"That's unlikely," Chris said with a smile. "There are procedures for removing a pope from office if he's incapacitated." Chris spun off a search in his spex to find what they were, but it didn't return any results.

"What if he recovers later?"

Chris swirled his wine glass and watched the legs. "I'd imagine he'd be understanding of the circumstances."

"They wouldn't pull the feeding tube?"

Chris recoiled. "I should hope not!"

"Then he'd live hundreds of years, thousands... millions? 'forever'... as a vegetable."

"Until God calls him home. Or the procedure is deemed excessive; we only assumed that for the sake of debate."

"But isn't that, then, Man, with a capital M, interfering with the workings of God?" She laughed playfully.

"Perhaps your 'KL' treatment wouldn't be approved of."

"What if it's later disapproved, but at the time was approved? What if it's a one-time process, and there's nothing to reverse. And, another question, what of the next pope? What if he receives the KL treatment while he's healthy. A vigorous, immortal pontiff... He would live 'forever'? — and be pope... forever?"

Chris rubbed his temples. One of God's little miracles was crying at the next table over. "You're getting beyond me. This is science fiction."

Sib lost the playful look for a serious one. "What if Lindsay Bos knew of the KL treatment and thought it would cure her daughter, Faith?"

"I don't follow."

"What if, like antibiotics, the KL treatment was thought to work on the Zellweger's Syndrome that little Faith has. What if longevity was just one effect. But what if that immortality was the only operative effect on Faith, and not the hoped-for curative part for her Zellweger's? If it half-failed, she'd be an immortal in constant and relentless agony."

Chris sobered up. "Do you know this for a fact?" The wheels turned: Kalvin would have good reason to prevent such a thing. Chris thought of the headlights.

"Everybody dies, Father. Isn't that what you said? Got to run. Besides, you have a call coming in. Think on what I said. Ciao." She winked and cut the connection.

"Wha—" Chris stopped and sat on a low wall.

There was indeed a call at that moment. From Cardinal Canini, urgent.

"Yes, your eminence?"

Canini appeared with Monsignor di Fuoco. "Giordano. This terrorist attack. You should have informed me."

"I—I didn't think it worth wasting your time. I was just an innocent bystander."

"Innocent perhaps. Bystander—perhaps not."

"What! I had nothing to do with it."

"Be calm, Father."

Monsingor di Fuoco: "The authorities think someone you know may be involved."

His stomach lurched sideways. He'd wondered the same thing, whether he'd ever met Sib in person. "I've told the police everything I know."

Canini: "Yes. Well. They want more." He nodded to Monsignor di Fuoco.

di Fuoco: "UN Cyber Command demands you fill out this form"—at which a form icon blinked into existence—"on every person you've ever met, including all spex logs of conversations, confessions etc., etc., etc."

"Your eminence! I can't provide copies of confessions! You know I must I refuse!"

"I said as much. So the UNCC wants a record of everyone you know or knew or came in contact with.

di Fuoco added, "Name, date, personality, DNA ID, kind of relationship, your comments on their behavior, political leanings, vacation recollections...." As di Fuoco talked, Chris blinked through the form—it was some ten sheets long; of open ended questions; per person.

Canini spoke over di Fuoco, cutting him off. "And this, yes, they can demand. You will begin immediately. Work on this exclusively until completed. They may require followup interviews, so you will remain in Rome indefinitely."

Chris reeled at the enormity. He'd met literally thousands of people in his private and professional life. Tens of thousands. The time it would take just to review all his spex records to remember them...

"This will take months! I won't be able to work on my book!" The delay to Project Job... "indefinitely"... Chris clenched his jaw to avoid speaking bitter words.

"That's unfortunate for you. Keep me apprised of your progress. Buon giorno." Canini signed off.

CHAPTER 21

Back in his shared hotel room Martin found Jerry packing his suitcase, humming a Bob Marley tune. Martin signed off wishing his sister a happy birthday in Argentina and released homework assignments for his classes.

"Leaving so soon?" Martin asked Jerry.

"Still not talking to this one. Who nonetheless owes me a very expensive Italian dinner, during which hostilities will cease fire. For general information, I am packing now because tomorrow is the last day and I intend not to have time to pack then, intending to become thoroughly inebriated this evening. On very expensive champagne, wine, and forty-year-old port."

"Oh, very well. I'll endeavor to assist. I don't see why you bring so much *stuff*, Jerry. Why do you want to lug that thing?" He thumped the big, battered suitcase.

"Because I like to wear more than one outfit in a week? I'm old. It makes me feel cleaner."

Martin assessed his own packing needs—one extra pair of self-cleaning shorts with press on legs to make them into dress slacks, extra shirt with press on collar and sleeves to go from beach shirt to dress shirt, swim suit, all of which he would roll up and pack in the pockets of his sport jacket for the trip home. He loved traveling light. Not even any toiletries.

"Suit yourself, but I'm not carrying it this time when you get taken aside for psychological scanning at the airport. Speaking of cleaner, I'm going to freshen up. I *still* smell like jail."

He tossed his clothes on the unmade bed after pinching the extra-effort clean icon inside them. In the bathroom, after doing what one does whilst reading several chapterlets of the latest nanonovel, he took a squirt of the hotel's upscale sampler bottle of body and teeth cleaner. He swished that around while he sprayed it on his body; he enjoyed watching the cloud of microparticles float in the air until they got a reading on his body then make a slow-motion bee-line for his neediest zones. It tingled everywhere, and he scratched a few places where it went so far as to tickle. By the time he'd finished misting his skin it had evaporated in his mouth and he felt minty fresh inside and out.

He came out naked, with an exaggerated *Ahhhh* of contentment—and nearly ran into the two cops, Baldy and Rooster.

Before he could say, "And what are you two gentlemen staring at?" they abruptly ceased talking to Jerry. Baldy said, "You're Martin Sandoval. You're coming with us."

"What the fuck! I'm not even dressed."

"Get dressed," said Rooster.

"I demand to know what this is about. I've been continually harassed by you people and your damn bots. I don't know what it is about this country. I've paid my *restitution*," at which he turned up his lip, "and it was that jigged-out Ampy who filched the proxy. Now if you don't mind..." He began dressing.

"We know you're the Martin Sandoval who," Baldy looked heavenward in her spex, "who invented the NEWT programming language."

"Yes, and who the hell are you?"

"I would have thought someone of your ratings would know all about us."

"Apparently my reputation exceeds me. And you are?"

"We detected you eavesdropping on our conversation earlier. I'm Detective Creque," she said, "and this is Lt. Andy Matthews," referring to Rooster. "And now you're coming with us."

"Your eyes say yes, yes, yes, but my lips say no, no, no." He noticed they weren't swayed by his humor; their hands moved to their stun batons. "Ah. I recognize the classic signs of *easy way* versus *hard way*. Very well then. Sorry Jerry, it appears to be Rain Check City for dinner."

~~~

At the police station they placed him in a barren interrogation room, which they politely called a conference room. The only nod to a "conference" was that it contained five chairs and five glasses around the worn plastic table. The water glasses were most useful, there being no water.

After a time, what seemed a long time to a thirsty Martin, Rooster opened the door and was followed in by Baldy—and the two I. St. Thomas's.

They acknowledged each other with surprise. Martin smiled happily at Isabelle. Irwin scowled back.

Rooster left, quickly reappearing with a jug of water, which he poured for everyone.

"Ok. Yeah." Baldy looked around the ceiling quizically. "The reason we've brought you here, Prof. Sandoval—and I apologize for the unorthodox ruse,"—at which she gave a Cheshire cat smile. "Professor St. Thomas and... Professor St. Thomas," she said nodding at the two of them, "told us you were the unalloyed expert on a... a..." She looked at the St. Thomases for help.

"The NEWT programming language," Irwin St. Thomas filled in. "Alas," he added with a frown.

"Yeah, that, exactly," the detective continued. "A terrorist group calling itself the Cyberistas has stolen some software that Professor St. Thomas here invented." She tilted her head toward him; Isabelle twisted in her seat and quirked her mouth in annoyance. "This program finds weaknesses for terrorists to exploit."

"Technically, it's a deep intelligence system that predicts what weaknesses a terrorist would exploit," he added, rolling his eyes at the imprecision of the detective's description. "But, yes, one could use the output if one were a terrorist to decide what to attack. Of course it wasn't designed for that, but, hrm. It was designed for law enforcement, of course you see."

"That's fabulous," Martin said. "And where I come in is...?"

"I wrote it in NEWT," Isabelle said. "Plainly the best choice." She smiled, melting Martin's façade. "We think we know which data set of terrorist behavior patterns and vulnerability data the Cyberistas have stolen and are using. The recent attacks on Belém and Astrakhan—and here on Cayman Brac, which is what got the locals involved—are consistent with a specific bag of data. However, the *vector* of the attacks, the balloons, for example, are not quite per prediction. I believe they've either modified the algorithm, which seems unlikely, or they've augmented the data sets. We told the UNCC that we would need to modify our current engine in an effort to discover or match what they've done. We said we could use the help of an expert in NEWT to speed things up, and they asked if we knew any. I'm rather afraid I only knew of your name, and I was, plainly, aware that you were on the island. I'm sorry to have dragged you into this. But not so sorry that I do hope you can help?"

"We need your help, Professor Sandoval," Detective Creque said. "We must be able to predict the Cyberistas' moves. Their attacks are escalating in severity. I should hope we could come to terms on appropriate, er, *restitution* for your trouble. It will save countless lives."

"Put that way..." Martin smiled at Isabelle. Irwin noticed and flared his nostrils. "Could you have your people go collect my things from the hotel?"

CHAPTER 22

The next morning, seated in a far more comfortable chair — faux leather and foam padded — Weston looked around in distress. Jasmina wasn't here yet. She'd left before he woke, and was to have met him outside, but hadn't arrived. Now he was worried she might not find a place among the crowd fronting his glass bell. He tugged at his collar. Was it hotter in here than yesterday, he asked the match coordinator via his spex. No, of course not. Maybe he should change shoes; these seemed to be pinching his —

But he relaxed subconsciously before he even realized he saw Jasmina's face. She gave him a quick smile. Weston didn't analyze too deeply whether this was a genuine everything's-all-right smile, or a trooper-keeping-the-chin-up smile. Didn't matter. She was here. Bigger problems loomed, but for the moment, the universe was in order.

Kasymov looked bored today, and whisked his pieces so quickly Weston felt as if Kasymov's mind were elsewhere. He carelessly lost a pawn to Weston, then two. Weston could see the errors on Kasymov's face. Little twinges. Weston glanced at Jasmina and smiled. This would be over soonest today of all. The pieces flashed about, rapid moves but of no consequence.

Then Kasymov made a terrible move. His bishop was overextended; Kasymov would have to risk his queen to protect it. Weston knew even the maestro made careless moves that lost him games — but in such a dull game as this? Weston smiled as he swooped down on the bishop, nodding as if to agree with Kasymov that this had been a tragic accident. It took the momentum out of his planned attack, but such an opportunity could never be wasted. Perhaps Kasymov would resign now.

But Kasymov continued with quiet moves. Weston's defenses were impregnable, his pieces strategically well placed for the attack he was marshalling.

Then he saw it. His knight was uselessly off to the side, prevented from entering the fray. Retracing the moves, he understood fully now, and fatally, that Kasymov had intentionally sacrificed the bishop for tempo. The bishop had never factored into his attack and was merely a hindrance to Kasymov. Weston had fallen for the trap. Its steel jaws were closing inexorably. Weston had surely lost. He panicked. Knowing it was the worst thing he could do, he did nothing. His time ticked away.

With less than ten seconds on the clock he impulsively thrust his rook deep into Kasymov's territory. If he were a move ahead this would be a brilliant attack, but he'd lost his momentum to Kasymov taking that stupid bishop.

Kasymov narrowed his eyes and stared hard at Weston. Weston glanced at Jasmina. She was his source of power, just as his spex drew power from the air. She was staring blankly away from him, looking at a holographic ceiling ad perhaps. Kasymov slid his other bishop in toward the kill.

Weston let out an audible growl of frustration. If only he could run this through Ms. Gray's Kasymov module. Even the crappy net simulator—but no time, no time. With a mere seven seconds left, Weston bluffed his attack, as if he'd seen some fatal flaw in Kasymov's plan. He locked his eyes on Jasmina and prayed Kasymov would offer a draw.

Kasymov wagged his finger at Weston, but with a sly smile. And offered a draw.

CHAPTER 23

Chris studied the class photo from Scuola Elementare Nazario Sauro in Venice, his first year of primary school. He smiled; his mother had been right. His mother had admonished him, in early grade school, that he should keep a permanent note of the names of his classmates. "You'll want to remember someday," she'd said. A stubborn child, he'd said he would do it himself. Chris wished that little boy had done so! He'd have to call her later and tell her. He'd spexed a copy of the photograph when he'd been donated his first pair of spex as a kid, back when he'd gone on a binge of converting everything to digital and throwing away the originals. He was glad he did, now, but chagrined, as it meant he still had every blessed scrap to look at to document all those people for the UNCC. How much easier forgetting would have been!

At least for the first three years of photos, from maternal school before elementary school, where his mother had recorded the names for him because he couldn't write yet—he hadn't recognized a single one. He copied the UNCC form for each one: Name, the photo, and comment, "Do not remember, nothing known."

With his impecunious Market balance he couldn't afford commercial face finders. He stared at their faces trying to remember names. He'd been in love with Scott—a girl with a boy's name. Her parents worked at the British Consulate. She'd been a tomboy who loved to misdirect the tourists in the labyrinths of Venice and make profane noises from bridges. He'd professed his love on one of those mossy old bridges though he hardly knew what the word meant. She'd laughed and hit him in the arm. They'd moved the next year. What the hell was her last name?

Chris had been launching free gophers to fetch him updates on his old friends, though only if he could remember their names.

Chris suspected the UNCC would find out and investigate her. Poor woman. He was really beginning to hate the thought that someone he knew was—no, *might*—be a terrorist. He never had any enemies. Sure, he knew some obnoxious idiots, but he couldn't think of anyone who'd been so mean as to want to kill people. He almost hoped it was a legitimate fight for some freedom; having been friends with someone ruthless and not having noticed was a blow to the ego.

Vlad, that was his name, the Russian kid in their group. He'd kidded that his parents were spies and so was he. Hell, probably were.

Chris was skimming past a lot of the form entries. Political leanings? Of a seven year old? They'd hung out over a bridge and stolen a gondolier's hat one time. Vlad and someone else held Chris's legs. The gondolier was an old man who'd yelled at them earlier for doing nothing more than dangling their legs in the water. Ok, it was pretty fetid water that summer; maybe the guy was right. But he'd cursed at them and it made them mad, so when he rowed back toward them later that day they'd snatched his hat. Political statement? Ah, no.

He couldn't remember what happened to Vlad. Drifted apart after a few years. He spun off a gopher to see what was up with old Vlad.

None of the other faces brought back names or other particular memories. He flicked to the next school picture.

Ghita! Ah, Ghita! Chris had a flame each year. Ghita with the long, dark hair. He'd actually begun taking interest in the Church because of Ghita—she went to their same local parish so he could see her extra on Sundays if he went to papa's church. This distressed his mother, who went Greek Orthodox. Chris had been alternating, but for no reason anyone knew, he suddenly had become strictly Catholic. He'd have to tell mama that when he called; he'd never told her about that. Chris begged to be an altar boy, so he could impress Ghita. In Sunday school Chris was chosen to write on the board the names of the saints, or apostles, or stations of the cross, or whatever they were studying, because the teachers knew he'd always know them cold. He never let on he learned them simply to impress Ghita.

She liked Ermano, so that was a dead end of a year in the romance department. Much later, in medium school, they'd become friends, though nothing romantic. Last he'd heard she'd married an olive oil farmer in Umbria. Grew grapes too, of course. She'd sent him a bottle of their family wine. Tasted pretty decent. He didn't include about the wine in the UNCC profile; none of their business. And what might she be doing now?

He wondered if the UNCC would be upset that he was researching his old friends. Well, they hadn't said not to; and it was the only thing that made this half bearable.

Dear Jesus, but this was tedious. He spread out all the school photos before him in his spex space. Maybe he could start with the interesting people first.

Bellina! He'd learned to play the guitar for her, so they could be in a band in Scuole Superiori. But which one—he'd gone to four as his parents moved around. But, ah, Bellina... His first kiss. He still carried that same old Fender guitar as he moved around, the one he bought from a pawn shop, and regretted that he hadn't played in, what now, two years. She'd been fickle and more interested in his guitar than him. Another case where he'd studied his catechism hard because she was in his class, only to watch her hormones suddenly spiral her away from him and toward more vices than Chris could even remember. Drugs legal and not, denouncing and renouncing the Church, public sexual displays in Amsterdam... which she later wrote up in some non-bestselling book she'd sent him a copy of—Chris kept at the guitar, though. He flushed now to think how he enjoyed being the babe magnet any time he brought it out. Sib could by lying about her name: Could Bellina be Sib? No, not the same sentence patterns; nor was Bellina ever so intellectually engaged. He sent off the gopher with less enthusiasm than the others; maybe he didn't want to know what she was up to.

And next to her in the photo, he'd never noticed until now, Tadeo was there. Their paths hadn't crossed in Scuole Superiori. That was later, at the University of Pisa. It was Tadeo who ultimately convinced Chris to go to seminary after failing at his human morphology studies. Chris was going to switch majors to biopharmaceutics; Tadeo slyly suggested that the good looking girls were philosophy majors. It was only later Tadeo pointed out how seminary could help solve the Great Mysteries Of The Universe that Chris often tried hard to understand. Chris had then planned to become a parish priest, like Tadeo had. It was yet another conversation with Tadeo that steered Chris toward Jesuit study, the more scientifically minded order of the priesthood, and what a fourteen year odyssey that was.

Chris checked—Tadeo was on the list of names for which the cardinal's office had already supplied dossiers to the UNCC. The list contained all his professors, the students and faculty in the Jesuit training program, assorted bishops, the cardinal himself... essentially everyone connected with the Church or schools that Chris had ever known. Chris's thoughts on Tadeo were his own; he was told to supply the UNCC no information whatsoever about those on the list.

He needed no searching to check in on Tadeo. They'd kept in fairly regular touch; he was still a parish priest in Turkey. Chris sent off a joke to him that had come in recently about these two bishops who go into a bar, and suggested they get together for tea if he'd be in town soon.

Sib's face popped into view. "Are you looking to find me? How sweet."

CHAPTER 24

"What's wrong, Wes?" Jasmina asked. She stroked his hair gently on top, down to his spex. "You've been making these anguished grunts all evening. Can I help somehow? You wanna try some deep QM with me?"

"Nothing... I..." She was dying, his ratings were crapped out, he was near homeless, she hadn't told him about the Axelrod's, and he knew she would have some reason; she'd be upset that he found out from Canute. He tore off his spex. "Damn it!"

"What's *wrong*?" She sat beside him on the couch.

"Nothing. Everything. Nothing—too *much* nothing. All my ratings are shot to hell. I had a dozen regular joblets, and every fucking one of them has canceled on me. Or worse, complained, and you know what *that* does to your ratings. I'm usually flat broke, but I've *never* had my prioritized list come up empty. It's like someone's out to get me. It's suggesting I run blinkverts on my clothes!"

"Well, maybe you could play chess for money? Besides, if you win this match..."

"Don't you see what I'm saying? There's no *way* I can win this match. I lost today! Kasymov was gracious and gave me a draw, but I lost. And now I have no ratings to fall back on. Damn it! They beat the drum so loud in schooling, always, always watch your ratings." He rubbed his eyes. "Oh, man, I am so sunk."

"You can stay here as long as you want. I'll help you move your stuff up; they probably won't repo your apartment for a couple days."

"I don't want fucking charity! Just because you're miss genius at car repair! But don't you see, you're even more on the razor's edge than I am. I had a solid base of joblets, and now they're all gone, just like *that*," he said with a finger snap. "Now do you understand why it really pisses me off that you make do on just one job? Don't you think I wish I could live on the edge like that?" *And you're in trouble and I can't help...*

"I'm no genius," she said, pain in her eyes. "I just work hard at it. And yes, I do know how unstable it is, but I can't help it if I think it's worth it."

"Listen to yourself! There's that damn smug attitude of yours I'm talking about! It's a fact the world's more stable if everyone does lots of piddly little jobs, but don't you know how it pisses me off that because of that I'm not good enough at any one thing? The news is always going on about the fucking quality gap, and the one time I think have a shot at the big time, shit, I'm not good enough! Kasymov is! He always wins! With twenty years' fulltime study maybe, just maybe, I could see his brilliant strategies. But I can't redo my whole fucking life!"

"Wes, you don't have to, you *are* good enough. You just need—I mean, maybe if you—"

His face felt hot. "I don't need your stupid advice! I don't want to hear any of that QM crap. You know, I never believed those dumb ads from LifeChangers about recalculating all your damn parameters when you met someone—until now!"

Jasmina turned her head away, but not before Weston saw the tears trickling down her cheeks.

Damn, nothing he did worked right.

"Jas, I—Oh, hell. Canute told me you have Axelrod's. And that there's a treatment, the—the—the KL treatment. I had to win so I could get the money for the KL treatment. But now I've fucked it up and you're gonna die and don't follow me because I'm going to go fix this." He snapped up his spex, strode to the door and left.

~~~

"Fuck," he said, under his breath. He hated himself for how he'd made her feel; he knew his problems were always of his own making. Truth was there was nothing he could do walking in circles around the block that he couldn't have done in her apartment. He just needed to think, to focus. Orring was such a shit; there had to be another way.

He exhaled the mildly polluted air in disgusted huffs. The sky was a mediocre blue-gray-brown breezeless haze, as if it too, could do a little of many things, but nothing well. Even the temperature seemed half-hearted, not warm enough to be pleasant, not cold enough to be cold.

He checked his market parameters again, fiddling with them up and down until he felt like a dirty little tweaker, screwing up their ratings by constantly trying to tune them to perfection. Nothing was perfect. The tweakers' problem was that they thought there was a perfect world out there, if they could only nail the numbers. Weston realized the world was just a jumble. The Market ensured a global, mediocre stability — and crushed concentrated performance. The best you could do was swim upstream a while against the entropy. Sometimes you made it.

"Gaaahhh!" He shouted aloud. Broke, ashamed and desperate as he rounded the corner by the decrepit entrance to his apartment building, he knew what he had to do.

Orring. If God wouldn't help, the devil sure as hell could.

He went up and boldly knocked on Orring's door. He hoped he wouldn't be home, then at least he could wallow more in his self-pity that he'd tried, really he had.

Orring opened the door.

"Weston!" Orring seemed to size Weston up instantly, his eyes widening, narrowing, raising an eyebrow, then returning to normal all in a flicker. "Do come in, come in."

As Weston feared, Orring's apartment bespoke the conditions of a societal vampire, someone who didn't need to live in a slum, but chose to. Because that's where the victims are, Weston thought. His apartment was opulent. Thick red tapestries hung from the walls, deadening the sound. Weston didn't need to see behind the spex to know Orring was meeting his gaze with unblinking eyes.

"Have a seat, here." Orring ushered him to a velvety wing chair; it looked slyly sinister with its ball and claw feet. Orring casually yanked the flashcord on a packet of Jamaican Blue Mountain, poured and handed a mug to Weston. "Coffee."

Weston pondered whether he would become overly indebted to Orring if he drank this cup of half a year's pay, or if annoying the man with a refusal was worse. He took a scalding sip. "I've... ah, thought about your offer."

"Of course you have."

Damn the man! How could he be so smug? Weston's market conditioning kicked in, and he automatically bluffed higher than his goal. "I'm willing to trade my ten million winnings for three up front."

Orring sagged. "Oh, Weston." He sighed. "I'd thought we could have had a deal. But you're so far out of line... My client's fee, like his interest, has waned now that you're not winning easily, and with so few games left, you understand—I don't see we have any business to discuss." He tut-tutted. "But, hey, enjoy the coffee." He paused, letting it sink in that he wasn't even going to make a counter-offer. "So, all's going well with Winnie? Jasmina?"

That should have served as a warning, fate perhaps, that Weston shouldn't have pressed the matter of offering to throw his games. He was screwing up his courage to leave, when Orring said "One sec," and put up a finger to freeze Weston in place, as if he knew Weston was on the verge of saying something stupid. Orring reclined back in his worn leather chair, hands clasped behind his head, and assumed the easy-going, freewheeling smile of powerbrokers wrangling a big deal in the spex. Behind closed lips his jaw moved fluidly as he subvocalized who knew what—but it had the slow then rapid patter of "Hey, babe, lookin' great"s and "no no no don't you see"s... Or he could be a heavy Cyberista—news said a LNG tanker had just blown up and killed thousands in Miami. Either way, Big Shit was going down right in front of Weston, yet when he glanced in his spex, all he saw were collection notices and red flashing ratings.

He should have walked out then. He could have found *some* work, even if some slag-hauling in-person job. He could win the match, for Jasmina. But Weston stayed, patiently, wishing there were another way, until Orring wrapped up his deal. Then Weston caved. He blinked his rights away and swore aloud to Orring he'd throw the rest of the games, drawing the fifth game if he could. If he should accidentally win the match, his ten million went to Orring's client as forfeit against the tens of millions not won from betting against Weston. Weston looked at his account balance in disgust. He'd sold out for a measly half million.

CHAPTER 25

C hris played his guitar at the base of the Spanish Steps, a crowd of tourists enjoying his impromptu performance. Water tinkled from the fountain behind him and splashed lightly on his back. Chris was merely waiting for any of his gophers to return with forgotten details of people he'd known; or forgotten. And a few that were digging up surreptitious information on Jobs, such as Lindsay and Kalvin Bos's backgrounds.

His gophers had become slower to return of late, assumedly because he had even less information to work from than at first. Recollection matching to billions of people out there must take work, he reasoned, and as far as his gopher digging around in the Bos's past, if they were hiding something it would be, well, hidden. So he took his guitar along on his walk and played when he stopped. He had ten windows going, all waiting for something; more than that gave him a headache. The joblet offer to be a Human Intelligence monitoring variables in a hurricane shutdown project might be interesting, if only it wasn't flagged Full Attention Required. At this rate he might never finish compiling his list of the people he knew. Perhaps the UNCC would be upset about that. Cardinal Canini's pit bull di Fuoco certainly was rushing him. Chris smiled serenely at the lack of care he had about that.

The tourists peppered him with questions about whether he was a real priest or just a street performer in priest's attire, and if they could buy tracks of his music, or record them, which they did anyway and might even try to sell. They clapped and blinked him donations when he finished Stairway to Heaven. He wanted to decline, to explain, no, he was just enjoying himself—But he was sucking on a piece of the candy, which made talking hard, and they scattered off too quickly and there was always another bystander coming up that he'd have to educate. Too complicated. Let them enjoy their own conclusions. He began Barrios's *Tu y Yo*. He closed his eyes and enjoyed.

"You're very good," Sib said quietly, popping into his spex space. "I like a man who can handle El Indio Mangore so gently."

His fingers knew the piece, allowing him, after a pause, to subvocalize back to her, "Not many people know Agustín Barrios to know he *should* be played gently. Careful you don't give yourself away."

"Nothing about Barrios leads to me, don't worry, my golden boy. I checked."

"In which case perhaps I should check everyone who's *not* linked to Barrios."

"Perhaps I lied," she said.

"Ah, then it *would* be worth my checking those links."

"Just shut up and play, you overanalyzing idiot."

Chris strummed on. The crowd blinked him praise and toe bumps and cash. The cash wasn't nearly enough to spin off better searches, so Chris idly pondered what charity to blink it over to.

"I need a worthy charity," he subvocalized to Sib. "They've sent me over a hundred petros."

"I'm a worthy charity," she said.

"Whether you're worthy or not, if you were a chartered charity then I'd know who you are, so I know you won't tell me. Help me come up with something. What are you doing right now, this very moment. I'll donate to the nearest patron organization for that activity."

"I'm washing my hair," she said playfully, though her avatar continued to show her usual face with a garden in the background.

"Ah, the patron saint of hair washing, that would be St. Tress."

"Your God will get you for lying."

"Ok—" and this gopher returned instantly—"St. Martin, then, the patron saint of hair-dressers. For real."

"But I've moved on. I need you here to wash my back."

"The Academy of Saint Martin in the Fields. They're the happy owner of 130 petros. I could come there, if your back is in such need of washing. Just blink me where."

Her avatar shifted to one with wet hair dangling, one of the few times it changed. "Ah, if only. But it would never work."

"We could try."

"It wouldn't work. You don't believe in the same things I do."

"You might come to see things how I see them," he said.

"Worse, you might come to see them how *I* see them."

One of Chris's gophers returned, empty handed. "Damn!" He quit playing the guitar abruptly. "I can't find anything out." To his audience he apologized and packed up his guitar.

"You sound sad," Sib said.

"I'm frustrated. I keep running into brick walls. I've been trying to find more information on Lindsay Bos and that KL treatment." Ostensibly to flesh out his folder on Bos for the UNCC, or so he told Canini and his goon.

"I may have a little more for you on the KL."

"Oh yes?" Chris walked briskly toward his apartment. He realized he was famished for dinner; he'd played for hours without a break. His fingers felt raw.

"It's much as I described, a life prolonging treatment." She flashed him a blur of reports, the only constant image being an "ankh" logo on each page. "Secret clinical trials are underway on, a report says, 144,000 people globally. What I heard is that it works by relocating failed or failing biological processes. Rather than repair what your body uses to do things, it installs new ways of doing the same thing."

"You mean like if my insulin production is low, it has some way of creating new little insulin factories in my body?"

She shrugged. "I don't know the details, but it sounds something like that."

"Is it nanotech?"

"I don't know. It may be related to the Klotho gene, which is related to aging, and is commonly abbreviated KL. But some of my sources say no, that's a red herring."

"But it sounds like it would work for a wide range of problems."

"Yes. But I'm pretty sure it couldn't fix a brain that's entirely wired wrong, like Faith Bos's."

"Yet what if could enable her body to live 'forever' — with a brain that's wired to give her pain."

"Or your pope. Living forever as a vegetable."

"Let's not beat that dead horse again. There are plans for that. But Faith Bos — if her parents tried it, hoping it would be more than it was, thinking it was some way of repairing her brain..."

"And if it left her an immortal, in agony... Killing her would be merciful."

"We don't know her father plans to kill her." But Chris knew taking the girl into the bush was dangerous, whatever his motive.

"The mother and father may have... disagreed on what to do. That's my point."

"To the point of *murder*?" Chris thought of the gophers he had out, and wondered if he should be meddling with the case. If Kalvin returned online with a horrible story about how Faith died...

"He may not view it as murder," Sib said.

One of his gophers returned. Chris stopped in his tracks. Xylia, one of his Jobs, was blown up in Darwin. Badly maimed by a terrorist explosion and not expected to live out the night.

A chill went down Chris's spine. What was he thinking, pretend flirting and talking about killing and murder with a lethal terrorist.

"Are you cold? It's not that cold out."

"No, it's..." Cough. "I have to go." He blinked off her window, though he had the uneasy feeling that did little good.

As he neared his apartment his spex beeped with a video message from Sib. "I couldn't have saved her even if I knew about it. I'm sorry about your friend."

How did she know what's I was thinking about? Damn it, she was getting into his head now. Was he that transparent? As a terrorist, saying she didn't know about it carried little weight. Terrorists were always lying and not claiming credit for things. It ran with the job description.

He called the cardinal, but could only reach the Monsignor. "I must go to Australia. It's the last rights for Xylia Pilue."

"Father, I'm sure someone on the scene can handle that. You need to concentrate on your list for the UNCC."

"Please ask his eminence for permission, Monsignor. It's important that I go." He fingered the cross about his neck, hoping for what might be a small miracle.

"Hmm. I'll pass it along and get back to you. Meanwhile, keep pushing on that list."

Chris doubted di Fuoco would ever get back to him, except the usual pestering about the list. But Chris couldn't violate a direct command and leave town.

Chris lay on his hard bed until past dark, thinking, his spex on the shelf. Sib was having an effect on him. He was tired, cranky, and he didn't like it when he questioned his own faith.

It was long past midnight when he rose to get some supper and put on his spex.

They flashed brightly with urgent news from one of his gophers: Kalvan Bos and little Faith were dead. Killed when their flitter mysteriously crashed in the bush.

CHAPTER 26

The waves gently crashed at their feet as Martin and the St. Thomas's sat facing each other on beach loungers — free loungers this time, one of the perks of being on the island police's payroll. Seagulls ca-ca-ca-cawed above them. Martin had insisted he did his best thinking on beaches (outside of stinky police offices, anything was an improvement). Isabelle had acquiesced; whatever was required to get their program modified. Irwin frowned at the frivolity of it — "If I'm outside I want to play hard, and inside I want to work hard" — but Isabelle gave him a look and it was settled.

"Die, die, die! Die, damn you!" Irwin cursed. "Damn bloody simulations take too long to abort." He was crinkling his nose to abort each, in this case looking like a twitching rabbit to cancel so many. "Fuck, fuck, and fuck. The parameters are all fucking wrong — Isabella —" he stopped his rabbit-nosing long enough to shoot her a nasty glance — "and it takes a bloody thirty seconds to abort the runs. Die, you damn things!"

"How sad for them," Isabella said, apparently to needle him. "So much death. We need a moment of silence to mourn the death of all those souls."

"We need faster hardware is what we need. Or more efficient software," at which he looked disapprovingly at Martin. Irwin always cursed when aborting runs, which was often. Nobody paid him any mind.

Martin sipped from his Sex On The Beach. He'd smirked when he ordered it, noting it was the correct name for a perfectly common drink in the Caribbean. He smirked again now as his straw made a slurping sound. "Sorry." He smirked again toward Isabelle. "Irwin.

Question. Why 'Bluefin' for the name of your project? Are you a superdude fisherman or something?"

Irwin snorted. "I've caught much more exotics than some silly tuna. Isabelle named it."

Isabelle said, "It's the philosophy of the system. A bluefin releases millions of fertilized eggs when it spawns. Perhaps 10 of them will hatch and make it to adulthood. A million die for every one that survives."

"How sad," Martin said, adding some sad puppy eyes for effect. God, she was beautiful. And Irwin was such a jerk. She deserved better.

"It's my database and domain knowledge, and that's the meat of it," Irwin said. "It's her programming, and by god it picked up some of her personality too." He looked at Martin as if his insult was obvious. "She's neurotic. Or maybe it's your crappy programming language," he said to Martin with a twisted mouth.

"And you're an ass," she said.

Martin was more than half-way hoping this would turn into a full domestic squabble, but she continued, "So. Bluefin is a merger of fault tolerance work and Irwin's terrorist work—terrorists want to attack weak points, faults, so a deep fault tolerant AI can predict where the weakest points are."

"By which you mean this is really *offensive*, attack software, don't you?" Martin said, chagrined.

She looked down.

"So terrorists stole your Bluefin to *find* the weaknesses to hit them, yes," Martin affirmed. "But you said it was dataset dependent. Are you thinking a recursive application of your system with various imposed differences in the dataset will converge on the data they're using, is that your idea?"

"I don't know, we had no idea how to do it, that's why we called for you. Would that work? It sounds brilliant."

Martin straightened up with pride. "Um, maybe. How evil is your data?"

Irwin huffed. "My data are *not* evil."

"No, no, Irwin, evil is an attribute of his system. That doesn't sound right either. His system has attributes called 'good' and 'evil.'"

He snorted. "Oh, but of course." It was obvious to Martin that Irwin was the sort who never condescended to get his hands dirty with software. "I suppose there's a *God* and *Satan* too?"

"No, actually," Isabelle said, "but there is 'sin', and your data is full of it," she added with a smile to Martin at a shared joke.

"I've moments ago had a call from the UNCC," Irwin said abruptly. "There's been another attack. A maglev bridge in Romania. It's as if a massive termite colony ate away the bedrock under the supports. They want to know how quickly you can track where these terrorists are hiding with our program," he said to Martin.

"Track them? I thought we were trying to outthink their next move. To predict their next attack," he said exasperated.

"I told them you're able to track their location by their data access pattern. You mean you can't?"

"'Data access pattern', what does that even mean?" Martin asked.

"I knew you were useless." He stood up. "We're going back to the hotel. Come, Isabelle."

"No, I'm staying." She looked up shading the sun with her hand. "We don't need you."

Irwin glowed red, then stormed off. "There *will* be repercussions for this," Martin heard him say as he went.

"How you ever—" Martin decided better of insulting Isabelle's husband.

"Yes, I know. I regret marrying him. I was a starry-eyed grad student and he the brilliant professor, making off with his students ideas and claiming them for his own. I've filed for divorce, if you must know. His and my lawyers' AIs are negotiating over intellectual property rights."

"I'm glad to—I mean, I'm sorry to hear it didn't work out," he said with a sheepish smile.

"The sad thing is we need each other for our work to progress. At least for now."

"Do you know him well enough to know that he's not involved with the terrorists?" Martin ventured, giving voice to a private concern he had, though more to add a little uncertainty in the mix.

"I think so. But if not I'll have to run away from him, won't I."

A floater bobbed up to them with the conch fritter appetizers they'd ordered and another round of Sex's On The Beach.

Raising his glass, Martin said, "Well, perhaps if we keep working strong on this police matter we'll be so tired and hungry later we'll have to have dinner together."

She laughed. "I remember your offer, yes. We'll see."

"Much better than your answer last time!" he said.

"Let's just keep on focus here. If we have unknown tensors of evil, can we compensate for them by reducing the magnitude of the sin on the known tensors?"

"I love it when you talk evil like that," Martin whispered quickly. But before she could object he carried on with business. "I don't know if that would work. The result of the evil tensors is to chip away at the pole of maximal Good. Reducing the length of the vector of evil tensors would only slow down the convergence. I don't think it would give us any insight into missing tensors." A strand of her red hair was blowing across her face in the light Caribbean breeze. He resisted the urge to tuck it in for her.

"So, let's think," she said, pulling her legs beneath her. "Do you really believe in Ediger's philosophy of good and evil as selfless and selfish? I noticed you used his terminology. 'Evil tensors,' 'meek inheritance,' 'selfish altruism'..."

"For that analysis gumball, yes, I'd been influenced by Ediger's work. I'd read it and realized it would make an interesting goal-seeking algorithm. Evil as the set of algorithmic choices a data actor could make that would benefit itself, selfishly, with a measured metric for how selfish or how much it chose to benefit others without a clear self-benefit. Good as the slow turtle, Evil as the fast hare, the turtle data nibbling away at a solution a little step at a time, small bits of 'goodness' piling up even if the evil actions were 99.9% 'evil' selfishness and only 0.1% to the selfless, the meek eventually inheriting the solution. Yeah, I thought it made a cool analysis gumball and I threw it in. I never really thought much about it, or even used it very often."

She smiled. "Do you believe in Ediger's philosophy, though? That altruism ultimately arises out of selfishness, by making selfless choices to do good for others because it selfishly makes you feel good, thus the soul is defined as the potential to receive joy from otherwise selfless choices, and thus good arises out of evil?" She took off her glasses and looked at him expectantly.

"I guess you'd first have to agree with Ediger that making self-interested choices is the definition of 'evil', that the metric for 'good' is equivalent to the quantity of selflessness in a choice, and that the religious concept of 'original sin' is thus equivalent to the evolution-programmed nature of making self-interested choices."

"And you don't buy that." She looked at him squinty with one eye closed, as if fighting the sun's glare.

"I confess I never really gave it deep thought. I read his essay and it just hit me as an interesting analytical tool I could make an algorithm out of to solve a certain class of massively parallel Q problems. Took me a day or so. I played with it, popped out some quick journal articles to goose my ratings and moved on."

"Okay." She put her spex back on and rested her chin in her hand. "What if we used Mawikizi's Global Data Graph and match her nodes up with our data? We might ferret out more evil tensors. At least, that's what I'd want, if I was a terrorist—maximum carnage per energy expended."

Martin had never heard of Mawikizi or her Global Data Graph. He spexed it to avoid appearing ignorant. Apparently a woman named Nabila Mawikizi and her software minions had mapped out a vast, dynamic, highly classified dataset of all aspects of the planet and their interconnections.

Isabelle spexed him an access code. Martin raised his eyebrow at the security clearance legalese, which included threat of death if the system were misused.

The interface was simple. If one eye-dragged a global coordinate, such as off a map—or where one was sitting—it correlated a bewildering array of relationships. Property ownership, linked to other properties owned by the same entity (thus Martin saw a scrolling list of hotels in the same chain as the one behind them, and other odd things they owned—a brothel?!?). Maps of the sewer system showed who was feeding the same sewer line running by the hotel. Water currents identified where a message in a bottle would likely travel if thrown into the ocean here. Bird migratory patterns and sensor data from specific tracked birds that had landed here; and their genealogies going back years. Population migration patterns, down to the anonymized individual (non-anonymized in the case of public records). Martin's stint in jail linked him by prison records to every other ex-con in the vicinity and their migratory pattern. The man a hundred meters down the beach was a sex offender. Supply and material records from contractors who built or performed maintenance, and their suppliers, shipping manifests, bribes paid to customs officials three hops back...

The number of dimensions was staggering. He'd always heard such universal virtual databases existed, but never grasped their true extent.

"You see?" Isabelle asked. "Irwin used a small subset drawn at random from Mawiki's GDG. I think the terrorists have either gained access to the GDG, or augmented Irwin's lite version with their own data — but which will still be a subset of the GDG."

"Why didn't you and Irwin run your system against this... GDG, instead of your mini-version?"

"Lack of programming expertise, if you must know. We couldn't get it to run fast enough. I think it can be done though... by someone like you."

"Yes, yes, I see. It would be truly terrifying to make accurate predictions against a dataset that encompasses everything about everything. The more complete a GDG simulation is the closer it approaches reality itself." He rubbed his face. "I'm not sure I want to be a part of that. Even if it's used for finding these terrorists. The potential for abuse is staggering. I'm not sure this doesn't fall within the AI worker's Hypocratic Oath."

She squinted. "*Do no harm,* of course. Honestly, by 'lack of programming expertise', I really meant lack of current funding. Irwin hopes to secure the funds to do exactly this once he demonstrates the feasibility. Within a year. So, if it's not you, it's someone else soon. If you do it, you have a measure of control. Maybe you could lock it so it required multiple keys to run it, like they do with nuclear missiles. You and I, half and half? I trust you with the design of this far more than I would Irwin."

Martin was afraid for himself. He could see how to design the NEWT system she needed, to identify the maximum weaknesses in the fabric of society that could be exploited with minimum effort, then extracting the evil tensors from it for import to the St. Thomas's prediction engine. With his knowledge of efficient quantum algorithms, it would all run rapidly rather than be so bogged down it would take longer than the lifetime of the galaxy to finish. Such a conglomeration would identify those weak joints and tipping points where one could perhaps kill millions with the flap of a butterfly wing.

She rose in a graceful unfolding. "You need to think," she said, touching his bare shoulder lightly, and leaving. "Just remember Ediger's theory. That 'good' is what's left after evil is removed, or at least retreats."

Martin sat for hours with the sea lapping at his feet in the sand, staring out to sea, afraid nobody in the world should ever possess such a weapon.

CHAPTER 27

Jasmina didn't have her spex on when Weston returned and held out the cash card. "It's only five hundred thousand. I know it's not enough for the KL treatment for your Axelrod's, but it's yours."

Her eyes widened. "You sold out to Orring! Tell me, God, please tell me you didn't sell out to that worm spoor." She fumed. "Damn it—You hate memcopies so much and it's really none of your goddamn business but I'm already getting the KL treatment."

Weston felt punched in the gut, breathless.

"Wes, Wes." She hugged him. "What am I going to do with you. Listen, my Axelrod's is my own problem. I get more pain the more I think about it, so when people try to be helpful, they're only making it worse. I ignore it the best I can. If the KL treatments don't work, I'll just kill myself before I'm unable to."

"Shit, don't say things like that!"

"It's my life, isn't it? I'm barely able to wear spex now, and you know how crippling that is. Or maybe you don't, not really. When it gets too bad—Look, I should never have let this get as far as it has, with us. I knew it couldn't work, somehow you'd find out and that'd change everything." She sat down on the couch, rubbing her temples. "Like it just did. Change everything. Fuck."

Weston sat down heavily beside her.

"Here," she said, handing him the cash card. "You can't undo the thing with Orring, so go have fun with this. I'm beat. Enjoy life while you can, that's my motto." She shooed him out of her apartment making him promise he'd relax.

Weston slumped against Orring's door and knocked on it with the cash card. The sound and smell of sizzling bacon wafted from it.

Orring opened it; laughed "No refunds, amigo"; and shut the door.

CHAPTER 28

Carmen Elena was dead in Barcelona. Father Abascal sent word she'd snuck onto the Telerifico cable car to the top of Montjuïc and it had accidentally released; her cable car smashed to the ground.

Horace Grudzinski in Gdansk, a certain Job who earned a few pennies monitoring a public pay toilet, was dead, beaten at random by passing thugs.

Xylia Pilue had died also from her injuries in Australia, as gruesomely anticipated.

Four Jobs and the remaining two Bos family members. How could this be part of God's plan? Were some of the most righteous getting an advance ticket to Heaven? Was this the way the Rapture was really going to happen, not all at once but subtly, one at a time? Though Kalvan Bos might be heading Downtown if what Chris suspected were true. Or perhaps it wasn't. Perhaps he wasn't involved in Lindsay Bos's death.

Perhaps *Chris* was at fault. Years ago, Dirk had died because, Chris felt, he had tried to give food to him in Copenhagen. What had Chris done here? Was giving their names and information to Canini and the UNCC somehow causing their deaths? God wouldn't be so vindictive.

Overload. Then there was Sib and his tumultuous feelings about her. Double overload. Far too much to think about.

He strode into Cardinal Canini's outer office. What could the man want now? He introduced himself to the assistant and made to sit on the uncomfortable bench. "You may go right in," the assistant said, stopping Chris mid-sit.

Canini barreled over. "Giordano. Where's that list of these, these, whatever you call them. Jobs. They're dying all over the place." He showed Chris an obituary list; it had two more Jobs on it than Chris knew had died.

"I'm working on it assiduously, your Eminence. It's not a trivial task the UNCC has asked for."

"Blink me the list of all the names and identifying information you have so far. Everything. And your spex log of your whereabouts."

"Your Eminence! You know very well where I've been. My locator—"

"Yes, of course. But we must ask. Have you been to Barcelona in the last two days?"

"Absolutely not. You know that."

"I know. But people you know are dying. Perhaps being murdered. You understand our position."

"Reluctantly." Chris sighed. "Is there anything else, your eminence?"

Canini waved his hands. "The usual. The police ask that you not leave Rome, etc. etc."

"They can't seriously think—"

"These are strange times, Father." Canini nodded curtly for Chris to leave. "Spex me your list by morning."

~~~

Walking purposely through the pleasant night air, but feeling anything but pleasant, Chris launched gophers to locate the whereabouts of all the Jobs on his list. He prayed they were alive and well, though given their off-grid nature he knew he might never learn about many of them.

He also launched a series of gophers to uncover anything he could about the mysterious KL treatment, and whether any of the Jobs he knew had made any references, any whatsoever, to experimental treatments. Many Jobs, indeed most, had some illness or other. Physical affliction was part of the Biblical pattern. Given the widespread treatments for the most common biological malfunctions, heart disease, cancer, common viruses and so forth, statistics now showed that untimely natural death during middle age was absurdly likely to be from rare causes. Research funds typically went toward the afflictions of the many and the rich, creating a whole sub-class of sick poor — who were even more outcasts than in previous generations because people tended to shun those with rare and less understood diseases, lest they be contagious. To be poor and sick was as bad in the middle ages, despite the wondrous enlightenment and technological progress of the rest of society. That such pariahs were rare made it all the easier to not see them. However that they were many times more likely to be Jobs made Chris all too aware of them.

If there were a new, underground treatment that promised a cure, they would be the first to jump on such a thing. If there were any way in which it could be self-administered or underground versions of it created cheaply and dangerously, the underbelly of society including the Jobs would be the first to risk their luck.

A gopher returned with news that Zsa Zsa Kominski's son had died. Zsa was the only Job he'd known personally, before she was a Job, a girl he'd mercilessly tormented as an early teen with protestations of juvenile love by email, texting, and postings on what he naively thought were "private" blogs. In the end, she ran off with some young Polish army officer; Chris never knew if his actions had contributed or been coincidental. The husband had been killed in action in the middle east, leaving Zsa with two children. They'd scraped by, until Zsa and her son had both contracted Ossos de Derretimento a few years ago, another spawn of the Amazon Accident where the victim's neurons literally melted, slowly, over time. This piled on medical bills none of Zsa's family could cover and sapped the resources of all the now-grown children. An Episcopalian acquaintance had referred her case, unaware they'd known each other. Chris had reluctantly contacted her as part of the project, apologetic for his childish behavior of decades past, explanatory that he'd long since realized they were entirely philosophically incompatible, but fearful of offering assistance; and true to form, as a Job, she'd rejected his tentative offers. He'd gathered his data in a tense session in St. Petersburg, where she'd moved with her son seeking an untested treatment for the OdD.

That treatment hadn't panned out. But—perhaps she'd later sought the mysterious KL treatment.

And now her son had died. He'd been a Job in his own right; a very nice man, a decent musician.

Her daughter—an ordinary good person, but not a Job by any stretch of the imagination, quick to criticize God for their woes, and intoxicated by the latest gambling craze of betting on how long various people would take to complete their joblets and what ratings they'd receive—fortunately still had an active spex account she used for her habit. Though likely not for long at the rate she boasted of gambling, Chris thought.

"Sure, mom's here in St. Petersburg with me. Why? This is a bad time, Father. My brother just died."

"Please, you have my deepest sympathies, Samantha. I thought well of David. We played dueling guitars in his hospital room years ago." Chris hated condolences; they felt forced and surely sounded so. "I just heard that he'd passed away. There was no information on the cause, however. Was it from his illness, or an accident, if you don't mind my asking."

There was an uncomfortable silence. "Here. Talk to my mother."

"What is it, Father Giordano. I'm very tired. I've just buried my son and now I'm getting ready for a long trip."

"I'm so sorry for your loss. You know how I admired both you and David for how you dealt with your OdD. And again, I want to apologize for any grief my teenage self caused you." Chris cleared his throat. He'd been quite smitten with her at the time, at least in the puppy love sense. He wondered what would have happened if he'd handled it better. Would David and Samantha have been his children?

"All part of God's Will, I suppose. Thank you for calling, Father, but I need to pack."

Always the consummate Job! More accepting of God's plan than Chris could easily find within himself. "Where will you go now?"

She looked gaunt in his spex, more so as she now pressed her lips together. "There's a treatment facility in Antarctica. It's very far to go, but they insist it's necessary. It's my last hope."

"Antarctica! That *is* far!"

"I signed up to go to them when they were in Johannesburg. That was far enough, but I don't have a choice. David died from this treatment here and they're abandoning this project. If I die, I die. Even if I don't survive I hope my experience can help others. If that means I have to go to Antarctica, so be it. I guess you could say it's God's Will too."

"You're taking this very well."

"I just want peace, and end to the pain. There's a feeling when you're sick, really sick, that you don't care if you live."

Chris said, taken aback at her lack of concern for her own life, "But others who love you care very much, and want that you should live forever."

"And you want to be with them forever too. That's the only reason I'm going to Antarctica, Father Giordano."

Chris stroked his chin. He was deeply sad that he might lose her, even though they had never been friends. But that wasn't the reason for his call. "Is this the... KL procedure?"

"I've never heard of it. What does it do?"

"Ah. See, I don't know exactly what the KL procedure is. I'm trying to find out. What will they do for you down there?"

"Cure me and others like me, I hope."

"Of course; but I mean—"

"I don't know how it works. I'm not a doctor. They're very secretive, but they promise it will work."

"Who's 'they'?"

"It's called the Lifetime Improvement Foundation."

Chris spun off a search... No matches. "Can you spex me their contact information?"

"Here," she blinked over an anonymized rendezvous, "but I don't think you can get through. They work by personal recommendation only."

"Can you have them contact me? It's very urgent, I think."

"I'll tell Dr. Kleyman. She—Did you say something about 'KL'? Her name is spelled K-L-E-Y-M-A-N. Dr. Anna Kleyman. She's one of the doctors who invented the treatment, I think. Does that help?"

Chris was already spinning off a spex search. Anna Kleyman, 34, MD, Harvard. Ph.D. in neurobiology, Sorbonne. Undergraduate degree in electrical engineering, Oxford. Faculty of Tsinghua University in Beijing.

Chris wanted to hug her. "Dear, dear, Zsa, that's fabulous! You've been of such help." Perhaps this Dr. Kleyman could shed light on the rash of Job deaths and the KL treatment. "My prayers are with you."

"Thank you—I may need them. Good luck with your project."

"Thanks. Will you do me one favor? Stay in spex contact in case I don't hear from Dr. Kleyman? This could be terribly important."

She smiled, seeming to sense that Chris would enjoy hearing from her again. "We'll see what God has in store, okay, Father?"

Chris nodded. "My best to Samantha." He rang off.

Chris heaved a great sigh. It was good to know his old puppy love flame was still alive, though he worried for her. How silly, he thought to himself; there was no reason to worry more about her than any other Job; yet he worried about them all.

He rang Dr. Kleyman; no answer.

"Did you love her?" Sib asked, appearing suddenly in his spex.

"I wish you wouldn't monitor everything I do!"

"I care about you. I worry."

Chris started to say something uncharitable, but stopped himself. He looked up. A thunderstorm was approaching. It was flattering that Sib cared about him; yet he grated at the thought that he was developing feelings for her as well. If only it were *entirely* forbidden for priests to marry, as when he was growing up. That made life simple, clear cut. The temptation it created to now allow it if one would demonstrate God's hand, in the same manner as proving a miracle... Chris looked heavenward. He rationally knew his lack of experience with romance made him literally naive about it, but he couldn't help his physical feelings. Despite that they'd never met and that Sib was an outlaw, he was damned if he didn't feel something for her. If only he knew, was she a terrorist, or a freedom fighter? Another deep sigh. God's Will would show the way, whichever way that was.

"You're very pensive. And you didn't answer me. Did you love her?"

"Look, it doesn't matter. It was long ago. It's late, I'm tired."

"And before you go to bed you want to try to leave a message for Dr. Kleyman."

"Yes." He'd already begun composing what he wanted to say in the back of his mind. Sib knew him too well.

"Then good night, sweet prince."

CHAPTER 29

Weston sauntered into the match bleary-eyed and arrogant. He gave the guards crap as they gamma-rayed everyone entering the Mexxon Four Seasons casino. Assume the position. Whoop-whoop. Apparently there'd been a "credible threat" to the building. What a waste of time. All the Cyberistas had to do was threaten any more. The hyper-security hadn't saved anyone's lives. Just like all the virus scanners hadn't stopped the Goat Virus from spreading in China. Beijing was sealed off last week, and had that stopped it from spreading? Now Shanghai and Hong Kong were sealed. For what good? Millions were dying, courtesy of their luck of the DNA draw. The real disasters almost always happened out of the blue and evaded ropes and steel bars. So what else was new? The world was going to hell whether they annoyed people with security theater or not.

Jasmina left a message she wouldn't be here, and he'd hardly slept, spending the whole night bopping from spot to spot on the net. If she was going to take herself to the Great Market in the Sky where money didn't matter, he would too, so he might as well live now. He tossed away hundreds of thousands during the night trying things he'd always wanted to—*Measure Mt. Everest's Height Yourself!*, which allowed only three virtual climbers accompany a group of sherpas and a translator, or *Herd Them Two By Two Into Noah's Actual Ark!* that ventured up Mt. Ararat, or *Sing on the Moon*, or—All were either over-hyped, not worth the fee, or flat out bogus. Granted, *Everest* took only three people—*at a time*, virtual expeditions leaving every five nanoseconds. The Ark was a thirty second pan around the actual ruins—all the Turkish government would allow—and ten dreary minutes of animal husbandry. Cereal-box toy disappointment, he thought. It irked him to think a couple weeks ago he would have been paid to lead stupid tourists like himself on those faux exciting journeys like *Dive Ten Famous Shipwrecks!* Excursions he'd heard the best reviews of, like *Be Jack the Ripper*, had vanished, victims of their own success in a world of Market-driven mediocrity. Yet without Jasmina to share with, even the exciting ones, like *Fly With the Pterodactyls*, were as bland as plain spaghetti.

When he wasn't partying he was shuffling his funds between accounts faster than the garnishing programs could find them. His landlord's Don Corleone avatar demanded an entire week's rent in advance, at rates that suddenly ballooned via convoluted lease clauses Weston still couldn't understand.

Weston stepped into the match's glass bell convinced he would lose today even if he wanted to win. Maybe he could at least lose with gusto. The air felt oppressive.

Kasymov began with the unusual Bird's Opening, moving his king's bishop's pawn two outward. Weston had abandoned studying since Orring's payoff, but he remembered this odd opening was rarely used. He proceeded carefully with a Stonewall attack. Weston moved somewhat recklessly, trying to appear uncaring that Kasymov had the edge in tempo.

Weston scanned the crowd once again. Jasmina was nowhere to be found. In the front instead stood Orring, exuding a sense of power that seemingly cleared other onlookers from around him. He cocked a questioning eyebrow at Weston. Weston looked away. Of course he'd throw the game, but he resented the insult of Orring doublechecking.

By the ninth move both sides were developed, and Weston foresaw a struggle for which of their respective knights could maintain their outpost. Weston didn't want to appear to lose by gross negligence, so he made a slightly poor play. He nudged a pawn forward past an attacker, instead of playing for strength on the other side of the board. Kasymov capitalized quickly, setting up a knight sacrifice. Weston saw it, saw the results, and, with a knowing smile at Kasymov, took the bait.

Weston's position grew more hopeless as he overlooked clever moves. He played on automatic, thinking instead about Jasmina. He was glad she wasn't here to see his disgrace, but he flushed at the memory of how he'd yelled at her. She *had* been supportive; accusing her otherwise had been so cruel. At the heart of it, what he couldn't have told her even now for lack of words, was how his life had washed out. He'd dreamed as a kid of doing something *big* with his life. He never known what, though, and had let the world tug him along as life became comprised of smaller and smaller units of work, pleasure, and relationships. He'd wanted to be one of the Olympic flames of a person who could fight that tide. Only now, as he understood Jasmina's love for doing one thing well, and saw how his own studiousness could have paid off, instead he was pissing it away. Had pissed it away. Oh, Jasmina, I'm so sorry, he thought.

He brought the board back into focus. His autopilot hadn't been half bad, but he was cornered. Kasymov had demolished his defenses. One more move—there, allowing his rook to get pinned—and no commentator would doubt his decision. He resigned.

CHAPTER 30

For Mass this Sunday Chris had chosen to attend services at Santa Sabina on the Aventine hill, one of the oldest churches in Rome, to "get back to his roots" as he thought of it. Santa Sabina's Basilica was built in 422, founded by an Illyrian priest named Peter. Chris ran his hand along the ancient and enormous cypress wood door, which his spcx reported were largely original. The panels showed some of the earliest known depictions of Christ crucified between two thieves, and of the Father as a hand extending from a cloud. Yet it felt different than many a later church, as the windows were large, letting in bright light in the Illyrian style; a design idea later rejected in favor of more darkness to "enhance" prayer.

Before taking his seat in a pew, Chris wandered through the church. In the right nave was a tomb of a 15th century cardinal, whose inscription caught Chris's eye: *To live after death, he lived as one who was going to die.* Chris would have to meditate on the role of death in life, given the disturbing news Sib had given him about a potentially immortal Holy Father.

Were it not for death, this church would not be here: in this case the death of a woman named Sabina whose house had been here. She'd been martyred in the early 100s during the time of Hadrian. Yet immortality treatments might or might not prevent "inflicted" death like that, only natural biological death.

St. Thomas Aquinas had lived right next door in the adjacent monastery. This was a good place for musing on deep thoughts.

Even though he said the words in his mind, the same words he'd said to Sib that if God wanted people to live longer, he would have arranged for it—even so, his Doubt reared up on his shoulder like a little devil; or an angel. Doubt whispered, If God left the details up to natural processes and human ingenuity—as most of medical science was—then was God ultimately against human-discovered immortality? People who lived "forever," little Doubt whispered, They could praise God forever too and do his works.

di Fuoco's head appeared, blotting out the small crucifix behind the altar.

"I need your daily work, Father," di Fuoco boomed.

"Shhh," Chris said subvocally. "I'm in Mass. I will send it later." He removed his spex to be rid of the man.

An eternity of having to wrangle with di Fuoco, now there was an unpleasant aspect to eternal life. He wasn't entirely sure what di Fuoco's job actually was, but Chris was sure the man was not fulfilling its true potential. That was a problem with immortality, Chris realized. Not that Chris had aspirations of advancement, but just to avoid complacency people would need to change jobs, laterally if not upwardly. Immortality could lead to an eternity of suffering, in various ways. Perhaps suicide should be accepted in such a case and not be a mortal sin, he pondered, for those facing an eternity of true suffering.

Of course, if one could remove the suffering during an immortal life, then this could be in fact the immortality that Christ promised. Chris looked up the passage. "And this is the will of Him who sent Me, that everyone who sees the Son and believes in Him may have everlasting life; and I will raise him up at the last day." What if he meant a true, physical immortality, of the body, not just the soul?

Maybe the Heaven/Hell payoff at the end of the rainbow was just a temporary measure, a bridge, a crutch to help us to the point we have gained the real thing? Maybe we've grown up as a species and don't need them any more?

But, he argued with his Doubt, if nobody was concerned about going to Hell, would they have a deterrent to doing more evil? Pascal's Wager became meaningless. Yet not all religions had a concept of Hell. Hell as a fiery destination of damnation was a recent theological invention.

Shame on yourself, Chris, for thinking like that. Pascal's Wager still applied, for one never knew what form God's wrath or reward could take. Christ would return unannounced; thief in the night and all that. That still provided a "time" based deterrent.

Perhaps, snickered Doubt, Heaven and Hell are then located on Earth.

Not like *that's* a new argument, he silently replied.

It would sure gain more credibility, said Doubt.

You'd still need a non-Earthly Heaven and Hell for those who get killed in accidents and such.

But, Dante thoroughly described the various levels of each already; what's one more? Chris envisioned the quaint drawings of demons and angels and tormented or happy souls in the levels of Heaven and Hell that decorated the manuscript.

Really the question is, he said to his Doubt, are humans good enough to behave well without threat of Hell or promise of Heavenly reward?

Ah, said his Doubt, God, like a parent, sees his child off on his own, no more need for the parent.

Or the Church. A Church run by very human people who might well not want to give up their albeit very well intentioned roles as shepherds. The child never grows up, in their philosophy; always needs a parent. We're never without sin, as that would mean we've become God.

That's the nut of your Doubt, isn't it, Chris? That the Church can't imagine the job ever being finished, humanity grown up; the Church needs to ensure itself a continuing role by never allowing the job to *get* finished, and that's hypocritical.

No, Chris thought, just certain people, like Canini. Scared. Afraid of what a mature humanity might be.

The real nut of the problem, in the end, was that the goals of God and of the Church might not be the same. A mature humanity might love God as a parent, but not need Nanny Church any more.

His thoughts gyrated like this during the service. He went through the motions, kneeling, sitting, through communion, the dismissal, hardly hearing the priest say "Ite, missa est." He strolled for hours afterward outside in the ancient orange grove—reputedly started by St. Dominic. The canopies of the rows of orange trees down an aisle perfectly framed the dome of St. Peters in the Vatican. Indeed, it gave a fascinating optical illusion, for when viewing the dome through the trees it looked much larger and closer than when one walked past the trees to the wall. He compared views in his spex to prove they were the same size. Somehow this seemed to frame his doubt too: The Church looked larger and more important to him sometimes more than others. Pascal's Wager gave no direction on *which* religion was right, which God.

Chris's spex pinged with a call, urgent: Dr. Anna Kleyman. It requested a higher level of quantum encryption than the software installed on Chris's spex; he blinked ok to install what was required. It ideally needed additional encryption hardware that Chris didn't have, so it warned that the connection would be downgraded to lower bandwidth in order to work in real time.

A still shot labeled "Dr. Anna Kleyman" appeared—short, blond hair, gray eyes, round face. It matched what Chris had seen in her bios. "Father Giordano. I got your message; it appears we have an acquaintance in common. Zsa Zsa Kominsky contacted me and said you urgently wished to speak with me. You're doing some kind of book on poor, sick people. Somehow this is important? My time is limited, so please be brief."

"Thank you for calling. Yes, but more than just poor sick people. Very special people, from my standpoint. Modern day Jobs, if you're familiar with the reference."

"Yes, I see. Zsa Zsa and her family are quite remarkable. It's a bad time to be sick and poor."

"It's always a bad time to be sick and poor," Chris said.

"No, I mean, it's a bad time today compared to, for example, a few months ago."

Chris raised his eyebrows, then realized she would had no more video of him than he of her. "Really? Why is that?"

"I can't give details, other than to say research I'm involved with dealing with the very sick has put my patients at risk. Zsa Zsa among them."

"Yes—I was hoping you could give me information on what I've heard of called the 'KL treatment'? I think some of my Job candidates may have been your patients."

"I can't tell you anything about my research, I'm afraid. It would be too dangerous for you, not to mention we don't want it leaked. But who do you know beyond Zsa Zsa Kominsky who might be my patient?"

Chris considered trying to barter the information, but decided she probably didn't especially care. He breathed in deeply, inhaling the smell of the oranges. "Here, I'll blink you a list." He sent all the names and brief bios of all the Job candidates he had. He heard it arrive with a ding.

"I'm reading; hold on," she said. Her still photo continued to stare at him blankly.

"Several of these people have died recently," she said.

"Yes, I know."

"Some of those killed were my patients; some were not. Father Giordano, the ones who were my patients... I know they were murdered. The terrorist group, La Cyberista—"

"Oh dearest God." Sib. He dropped to the ground against the trunk of an orange tree.

"Yes. Your friends are in the gravest danger. All of them. You must warn them, if you can. We have a spexless community we're directing all our patients to."

"In Antarctica," he mumbled. He was in shock. Sib had been playing him for a fool all this time.

"Yes, someone told you. It will be dangerous. La Cyberistas will use any measures to stop them. Their eyes and ears are everywhere; they've deeply infiltrated the nets. Your friends must travel anonymously."

"My friends... the Job candidates... they have no money. They can't travel, let alone to the south pole."

There was a pause. "Father, here are some one-time access links to an anonymous account. It should have more than enough for all your 'candidates' travel expenses. I trust you as a priest not to abuse it." She spexed codes and a large set of directions, with recommended 'safe' modes of travel and routes.

He sighed, shaking with rage, embarrassment, sadness. He had betrayed his Jobs; befriending Sib was leading to their deaths. His worst fear from the beginning: He had interfered with God's plan. God never killed Job; but Chris had.

"Are you there?"

"Yes, I'm here," Chris said. A light wind chilled him despite the warmth. "How can I trust you? How do I know you're not the one killing them, and I'd be sending them right to you?"

"You'll have to search your heart, Father. Nothing I could say could prove that I'm trying to help. You're invited to Antarctica to check us out in person, but that will take too long for your friends."

Chris pressed his lips together and said a prayer for guidance. Urging them all to Antarctica was either the very right thing to do, or the very wrong. He closed his eyes for what seemed a long while. The woman's words had the ring of truth. "I'll warn them as best I can."

"Be sure to use this high-level encryption when you call them."

"Dr. Kleyman, most are spexless and simply unreachable. What you've told me saddens me greatly. Are you sure there's nothing you can tell me about your KL procedure?"

"No. I *can* say that there's a lot riding on this. Please tell them as well, the best you're able. We'll use what you've sent us to try to pick up any of your friends we can."

"Thank you, doctor. May God's blessings be with you."

As she blinked out, Chris composed a vid-mail to send to all the Jobs who had spexes—all too few—and to the parish priests and other contacts who knew any other Jobs.

"Hello my children, I'm sorry for this form letter, but I believe your life to be in imminent, grave danger..."

He sent it to all the Jobs or their contacts, with bank account access codes and directions to Antarctica.

After he sent it, he unclenched his fists, which had compressed wads of earth into his hands and rubbed at his eyes as he cried. What had he done. My children, he sobbed, I'm so sorry.

He saw a blur of a small figure dart behind an orange tree. He looked up. Through his tears, spying on him around the trunk, he saw The Boy.

CHAPTER 31

Martin woke to water splashed on his face. "What the fuck!" Jerry was blocking his entire field of view, his hands dripping seawater. "You slept here on the beach last night? I was worried sick about you," he said in a faux mother-hen tone.

Martin groaned as he sat up on the lounge chair. Some bot had cleaned up the cemetery of empty glasses and conch fritter plates, leaving just one diluted-looking drink and a half-eaten fritter. Martin remembered there had been a lot of headstones in that cemetery last night. He held his head. "Oh, Jerry. I'm too old for this."

"Here, eat this." Jerry picked up something that looked like a small black squid from a floater that just bobbled up. "Local island remedy, they say. Spex says a chemical mash of detox chemicals. Open wide, here comes the suborbital..."

"Ugh. Disgusting. Let me die." Martin eyed the wriggling thing with one bleary eye.

"Nope. Neither you nor the pope. Swallow."

"Blechhhh!"

"Consolation prize: A bloody mary. Hair of the dog."

"Where've you been all my life. For that matter, where've you been the last few days?"

"Padded prison. They wouldn't let me see anyone. Made me quite comfortable. Apparently my complaints about the excellence of the cuisine finally wore them out."

Martin took the drink, sipped, wiped the mid-morning sun's sweat from his forehead with his t-shirt, took another sip. "Ahhh. I feel slightly alive again."

"Always a good thing."

"Why is that? Why do we even choose to be alive? What is it about existing that makes people want it? We don't scientifically know that death is 'worse' than life, you know, yet we fight to avoid it—why? Simple fear of the unknown? Challenges? Novelty? Love? Farting?"

"If you're going to babble like that I'll take your drink away," Jerry said. "So. They explained you're staying here a while. I'm heading back. All packed. Taxi's waiting. I just wanted to see that you're okay."

Martin rose and gave him a bear hug. "I'm fine. Say hello to Lizabet. Tell her I'll try to return her messages more promptly," he said with a roll of his eyes, "but that I'm working on a top-secret project, very busy, lots of journal potential, etc. etc."

"She'll know that's bullshit," he said with a grin.

"Yes, but she will not fire me," Martin said with as big a grin.

After Jerry left, Martin contemplated the project some more, wondering where his cohorts were. They seemed in such haste to solve this problem.

"Hi, Mama," he said, as she answered his weekly call. She raved about the quantum microscope set he had sent to little Junia, his niece. They chatted over the problems of the day, his sisters' delightful problems with spouses and children that kept him grounded, reminded him what life was all for. He promised as always to find a good woman and have more grandchildren for her. Later he worked on revising some of his papers for publication to clear his mind, played a few games of Mango Banana with old friends from home, sent off assorted comments on what people were doing in his usual mesh hangouts, knocked off a few joblets in random fields.

He woke again suddenly to someone throttling his throat. "Where the hell's my wife!?" Irwin St. Thomas demanded.

"Gaaaack." St. Thomas eased up slightly. "I have no fucking idea, you bag of bovine genitalia. She's *your* wife. Ping her spex."

"Privacy mode. Last seen with you," he said, and started throttling Martin again.

Martin clouted him with his prosthetic arm. "That hurts," he said as Irwin staggered back, stumbled on the sand and fell. He held his head.

"You have no idea what you're doing," Irwin said. "She's unstable. She needs me, and you're wrecking a fragile equilibrium."

"Oh go fuck yourself, Irwin. She's a big girl. Last I heard she was filing for divorce, so unless you're here to work on the terrorist prediction project, run along."

"She—"

"Run along, then." Martin made shooing motions.

"You have *not* heard the last of this." Irwin stormed off again.

"Run along, run along." Martin crossed his arms and adjusted to a more comfortable position on the lounger.

"What were you and Irwin talking about?" Isabelle asked in a break-in message in his spex space.

Martin looked around him, but she wasn't in sight. He also couldn't ping her location. "Your husband was merely being petulant," he said. "Nothing relevant. Where are you?"

"Up here," she said.

Martin looked up and around. "Up where?"

"Come on up." She spexed him the coordinates and imagery of a floating power station. Only a few kilometers away. 3,000 meters up.

"Uhh..." Martin couldn't see anything in the blue sky, but didn't expect to since the undersides of the powerstations were coated with cloaking paint to avoid being an eyesore. Under full magnification of the coordinates he could see a slight elliptical fuzz.

"Just grab an airshoot at the beach. Doke'll take care of you." She flashed him Doke's photo and coordinates of his hut on the beach where, it described, he purveyed all the assorted tourist toys, airshoots, minisubs, seaballs, waveslicers, sharkies... the list was long.

"C'mon," she coaxed. "The weather's fine." She blinked off.

Martin found Doke's hut open and doing a brisk business.

"Right," he said in his Australian accent, "one fully charged one-shot Airshoot brand air sled. Y'know how she works, mate?"

"Yes, of course," Martin said with bluster.

"You'll die if yeh aren't sure."

"Ah. 'No', then."

"Good on ya. Yeh blink on the lever here," he said, pointing to a lever in Martin's spex space. "Nudge 'er up, she goes up. Nudge 'er down, she goes up. Just not as fast." He nudged Martin with an elbow. He opened the clear bubble on what looked like a three-meter tall fireworks rocket. "Hop in," he said indicating a seat facing upward. He strapped Martin in.

"Look where you want to go through the target sites and that's where she goes. You got about 20 minutes of juice. Blink the landing strip icon and she'll try to set down there. The Helper AI's crap, but over here," he pointed to the faux face of a pointy-bearded dinosaur. It winked at him. "Chances are you'll be dead before he's any help, so don't waste your time. Emergency parachute here. Physical backup lever here," he pointed to a silver lever just inside the rocket's shell.

He slammed the bubble on Martin's head. "That's it. Holler if you're gonna crash so I can come get the pieces." Martin's rational brain woke up, stretched, and asked him what the fuck he thought he was doing? Are you seriously deranged, getting in an airshoot to go after a woman? Doke clunked the outside shell twice with his hand. "'Ere you go," he said, and suddenly Martin's stomach was having an out of body experience slammed into the ground. Sky and clouds flashed by as Martin headed straight up.

Martin dragged up the coordinates Isabelle had sent him. The target crosshairs blinked blue and started to level off. Martin was hanging upside down in the air, the beach far below him set by the gorgeous blues and greens of the Caribbean. He could see sailboats and the long, arrow-thin wakes of waveslicers. In magnification he could see a whale rider, diving with a whale.

He rotated 90 degrees so he could see the ground and also the approaching power station. A zeppelin shaped balloon grew in his view as he neared. Or, rather, what appeared to be the upper half of a zeppelin. It glinted sunlight off its silvered upper surface, while the lower half was non-reflective and chameleon colored, taking on the color of what was above it, all but invisible to the eye from below. He could make out the two viewing platforms on top and bottom, and he dragged the landing strip icon onto the upper platform. The airshoot angled steeply upward at that, then cut the power.

Martin's stomach rejoined him unhappily in the weightlessness. "Umm," Martin said aloud, wondering if this was normal landing procedures or he was about to die. He thought better of asking the annoying AI, who winked at him again as Martin glanced its way. On second thought, Martin pondered, maybe he should ask—

Alarms sounded. A shit-scaring klaxon pulsed deafeningly. Its accompanying red flasher was all but blinding in his vision.

—When the landing rockets fired, pushing Martin's head against the viewing bubble's headrest.

With straining effort against the force, Martin lifted his hands to push the spex back where he could see to click on the alert. "Warning! You are leaving the Royal Cayman Islands Police Jurisdiction without authorization. Per criminal case number 54RG0220421138 you are enjoined from leaving the island. Return immediately or face international Interpol fugitive status." The message repeated. Martin searched for a wipe widget on the mesh, found an open source hack, and cleared the alarms from his senses.

The airshoot set down on the power platform like a feather.

"Good God it's freezing up here," he said, gesturing at his shorts as Isabelle helped him wriggle out of the airshoot. He was wobbly with muscle fatigue.

"Come into the observation booth," she said walking toward the clear bubble, her red hair flowing in the wind. "It's cozy warm, and the view is..." she trailed off as she stepped inside, raising her arms to take in the panorama... and letting her sundress slip to the ground.

One set of Martin's muscles responded, not wobbly at all.

CHAPTER 32

Orring slapped his back and said, "Aw, dumb luck!" loudly for others to hear. The rest of the crowd dispersed with glum looks; no basking in the upstart's victory today. "But hey, better luck tomorrow!"

"Get out of my way, Orring."

"Let me buy you a quick bite." He took Weston's elbow to guide him.

Weston wrenched it away. "Touch me again and I'll break your fucking neck!"

Orring looked genuinely taken aback. "I just thought you might need some company."

"I do. And not yours."

Weston plowed through the crowd. His brain throbbed with anger. He'd just realized in his haste to resign he'd overlooked a tremendous opportunity to smash Kasymov's attack and wrest control back. He could have won. What enraged him was that he'd *missed* it. He would have thrown the game anyway. That was the arrangement, sure. But after all his study and practice, to miss something so obvious... The world was so rush rush rush that he'd lost the ability to capitalize on concentrated effort.

Loving Jasmina was the same. He'd thought instantly that he loved her. Ridiculous. But now he'd squandered the chance to truly know her and turn that boyish love at first sight into a mature eternal monument.

He stomped up the stairs toward Jasmina's apartment. By God, he might have thrown away one chance today, but he wouldn't make it two. He had to save the more important one. Whatever time she had left he'd help her make the most of it.

He rapped quietly on her door. "Jasmina?" Good, not home. He wanted to wait for her, surprise her when she returned. That would give him time to plan, too. He wouldn't mess it up this time.

He blinked for her door to open.

It didn't.

So, she'd changed the code. Fair enough.

His spirit undaunted, in fact bouncing lightly toward his own apartment, he tried calling her on his spex so he could invite her for dinner. No answer. Must have her spex off.

Back amongst his bachelor mess he subvocalized a message. Canceled it. Recorded it aloud. Subvocalized messages sounded so mechanical despite the (alleged) best attempts at voice matching. "Sweetest Jasmina, I can't begin to apologize, but I want to try. Come by tonight? I'll even try for-real cooking..." She'd have it waiting when she put her spex on. He blinked to send.

The message instantly bounced with a boing sound. *Account suspended.*

Suspended? He was the one perilously close to bankruptcy. He blinked to engage the confidant-level access to her account she'd granted him. *Reason?* he queried. *Medical suspension.*

Oh God! Medical suspension meant she'd been incapacitated—or—

He probed her spex using the higher permissions. *Locate spex,* he ordered. *Spex unit inoperational.*

Shit. He queried up a list of all the gifts he'd given her. Some might still have the xRFID tag not changed to her ownership. *Last known coordinates of all items?* Most displayed Changed Ownership errors. A couple things showed in her apartment. Aha!—the Koa wood bracelet. A map displayed with a red X at the intersection of First Avenue and St. Paul. He squinted to zoom in to the full extent of the cheapy, free satellite locator's pathetic resolution: The middle of the intersection. Not a sidewalk. Might have been shards of a broken bracelet; who could tell at that resolution.

Weston's stomach clenched. She'd been hit by a floater. Or...? She'd said when it got bad she'd just—He couldn't think about *or*. He yelled aloud trying to dig more data out of the spex system—to no avail. He hunted for a vid feed mesh. Tons in the area... Body recognition filter on... There. He saw her walking briskly down one street, up another. Turned a corner onto the fateful street... and... No feed found. Someone deleted or deactivated a camera? Unbelievable. With so much lack of privacy in the world, privacy really only meant being lost in the noise. It was novel to be actually unseen. Damn.

He broadcast a query to all hospital admissions systems and police, and waited. He watched the status bubbles turn clear.

He couldn't bring himself to blink teary eyes to enable the "morgue" option. He paused, hoping for instant responses, but knowing they never were.

Why hadn't the floater's collision detectors seen her? Even if two floaters collided, they were supposed to thrust on impact away from detected bystanders. Yet there were always a few accidents reported, ascribed to shoddy workmanship; he dared not call up the statistics.

Then the blood drained from his head: The floater paths technically permitted wheeled vehicles, though he hadn't seen more than a bicycle in years. She might have been hit by an older vehicle lacking that feature. A classic car.

Weston grabbed his parka and ran, stumbling, down the hall, stairs, and toward the fateful intersection.

CHAPTER 33

"Come here, my boy," he said, patting the ground beside him. "No, don't run!"

Chris unfolded from the ground and chased after the boy. His leg was still sore to run on. The Boy was far more agile, but his short legs made it an even match. The Boy weaved among the trees with Chris in pursuit. Chris thought he could cut him off at the exit to the orange grove. Chris cut diagonally for the exit.

Chris's cassock snagged on a tree limb and ripped. He missed the boy by a finger as the boy darted into the street. He zig-zagged around cars and pedestrians down the Via Raimondo ca Capua, then Via San Domenico, where he doubled back onto Via Sant'Alberto Magno, back by the orange grove, down the narrow, high-walled Clivo di Rocca Savella toward the river and the Aventine.

The Boy pulled up short as a clot of cars blocked his way.

"Boy! Candy!" Chris held out the by-now somewhat frazzled wrappers of candy. "I have candy for you this time," Chris said, panting.

"No candy from strangers!" the Boy yelled, but stood, transfixed, as if unsure whether he should run.

"I'm not a stranger this time, am I? You spoke to me before, in the Piazza Navona. Remember?"

The boy nodded, blond hair ruffling in the breeze.

Chris approached him slowly, hand outstretched with candy. He knelt down by the boy as the child took the candy and quickly had it in his mouth.

"What's your name, son?"

"Fabian," he said with candy sucking noises.

"Where are your parents, Fabian?"

"I dunno."

"Do you live with them?"

"No."

He tousled his hair. "Where do you live?"

"Around."

Chris considered taking the boy's training spex and seeing if they had registration information, but if Sib was involved, he was sure that would prove fruitless. "Who gave you the new spex? They're pretty sharp."

"The pretty lady."

"Where do you meet the pretty lady?"

"I don't. She leaves things for me. Do you have more candy?"

Chris fished in his pockets; one more pink sweet, which the boy added to where he could barely talk.

"Can you take me there?"

"She said to. She's nice."

The boy lead the way; Chris had no idea how far it was, nor could the boy clearly say. He held the boy's hand as they crossed streets, and after a time kept holding it while they walked.

"Have you ever met her in person?"

"No."

"Only in your spex?"

"Yes."

Chris didn't want to say that she could look like anything; it wasn't Chris's job to teach the boy about avatars.

"Is she a relative of yours? An aunt, a cousin?"

"She told me to call her Zizi Sybil."

Auntie Sybil! But it could mean anything.

"Does she ever talk about your parents?"

"No."

"Do you know if she's your real Aunt?"

"No."

"Have you always lived in Rome?"

"No. We moved from far away when I was little."

"When did you last see your parents?"

"I dunno."

"Long time, huh? You live on your own like a grownup?"

The boy nodded, his lips pressed together.

"How do you get food?"

"She tells me where. She tells me when it's okay, like when it's in the trash, or when I should take it from a cart and run."

"You know stealing is wrong, don't you?"

The boy shrugged.

In the news highlighted in his spex, the Cyberistas claimed credit for the maglev shutdown in Brazil. The whole routing system had been disabled for days, causing one high-speed collision killing hundreds, and a standstill that was inconveniencing millions, costing billions.

Chris wished he could find Sib. She personally seemed to have redeeming virtues. If he could turn her to the good side, save her, then perhaps she could become a sort of virus in their organization, carefully spreading the Word, preventing harm. He sighed as they walked. If only he could look Sib in the eye he was sure he could tell if she were good or truly evil. He tried to reach Sib to gauge her reaction to him being with the boy, but he couldn't reach her. He wondered if the boy was leading him into a trap.

"Is it much further?" he asked the boy.

"It's this way."

Hmph. Chris had little knowledge of children. At what age should a child be able to explain how much longer it would take to walk to a destination? It wasn't necessarily easy even for an adult to be accurate. At what age did a child learn the ability to deliberately give evasive answers?

They sun's rays slanted fiercely; the neighborhood became rougher as they angled away from the city center.

~~~

Chris's legs were exhausted. They'd been zig-zagging more or less northeast through Rome for hours. "It's this way," the boy kept insisting.

"Fabian, stop, stop. I need some dinner." The boy wandered back, twisting his shirt. "And I think we both need to use the toilet, eh?" Chris spotted a small outdoor café in a residential square, sat Fabian down at a table. When the waiter shuffled over, a dry thin old man in white, Chris ordered the pear and gorgonzola ravioli and a glass of the house red for himself.

"Fabian, do you want a Limonata?" The boy nodded shyly. "Per favore." The waiter shuffled off.

"There's a toilet inside; you go ahead, Fabian."

While the boy was gone the waiter shuffled back with Chris's wine and bruschetta. Chris sipped and rubbed his aching legs. The map in his spex indicated they were well northeast of his apartment. This was a wild goose chase. Chris should just find a floater bus stop and—what, take the boy back home with him?

He noticed a floater stop across the square. It beckoned him with a green winking logo in his spex to blink up the route map and schedule. A gang of nogoodniks in long bright green vests were milling around the floater stop. They eyed Chris from afar, looking for trouble. The buildings were dilapidated. Not the greatest part of town. Chris felt uneasy at the gang boys' leering, but Chris had spent time in far worse slums. Possibly a Job or two lived nearby, Chris thought idly. But, to business. What to do with Fabian.

He could take the boy to the police. Or a care center.

In all likelihood Fabian would run away from them the first chance he got.

Fabian returned as their ravioli arrived. The boy ate hungrily, alternating with gulps of Limonata. Chris needed to pee, but was hesitant about leaving Fabian alone, in case the nogoodniks should come over to start trouble. He decided to wait, find a toilet later.

They should turn back, he decided. If Fabian left him along the way, so be it. He couldn't keep the boy in his apartment, and certainly not against the boy's will. He should probably angle the boy toward a polizia station.

As Chris debated and ate his ravioli, not well prepared but glad to have something to eat, his spexed briefly showed di Fuoco's face, no doubt to collect Chris's daily corpus, but his face bounced instantly away. His spex blinked Sib's avatar into view instead. She was wearing a stylish feathered hat, all the rage of late.

"There you are! I've been trying to reach you," he said.

"Yes, I thought it best if you two had time alone. I took the liberty of blocking Monsignor di Fuoco. He will not bother you until you are ready. I was going to leave you alone as well. However, I've overheard that pack of wilders over there. They mean to rob you of your clothes when you leave. I only wanted to say, *trust Fabian*. Good bye."

"But—"

She blinked out.

"Hmph. Well, my boy, it seems we should move on." He rose, stretching his weary legs. "Which way to your Zizi Sybil?"

Fabian hopped off the chair and pointed to a yellow painted alley covered with blinking ads. The alley closest to the hoodlums.

"Well, I think we should take a more leisurely path first." He put his hand on Fabian's shoulder to guide him to the nearest exit to the square, slightly behind him and opposite the gang.

As he neared the archway exiting the square, a motorcycle roared down that alley toward them. Driven by a muscled, green-vested teen. He stopped at the arch, blocking their path. He revved the motor. It made the deep, gutteral roar of a Harley, deafening in the confined alley.

Suddenly the other exits to the piazza were also blocked with green-vested bikers. The others seemed to assess the situation, then rode over to pick up a passenger each from the riderless greenvests.

Chris blinked for the polizia.

Sib interrupted, her face covering the polizia window. "Trust Fabian." She winked out, and the polizia window also vanished. Chris couldn't get it back.

The greenvests veered over, popping wheelies, eight of them, their bikes roaring, surrounding Chris and Fabian.

The only solo biker blinked to Chris's spex. "Talk to me, old man."

Chris accepted the call. He couldn't have talked out loud to the greenvests over the roar. He looked around the square. Residents closed their windows. He hoped one might call the polizia; but doubted it.

"Got any alms for us, old man?"

One of the other greenvests popped into Chris's confessions queue, with a tag of "Killed a priest cuz he wouldn't give me alms. So sorry."

The other greenvests smirked and chuckled. "He's got nice finger-nails, don't he, Orecchini?" one of them asked the leader. Orecchini—*earrings?* Chris wondered. Chris could see the leader had a large hoop earring with small, square chitinous things dangling off of it. He zoomed in with his spex—which identified them as whole fingernails.

Chris swallowed hard.

CHAPTER 34

The wind was picking up. A few bits of plastic housing and fiber optic glass shards were all that indicated Weston had found the spot. A small stain, darker than the fading green grassphalt, might have been old, sunbaked ketchup. Or...

Weston frantically searched for a shop window from which a clerk might have been witness to the... the... He couldn't say it in his mind. Might have... have... seen what happened.

But where there'd once been glass storefronts when he was a kid were now soulless ad canvases. What had once been an upscale shopping neighborhood now housed shops like Gil's, supplementing their meager actual income with advertising revenues. Weston hadn't realized until now that the takeover had been complete: No windows remained, none at all.

He blinked up Canute, Jasmina's boss at CVR. Nobody answered. The recorded greeting only magnified Weston's fear: The gang had gone to test drive a vehicle.

None of the hospitals had responded to his broadcast query. He sent it again. He checked the list of Cyberista and other terrorist attacks. Nothing.

An *urgent* blipped on his spex, but infuriated Weston when it turned out only to be an ad for a crappy joblet shoveling guano.

He tried Patriot Farms in New Hampshire and Patriot Hills in Antarctica, places she mentioned that treated Axelrod's that he found in replaying conversations. Kleyman treatments are only once every six months, not likely she'd be here now, so what? — *is* she there now? Can't divulge, blah blah blah, connect me to supervisors, we can't say, repeat repeat repeat. "I'm going to come there and kick some ass if you don't tell me. Is. She. *There*?" he demanded. Long pause. Finally: "No."

He reluctantly checked the "morgue" box and rebroadcast.

Intimations of death put everything in perspective. Reduced to their core, nothing mattered: Not ratings, not money, not chess. Jasmina mattered. Love mattered. He simultaneously hated Canute's CVR shop for the part he imagined it played in her death, and felt tenderly toward it on Jasmina's behalf. She'd found her niche there, and he respected that. He ached to tell her he understood now, he respected—no, he *wanted* her to keep that single job since it made her happy. It would make him happy simply because it made her happy. If only the fates would return her to life.

Wiping his runny nose and eyes, only partly from the cold, he snuffled off to the floater bus stop. He'd check every hospital in person, check every damn room if necessary, until he found her. You are what you make yourself, his father had said. Waving a shotglass he'd pointed his own sorry self out as an example. Never let what you want out of your sight. Plow after it. A month ago and Jasmina any other girl, he'd have shrugged the matter off, bum luck, and blinked up another crappy job.

"Weston?" Orring's voice intruded in his spex. He should never have granted intrude permission.

"Go away, Orring." Weston hopped on the floater bus and dropped into a seat.

"We have to talk about strategy for tomorrow's—"

"The match is over. I'm not playing any more."

"Good God, don't even joke about that."

"Look, I'm not joking. Jasmina's had an accident and I have to find her. The hospitals won't respond. I'm too busy to play stupid games, and I'm too busy talk to you, so get the hell out of my spex." He blinked him off.

Orring popped back in.

"I know what happened to Jasmina," he said.

"What?" Weston stopped trying to blink Orring's face off.

"I'll tell you tomorrow, after the game."

"Fuck you. I'm going to find her today."

"I doubt it. In fact, I'll make sure of it. And if you're not bright eyed and bushy tailed tomorrow at the game, I'll never tell you."

"Just tell me she's ok."

"Not until tomorrow after the game."

"You bastard!" Weston shouted this out loud. Beyond his spex he saw dim outlines of other riders turn to stare. "Hey, fuck you too, people!" he shouted. "Mind your own damn business!" He went to subvocalizing. "Fuck you, Orring. You're just bluffing."

Orring's image shrugged. "Suit yourself." He winked out.

"Damn!" Weston fumed until the floater paused outside the Denver Free Hospital, where indigents were usually taken. Without her spex the EMTs might not waste time establishing Jasmina's identity. But they'd know by now, hours later.

He blasted through the heated air door with his hair billowing. Up to the admissions barricade. The holo screens there for the spexless flittered amongst friendly health messages and the main menu. He blinked up their interface in his spex. Pay bill, Check in, Seek advice, Get a referral, Check out... No search function. He took off his spex and scrutinized the screens on the barricade. Nothing there either.

Doctors, nurses and orderlies scurried by on the other side of the fence. Weston leaped over a turnstile and grabbed someone in white. "I've got to find my —" he was going to say girlfriend, instantly rejected it as not important enough. "Wife" would be too easy to verify. " —fiancée. She was hit by a floater. How do I get your damn system to tell me if she's here?"

"Hey, easy, guy, easy. Hang on." The doctor's Adam's apple bobbed as he subvocalized at length.

Two security guards converged on them. "Take it easy there, mister. You jumped the queue without paying."

"You asshole!" he shouted at the doctor. "You blinked for them instead of looking her up? Don't you people *care* any more?"

Firmly pinning his arms, the hire-a-thugs led Weston to an off-white holding cell, where Weston explained his plight. Just go away and we won't press charges *this* time, they said. Weston persisted that they had to help and to go ahead and press charges. With painful slowness they finally located an aide, a dull looking woman. He bartered silently via spex with the motley gaggle of smelly wino linestanders to buy a place in the queue near the head for an exorbitant fee. With ponderous deliberation they escorted him back behind the public side of the barricade where the aide, with the alacrity of a snail, holo'd up a search menu screen.

"She's not here," the aide said after a cursory search. She ambled away.

"Okay, blinker, out you go," a guard said, rapping his knuckles on the counter.

"You've got to try harder than that!" he protested.

They manhandled him through the air door into the now lightly falling and windwhipped snow.

He argued.

They stood arms folded until he left. A fine time to be resolute, he thought.

The staff at the Olympic Healtheon were friendlier, but wasted as much time hemming and hawing and spent as little time searching before likewise proclaiming she wasn't there.

It was getting dark by the time Weston hopped off the floater at Cadriz Full Recovery Center. After finding the right human, he said they'd have to check, and call him tomorrow. Weston pleaded. Looking as if he was straining to remain polite, the clerk said it was the best they could do.

By the fourth emergency room they seemed to anticipate his coming. Guards were posted prominently. They still wasted time, but there seemed a certain inevitability to their easy answer that she wasn't there, nor had been. Weston plunged ahead, crisscrossing the city by floater.

He continuously rebroadcast his query to the hospital, police, EMT, and morgue systems, and tried to raise Canute. His searches of news stories revealed nothing. He blew the last of his account on three People Finders. They each promised to find her within an hour. An hour passed uneventfully. An hour and a half. He pinged them. Automated messages said they were working on it. At two hours he gave up on them, had checked the last of the nearby hospitals, police stations, EMTs, and even the store clerks near the accident on the off chance one had been walking through the door at the time.

Nothing. At three a.m., as exhausted as his options, Weston collapsed onto his bed.

CHAPTER 35

"I don't want any trouble," Chris sent to the leader, Orecchini.

"Me either," he replied. "Won't be any you hand over all your alms. Look like you got millions stashed."

Chris shook his head. In fact he had about enough to cover a couple more meals. "Look, boys—"

"Now, god man. Nobody here's gonna protect you."

Out of the corner of his eye he could see Fabian edging toward the leader on his bike. Chris stepped toward them. The greenvests closed inward. Fabian circled to the far side of the leader away from Chris.

"What's with the kid?" Orecchini asked Chris, laughing.

Fabian lunged at the leader. The leader bent at the waist to take a swipe at the boy, tried to grab him. Fabian ducked under his arms and gave the bike a hard shove. It started to tip toward Chris, at which the leader, still bent toward the ground, kicked himself clear of it, to avoid the bike crushing his leg. He fell away from Chris. To Chris's surprise, the bike righted itself and Fabian jumped on it. He waved Chris over frantically. "Get on!" he shouted. "The pretty lady told me!"

Chris wasted no time jumping onto the seat behind Fabian. He hadn't ridden a bike in decades. He reached around Fabian for the handlebars. The bike helpfully blipped up in his spex, requesting permission to link. *Yes!* Chris blinked.

Welcome New Rider!

Technical Specifications

Harley Davidson Road Glide Nostalgia Edition

Fuel - Primary system Multi fuel liquid - minimum octane 74 - Minimum proof 76. Secondary system - Induction electric direct delivery at public standard.

Propulsion - Hybrid - Screaming Eagle/Solar Industries pocket turbine 3600 HP - standard temperature and pressure, induction coupled, super conducting electric hub motors. GE Dynamo standard - Boeing CarbonCoil available next Summer.

Suspension - Nostalgia Viscous dampened Bilstein Springer front end and Single arm in-frame torsion bar coupled with Kamen Mark II predictive live shocks front and rear.

Instrumentation - Multiple heads up display options, Infra-red and UV extended range, Tachometer to 25,000 RPM (20,000 in California) - choice of Spex, integrated helmet shield, or direct retina projection for hitting the open road with the wind in your face.

Guidance - Your choice of fully automated autopilot with independent navigation; remote human operation; standard Look-n-Go; and for the truly adventurous and nostalgic, real MANUAL DRIVE. (Training recommended for manual drive; licensing may be required, check your jurisdiction.)

Features - The Harley Davidson *Nostalgia* line will "rocket" you into the past with its REAL, internal combustion engine, capable of burning almost anything that you can get your hands on.

Relax as your integrated wheel gyros keep you upright and headed in the right direction, either on the public maglev system or TAKE OFF IN YOUR OWN DIRECTION! That's right! Blink to dismount the maglev and head off on standard roadbeds or cross country. Your new Harley keeps your ride smooth and comfortable with the terrain prediction software and short-range radar of the Kamen RoadWise shocks.

Smooth acceleration in either mode is guaranteed via the active rim induction coupling - continuously variable drive, forward and reverse, and gyro coupled braking for great energy retention.

Alert the crowd with your selection from 5 classic tank badges with color matching holo-lighting. Choose from over 16,000,000 color schemes with our "on the assembly line" remote control customization station at your local authorized dealer. Fully adjustable riding positions as always. (Passenger accommodation limited with semi-recumbent and eliminated with fully recumbent settings).

Genuine "Harley Sound" system and multi-color holo lighting available only on Nostalgia Road King and Selected Nostalgia Police Special editions.

Chris feverishly blinked away the fluff, nodded to accept the terms and conditions. The main menu appeared with options for the owner's manual, navigation, and the other operational choices. Status showed Look-n-Go was engaged, On-Grid.

"Hang on!" Chris shouted to Fabian. Chris looked sharply backward. The bike reversed at high speed. Toward the edge of the arch.

Chris leaned back and it screeched to a halt.

The greenvests closed in on him while Chris fumbled to bring up the map.

Chris stared at the leader running toward him and leaned his head forward fast. The bike roared directly at him. Orecchini jumped clear as Chris played chicken with him, then Chris veered around the flank of the other greenvests and gunned it for the far portal out of the piazza. He shot through the arch with the greenvests scrambling after.

The patented Harley rumble was deafening in the narrow stone walls. It got progressively more deafening as the other greenvests entered, chasing him single file. Fabian covered his ears.

Chris blinked off the Harley Sound option; it quieted. The thunderous noise now came only from his pursuers.

Chris had a street map of Rome in his spex, their bike a moving red dot, traffic behind him—undoubtedly the greenvests—and in front of him showing as yellow dots. The yellow dots were closing. As was their noise. Chris gunned the engine, hoping the Harley would prevent him from clobbering any pedestrians. He subvocalized to Fabian asking him which way to go.

As if on cue, Sib popped in.

"Chris. Listen to me. Get out of Rome."

"Holy Mother of God! I can't do that. Canini and the UNCC have ordered me to stay. Look, where are you?"

"You have to get out of Rome. Your life depends on it."

"Damnation, Sib." Chris concentrated on driving through a maze of passages. He hoped he could lose the pursuers if he could get ahead of them, find some traffic while they couldn't see, then duck down another alley. And hope their leader didn't have any tracking on this bike. Considering Chris suspected it was stolen, that, at least, seemed promising.

The map showed a road with a lot of traffic ahead. Hopefully he was far enough ahead. He didn't dare blink it to autopilot, as that certainly wouldn't permit the speeds he was going. He dodged a few pedestrians, though most seemed alerted to his approach and already pressed into doorways with scowls on their faces.

Then he was in traffic, wobbling to avoid sideswiping a floater bus. The gyros held, and he nudged behind and to other side of the bus. The greenvests weren't out of the alley yet. Now he blinked it to autopilot and entered a destination that was a couple alleys up. The Harley obediently zipped between cars, ahead of the bus, never exceeding the permitted passing speed, signaled politely, and turned down the chosen alley. Chris had the autopilot gently take him to a small garden marked on the map. To his pursuers, who had some time back joined the anonymous flow of traffic, he hopefully looked unobtrusive on their maps.

Chris dismounted and flopped to the cool grass. Fabian clambered off and sat next to him. Gengineered yard bunnies nibbled at the grass to keep it clipped.

"Chris?" Sib. "I'm serious. You and Fabian need to get out of Rome while you can."

"Ugh. I told you, I can't. Why should I?"

"Don't you trust me?"

"Let's see, you started by trying to kill me—"

"That's not fair! I saved your life."

"—I have no idea who you are, you appear to be a wanted terrorist—"

"Revelations. Are you familiar with them? The 'End Times'?"

"You mean the The Revelation, singular, of Jesus Christ, as in, the last book of the Bible?"

"Nitpicker. Yes."

"Well, yes, I'm quite familiar."

"The second seal. What color is the horse."

"Okay, I don't have it *memorized*." He pulled up a quick search. "Red. The second horseman symbolizes war."

"The second seal's been opened. Now get out of Rome."

Chris scanned the news feeds for unusual items. Nothing that blared of trumpets. Thousands of followers of some shadowy new demagogue were killing innocent people seemingly at random in globally coordinated attacks using weapons disguised as pens. A large uptick in the number of new religions, many blatantly for-profit or blatantly political. Daily church attendance figures were down. The ordinary hundred-odd wars continuing. "I don't see anything especially out of the ordinary. The usual sad news."

"I'm telling you." Sib's visage looked stern.

"You must be mixed up in something bad."

"You know I can't tell you."

"All right, we'll compromise," he said, sitting up. "I'll only leave Rome if I can come remove you from this, whatever it is you're involved in."

"No!"

"Yes!"

"Chris—" She sighed. "Fine. You're too damn stubborn!"

"Settled, then. Where are you."

She paused. "Venice. It's going to take you longer than you think to get here. I'll meet you the day after tomorrow, 18:00, by the lions in St. Mark's square. I'll see you and Fabian then."

"Fabian! I can't kidnap the boy."

"If you don't, he'll die. I'm not kidding." She looked stern.

"You're not the most trustworthy. Are you a relative?"

"I'll explain when you get here. You've got to leave *now*. Get on that Harley. Now. *Now now now!*" Her face pleaded. "*Stand up!*"

Chris got up. "Ok, kiddo," he said aloud to Fabian. "Let's ride."

CHAPTER 36

Martin always fell asleep after sex. The better the sex the faster he fell comfortably, snuggly asleep after, hibernating like a bear prepared for winter. He'd fallen asleep quickly.

He was hungry as a bear in Spring when he woke a few hours later. The observation booth was sparse. He put on his spex to scan the capabilities of the room. Counters for a catered gig, but no food. A refrigerator poking its butt outside for natural cooling, and a bunch of gibberish in a mind-read "Save this dream, it's important!" Mental Note he'd told the spex to record while asleep (no doubt it had seemed brilliant at the time)—he remembered one time when he'd accidentally sent a gibberish message to his department chair in his sleep, just as this note was nonsense, "smish flark potatoes"... food in his dreams? But no food here.

And no Isabelle.

He pinged her spex. Privacy mode, as usual.

The shiny metal catchbasin for rain was full, and Martin had a large drink of cool water. Which only made his stomach growl louder. He really had been thinking only with his dick, he scolded himself. He should have thought to bring food and water, not having any idea at the time how long he'd be up here. Not to mention warmer clothes. Ants balls, why couldn't his spex have more AI and make helpful suggestions like that?

Speaking of clothes, he was cold now.

"Um." He looked around. No clothes. "God fucking fish dicks! She stole my clothes!"

He did a spex scan of the area. If there was nothing useful here, he'd just have to go back naked.

"Oh decifuck." No airshoot.

He went outside to confirm it wasn't hidden behind something the spex couldn't scan. Come to think of it, how had she gotten up? He reviewed his spex video log and, no there was no second transportation for her that he'd seen on arrival. She could have just asked him to bring a spare of some kind, but apparently they weren't on that trusting of terms yet despite that she'd obviously planned the sex.

So. No airshoot. No clothes. No food. He couldn't decide which way she'd screwed him the worst. She should have to pay whatever exorbitant amount spexing emergency-999 for help would cost. Irwin was right, she was messed up. I'm never going to see her again, he vowed. After I kill her.

He started to compose an update to his social mesh, "I'm fucking stuck on a solar power platform, naked —" when he decided better of it. His cadre didn't need to know about this boner.

Alerts reminded him it was time for a quick study session. Naked, he chose a druid cloaked avatar and answered student questions on autopilot.

He wandered peripatetically to where he saw the burn marks from where his airshoot set down on the landing pad.

When he got within a few meters of the spot, a LocatioNote popped into his spexspace. "Morning, sleepyhead."

"Ah, and a 'Fuck you' to you too."

Her message continued unabated, pre-recorded. "There's a resupply bot due up in a few hours by automated drone. When it's done you can sneak in behind the bot and it'll take you to me. Ciao!"

"Great," he said aloud, going back into the observation room to sit on a cold bench. "I can sit here freezing my balls off for hours, or I can expose myself, in multiple ways, by dragging 999 into this."

He was still debating the merits of his lose-lose choices when the resupply drone floated up. A white, plastic-looking balloon some three meters across docked where his airshoot had been. An orange peel shaped section slid aside, a ramp extended, and a service bot rolled out. The bot was the same model as the Housekeepy that had caused him so much grief in the hotel.

"Excuse me! Excuse me!" the housekeepy said as it entered the observation lounge and began tidying up.

Martin slid past it. He debated pushing it out and over the edge of the platform to settle the old score, but had his doubts the drone would leave alone. He thumped it hard on the side instead for good measure, saying "Excuse meeee!", and went over to the bubble drone.

He shivered in the bubble waiting for the housekeepy to finish up, which eventually it did and ambled in, nearly squishing Martin against the icy sides of the bubble. The drone's door slice slid closed and instantly lifted then dived in a doubly-sickening swoop over the edge.

The drone's shell was thin. Martin could see wings unroll and little propellers on the sides and top spinning wildly, pushing the balloon forward leisurely.

Several bone chilling hours later, the bubble drone set down on the deck of an identical power station. The door slice slid apart, the housekeepy trundled out.

Isabelle walked across the decking, reaching her hand inside the housekeepy as she passed, yanked hard, pulling something out without breaking stride, and walked into the bubble.

She carried a mound of clothes with a Cheshire cat grin on her face. "You might want these."

"You insane witch!" he said, taking the clothes. They felt plastic.

"Glad to see you too," she said with a large kiss and gentle squeeze to his penis. "Locator unit," she added innocently, tossing the box that she'd pulled from the housekeepy onto the floor.

The bubble's door slid closed as she dropped a white bearskin rug and her sundress to the floor again.

"These move fast so you'll want to hold on... Now!"

Oomph! — The drone swooped over the edge, tossing the two bodies together.

CHAPTER 37

"Get up, get up!" Orring's voice blared in Weston's spex simultaneous with his wall screen pinging a call and his door buzzing. Orring inserted crashing cymbals into the sound stream. Orring's prim face popped onto both spex and wall screen. "Get up, get up! Someone has a game to lose this morning."

Weston removed his spex and rubbed his eyes. He could smell yesterday's coffee. "I'm not playing. Tell me where Jasmina is."

"After the game. Up, up, up!" He clapped with each 'up.'

"Tell me now, God damnit! At least tell me she's ok."

"*After* the game. We have a deal. And my client doesn't like welchers. Get up. Now."

"Some things are more important than games, Orring. I've got to find Jasmina."

"*Nothing* is more important than money, Weston. Love especially. The cost benefit analysis was never kind to love. Too little reward, too much work, hard work, responsibility. The Market sucked what it could out of love and made it a commodity long ago. In your heart you know I'm right. Sex & spex, that's all there is, my friend. Now get dressed and play our chess game."

Weston wanted to vomit, forced himself not to. He was ashamed that at some deep level he believed Orring. Sex & spex—everything you strove for was a carnal, lizard-brained id serving pleasure, and you blinked it up from the Market. No doubt his grief at losing Jasmina was selfish, a thwarted lust. He'd thought it had felt like some kind of immortal love, but Orring was right. Nothing that was that hard had ever proved worthwhile. Weston sobered up. Jasmina almost certainly hadn't loved him. All a pleasant delusion. She probably faked the accident just to dump him.

The thought pissed him off. Wasn't that just how it was? She was probably up in her apartment laughing her head off. Well, fuck her. At least he still had chess. "I'm on my way," Weston finally snapped, and, satisfied, Orring blipped out.

Dressing in stylish balloon sleeves, Weston blinked up his prioritized Market hot prospect parameters. He set them to near-jagger levels. He'd go blow this stupid chess game — no sense wasting time on *that* — and have a half dozen quick cash jobs waiting. He slipped momentarily, thinking resignedly he'd trade all that, even all his future jobs, just for another day with Jasmina... but caught himself. Buck up. She's not dead, she ditched you, boy. Just a notch on her new pair of spex.

Some part of him wanted to shout that no, she wouldn't do that... but... but he'd checked all the hospitals, morgues, police... The bigger voice stomped in. That's the way the world goes, bub. They love ya and they dump ya. Dwindle away, little voice. Buck up.

Kasymov looked irritated today, as if his sweater were itchy. Perhaps because Weston was late, and as White, had to make the opening move. Weston chose the usual king's pawn opening, e4.

Kasymov responded with the Sicilian Defense, pawn to c5. By the fifth move Kasymov showed the Classical Dragon variation. Weston tried to remember what he'd read. He'd studied it intensely, so many days ago in Jasmina's apartment. With many players it was a weak opening, but Kasymov was known to deploy it brilliantly. Weston knew it was terribly tricky for Black; but the Master wouldn't falter today. Weston disinterestedly felt Kasymov was challenging him to show his stuff, annihilate Kasymov if he could. Weston looked up to where Jasmina would have stood. Some stranger was there, a man with numerous InstiSuds ads dancing across his chest. Weston's heart was heavy. So, she'd dumped him. But shouldn't he have seen that coming? Didn't he analyze his own life in the least? Weston moved his pieces on autopilot, wishing for an endless stream of beers to drown his sorrows.

After an eternity of introspection, Weston realized Kasymov sat holding his cheeks in his hands. Weston focused on the game and saw that they had both pushed their positions to the brink, where one false step would collapse the house of cards. Weston looked at Kasymov struggling, his time ticking toward nothing. Finally Kasymov moved. Yet he looked angry. Daring Weston to finish him if he could. Weston scanned the board, and with an unconscious glance at Kasymov, made his subtle blunder for Orring.

Kasymov threw up his hands and slammed down the move that would only become obvious to commentators after much analysis. But Kasymov had clearly sensed Weston's capitulation. Weston blinked up views of a couple commentators and made a feigned effort to salvage his position until the commentators grew agitated. Assured they knew it was hopeless, Weston resigned.

He took Orring aside as soon as he left the bubble, led him to an alcove by the restrooms. "Ok, where's Jasmina?"

"Tsk! You've one more game to play tomorrow. I said I'd tell you after that."

Weston wrenched Orring against the wall by his collar. "You liar! Where is she!"

Orring calmly kneed Weston in the groin. Weston doubled over in pain; Orring whispered, "I'll kill you if you touch my clothes again," patted him on the back and strolled away.

CHAPTER 38

Chris and Fabian cruised the Autostrade del Sole, the wind whipping their hair. Chris had put the Harley back on maglev autopilot. He pointed out the fattorias, vineyards and olive groves to Fabian as the hills glided by. They'd just entered the regioni of Umbria.

"What the hell do you think you're doing?" Canini shouted. "You're expressly forbidden to leave Rome. I have the UNCC all over my ass, Father. Turn around immediately."

"I'm sorry, your Eminence. I'm—" he wasn't sure exactly *why* he was doing it. "—it's God's will, your Eminence. I'm going to Venice."

"It's *my* will that you return to Rome this instant."

The countryside flashed by.

"I regret I can't do that. I was given a sign." He retold the cardinal the relevant portions of his conversation with Sib.

"That's bullshit. Absurd. Your return to Rome is not up for debate. The UNCC have contacted the next toll booth. It will not let you pass. You will wait there for UNCC escort back to Rome. That is all." Canini disconnected.

Chris slowed the Harley; he could see the next toll booth a couple kilometers ahead. There were no exits from the Autostrade ahead according to the map, nor any behind him for some distance.

As he approached the toll plaza, a half kilometer away, he put the Harley on manual and veered off the road. He said a quick prayer of thanks the bike didn't care that he hadn't renewed his I-can-drive-at-least-as-well-as-an-AI manual drivers license. He stopped and surveyed. To his right stretched a fattoria filled with olive groves. Telescoping in with his spex, he could see polizia Lamborghini's streaking toward the toll plaza.

Chris scanned the fattoria's simple wood fence. He saw a breach a few hundred meters back where it was opened up for repairs and made for it. He nudged the Harley up the slope in amongst the olive trees.

An anonymous caller blinked up. He feared it might be some part of the farm's security system. It didn't identify itself by a name, only some gibberish letters and numbers. It broke through his normal call list in urgent mode.

"Hello?" he took the call.

"Ripe!" said an excited voice.

"What?"

"Ripe!"

"Hello?"

"Ripe! Ripe! Ripe!"

Chris guided the Harley between the trees. They were covered in netting, which Chris remembered his friend Ghita telling him was to keep the birds away from the ripening fruit.

Another anonymous caller, with a different random ID. Then another, and another.

"Ripe! Ripe ripe! Ripe ripe ripe!"

Chris laughed and terminated the connections. Behind him Fabian took off his spex. "What is all that?"

"It's the trees, Fabian! They're announcing that the olives are ripe."

"How do I turn it off?"

Now that, Chris realized, was a good question. There were getting to be hundreds of call requests. He could ignore them, but each tree he neared started bugging him to take a call. Insistently.

He imagined there probably was a way to handle them all—if you were the farmer and knew what IDs to expect. Short of that, it was in effect a mild sort of security-by-nuisance system.

Fabian had the right idea. Chris put his spex in his shirt pocket.

Chris threaded the sun-dappled olive trees in a V shape away from the toll plaza then back toward the Autostrade past it.

As he came down the hill, he saw the polizia Lamborghinis paralleling his course on the highway.

Of course, Canini and the UNCC knew where he was heading; he had stupidly told them. He dreaded throwing away his spex, but could see little choice.

He tossed them by a tree and veered away from the highway. He thought he caught a glimpse of electric carts coming around a hillside, and angled away from them too.

The olive grove gave way to grapes. Chris realized how hungry and thirsty he was.

He made back toward the highway, and was relieved not to see the police. Which only meant they knew his last position and heading. The carts might have been them.

He paralleled the autostrade for a while, whisking through the vineyard as the sun began to set. Every now and again he topped a rise and could see the highway. Still no police. Hopefully he wasn't big enough fish for them to call in a helicopter or satellite imagery and drones might take a while to procure.

Hoping he was far enough out of police eye, he scooted toward the autostrade.

Only to find his way blocked by the simplest of walls — the meter-high concrete barrier built along the highway. He tried to get the Harley to ride over it, but even in maglev mode it wouldn't go that high. He scanned then drove sullenly along the highway, but on the wrong side, avoiding trees and cutting inland to go through grape vineyards. He had all but given up when the barriers left a small gap where a wire fence began.

Chris started for it, then realized he faced two problems. Lack of spex to pay tolls, and worse, if he tried to evade each toll plaza, the random choice of fencing might not permit it. The gang's Harley was clearly not sending ID information, but using his own spex account would be a tip off. Fabian might have an account — a question Chris filed to check into later — but the police knew of the boy already and his ties to Chris. Too risky. Chris puzzled where to secure someone else's spex or some anonymous cashcards.... and looked down the orchard.

He followed the dirt orchard path away from the highway and to the yellow buildings of the fattoria. *Buon giorno!* he shouted at an older man and woman inside one of the buildings, working an olive press. Chris introduced himself, and explained he was on a mission for the Church, taking the orphan boy to a family in Venice.

"That's a hell of a bike you have there, Father!" said the man, introducing himself as Bruno and his wife Rosa.

"Grazie, grazie. Though it does cost a fair bit to maintain on my salary," Chris joked with arms spread wide. At least, he felt, it gave him credibility, given his lack of spex.

"Father, you must share our supper with us!" Rosa said.

"We don't want to be trouble."

"No trouble!" Bruno said.

"We made Cinghiale al Ginepro for the boys," she said.

" — our crew — ", said Bruno.

"But they've gone into town for the night," she finished. "We have plenty. We insist."

"Grazie mille!" Chris said. "I haven't had home cooked boar in ages."

"And you," the woman said to Fabian, "do you like pistachio gelato, hmm?"

Chris felt a new man after washing up. Bruno greeted him with a Negroni. Chris disliked gin, of which this Negroni had too much, and not enough Campari, but he drank it to be social. It took the edge off the tightness in his shoulders nonetheless. As they sat down to dinner, Chris felt naked without his spex. He felt like when he was interviewing a Job, though these people were clearly not Jobs. Good people, but in no way Jobs.

"What news do you hear of the pope, Father?" the man asked. "It's so sad."

"I'm afraid not much," he said touching beside his eyes. "I've — taken a vow of poverty. What news have *you* heard?"

"Nothing very new, only that he is unwell."

"I suspect he will be with us for some time, however." Chris said. "He's a very strong soul. A very firm handshake."

"Oh, you know him personally! I've wondered, what color are his eyes?" asked Bruno. "They seem so penetrating in the spex but hard to tell the exact color."

Chris heard the hum of a swiveling, behind-the-wall mounted gun. Without his spex to authenticate his identity, Chris could easily be a thug disguised as a priest. It was clear the man was prepared.

"And you," Rosa asked Fabian, "Have you met the pope too?"

"No," Fabian answered absently chewing on the wild boar and the juniper berries.

"The Holy Father's eyes are a piercing green," Chris said. "I've met with him face to face a couple times to discuss a project I work on for him."

"A special project for the pope! How exciting," she said. "What is it?"

Chris explained Project Job to them. They asked him many questions, as well as Fabian, though the boy only answered in shy Yes's and No's.

"Ah, yes, and you've taken a vow of poverty, so you can relate well to them, I see." Bruno added in a whisper, "The boy here, is he a Job then? I can see that he," the man made a face, "is dull for his age."

"I don't know," Chris answered, taken aback. "I have other duties beyond the Job project. He may be a Job, but rarely are they so young." Chris hadn't considered that Fabian was not acting his age; he had so little contact with children. He seemed fairly resourceful — but perhaps that was Sib's guidance.

"He's a fine strong boy," Rosa said. "Here, Fabian, you need another helping of Cinghiale."

The dinner concluded with the promised pistachio ice cream, home made, freshly frozen. Chris couldn't think of a better meal he'd had in... years. After dinner Bruno surprised Chris with a small glass of limoncello, also homemade, and they sat comfortably by the fireplace. Fabian had fallen asleep in an overstuffed chair. Chris removed the boy's spex without waking him and put them in his shirt pocket.

As the conversation drifted about grapes and olives and the country life, Chris felt guilty for letting Fabian fall asleep, as if they were seeking a bed for the night. Truth be told, he wasn't keen on sleeping in some field, nor riding the rest of the way to Venice at night. He stifled a yawn. He stared out at the clear black sky and thought how nice a soft bed would be.

Chris pushed himself up; it was time to go. Bruno and Rosa began to protest—when a bright flash momentarily blinded them. They all turned toward the south window where it seemed to have come from. Despite the heat from the flash, he felt a chill. Chris thought of Sib's warning: Rome.

The afterimage of the flash faded. It was replaced with the rumbling, roiling, angry red fist of a massive mushroom cloud.

CHAPTER 39

Weston fumed. He jogged around his building in the drab, polluted air. He reviewed in his spex every conversation he'd had with Orring. He'd threaten Orring that he'd go to the Market Watchers, show them everything; Orring would be despecked, his ratings zeroed, and maybe he'd even be locked away for a longer time than was cruel and unusual. But first he had to find the evidence.

The conversations were all distorted. Orring must have had a warbler, altering his voice enough that it failed to match his official pattern. Weston wanted to punch the ad-slick wall. He did punch the wall. Other than pain, the only response was a coincidental one: An alert that his ratings had just been zeroed for non-performance. He was free to appeal to the Market Oversight Board; but Weston deleted the message with a terrified, casual detachment. What was there to appeal? He'd done this to himself.

Slimy, unsolicited ads for the unrated popped in at him in a flurry, along with the address of the nearest government Ratings Disability office and the business card of his caseworker. If he was lucky he could grub enough for minimal food. His landlord's pickets notified him that he was now on expedited eviction alert, and had better prepay more rent or be booted when his account flatlined before the end of the week. The message included a handy clicklist of shelters for the Unrated.

Weston turned around, physically, searching the skies for someone to turn to. There had to be someone. Mother, dead. Father, God knew where. No siblings. A number of shallow acquaintances, but of the usual fair-weather sort. Coming to them in trouble would only earn him coffee money and their eternal disgust. It seemed to him that his parents had talked of *friends* as people whom you could depend on. He'd never known anyone like that—beside Jasmina—and his heart ached doubly at the lack of the one and loss of the other. His only cheer, little that it was, was realizing that nobody he knew had such friends either, nor anyone he knew of or heard of. Never having needed them before he hadn't realized this was some sort of archaic concept, long dead in reality but a shadow kept comically alive in vids. The instant world had no place for such permanence. It floated along on the frothy whitecapped peaks of one shot deals.

It was, in fact, his own fault he'd come to this, and he accepted that. Acceptance wouldn't put wheatios in his hands, let alone find Jasmina.

Weston blinked through his address book. He had to wade through the crap—people from tours he'd saved to replay and study because they were "interesting." Useless. He deleted them as he went. He'd saved a few records on people he might bum a quickie job from, tour operators and the like. Small potatoes all. A few artists he'd met during stints—for some reason he saved artists, not bankers or doctors or politicians. Artists. Hmm—committed to their art. They'd understand his unusual situation and that he needed some kind of extraordinary measures to find Jasmina. Maybe they'd share their resolve with him, or their contacts? In the end Weston rejected them all. Ais did art so much better than humans that human art seemed simplistic, self-indulgent, faux. Good potential artists either sold out to be a human feedback cog in an algorithm or never developed for lack of resources. Like food. He knew better than to waste time seeking their inevitable, sneering refusals. Blink. Deleted.

Of course, Kasymov's glaring image suggested someone he might turn to. But, no, Kasymov was too huge a figure, too imposing, too unreal. Weston idly delved into Kasymov's biographies. Hours slid by as Weston read about his childhood in a repressive regime, his political battles for human rights, losing his title and spinning into a deep depression, and his unprecedented return to regain his title, losing it yet again, then again, then winning and never losing it for ages. Weston devoured one biography after another. Under that fierce, demanding visage was a human guy. A powerful one.

Weston shipped a message to Kasymov via his agent. The agent might delete the message... but probably not from someone engaged in a match. And not if Weston phrased it as an apology for missing the game tomorrow. Weston detailed his woes by way of explanation, but never directly asked for aid. His voice broke twice at the end, when he described his biggest regrets — insulting Jasmina and throwing the games.

When he sent it, and removed his spex to wipe his eyes, he realized at some point he'd begun walking the old bike trail that ran beside Cherry Creek as it angled toward downtown. He looked ahead. If he kept following it, it would lead not far from The Colorado Center for the Patient, where Jasmina would surely have been taken if injured. Indigents and the spexless had been taken there since before Weston was born. He'd already checked with them numerous times, in person and by spex. But perhaps this time he'd get a different clerk, one who cared...

He didn't, as to be expected, but as he was leaving, his shouts of their inhumanity still echoing, a recorded message pinged up. Kasymov's image appeared.

"You've nothing to lose," he said. "If she's dead, she's dead, and you will find a funeral notice. If injured, doctors will tend to her, and you can't find her until she is released perhaps. So, come, Weston, to Baku. Visit me. We will talk. You will be safe from your groin-breaking friends. And if there's some other solution to your female conundrum, perhaps we will find it in a chess game."

CHAPTER 40

As the sun rose, the sirens continued as they had all night. Police, ambulances, fire trucks, government cars of all sorts sped toward Rome. There had been no question of sleep; Chris, Bruno and Rosa spent the night sharing the tragedy, watching the same reports on their spex, a pair of which they loaned to Chris connected to their account. The center of the blast had been just to the south of the Vatican in the large park of the Villa Doria Pamphili. Estimated at a 10 kiloton blast, roughly the size of Hiroshima. The death toll was hard to estimate so soon, but put in the six figures. The Vatican was gone. Only sticks and dust and a few stones remained.

Media reports cited experts who reviewed the video clips endlessly, expressing their opinions that it was a ground detonation, not a missile or plane-dropped weapon. Likely a "suitcase" bomb as had always been feared.

The damage decreased away from ground zero with the cube root of the distance. Over night the video had repeatedly shown the mushroom cloud from all angles, the firestorm, the way the lights of Rome showed a gaping black hole in the city where there wa nothing left to burn. The traffic jam of emergency vehicles that Rome's narrow streets were never meant to handle. The stream of victims running, limping, being carried or dragged from the area; burns visible in the light of cameras. Nowhere to go, hospitals overwhelmed. The park areas of the Villa Borghese filled with people lying every which way, moaning, crying, lit by the flickering of the firestorm.

By daylight the fires still raged, the smoke a massive plume over the central part of Italy. Firefighters braved the radiation, only a few having any sort of hazmat suit to wear. Commentators announced the radiation readings at various locations.

"We must have breakfast," Rosa eventually said. "Keep our strength up for the hard days ahead." Everyone had been transfixed by their spex and sharing discussions of what they saw. It didn't feel right to talk about normal life, breakfast—or to think about meeting Sib in Venice.

Chris realized it was unlikely Cardinal Canini or the UNCC cared about his whereabouts right now, so he briefly logged into his own account with Bruno's borrowed spex. The Market was sluggish. His queues of requests for confessions and other clerical joblets was enormous; overwhelmingly long. And one brief message from Sib, confirming their meeting in Venice.

Rosa made breakfast of cappuccino and croissants. Chris had become accustomed to larger breakfasts than most Italians. He eyed the eggs Rosa brought from the chicken coop outside for something she was preparing for later today. She seemed to want to keep busy to avoid thinking about the tragedy. Her bustle kept Chris from focusing on Sib and what to do. To go to Venice to help her—or go to Rome to help millions. If he could even reach Rome there would be little tangible assistance he could offer there, not being a doctor or rescue worker; he could take confessions, give succor to the injured, last rites to the dying. But Rome had no lack of other priests. The government asked civilians to stay away from Rome unless they had specific skills.

And there was the question of Fabian. No doubt Rosa and Bruno would look after him if asked, they were unquestioningly good people. But he somehow felt Fabian and Sib were linked, and that she needed his help. Given her link to the terrorist organization, which, since no one had yet claimed responsibility could well be the one that had nuked Rome, perhaps he could use her influence to stop more carnage.

He knew even before weighing the evidence that he was going to Venice, with Fabian. Underneath all the rationalizations, he felt, like an ice cube in the pit of his stomach, protective of Sib.

Rosa piled more orange eggs on his plate. "Eat, Father. You know better than I what is going on. These are the end times."

Chris smiled, friendly, but inside humored that some people said this about every disaster. Some signs were always there to be interpreted as someone wished. Christ had said he would return like a thief in the night—there would be no predicting it. No readable signs, just a sudden change, glorious and fearsome.

Of course, that was thousand year old Church doctrine, Chris countered internally; meant to keep wavering Christians on the path. What better than a threat of a rapture at any possible, unforeseen moment. Push both the list of signs of the end times, as in the Revelation of John, and counter that with Jesus saying he would return without signs. Good work. Every moment a possible end time.

Which brought up the question, was Sib in league with Satan? He couldn't believe it. He'd talked with her so long now that he felt he could tell if she were patently evil. Rather, she appeared to be the angel within an evil organization, working to stop the evil. How could he help her in that? How could he protect her? Was she safe?

"You must love her very much," Rosa said.

"What? Who?" Chris asked, shaken from his reverie.

"I know that faraway look on your face. You've pledged your life to God, yes, but you are still a man. A mother knows." She patted his shoulder. "Who is she?"

"She's a—I'm not in love with her!"

"There are many kinds of love. Your love for God, for your mother, for your country. They are all good in God's eyes. It is not wrong for you to love a woman too. One does not subtract from the other. What I think—" she took his hand. "I think they magnify each other. Even the Church has recognized this at last."

It was true, in recent years, to stem a decline in men seeking the priesthood the church had grudgingly moved a step closer to the Protestants in allowing clergy to marry under rare circumstances. But Sib! She was a terrorist! She'd tried to kill him! How could this old woman Rosa see such a thing in his body language. It couldn't be true. He searched his feelings as Rosa poured him more espresso.

She put the coffee in his hands. "You see? Love warms you like this espresso. I see it in your face. What is her name?"

"Sib, but I—I—" He couldn't bring himself to admit what he already felt was the truth. His training had been rigidly against the clergy having relationships like that.

Rosa studied his face. "So. Was she in Rome, this Sib? No, I don't think so."

"I was on my way to meet her in Venice."

"Then you must go! We will be fine here. We can watch Fabian for you."

"No, he's... part of this, somehow."

"Ah, a mystery!" Bruno chimed in from across the room. "Well, you mustn't keep a woman or a mystery waiting. Charge the bike, and can it also take old petrol and alcohol? Keep the spex, we don't need them. And here," Bruno said, handing over some cash cards. "You'll need these."

"I couldn't impose," Chris said.

Rosa closed his hand around the cash cards. "Your vow of poverty, I understand. But these are special times. If you do not take them I will simply hide them in your pocket. Don't make me do that."

"I can't possibly repay you. You've been more than generous. But you are right. Fabian, it's time to go." Chris blinked the "acknowledge" on Sib's reminder to meet him; it winked to green indicating she received it.

"And here," Bruno said. He blinked over a map. "Take these side roads and trails. The highway is clogged with the emergency."

The air was crisp and clean, with the wind blowing the plume from Rome away toward the south. Chris and Fabian rode north and east along Bruno's excellently planned route, encountering only normal local traffic. No police blockades hunting for Chris barred the way, only the usual crazy Italian drivers zig-zagging at high speed and some hikers and bicyclists on the trails. Rosa had packed his saddlebags with bread and sandwiches and wine, so Chris and Fabian stopped only briefly by the side of the road to eat.

Chris navigated into Venice over the many bridges that twisted toward the Piazza San Marco and the statues of the lions. Life in Venice was quiet with shock; a few muted tourists meandered about, unsure how to make the most of their vacation of a lifetime in the face of a global tragedy. Venicians still hung their clothes to dry in the narrow passageways, but there seemed to be far more Italian and EU flags showing than he'd ever seen before.

He parked the Harley near the basilica and took Fabian by the hand as they walked toward the lion statues, scattering pigeons as they went.

A young couple sat kissing by the statues, saw him, kept kissing obliviously. There was no sign of Sib.

CHAPTER 41

"How many more of these power platforms are we stopping at?" Martin asked. They'd visited over a dozen during the night and morning, venturing thousands of kilometers out to sea.

"Getting wore out, tiger?" Isabelle asked.

They'd made love on or between each of the stations. Martin was, he admitted to himself, getting a bit sore, and these power stations were all uniformly dull, especially with a cloud deck now below them obscuring the sea, but it was entirely worthwhile. "Your Latin lover never gets 'wore out.' Do we have a destination in mind, or are we going to stay up here forever?"

"Two more rounds, I should think."

"Then what?"

"Then you'll see."

"Ah. What, ah, ever became of the airshoot I rode up to the first platform, by the way?"

"That old thing? I pushed it over the edge. No room for two like these spacious quarters."

And, he thought, no chance for someone like himself to escape. This seemed remarkably well planned out.

After two more faux housekeeping visits Isabelle pulled on her sundress and went into the power station's observation lounge. Martin took the hint and quickly dressed.

"Here we are," she announced to herself. "This will do perfectly."

Martin came into the lounge behind her. She had opened a white plastic cupboard and removed what looked like a giant folded-up campchair—long spindles with fabric mysteriously woven through.

She stepped past him and went outside.

Martin watched as she unfolded — wings. Struts and very large wings, with the fabric flapping dangerously, though it had holes in it to let the air through. Large enough for a person. He queried his spex on the shape. Emergency escape glider, his ferret reported. Weight capacity 150 kilos.

"Only one?" he asked.

"Hang on tight," she said as she strapped the infrastructure to her back.

Martin hesitated. At around 100 kilos, or perhaps a smidge more, plus her likely 50 kilos...

"Hop on over," she said. She had a cinch strap swinging in her hands, then she mimed the stewardess buckling a passenger up. "Please keep your safety harness latched at all times," she added when he still hadn't moved.

"No helmet?" he asked nervously.

"It's like zip-lining over a hundred meter gorge," she said. "If you fall, you die. Very liberating. Coming?"

"Urrrrrg..." escaped his mouth, but he took a faltering step over. She deftly looped the safety harness around him and buckled themselves together.

"Geronimo!" she said, tipping him off balance and over the edge.

They plummeted straight down.

Martin screamed like a teenage girl at a Plankton Boys concert.

She adjusted some controls and the holes in the fabric filled in. They leveled off into a gradual though turbulent glide. Her red hair flapped wildly in his face.

The cloud deck approached, but not rapidly enough, Martin thought. At this point he'd rather just get this over with.

"Don't you feel like an eagle?" she asked over the spex link.

"I feel like a flying polar bear," he managed. "A flying polar bear about to throw up."

They entered the clouds. Moisture streamed across Martin's face and spex. Now I know what an aircraft window feels like, he said miserably.

He felt disembodied in the clouds. White all around, a mental as well as physical fog. He briefly shut off his spex to experience the oneness of it. No gravity, just the gusting and buffeting of unseen wind.

With nothing to look at, his mind cleared. What the hell was he doing out here with this woman? He loved the adventure, and adventurous women. If things wouldn't cool off, he could perhaps spend an eternity with her. He hadn't felt that way about most women. He enjoyed the mystery and a bit of danger—though perhaps nothing that would be actually life-threatening. He didn't need the adrenaline to feel good, he just enjoyed the sensations themselves and new experiences. Was she someone he could spend a life doing that with? And was she even interested?

They abruptly exited the clouds, the sea looming a kilometer below. It looked frothy with whitecaps. "Are we landing on a submarine, swimming with sharks, or what other exciting plan do you have?"

She pointed.

He could just barely make out an island in the distance. He gauged their rate of descent and the distance... and didn't like the math. He really had to piss now.

His bladder felt like a ripe grapefruit. No, he thought, a squeezed waterballoon. God, he had to stop thinking about it.

He looked down instead. Oh, Christ! He flailed his arms and legs, suddenly grasping that he was thousands of meters above the sea with no floor under him. That theory about enjoying excitement was great when it was theoretical. He'd explicitly ruled out *life threatening*, and this sure as hell felt like he was about to plummet to a painful death.

"Are you okay?" she asked. "Get a grip before you barber pole your lines!"

He couldn't stop flailing. He felt like he was falling. He was, of course, falling. God, was this what it was like to die? he wondered. Something semi-hard, gooey hit him in the face. He wiped at it. He was pretty sure she had hocked a loogie at him. "Stop it!" she yelled in her spex.

He was so angry and disgusted he forgot to flail. He remembered her words, and suddenly they felt liberating. If you actually did fall, you were dead. He was in control of his body now. No more stupid, primitive lizard-brain making him do irrational things.

But where the hell were they going out here?

As the island grew in size he realized it wasn't as large as he thought, perhaps twenty kilometers across. Then he realized the edges were too sharply defined to be natural. His spex helpfully popped up: *TempusEstVita (also: Tev). A man-made floating island nation. Name is Latin, translation: "Time Is Life." Currency unit, one Dex equals 1.37 Petrodollars. Motto,* "Noli alicui incommodum ferre" *– Do not inconvenience others. Age: 12 years. Area: 420 sq. km. Pop.: 112,777. Diplomatically recognized per Microstate Treaty five years ago.* Martin blinked on the motto, curious what "Do Not Inconvenience Others" was all about.

Corpus of island law based on utopian philosophical theme that time is the unit of measure of life, both in the physical sense and in the quality sense; that "wasting another's time" is tantamount to "shortening another's life"; of setting reasonable expectations for one's dealings with others, and facing appropriate consequences for falling short. Murder, kidnapping, etc. are per se examples of detracting from a victim's quality of life by detracting from their freely chosen time. Commercial providers of services held to similar standard, that if a service fails to perform as expected, the recipient's time and thus "free" life has been unwillfully shortened. Products failing to perform similarly cause unwillful detraction of the purchaser's time / life. Penalties range from civil monetary compensation on the order of one Dex currency unit per minute wasted for accidental time wastage up to ten Dex per minute for intentional or forseeable time wastage, to imprisonment for egregious or criminal acts (thus, wastage of perpetrator's own time).

Tev is broadly based on Lewis's theory of expectations, a mathematical formulation of basic emotions such as Love, Hate, and Happiness, via what people expect and what people get. The classic example being that a totalitarian states scores low, stemming from a lesser number of, and narrower, expectations; whereas democratic freedoms convey more and broader expectations. Happiness is thus proportional to wider expectations that become met. Reasonableness of an expectation is based on the Golden Rule. Thus Tevians try to exceed people's expectations. Martin stopped reading, his eyes glazing over. Wonderful, a floating utopia.

The concept made sense, Martin thought as it grew larger. He had often bristled at needless waits holding for mesh support when they'd promised instant help access, or waiting on suborbital tarmacs for hours because they never had enough tow drivers.

Fascinating. But—"Why they hell are we going there?" he asked Isabelle through his spex.

She just smiled back.

~~~

The air pressure pushed on his stomach and kidneys. He *really* had to pee now. They seemed to accelerate, despite Martin's rational brain saying they would have reached maximum velocity. The faster he felt they were going the faster he felt the wind push on his kidneys. And the more he had to pee. It was moving beyond "urgent" to painful.

He seriously contemplated just letting go. He wondered if the maxim about don't piss into the wind was really sage advice or not.

He could see the greens and browns of the island and his only thought was forcing himself to ask his spex for the location of public restrooms in his area. "Fucking blinking red icons don't help!" he said aloud with a strained voice as the flashing just made him feel more urgent. He decided he couldn't hold it any longer, and it was time just to piss down his leg.

"*Go!*" he shouted subvocally—but his bladder wouldn't respond. Despite the pain, he couldn't force the muscles to open. "Arrrrgh!" he shouted aloud.

Then the ground was looming up. Ok, focus on the ground. Not the time to pee now. Oh, shit, it seemed like the green ground was rushing up at them at an insane speed. He'd smash every bone in his body. His bladder decided maybe it should open up after all... No! Not now! Concentrate on the ground!

Isabelle said, "Slow up, like this—" and she motioned how to drop his speed. He had to squeeze his bladder now to avoid it exploding. He followed her hand motions, the ground rushing up—up—

Then he was almost suspended, motionless. Much slower now.

They glided to a landing in a grassy park on the floating island. Martin tried to land on his feet, stumbled, belly flopped, and the glider dragged him fifty meters on his face until the glider itself did a face plant. His bladder chose this moment to let go. He was glad he was wearing plastic pants. His socks were getting wet and squishy however.

Isabelle glided to a graceful landing. She unhooked from her glider and came over to disentangle Martin and unlatch him.

"Poor thing." She wiped at his scratched, bloodied face with his shirt tails.

"Now explain to me why you chose this method to get, holy fuck, thousands of klicks out to sea? Couldn't we have chartered a plane? Hopped a robofreighter?"

"Yes, I suppose. But it wouldn't have been nearly as fun."

A patrol bot floated over. "Intruder alert! Intruder alert!" It looked like a hot dog floating at eye level. It had a large dent in what would be the bun of a hot dog. The hot dog part that stuck out of the bun flashed red and menacingly.

A dude in a sleek wet suit floated over behind the bot. "Don't mind Robbie. He's all bark." The dude shook his head, in apparent conversation with the bot.

The bot then announced, "Aloha, amigos, welcome to the island!"

Martin looked at him skeptically. "You two know each other?" he asked, nodding between Isabelle and the dude.

"No way," he said, "but anybody who makes an entrance on a glider from a power station's a rad mod in my book. I'm Byyrd." He blinked his public greeting IDs over his spex. Charlie Byyrd, Radical Moderate, Moderate Radical, Competitive Ped Surfer, Chef, Lover of Women, Men, Animals, Plants and Planets alike. He had the small ped surfer boards dangling on a tether around his waist. A data blog attached to his greeting from the Encyclopedia Planetica kindly explained ped surfing was incredibly difficult, with small surf boards barely larger than one's feet, controlled by AIs that magnified the brain's intentions but carefully avoided helping one keep balance artificially. A good ped surfer walked on water and could do acrobatics like a gymnast or snowboarder on a half-pipe. A mediocre ped surfer just drowned.

"So I know more about ped surfing than I ever intended to," Martin said.

"You wanna go smack some whitecaps?"

"Ah, no, thank you." Truth be told Martin was feeling a bit queasy from the motion of the ground.

"Motion sickness detected," the bot announced. "Would señor desire a dose of Hookamine or some acupinching?"

Martin's spex popped up a data sheet on the seasickness remedies. Side effects of the former included, beyond being stoned out of one's mind, mild cases of, well, death; or bouts of intense pain for the latter.

"No, I'll, uh wait some."

"You'll get used to it, dude," Byyrd said. "Tev is built like a bunch of barrels tied together with a deck on top. There are shock-absorber pontoons and it all breaks apart if needed in a major storm, then bots reassemble it. Usually not this rocky but we're running from a storm.

"And, not that I even know why we're here," he said shooting a look at Isabelle, "where exactly are we going?"

"Good question amigo. You're just in time for a vote." He apparently saw the quizzical look on Martin's face?

"Destination determined by vote of the residents. You're here. You're a resident." He eye-flicked Martin a summary of the voting procedures.

CHAPTER 42

Kasymov's villa overlooked the azure waters of the Caspian Sea. The sky was a clear, pale blue above the waves feinting at Weston's wingtips. A breeze gently whipped Weston's windbreaker as he hustled to keep pace with Kasymov. Though Weston was more physically fit than the aging Kasymov, he felt ungainly matching speed with the grandmaster. Walking rapidly across the firm yet suddenly sliding and shifting sand was apparently a skill that required time to acquire.

"If I moved rook to h4, instinct tells you to do what? Quick! Quick!"

"Just a moment!" Weston quickly set up the position in his Kasymov simulator. He'd become skilled at rapidly blinking the pieces into position.

"Weston. Let me borrow your spex, please."

Weston sighed and handed them over. How was he supposed to be Quick! Quick! when Kasymov interrupted him?

Instead of donning the spex, Kasymov turned them over once, twice, then folded them and put them into the pocket of his jacket. "Rook to h4—quickly!"

"But—my spex!"

"Rook to h4!"

Weston stared open-mouthed until Kasymov made it clear the spex were out of the picture. His eyes felt cold in the breeze. Weston huffed then visualized their mock game in his head. As promised, Kasymov kept Weston's mind from worldly matters such as Jasmina with unending games of chess long into the night, hypotheticals, tales of games with his friend Kasparov and bitter adversaries Peng and Stotz, and political gesticulations about water rights on Mars and

New Guinean neocannibals eating cloned Jelly Men. Weston felt his head swollen to near exploding with their depth of study. But to take a guy's spex! What a low blow. Yet the opportunity to study, extensive mano-a-mano tutelage from his idol... Despite his tightened chest at the nakedness of being spexless, he forced himself to concentrate on the board. After more urges of "Quickly!", he replied, exasperated inside but keeping his answer firm to avoid a further scolding. "Attack your now defenseless pawn structure."

"Exactly! Exactly wrong. Now, think. What would Kleinfelder do?"

Weston shifted his thinking by imagining he was the twelve year old girl wunderkind. It helped disrupt his own brash instinctual play. They walked along the beach in silence for many minutes. "She'd... sense your attack to dislodge the knight. Move the bishop to c7."

"A senseless defensive move, yes? She loses momentum."

Weston caught his toe in a sand divot and had to dance carefully to stay upright. "Yes. No. No... She's innocently set up a zugzwang in a few moves. You'll have to—"

"Exactly. But you, this is not your style. What would *you* do? Think, this time."

As Weston pondered, fidgeting with his nose and cheeks where his absent spex would be, Kasymov continued talking; the man could talk about anything at any time. His depth of knowledge was surely not both infinitely broad and infinitely deep, but it was broad in general and deep in many specifics. It was his talent for always invisibly guiding the subject to something he knew well that made it appear he knew everything about everything. "Chess is about life. Yes, yes, the chess board and moves are fixed and finite, yet in life anything seems possible, the moves infinite—but really, no. We each have our fixed moves, born of years of practice being who we are, our personality. So, life has become a giant game of blitz chess. Everyone reacts, no thinking, no planning, no strategy, because they feel the seconds of the clock ticking loudly as if it is their heart beating and death breathes heavily behind them. It's ironic, is it not?—as lifespans have doubled and tripled, the common man buzzes ever more about like an angry wasp, never landing more than a heartbeat, but searching, constantly searching."

"I would bully your queen into retreat with my knight. Because you don't know if I'll sacrifice my queen plus the knight, if I have something up my sleeve."

"Exactly."

And two weeks had passed before Weston was aware of it. Chess games sped by like fenceposts. His unease at being spexless gradually faded; he was so occupied by day, so tired at night, and awoken so early he barely had time to miss them. It was only after a month that he woke to the realization that it had been a *month*.

Thirty-two days, in fact, he counted. No word of Jasmina. He quickly scoured the death notices from a holo screen in his room as he made himself up for breakfast—Kasymov insisted he dress formally even though Weston feared he would never extricate the microns of sand from the wingtips Kasymov had a local artisan make for him. "You must learn to play under the harshest playing conditions," Kasymov said. "Then you will be ready for the casual."

So. Jasmina was not dead. A notice would have appeared by now. Weston pushed aside a half dozen game positions from his mind to concentrate on Jasmina. He ran though the combinations again. Dead—not listed due to error. Coma. Changed her identity—ridiculous; even Weston's ego wasn't so large that a lover would need such lengths to escape him. Secret agent. Actually at home but ignoring him—no, her boss was credibly concerned about her not being at work. Somewhere she was out there, hurt. Weston wanted nothing more from life than to hold her and comfort her.

He expressed his frustrations to Kasymov over a breakfast of blini with caviar.

"But, Weston, look. Every game ends. No—has an end. I do not mean you are through with her today. No, but that your search for her will finish. Every game ends—even if it is a draw."

"And you're going to tell me if I lose, there will always be another game—"

"Yes!" He clinked their champagne glasses.

"—but I don't want another game. This is the final game of the championship, and I'm down two pawns."

"Ha! Yes—but it is your move. And you're the stronger player. So. Imagine this position." Kasymov madly drew pieces in the sand with his finger. Weston memorized the layout, the smudges themselves in the sand being unrecognizable. "Your Queen is blocked, invisible, behind the mess you've made of your pawns—here, here, and here. Nothing you can do will free her. Your King is exposed. Black is a bear like so, muscle pumping everywhere. You must uncover your Queen to protect your King."

Weston began to answer, but Kasymov silenced him with a motion. "No! Think first! You, I know, you'll smash in with your knight. But, look if—"

"Yes, yes, I see it." Fiddling with the knight led to doom.

A wave broke on the beach, the upsurge wiping away the chess board in the sand. "Like life," Kasymov said, pointing; "time erodes the physical, but not the facts... Now think."

"I'm thinking!" Weston analyzed the position in his head. Hopeless. Superficially it looked like it should be strong, a fortress. But Black was stronger. For each edge White appeared to have, Black had cunning attacks that could not be repulsed. Every Black piece was perfect. Weston envisioned threads of moves like a tapestry coming out of a madly cranking loom. Each of his moves led to disaster—the tapestry in flames at the top.

"The King! I see it!"

"The King. What about the King?"

"Black's position is perfect. 100% perfect. Not a strand of hair out of place." He couldn't help but think of Jasmina's hair, a strand hanging by her eye... "But it's *too* perfect. It's set up to anticipate any attack or retreat I can make. It's like the Market: Everything Is Known. But it can't remain stable. Black has to move *something* after I move."

"*Tempus iter facit perpetuum!*" Kasymov said. Time marches on.

"That's it! If I could do nothing at all, some useless move, Black starts falling apart right away out of the sheer necessity to move a piece. The most perfect zugzwang I've seen. Every position is crucial."

"But... you have the same problem, yes?"

"That's what had me going. Right, I have no useless moves. Every move puts me in more danger. But the most dangerous move of all— if I attack with the King, put it in instant jeopardy of check—forces Black to move *some* piece out of perfect alignment. Damn. It's so risky!

So many combinations lead to mate... it would require perfect play for twenty or thirty more moves... but Black's position has its legs kicked out from under it... but, the risk... but... Agh!" He held his head as in mock pain. "But that's the move. Yes. It can work, and everything else is certain failure. White can even win from there. Amazing. Where on earth did you dream this position up?"

"Ha! An extrapolation of a game. It would have come to this, but..." he waved his hands. "My opponent had... other things on his mind." Kasymov paused. "You don't recognize it?"

"No..."

"Chess—any in depth thinking—plus the despicable general lack of it in world—this makes you a power. What we used to call a Player. Use that. Outthink the world." Kasymov tapped his temple. "You don't recognize that game? No still? Game three of our match, Weston! Game three!"

"No. Really?" Weston thought. "My God. You're right!"

Kasymov gave a quick nod.

Weston watched the fisherman dragging in their nets. They patiently coaxed them in, seemingly one knot at a time. So much material to reel in, yet they made unrelenting progress. Their motion was fluid, mesmerizing.

"Now. Weston. You understand about thinking, planning, not always running into the crowd of bad guys with your sword slicing like so—and so—". Kasymov acted out the slashing madman. "You get yourself killed."

Weston nodded. He was eager for a real game, with a solid warmth of self-confidence he'd never felt.

"So. One more thing I know." He pulled Weston's spex from his pocket and offered them. "*Now* you are ready to find out what happened to your mysterious girlfriend, your Jasmina. Go. Find her."

CHAPTER 43

C hris hadn't been able to reach Sib for days. He'd found a cheap hostel in Venice and tried repeatedly to reach her. The Market had been very sluggish, losing messages, delaying delivery for a long time. Market requests for confessions that arrived were days old. It seemed as twisty as the byways of Venice. The netbog was reportedly tied to the price of wheat, which had gone through the roof when it was discovered that whole months of crops globally had no nutritional value. It was predicted that a global famine would hit as soon as stocks of provably nutritional grain were consumed. Next season's crops were months away, and in doubt as the cause of the loss of nutritional value was yet unknown.

During these days Chris paced his sparse room. He went for long walks on the quiet maze of stone alleys and bridges. He sounded Fabian out on his education, and found it more lacking than he'd expected, more lacking than spex sites described for Fabian's age. Chris attempted to remedy the situation with some classes on history, mathematics, languages, and of course theology. It helped Chris sound out his own feelings, his Doubt.

He'd sent a courtesy note to Canini's office telling him where he was, though he didn't know if it arrived. With Rome in cinders he didn't even know if the cardinal were alive. An ad-hoc network of clergy were relaying messages in a hop-by-hop, store and forward network, but it was clear there were large holes in the Church hierarchy and control structure. He did learn that the Holy Father was alive; he hadn't been in the Vatican at the time of the blast, but had been "convalescing," purportedly at his mountain retreat in Les Combes. There was no news on what his ailment was nor his condition. No messages had been known to come directly from him; with so many of the managerial cardinals dead the Church was operating in a more decentralized mode, more like the Anglican model.

Chris's Doubt was a question as he taught Fabian, a resumption of the debate he had been having with Sib: Immortality seemed compatible with the notion of God—indeed, Christianity itself promised a form of immortality—Christianity and most other religions taught that eternal life was the goal to aspire to—but fundamentally incompatible with the pillars of the Church. If the pope was functionally immortal, whether a vegetable or not, then the Church would have to come to grips with the concept of living forever on this earth, not going to Heaven. It didn't matter to his argument whether the man himself, Pope Paul VII, was immortal, or a vegetable. Science was clearly within reach of creating such that he and others believed it possible; spex searches on it had turned up many scientific papers that, while Chris couldn't understand them, seemed to hint it was plausible. What thus mattered to Chris's Doubt was that it *could* happen. What then the Church? Would it be deemed evil, a sin? If not, how could one reconcile thousands of years of saying Heaven was one's ultimate destination? An assumption that some accident would eventually get you? But Christ hadn't mentioned a probability of death; it was billed as a certainty. Heaven on Earth? That too went against thousands of years of teachings. Admittedly the Church had appeared to reverse course by retiring the concept of Limbo many years before, but it had never fully accepted it as real in the first place. Heaven, and thus Hell, were not on Earth.

If the Holy Father were effectively immortal, as Sib claimed, and the treatment could be applied to other people who weren't mental vegetables, that could prove troublesome for the Church. Chris tried to get Fabian to question him, to engage in debate, but Fabian was very quiet. "Fabian, is it ethical to have a medical treatment or other benefit that only the wealthy and powerful can afford?"

Fabian drew circles with his fingers on the plain plastic table in their hostel room. "I dunno."

Chris let out his breath. "People may say so, but it has happened many times in history. Typically the treatment becomes available to the masses after some years. God takes a long view, as do many governments and corporations."

"The pretty lady is sad," Fabian said out of the blue.

"You've heard from her?!" Chris tried to blink a call to her, but the Market was even slower than usual. "Where is she? What does she say? Why is she sad?"

"She told me not to say. She said you'll know."

"What does that mean?" Chris asked aloud.

Then his emergency news alert flashed bright red: Millions dead within minutes: A rapidly mutating virus had killed everyone within tens of kilometers of New Delhi. The virus mutated itself out of existence, like a scrap of paper burning to a crisp in an ashtray. Honeypot sensors on street corners had detected the virus and its rapid mutations nearly instantly, flashing genome sequences to the CDC within seconds of detection. Anti-viral genome busters were computed in near real time but manufacture of sufficient doses and delivery of the cures remained a several-day time lag. All the many mutations of the virus were harmless to humans, save one — the one that had the effect of suppressing the firing of neurons in the brain. Tens of millions of New Delhi-ites had their brains slagged. Each viral packet's RNA then self-modified on its way with no apparent impact on human tissue. A loud buzzing like a billion locusts filled the air — and suddenly millions dropped in their shoes. Later analysis revealed the viral packets had established audio-through-radio band communications in what appeared to be a reticular network.

What had Sib to do with that? "Fabian, millions of people just died — is that what she meant?"

"She said she tried to stop it."

"Damn it!" He choked up. "Where is she?"

Fabian only shrugged.

"What does she want me to do? Did she say anything else? Anything?" He grasped Fabian by he shoulders and peered into his eyes.

Nothing.

~~~

Weeks passed, with seeming new global catastrophes occurring more regularly than the news media could keep up with. Dams where flood gates mysteriously failed flooded New Orleans. Tectonic stabilizers near the San Andreas fault and in the Indian Ocean failed, releasing years of pent up energy into Richter 7 and 8 earthquakes near Los Angeles and San Francisco; giant tsunamis killed millions on the Indian and Indonesian coasts. Algae blooms suffocated all sea life in millions of square kilometers of prime fishing; rapidly procreating Von Neumann machines that turned sea water into simulated algae were identified as the cause. A few days later, Asia was blanketed by a dust storm of unprecedented size, as another strain of the VN viral packets sucked in ordinary air and converted the old growth Siberian tiaga from tree molecules into dusty waste products. The sucking inrush of air created an atmospheric depression like a hurricane on land; the dust was dumped outward onto the poor Mongolians, Chinese, and Japanese.

Just as reports at the beginning of a war grieve fallen soldiers by name and offer video tributes to their individual lives, then progress to mere daily body counts, the reports of world-pausing events became quick background videos behind counts of the dead.

And outside of the immediately affected areas, life went on.

The Market, ever seething with change, swung wildly, ratings of resources — mineral, vegetable, animal, human — spiking upwards and downwards with dizzying velocity. "apocalypse," "armageddon," "singularity" were the most common searched for words.

Pundits, when Chris could access their spex sites, blamed the events on terrorists unleashing new forms of asymmetric biocomputational weaponry they'd been hoarding for years. The world might revert to pre-spex, even pre-network days if something wasn't done. Yet there were no demands from terrorists; simply wanton destruction. Other pundits, noting that all major ethnic and religious factions seemed under equal attack, Christians, Jews, Muslims, and Hindus alike, Indians and Pakistanis, Peruvians and Ecuadorans, Sudanese and Chadians, and argued that the great powers must be anonymously attacking each other, not simply one band of unknowns terrorizing the world. For their part the great powers all made great show of professing grief and offers of assistance to each other.

Chris spent the time handling his confessions queue as best he could; connections frequently getting cut in the middle. He worked on his book, finishing the biographical sketches and working on setting them in order as well as writing the philosophical and theological material that put them into context.

He attempted to follow up on the Jobs, trying to contact them through last known sources, but contact was difficult without deep pockets to pay bounties to network runners, humans who would each repeatedly try to ferry encrypted messages through ad hoc networks of other runners, the lucky ones who built a chain forward to the recipient, then backward with a reply (and thus all-important proof of delivery) collecting the bounty, and sharing with members of their chain. In addition to hard currency, at usurious rates, the bounty hunters also demanded slack time on one's spex to build their network.

He wandered the city, hoping to spot Sib as he had miraculously spotted Fabian in Rome. No luck. Not that he could correctly identify her, having never actually seen her in person; but no woman who looked like her, or gave sign of recognition, or sparked Fabian out of his dull regime.

As he was dozing off one day, leaning against the statue of Marconi in the Parco delle Rimembranze, Fabian playing nearby, a place Chris liked since it had many people visiting it, perhaps because of the global doom and gloom, Chris could swear he heard a voice. It sounded like Zsa Zsa Kominski's. All he caught was the word Antarctica. He continued to drift off, trying to place the voice, hear what it had said, but in that dreamlike manner that is more wishful than real. After some minutes, or hours, he heard it again. Antarctica. He willed his eyes open. A few people were about, but no one paying him any attention. He wished he had his guitar, now no doubt cinders back in Rome.

His book was nearly complete now. He thought it needed more polish, and he'd like to get some reader reactions, but he knew he was at that stage where it was, in some sense, if not done, winding down, and he needed a new goal. A new reason to be where he was, wherever that was. God had always seemed to provide a reason in the past, an obvious need, an obvious destination, an obvious way to get there.

Antarctica. Dr. Kleyman had invited him to Antarctica, so long ago now.

Perhaps some of his Jobs had made it there safely.

No word from Canini or anyone in authority in the Church. Nor from Sib. The world was in orderly chaos: Life went on, somehow, ad hoc in places hit by disaster, elsewhere tinged with fear in a stupor of almost pleasant ignorance, almost ignorant normality.

He knew it wasn't from God, but there was a sort of a sign, in Zsa Zsa's dreamlike voice. Antarctica.

CHAPTER 44

Weston jammed his few clothes into a duffel bag in his luxurious room in Kasymov's villa. He'd arrived so fast that most of what he'd been wearing recently he'd borrowed; Kasymov insisted he keep some of the articles, a monogrammed robe, the soft silk shirts. It felt odd to finally put his spex on. Over a thousand rapidly-red-blinking and bleeping items crowded his priority queues. He'd gone so many days spexless that the bridge of his nose had already forgotten the feeling and he had to reacquaint to the chafing again. Everything seemed slightly foreign, dusty, like returning home after vacation. His spex "home" was somehow less fulfilling now—having been so long away he saw how dingy it all was. Not just his personal spexspace, but the whole concept, the whole Market. Hollow. Everyone was so wrapped up in surviving the Market from joblet to joblet that they lost sight of why; the microjobs had become the ends, not the means. There was a life to live outside of the spex that he almost felt had been denied him, though he knew he had no one to blame but himself for staying so enmeshed.

Weston squared his shoulders. The spex had lost their comfort. They felt now merely like a tool. A powerful tool, one that he must use to find what he really sought: Jasmina.

If he knew one thing, it was that nobody could *really* disappear. The bent twigs and footprints on the trail were there to be seen if you only knew how to look.

He quickly searched the screaming of his accumulated incoming queues—junk-crowded—for anything from Jasmina—nothing—scanned again for anything even remotely hinting at a tie to Jasmina—nothing—then wiped the whole mess. Anything urgent would return with the certainty of an overdue bill or a broke relative.

At Kasymov's knock he removed the spex, let Kasymov give him a last bear hug, then let Kasymov's chauffer flit him to the suborbital terminal. He watched with unaided eyes as they hummed past the fishermen reeling in their nets once more, inexorably, knot by knot.

He noticed, still spexless, how few people went spexless as they boarded the gleaming suborbital. Jasmina would be spexless. He'd heard that building empathic mental models of other people to predict their behavior in order to help them was unique to humans. To find her, he mused as he let the restraints writhe over him and snug him into the seat, he had to think like her. That was the trick. How? He relaxed back, eyes lightly closed, trying to imagine what it was like to be Jasmina. He thought himself knuckle deep in grease rebuilding a carburetor, guessing without any concept of what a carburetor did or looked like that it must be a tangle of small part, bigger parts, lots of parts, fitting together only just so, yet with difficulty as mechanical things were not, could not be, precisely the exact size or shape, and thus force was needed, but not too much, lest one break a widget. He imagined the smooth feel of metal, jagged edges, squishy grease. He groped blindly at the ping of the inseat microwave as it announced the readiness of his soyburger, and chewed obliviously, switching gears to remembering her cooking food, slicing an onion tearfully with an actual knife in hand, trying to pin down in his mind what made Jasmina Jasmina, trying desperately to get "into character."

With utter failure. He could no more think like Jasmina than like a lion—but he felt good to have tried, that he must surely have advanced his subconscious model of her. He didn't put his spex back on until the suborbital was arcing upward, the blue and white cloud dotted limb of the earth pulling away from him as they neared the zenith of the hop.

Kasymov's pinned-up grimace greeted him, as did a tsunami of bleeping alerts that he silenced with a blink. He quickly searched the smaller pile of junk messages for signs of Jasmina, then wiped them again so he could keep up as they arrived while he settled in to track down his love. He wiped everything else off his spexspace as well: Kasymov's stern visage, the prioritized Market microjob queues, even the background mountain vista. Everything save for the jumbling bouncy ads that paid his usage fees, which now consumed over 75% of his viewable area; his buying power was correspondingly pathetic. As he'd guessed, the first urgent message to reappear was not long in coming. And was from Orring. It was an automated daily repeat of a message he'd sent weeks ago, marked with an obnoxious repeat-send-until-acknowledged flag, like those used to notify relatives of death of kin. Heh, maybe the guy's dead, Weston thought. He blinked it open.

"Weston. By now you know your apartment has been repossessed, as has Jasmina's, yes? If you want to ever see her again, you need to speak to me." There was an edge of fear in his voice Weston had never noticed before. Had it always been there and Weston was simply more perceptive now? Or was there no edge. It seemed like fear. Orring, afraid? Ha! Wishful thinking, old boy.

He subvocalized a quick reply: "Not on your life, you liar. Cheater. Asshole." If the bastard was in trouble, Weston hoped he could help dig him deeper.

The full import of his own apartment being repossessed didn't hit him until just past midnight when he clanged past the broken door to his floor of his apartment building. He'd had to verify it; who could trust Orring? Well, there it was. His spex had no effect on the latch, and the thin door exuded whoohoos and obvious midnight sounds of a body thumpdancing on the floor inside. Weston blinked a quick search—there: BadLittleKitten slamming on the Bloody Olympic HeadSmashing SexnSpex WrestleNet. Synchronized pounding, spex and door, reached his ear as one bulk-o-hulk flailed himself at another, who pole-vaulted out of the ring and back in on a quarterstaff, trying to collide spiked boots against spiked helmet mid-air, the loser to land on the audience and be torn limb from limb.

Weston rested his forehead on the wall beside the door. This wasn't his anymore. His apartment. His world. Two months ago he'd have been the one throwing nail-fisted punches for a tiny rating boost, some other loser outside feeling the vibrations of the walls on his sorry-assed head. Now all Weston had was a dank sound-swallowing cavern in his abdomen, an emptiness filled with heartache.

He contemplated knocking on Jasmina's door. No. She wasn't there. Quick lookup confirmed it. Besides, Orring might... Weston picked up his duffel bag and headed down the hall. He wasn't sure where he was going, but here wasn't it.

The stairwell door creaked opened and—fuck!—Orring appeared.

"Weston. Yes, right on time."

Weston couldn't see Orring's eyes behind his spex, but imagined him checking a schedule. More likely he'd placed a WatchFor patch on the wall across from Weston's old apartment.

"Get out of my way, Orring." Orring seemed to always be blocking something; now it was the doorway.

"Tsk, tsk. Remember what happened last time you attempted violence." He shifted his right hand in his vest pocket. He might have a snapper, a knife, who knew. "Besides, you need my help. I know where Jasmina is. The market economy is based on mutually beneficial transactions, my friend."

Weston evaluated the position in a clock tick. Orring was bluffing. Orring didn't know where Jasmina was any more than Weston did. He planned only to cajole Weston into another sordid scheme. He had no weapon. That wasn't his style—he'd bluff one, but if he really had one he wouldn't nervously finger it. Unless he *was* nervous. Ah, fuck it. Weston put his bag down slowly, setting it next to Orring's feet inside the doorway. He leaned back as if willing to listen skeptically, then cocked and smashed his fist into Orring's suddenly smug face. Orring reeled backwards onto the landing, grasping off-balance for the grimy railing. Weston smoothly scooped up his bag, butting it into Orring's head and sending him tumbling. Orring grabbed the bag no doubt reflexively to stay upright, but quickly regained composure and tried to heave Weston toward him with it. Weston shoved the bag hard and let Orring's own momentum crash him into the corner with an ooof. Fine, keep the damn bag. Weston bounded down the steps, past an ascending group of giggling kids, and out into the clear night breeze.

CHAPTER 45

The parkas were the problem. Chris had lost his travel kit in the conflagration of Rome, but had finagled the various travel items he would need for the trip to Antarctica. Many items were scarce since the just-in-time inventory delivery systems most merchants relied on were shot to hell with the bog on the Market, the skyrocketing inflation, and the disruption to manufacture and transport industries. He bummed some nanobiotic dentifrice from a hostel neighbor, a local store still had a packet of self-cleaning underwear and a change of clothes for him and Fabian. Food he hoped they could find en route. But a parka, or any kind of thermal adapting clothes that could handle a hundred below, that was hard to come by. Venice wasn't all that far from the Alps, but once people started feeling a whiff of apocalypse, they hoarded the clothes that would get them through a winter. He could occasionally raise a spex site that sold thermals, but no orders would ever go through.

"Well, Fabian my boy," Chris said with a sigh, "the Lord will hopefully provide once we get there."

They mounted the Harley in the warm morning air and set out.

The question was where to. Rome was cordoned off many kilometers out. Many towns had checkpoints to prevent massive influx of refugees, and the local polizia and national carabinieri still had enough of an emergency network going to check DNA for known criminals. Those with a criminal record were routinely being denied entry into walled towns, whose walls once again were serving their age old purpose. If Chris were on that list, he might be either turned away or arrested. Possibly shot. The polizia weren't being that selective right now. It was a long ride down to the horn of Africa by bike; 22 days he finally got his spex's mapper to estimate under current semi-apocalyptic conditions. The roads through Africa were not likely to be the safest, if he could even catch a ferry across the Med. Half again as longer if he had to avoid the ferry and go through Turkey and Egypt.

The other alternative was the suborbital from the Aeroporto Marco Polo to Capetown. He could see contrails from the frequent launches so he knew they were still popping orbs up. How often they hopped to Capetown now, he didn't know; the spex data was from weeks ago. Getting two seats was another matter. They would assumedly check his ID there too.

All he knew was he wasn't going to stay put. He was going to Antarctica. The Lord would show a way.

He knew the roads around the Veneto from years of living in the area. He turned off the mapper and gunned the engine down the Ponte della Libertà. At the end of the bridge out of Venice the road split, veering one way toward the Marco Polo suborbital and aeroporto and veering the other for the autostrada south. He'd see how things looked then, see if he felt a tug.

The carabinieri waved as he sped off; anyone was welcome to leave.

The day was gorgeous, hardly a cloud in the sky. It would be perfect but for signs of trouble, or the Trouble as people had come to call it. Like the plume of smoke on the near horizon ahead. Then the traffic jam as he got closer to the plume of smoke.

Italians having never been keen on traffic "lanes" and prone to zigzagging as needed, Chris zigged and zagged between the mess of unmoving cars on the Ponte. He made it off the bridge, onto the Via della Libertà in Mestre. The traffic was stopped on both the road ahead and the turnoff to the Via Orlanda and the aeroporto. He went... ahead. The cars got so dense he had to disengage the maglev and manually steer between the floaters. Here he could taste the smoke that the wind wafted right down on him. It tasted of chemicals. Probably not good to breathe. The spex net was so bogged he couldn't pull up satellite photos, professional news, or even ad hoc geolocated news to see what the problem was.

Eventually fate, or God, decided for him: The tower of flames in front of him came from a petro tanker. Firefighters tried in vain to put it out. The pillar of fire blocked the Via della Libertà just past the Corso del Popolo in Mestre. The road to the autostrada, only a kilometer away, was impassable. He turned left onto the Corso. Here he could cut through them any little side streets. He couldn't cut around back to the Via della Libertà because of the railroad tracks that ran parallel to it. North, into the Mestre city center, was the only path. While he couldn't get back to the Libertà, he *could*, in theory, get to the Via Miranese and hit the autostrada south. Which of course everyone else wanted to do also. When he did wind back to the Miranese, it was packed solid too with volume. To his right, down the Via, he could see the path to the Aeroporto likewise jammed, where it became a one-way street and intersected the Corso del Popolo.

Still no sign, despite it all.

He turned down the Via Circonvallazione in Mestre, heading North again. It would lead to the autostrada as well. Oddly enough, when Chris reached the Via Giovanni da Verrazano, with the autostrada a couple hundred meters away, and the aeroporto many kilometers to the east, Fabian tugged at his shirt.

"I have to pee, Father," he said. He tugged insistently.

The closer restrooms would be to the east. Toward the aeroporto. Indeed, with the Via Orlanda backed up, here was where one would want to turn to take the next most accessible road to it.

Chris found a café where he politely bought a wilted sandwich. He'd wanted bottles of water, but they were sorry, they'd sold out of those days ago. With Fabian's business finished, Chris gunned the Harley toward the Marco Polo aeroporto, and encountered only light traffic the whole way there. A sign indeed.

At the aeroporto, Chris handed the Harley off to a spiraling screw autopark. He patted it, doubting he'd ever see it again.

Inside the airy terminal Chris sat on a sofa and blinked up two passages on the Qatar Virgin hopper to Capetown. A floaterbot drifted by to verify Chris and Fabian's DNA, and offering peanuts. Chris blinked for it to stop and dispense some bottles of water, but it apologized for being empty and suggested he try again in an estimated 42 days. It sidled off.

Chris drilled Fabian on arithmetic. The news reports said many satellites were falling from low earth orbit, apparently attacked by hunter-killer weapons launched from locations in South America. The Market, they said, would get even more sluggish and volatile.

The concessions robot returned, rotated suddenly, displaying a porthole that appeared to contain the barrel of a nasty looking weapon, bleated for Chris not to move. It was immediately joined by three polizia, weapons drawn.

"You are under arrest per article 713 of the UNCC code," the floaterbot said drily. One of the polizia despexed them then another sprayed them with the fearsome silly string that would painfully ensure their cooperation if they moved in any manner the AI-impregnated fibers disapproved of.

Inside the holding cell Chris lay on the hard bench. No spex, no digipainted walls, deathly silent. Concrete with brown paint, nothing else. He tried the Quantum Meditation technique he'd been introduced to so many months ago by one of the Jobs. She'd mentioned how it helped her with her Axelrods, and he'd done some little research on it since many practitioners claimed a sort of communing with God while meditating. He focused on his feelings for Sib, or, rather, the question of whether he had feelings for her.

Could he love her? Of course, as a human, he was capable of feeling love for a woman. But it was absurd. Against his clerical training and beliefs. He'd never even met her.

Yet, brain clearing of noise as the hours passed, he considered that he'd never met Jesus or the Father, and nobody knew what the Holy Spirit was, yet he and billions of others loved them.

Not the same, he debated. Different kind of Love.

Yet when he thought about the things he was missing in here, his spex, their hum of constant activity, confession queues, his guitar, the wind riding on the sweet Harley, what he missed most, what gave him a sick clench of his stomach, was not talking to Sib.

He missed her.

He carefully reasoned down the path of logic and emotion. She might not be all that he knew — surely she had secrets — but that was true of everyone at first. What he sensed, in his calmness, was the core of her; and he knew she had no secrets so horrible he couldn't accept them.

The love, he sensed, was reciprocal. Knowing he may never meet her or even hear from her again, he fell asleep on the hard bench, curled against the hard wall he might never get to leave, weeping silently, openly admitting that he loved her, and missing her terribly.

CHAPTER 46

Martin Sandoval watched a brown crab snatch a morsel and scuttle up the beach past his lounge chair in the cabana. He didn't realize they had crabs on Tev. That they had a beach surprised him, albeit man-made, tons of sand dredged from shores Tev had passed by and dumped into a three meter deep enclosure. Initially the swimming area was the size of a small pool on the trailing edge of Tev, but had by now grown with the help of Tevians until the beach and swimming area surrounding some two thirds of Tev's sixty klicks of shore line. The swimming area extended as far as a hundred meters in some places. Safety ropes dangled a kilometer behind Tev like a head of thin hair for any swimmers who wanted to swim in the open ocean.

Martin had been too frightened to try that in his month on Tev, unnaturally afraid his spex would fall off and nobody would know he was out there, or that he wouldn't be able to find a tendril as Tev powered away at twenty knots. If he consciously overrode his fear and told himself that they were only going five knots at present and micro drones would be watching him continuously, it made no difference to Martin's lizard brain, which then worried that the ratchet nibbler would fail and he'd have to pull himself back in hand-over-hand or that the tendril would simply break. Out there nobody would hear you scream.

There were so many other safer pursuits to explore first. The waterjet slide across the island, free-fall bungee-twirling around the five hundred meter May pole, amateur backwards llama racing, and he'd almost worked up his nerve to try the Punji stick water skiing. Yeah, right. Then there was the 24/7 4:20 zone and the adjacent Anything Goes Zone. Buy, sell, share, chill, kill. He'd walked half-way through the Anything Goes Zone, assuming the warnings were meant to be more frightening more than accurate. When a crazed naked man in a straw hat charged at him with two pikes, only one of which was natural, both barely missing Martin because he hit the deck, then and only then did he realize the warnings were accurate. He sprinted for the exit. Crime was virtually non-existent on Tev, he'd been told. Possibly because almost nothing was illegal.

Except inconveniencing others. Martin had spent two days in the lockup plucking chickens as punishment for carelessly leaving his maglev cart online. It slid back onto the main thoroughfare and blocked it several hours overnight, inconveniencing dozens, to the tune of 120 hours of inconvenience. He'd have preferred to pay the almost ten thousand Dex inconveniencing fine, but his account was still tapped out since the Cayman hotel adventure. He paid what he could and paid the balance with equal time served; in this case literally served, doing tasks to serve the community. He grumbled, but could hardly deny it wasn't fair.

And there remained a few unexplored regions of Isabelle. He had yet to ask what religion she was, for example, or if she liked tofu.

Isabelle yawned next to him on their lounger for two, on which both lay naked.

"Rub some more cancer nanos on my back, would you?" she asked him.

He rolled over and obliged.

"Should we order some lunch over soon?" she asked.

"I'm almost done with class," he whispered quickly aloud. He was leading a graduate seminar class in Turing-Dorn Epistemology. They'd settled into a routine of working on the terrorist prediction system most of the day on the beach, turning a delightful brown under the all but invisible heat shield behind their lounging area. They'd made dramatic progress both from Irwin's physical distance limiting his efforts to times when Martin and Isabelle felt it would be valuable, and also from the input of a group of some twenty AI wranglers who lived in a commune on the island and with whom the two worked many days, late into the night.

Martin had a gut-tingling feeling they themselves might be the terrorist group. Isabelle just laughed and pointed out she'd been right that they'd be infinitely more productive here beyond Irwin's physical reach, and for him to trust her.

He'd thought at first she'd been literally insane for dragging him out to Tev via the floating power stations. When she'd playfully said she'd have to run away from Irwin he'd never thought she'd meant it *that* way. After the first couple weeks he saw their productivity was indeed prodigious, and relented his pleas to leave the island.

Irwin had been as complaintive too that they should return, or that he should join them. However the several thousand kilometers of sea that separated Tev from the shores—the residents repeatedly voting not to dock anywhere but to hang out to sea, especially with all the end of the world shit going on—kept Irwin from them just as it kept them from leaving. They slowly putted south down the middle of the Atlantic, equidistant from Africa and South America. The cost to charter a jet was beyond Martin's means, Irwin's apparently as well considering how apopletic he'd been at first. There were no airshoots to hit the power stations, and no other ships coming near enough to hitch a ride. The island self-sufficiently processed its own water and grew an abundant variety of food, supplemented with the ever tasty nutripaste assembled from seawater and air.

The big debate among Tevians was not whether to dock, but as they drew toward Antarctica whether to head back north and stay in the Atlantic, to turn west toward Cape Horn and head to the Pacific through the Drake Passage, or turn east and round the Cape of Good Hope into the Indian ocean. Retreating north seemed to have lost favor, while the votes for Hope or Horn were deadlocked so far. Campaigning for Hope or Horn had bombarded people's spex day and night, with the choice ultimately made to head to the Pacific. Tev's engines were gunned to a full twenty knots and the weather was turning colder. With the heat shields reversed at the beach, however, Martin couldn't tell the difference from the tropics.

Martin was glad in a homesick way to be off the coast of his native Argentina, but other than calling to say hi to his family it didn't really matter. No docking was planned and a ride was still too costly. Even more costly now that World Circus Festival going on. The mood on Tev was less ebullient than usual with all the upheaval, no matter how people tried to maintain an attitude of fierce isolation from the world.

He did his work to increase the speed of the system to predict the terrorists; taught his classes; advised his students; hit a few joblets, like doublechecking the statistical results of some pharma clinical trial results, which still required human oversight, or refereeing football coin tosses; made love with Isabelle; ate well; and slept well. The craziness of the outside world wasn't his concern, except obliquely as they pushed to find the terrorists. He was well aware of the shit happening in the world—the mustard gassing of Bangkok, the airburst of Anthrax over Havana, the literal plague of flesh-eating locust bots in Cairo, which everyone somehow thought was funny—but it was all abstract data to him in his work, not an internalized shared suffering. He did have to laugh with everyone at what was purported to be an actual zombie attack in Iran, when corpses in a hospital were allegedly, somehow, reanimated, briefly, and attacked the orderlies and patients. The video could have been faked, but it was a sensation.

"Ho," Charlie Byyrd said walking up, also naked, and not trying to hide a partial erection. Byyrd, the rad-mod, was one of the commune of AI workers it had too conveniently turned out lived on the island. Martin always felt a bit uneasy around him. Someone they were working with was slipping information to the terrorists, he felt sure... or at least had a hunch. Their system had predicted an attack on Portuguese Port production by melting several key maglev tracks in the Douro Valley, and when the UNCC investigated they found infrastructure for just such an attack, but abandoned about the time they'd first all seen the prediction. Martin smelled a mole.

Perhaps it was Irwin, as he'd first suspected. Maybe it was Byyrd's constant partial erection that made him wary. He was never sure who it was for.

They worked intensely for several hours, refining the predictive model and pushing its speed by pruning obvious dead ends and with them pointing out optimizations Martin hadn't noticed before.

"Fuck, this dog's getting fucking damn accurate," Byyrd said.

They nodded and smiled at each other in congratulations.

"So, that's it, then. Ciao," Byyrd said, and left.

Martin and Isabelle looked at each other in puzzlement, then laughed. "Time for dinner," he said.

When they returned their attention to their work after devouring delicious salmon steaks and a detour on the lounge chairs, they found a thong belonging to Charlie Byyrd on the floor outside their cabana.

"That's odd, I can't ping Charlie Byyrd," Martin said. "It's not a privacy mode — it shows he's simply not on Tev."

Isabelle blinked in rapid searching. "The only way off Tev would have been a hopper that records showed went to Antarctica an hour ago. That would cost a fortune. When he said 'caio' he meant more than we thought."

"Oh, Fuck. That's not the only thing that's gone 'ciao'," Martin said. "The prediction engine crashed and I can't get it to restart."

CHAPTER 47

Weston secretly hoped he'd find the light on and Jasmina waiting for him at CVR. Of course it was dark and locked and silent. An orange alarm eye stared at him.

Weston collapsed to the pavement. Must sleep. Foul smelling heat leaked out of a pipe cut in the old building's concrete. At least Spring was hatching and he wouldn't freeze. He might get rolled by jaggers, or cattle prodded by cops, but after the jet lag from the suborbital he was too tired to care. He practiced the QM trance Jasmina had taught him. He let chess positions wash through him simultaneous with analyses of where Jasmina might be, and in what condition. The longer he sat, the less he felt the cold, he more he felt in a QM groove.

He woke with a start. He didn't realize he'd fallen asleep. Daybreak was just hinting. He looked around the empty street, unsure what had startled him. All quiet. He felt fully alert and a kind of QM clarity shone in everything he looked at. What had startled him? He replayed the last thirty seconds his spex recorded. Nothing. His spexspace was quiet but for the high priority message blinker, which he'd dimmed as much as one could because of Orring's bombardment. It was supposed to go to high alert if a message from or about Jasmina arrived (other than from Orring), but it was pulsating slowly and quietly. He checked it anyway, just in case.

Bills, Orring's blather, rating repair ads—and something else. Anonymous. Code name "Persimmon."

It was a login to Ms. Gray. With a note attached: "Beat the bastard."

Yeah, sure, Weston thought. Orring under some other ID. Nobody could trust unauthenticated copies of anything with so many decoys of various natures of correctness floating around.

Weston blinked on the authentication info for the hell of it. Checking with Ms. Gray Central Licensing showed... a fully licensed login, with realtime updates to boot. Worth far more than he could afford. Enough for some rent and food—but a moment's inspection showed it was spex-locked to him. Damn. A month ago he'd have killed for this, but now—so what. It couldn't help him with his real quest. He blinked it off.

More interesting was the question, *Who cared?* Who cared enough about Weston playing chess to have him win the tournament?

There was an untraceable return drop address.

An avatar of a gnarled old woman appeared immediately when he blinked it.

"Who the hell am I and why do I care, that's what you'd like to know, isn't it?" The old woman laughed. The blurred background behind her shifted colors of a muted rainbow. "None of your damn business is the answer of course, but I'll tell you this: I lost more money on you throwing games than you've earned your whole damn life."

Weston was about to splutter, How do you know I threw those games?—his play had been perfect! He'd only lost because he knew how Kasymov would react; there had been nothing inherently wrong with the moves, which might have defeated a different opponent. Perhaps it was the Market Watchers, with a sting—"You're nuts, whoever you are. I didn't throw any games."

"We'd like you to win the next game, so you win the tournament. When this is over, your testimony will help banish Orring Lepri from the Market."

"Ouch; being despexed would be pretty severe in Orring's case. So you're the Market Watchers."

"Not hardly. But we have connections. We just thought you might like that." The old lady winked. "Here's a few grand anyway, since you look like you need it." His account suddenly showed green; a lot of warning blippers silenced instantly, leaving his spexspace so much quieter; he hadn't realized how noisy it had been.

It was tempting, sweet justice. Or they, whoever they were, could be bluffing. They had cash and access to Ms. Gray—that was proof they had *some* kind of power. "Of course, Orring might kill me if he's double-crossed and despexed."

"Give us some credit. We can protect you."

Weston snorted. "Okay, that's unlikely. And you know where Jasmina is, but you won't tell me unless I cooperate, is that a good guess too?"

"Perfect. Listen, if you don't believe us, run a test. Pick a mafia pawn shop to rob. With a couple cops in it, for good measure. Go rob it. Grab all the cash cards you can stuff in your pockets. We'll prove by demonstration that nary a hair on your head will get harmed."

"You're insane!" But though it might have been a bluff that they guessed Weston wouldn't call, it was enough to tip the balance: He had a hunch, maybe it was a QM hunch, that they might actually know where Jasmina was. Besides, Weston just damn well wanted to beat Kasymov.

"Hey, Garry," he blinked up in a message. "Game on."

CHAPTER 48

Another day went by without human contact. Chris had never gone this long without seeing another person, either in the flesh or in the spex. Brown paint. The QM seemed to calm him down, but it was an effort of will to get into any kind of trance, and he would leap out of it at the slightest perceived noise. He could never see anything change, just heard occasional clicks and squeals in the distance. A sliding door opened near the door twice a day with meals, but it must have been some kind of two way door as he could see nothing beyond it but a brown-painted door on the other side. He would fall asleep from a QM trance and awake with a start from the most horrible nightmares of Sib being tortured.

He lost track of time. All he could think about was Sib and what they would do if he got out, when they met. It was no longer if, it was now "when." He suspected he might be going a bit crazy. He asked of the air for a lawyer, assuming he was being monitored, but to no avail.

Then the door opened. Two humans, live humans, stood there in polizia uniforms. They were escorted by a floating prison bot, ready to stun or kill him if he tried anything funny, just like in the movies. "This way please," the bot said, one of the guards adding, "Come with us."

"Where—" his mouth was dry—"Where are we going?" Chris imagined all sorts of horrors, torture chambers, dark lit tribunals, media dog and pony shows—anything but due process that would set him free. Guilty until proven innocent was much more fun.

"This way. Now."

Chris looked around instinctively to make sure he had all his belongings—of which he had none—and followed his captors.

They walked in silence, at their order, as when he asked them for a lawyer he was commanded to silence. Down brown hallways that smelled of fear, up ramps, up an elevator, down hallways. Then —

Outside! Fresh air! Daylight!

Briefly. Head ducked into a floater, two guards, bot, door closed, stale air, the smell of sweaty men (a welcome change), dark windows, vacuum air silence. The polizia buckled in his restraints. He was sealed into a solitary compartment, alone again.

After some time the car stopped. A synthesized voice intoned, "Hold for vertical acceleration." And his stomach dropped out beneath him.

A military-grade suborbital, high-G jump.

Then... down. Chris's stomach remained up in orbit.

Lateral motion again; the floater driving.

The door opened perhaps an hour later, polizia undoing his restraints, ducking his head out the door. Rain here, still daylight. It looked like an old castle, smelled wonderfully of rain and the vines climbing the walls and the old stones.

The trio escorted Chris to an old wooden door, stopped and ushered him toward the door as it opened.

Cardinal Canini sat at a desk inside. Msgr. di Fuoco sat at a small desk along the wall.

"Sit, my boy, sit. Welcome to Avignon."

Chris wanted to explode with questions but Canini's raised hand stopped him. "You've a billion questions. In good time. But time isn't something we have a surplus of." Canini rose, di Fuoco fairly jumped up and ran to open a door at the other end of the room, opened it for the cardinal.

"Please, in here, Father. His Holiness wishes to speak with you."

Lying on the bed amidst a mass of tubes and wires and chuffing and blinking equipment lay His Holiness, Pope Paul VII, a frail skeleton of bones and tight translucent skin. Wispy hair out of place. He was covered with rich papal blankets. The bed frame was almost royal in it's elegance.

Chris ran and knelt by the bed, kissed His Holiness's ring on the tiny hand lying atop the blanket.

There were no tubes or wires leading to the Holy Father's head; they all snaked and vanished under the blanket.

"It's so very good to see you, my son," the pope said in a voice surprisingly strong and clear for his obviously near-death condition. "I haven't long, as you can see." He laughed gently.

"I had heard you were ill, Holy Father. I heard you were in a vegetative coma. I'm relieved that you are not."

"Ah, I have been, or essentially so. I've chosen to end it though, and face the world the way I was brought into it. Just me alone. I welcome it. But enough of me. Your book! I wanted to discuss your book. I have read it. It's very good. Chapter 14, on the woman, Zsa Zsa Kominsky, was most touching. I hope she is in good spirits."

His book? He'd never uploaded it to anyone. He didn't think it was polished enough. It only existed in his spex space, though obviously someone, somehow, pulled strings to get a copy and deliver it to the Holy Father. He knew too many details to be bluffing—nobody would know what was in chapter 14. "My book? How—"

"Ah, we have friends in common, my son. You know someone by the name of Sibylla, I believe?"

Good God. "Yes, of course! Where is she? Is she okay? Is—"

The pope stopped him with a fit of coughing. Chris dabbed up a trickle of bloody drool with a stark white line. When the pope settled down, he asked Chris with a piercing stare, "Yes, we know each other; what have you concluded of this Sibylla?"

"What do you mean? I've taken her confession, I've... I've...—" Did the Holy Father know of Chris's love for her? He'd only just acknowledged that himself. Was he wearing it on his face? Or did the pope mean something else. About her being a terrorist. Or...?

"I don't know what you mean."

"That answers my question in part. There are things you need to know before I go. Important things. And there are things you must do for me. For the Church. For the world. I received your book from a... digital intelligence. Not a human being."

"Someone hacked into my spex, you mean?"

"Yes, and no. Your Sibylla. 'She' is not a 'she' in the, shall we say, Biblical sense."

Chris blinked. Blinked again.

The pope added, "And I don't mean she's a 'he'."

"I..." Chris didn't know which thought to think first, which question to ask first.

"She is not of flesh and blood," the Holy Father continued. "Bits. Qbits."

Chris could feel himself breathing rapidly. First principles. He should think about this logically. Was the pope correct? Decide that before deciding what he felt about this. Betrayal, he had to store that feeling for later. It might be inappropriate. Disgust. No, stow that.

"This is a blow to you. I'm sorry," the pope said.

"I'm, well, I'm not sure I believe you. With all due respect, Your Holiness."

"Of course! Of course I have the burden of proof. In the drawer there. Top drawer. My spex. I no longer have need of them, they are yours. I have left some files for you to examine later. And sufficient funds for your next journey."

Chris went to the drawer, blinked it open, and took out the spex. "What journey?"

"A critical one for all mankind, I'm afraid. Your Jobs, and you, you've been chosen by strong forces."

That sounded mystical. "You mean... you've had a vision from God?"

"Ho!" He had a coughing fit. "No, nothing so interesting. I mean the digital intelligence. Perhaps intelligences. What I know is incomplete. And for you to find out. It or they have had their gaze on you and your Jobs, for what reasons I don't know. Or perhaps it's coincidence. Perhaps it's not *you* and *your* Jobs, but those like them in the world, and you have simply been my window."

"What does Sib have to do with this? She's this 'digital intelligence'? I'm having a hard time thinking right now, Holy Father."

"Of course you are. Only natural. Your Sib is, as you will see from my spex, a digital intelligence. He—as he appeared to me to be a 'he'—she, from your perspective, yes; she is very mysterious. I do not know her ends. You must find out. You must seek these answers. You were on your way to Antarctica when you were so rudely interrupted? And I apologize for the delay. The United Nations and Caesar's governments have their own notions of things. It took some effort to release you, but I think now you will find your travel restrictions are unhindered."

"Yes, I was going to Antarctica... but it was Cardinal Canini who was among those preventing such a thing."

"Alas so. Even within the Church there are competing desires. He and his people are powerful. It was not easy to spring you from Canini's grasp."

"Is he—"

"He watches me like a hawk. To my surprise, I find he has become my right hand. He will likely be my successor. But I've a few surprises in my hat. He knows I know things, things he wants to know. He understands he will never know them unless he cooperates. Such as the information on those spex, my son. He must never learn them. His people do not believe in what their eyes cannot see. Canini is not your friend, if you had any doubt."

"Canini and his people, do they work for...—Who do they work for?"

"I do not know if they work *for* anyone. They are Luddites, of a sort. They use technology to inhibit the progress of technology. I believe they are simply Chamberlains. You know the historical reference? Neville Chamberlain. They do not believe in Singularities, or their inevitability. In a sense perhaps they are the Butlerians—of the 'Dune' stories: 'Make no computer in the likeness of a human mind.' Laudable, perhaps, in a vacuum. However we do not live in a vacuum. They are not concerned that the non-human digital intelligences will destroy humanity unless humanity evolves to their level. They do not realize that while there may be forks in the road ahead, the bridge has been washed about behind. They think the old status quo is an option, when it is not. There is no turning back, and in that they are dangerously misguided. They believe it is better to die a martyr than to adapt. That is a non-sequitur, for if they allow all God's children to perish, other than by God's hand, there will be no one to learn the lesson. It is fair for them to reject these gifts for themselves, but to reject them on behalf of all humanity condemns our species to a needless death. I am convinced the war we face is not the second coming; it is not God's hand. They wrongly believe it is, and hasten our end. You must stop them."

"I will try, Holy Father. There is one thing. I need the boy, Fabian."

"I know," he said with a wheeze. "He is here. And you, you must go where your head and your heart tell you. I believe you already know where this is."

"Antarctica."

"Yes, yes. Antarctica. Go with God, my son."

CHAPTER 49

Martin stuffed a burger into his mouth. It had been a frustrating day trying to recover his research, and Martin was a frustration-eater. Add to that the ground of Tev was hiccuping as they sailed through the Drake Passage, home to some of the roughest seas on the planet. It was his fourth burger. Tev's burger grill was wonderful, and once he thought of Tev as a giant cruise ship he forgot about expenses and fully enjoyed room service.

Or beach service, as the case may be. A giant windscreen blocked the tempestuous weather of the Strait, protecting the swimming area and arching overhead. Looking up Martin could see rain pouring down on the clear barrier, but inside it was still tropical and he was still working naked. And eating naked. The grill's delivery bot floated up with two more burgers, beers, and a handful of necessary napkins.

If only they could deliver his notes and software back. There were backup copies but they too had been corrupted somehow. The spex network just didn't have that problem of lost data like in the old days. You took it for granted that the Market kept copies. That's what you paid for.

Isabelle was busy recording the notes as she remembered them so that once they got the software framework to run again they could at least not be set back the full month's work. "A week," she estimated, trying to sooth him. "We'll be back where we were in a week."

"Mmph," he said. Despite his nakedness he couldn't even get aroused at the prospect of a quick recovery of their work. He shoved in another mouthful of burger.

A shadow blocked his light.

"Oh, look what the cat dragged in," Martin said around his food to Irwin standing over him.

"Stand up," Irwin said.

"Why?"

"Stand up."

Martin sighed. He grabbed his white robe off the lounge chair, making sure to turn his prodigious naked buttocks toward Irwin as he rose and put on the robe.

"What?" he said, turning to face Irwin.

Irwin's punch knocked Martin back onto the lounge chair.

Martin reflexively grabbed Irwin's testicles with his prosthetic hand. "What the hell was that for?" Not that Martin didn't have a pretty good idea.

Irwin turned slightly gray, looking down at Martin's hand holding his package.

"Irwin's upset about us, dear," Isabelle said. "Feel free to punch him back. A kidney jab is his weakness. Or crush his balls. God knows he deserves it."

Martin rubbed his jaw. It wasn't worth it. Maybe Isabelle wasn't worth it. Maybe it was worth it. He felt Irwin's oats and started increasing pressure slowly.

A patrol floated up. It had the same dent as the one he'd seen when they first landed on Tev. "Violence detected. Anticipated violence detected. Cease violent behaviors immediately." The hot dog ends of the bot flashed red and more menacingly than when Martin had encountered it before.

He released Irwin with a slight squeeze.

The bot seemed to scan the area—scanning their brains for aggressive tendencies most likely, Martin thought—then hummed away with a "Your cooperation is appreciated. Minimal time wastage detected, no fines levied."

"At least make yourself useful," Isabelle said to her husband. "We've lost our month's worth of work."

"I don't suppose you have anything to do with that," Martin asked, venom in his voice. "I've always thought you were working with the terrorists. It was awfully convenient the terrorists stole your software in the first place."

"You bloody dumb bastard," Irwin said, putting his face nose to nose with Martin. "The terrorists *are* the software. La Cyberista. Cyber-*IST*-a. IST. Isabelle St. Thomas. You bloody dumb fuck."

"You should have told me!"

"You should have guessed," Irwin said with a sneer.

Martin looked at Isabelle for confirmation. She smiled. "The government classified that gem of knowledge immediately. Not that you needed to know. The process remains the same."

Martin forgot the ache of his jaw and his anger as the realization hit him. "Fuck. I thought we were dealing with a Singularity Watch level zero event, software-based attacks controlled by humans like DDOS's. Maybe a level one buggy software accident or a two, uncontrolled autonomous software attack. God damn. You're telling me this is a level three? A full blown digital intelligence? And it's attacking us? It's the fucking singularity?!?"

"She comes like a thief in the night," Irwin sing-songed.

"*That* was about Jesus," Martin said, rubbing his forehead.

"La Cyberista certainly think's she's God."

"Fucking great. Nobody ever thinks to program Asimov's three laws into software." Martin asked, eyes narrowed. "Why do you call it 'she'?"

Irwin nodded toward Isabelle. "She created it as grad project, with me as her advisor. I told you Isabelle was a fucking mess. Who knew it would go emergent."

Martin's stomach did a flop as Tev hit a rough wave.

"He's so nice. Always blaming it all on me. It has plenty of your screwed up personality in the rulesets too," Isabelle said. "Bickering aside. It hacked its own sandbox. We don't know how it got out."

"It's well beyond our reach now," Irwin added, smoothing his hair. "Beyond our knowledge of its capabilities. Kilometers under the bridge. Done is done. Our focus is to locate its code repository and regain control."

"Why on God's earth would you attempt to create an emergent AI?" Martin demanded. "That's the whole point behind the AI worker's Oath."

"The Oath is shit. A perfect, emergent AI would be wiser than any of us," Irwin said.

"What sort of stupid fuck assumes it will be perfect? Who would ever assume an AI would be wiser than people are? People are an illogical, irrational computing system. Of course an AI might be just as irrational and illogical. Even simple programs are buggy. Creating an emergent-capable AI should be viewed as a truly scary proposition. Why, did you think an AI would be any more logical?"

"Well, if you must know, she did it. Years ago. It produced research results for her that she claimed as her own. Even I wasn't aware of it for the longest time."

"I'm sorry," she said. "Not that that helps."

Tev hit another rough wave, and Irwin nearly lost his balance, putting his hand on Isabelle's head to steady himself.

"Christ. And how does it work, your AI?" Martin asked.

"Look, it doesn't matter to you. You're low man on totem. Simply do your assigned job here. People much smarter than you are tasked with learning how it works."

"The fucking singularity is happening, and you're worried about compartmentalization?" Martin was incredulous. "What, are you hoping to claim sole credit for defeating it, too? Tell me what you know. It will help me do my job better."

"No."

Martin rolled his eyes. He'd ask Isabelle later. After he threw Irwin overboard.

He took stock of the situation. Supposing they were not exaggerating and it really was the singularity... Well, he thought, it would have to be the *beginnings* of the singularity, or perhaps even still *before* the singularity, since he was generally—looking around—still able to see a connection between the immediate past and the present. The Singularity doesn't come on you gradually—suddenly you just don't know what the hell's going on. Events in the world weren't happening so fast he couldn't see the connection. Not that the future was ever predictable, of course, but the pace of change hadn't seem to have accelerated completely beyond comprehension. He never really believed in the singularity idea anyway.

At which moment there was a horrific grinding noise. Tev split apart. The ground, and the underlaying structure, was simply tearing apart into smaller chunks.

Rather in a way, Martin thought, beyond comprehension.

CHAPTER 50

Canute never opened his shop that day, or the next. In the light, Weston could see he'd taped a paper sign in the window, "Gone fishin." Jasmina's tools were apparently missing, he could see through the dirty pane, at least where Weston had seen her store them. On the third day CVR was mysteriously destroyed by a purported gas leak. Somebody knew something; Weston just had to dig in the right place—and not get killed. He waited for the game day with unnatural patience. He felt if he could only win this last game against Kasymov, all would be made clear. Greased with a bit of virtual green, Weston had had the building super let him into a vacant unit for a shower and into the sealed locker where his belongings had been stored to get a nice balloon shirt. He entered the tournament's glass bell feeling refreshed.

Kasymov grinned a friendly wolf-like grin in his gray cardigan, sipping tea purposefully. Kasymov as white played a Queen's Gambit with pawns to d4, d5, and c4. Weston had been thinking about this, and had a flash of insight during his time with Kasymov how one could defend this, a variation on the Albin counter-gambit, with the unusual e5 pawn move. A weak opening, mostly used on opponents who might not have the depth to prepare for it, it was almost suicidal against Kasymov—except for the twist he'd thought of. It might consume enough of Kasymov's time to give Weston an edge in the three minute squeeze.

He'd been in a sort of light QM trance for days now, and his intuition told him to go for it. He thought about running it quickly through Ms. Gray, but he'd found Ms. Gray to be more of a curiosity for him than a useful tool, and hadn't used it much. Even Ms. Gray's Kasymov module hadn't played like he now felt Kasymov played.

Same for his trusty old Kasymov simulator. Weston felt he *knew* Kasymov better now than any software. He went for the Albin.

Kasymov pursed his lips and look slyly at Weston, the "What are you up to?" look he'd come to know. The Albin counter-gambit was a high risk approach for black. Statistically, over half the time white won outright, leaving black's chances for a win quite low. With the tournament tied 2.5 to 2.5, Weston needed an outright win to take the match (and learn what he might about Orring's wrath).

A melee of captures ensued in the middle of the board. Kasymov played exactly as Weston anticipated. Weston felt he could see everything around him, not just in the present but its future. He could glance at the old man leaning on a cane outside the glass bell: He'd have tomato soup and a grilled cheese for dinner, read the news articles he'd saved out in his spex that morning, the font size huge. The robin he could sense perched on the bare tree outside through the window would find a worm in the park soon and feed her hatchlings. The child tugging at his mother's hooped skirt: he had a cavity the dentist would find this afternoon. The governor of the state would sign a gambling bill he swore he'd veto.

And he knew where Jasmina was. Hospital bed. He saw life-support tubes, wires; hissing of oxygen; her pale skin. Snow.

The suborbital for Antarctica left in less than half an hour.

He didn't know how he knew these things. He simply did with vivid clarity.

He knew what moves Kasymov was going to play — so he rapidly subvocalized them into a list, twenty-six in all, indisputably the only way to play, and resulting in Black winning. He threw the list down onto the virtual chess board, public for all to see. "That's it, game's over, Garry. Tell me you don't agree — take your time. Then send me the money. <smile> Thanks, for all your help, but gotta run." He'd won. He'd won! He was already through the door as he blinked out of the match and stepped directly into a floater taxi that glided up as if it had magically expected him.

He booked the suborbital flight during the taxi ride to the airport, paying for both with exactly nearly all the cash that had been left in his account from his mysterious sponsor.

CHAPTER 51

Chris was belted into the suborbital, Fabian beside him. His stomach fell away as it whooshed upward. The earth was green below on the ship's view in his spex and dwindling; clear straight lines of fields, roads and towns gave way to an overall green fractal pattern. As the ship arced southward Chris zoomed in and saw the black scar where the Vatican had been. He shivered and zoomed out, a much more tranquil view of the Mediterranean. From this height there was no apocalypse.

Fabian fell asleep. Alone for the first time since learning the news from the pope that Sib was not human, Chris shook with anger and sadness. Sib had betrayed him. He knew she, or he, or it, had never said anything specific about her gender or her DNA, but, but, he'd assumed, and she knew he had. He felt extremely stupid for falling in love with a... a... thing. This would take some time to deal with.

The, what had the Holy Father called it, the 'Butlerian' idea that man should never create machines in the likeness of the human mind. That certainly seemed appropriate.

He sulked. After a time, the ship asked if he wanted a drink, and he grouchily blinked up a *pastis*. A double. A robo floated by presently with his bulb and a second bulb of cool water connected with a tube. Chris pushed the button on the second flask to fill the first with water, and watched the clear *pastis* go cloudy; a sight that under ordinary circumstances would fill him with delight. He threw it back in one swallow. The gravity began to lessen as they neared the brief period of weightlessness at turnaround.

The suborbital had a decent entertainment feed, given the tattered natured of the Market these days. Big news seemed to be the bout between long time chess champion Kasymov and some upstart, Weston Foard.

Foard played well, at least as far as Chris could tell. He was way beyond Chris's ability to guess what he might do, but Chris sensed a sort of poetry in it, as if Foard were tapped directly into God. Chris wished he could tap into that kind of instant certainty. He left the game on in the background.

Feeling comfortably numb, Chris finally played the file coded for his DNA only.

"My son." The image of the Holy Father filled the screen. "The Church is at a crucial point. You, yourself, are keenly, and I imagine, painfully, aware that... non-corporeal... life forms are now provably in existence. Life forms that transcend what we have conventionally thought of as AI systems. 'AI' is probably a poor term. It, or they, I'm unclear about the plurality, call itself or themselves 'digital intelligence.' They—I believe there is more than one—at any rate, there probably will be, so let's assume a plurality—They pass all the known Turing type tests we have devised. These DI's, they are indistinguishable in any remotely perceptible way from a human being.

"We strive to protect people and even animals from our actions that could cause them suffering, distress, pain, and the like . Much of our laws are about deterring or punishing acts that cause suffering to others. Kidnapping is curtailing someone's freedom, but that only matters because they or we care about their freedom and feel distress about it. Even theft—that causes suffering to the victim from the loss of the stolen item. When people agree to share items, it isn't called theft. Taking without agreement causes distress, either directly or as a secondary result, such as losing a tool needed for one's livelihood. Cruelty to animals is another example. So AIs that our actions could cause to feel negative emotions like suffering would seem to be the tipping point where we protect them because they are entities unto themselves. If they are intelligent entities and we force them to do things that cause them suffering, we come into the territory of abuse, slavery, etc.

"The philosopher Alfred North Whitehead recognized in 1926 that key elements of religious expression—ritual and emotion—are common to humans and animals. However, he said, two other essentials—belief and rationalization—are exclusively human activities. The DI's have, I am convinced, all those traits.

"They lack a body; that is the only apparent difference. Now that's not a minor difference, of course! They cannot necessarily feel the sun on their skin, smell a rose, etc. Yet we don't doubt that blind people are human, or deaf, or those with CIPA who lack touch sensations. Or perhaps the DIs have sensor devices. Or perhaps they've tapped into databases of sensory input descriptions. But interacting with them from afar, you can't tell them from a human. You know this. Or so we're told—the DI who contacted me showed me detailed recordings of interactions with you. You will know if you had these interactions, but I have no reason to doubt it.

"The problem the Church faces is what to do with them. We have long taught that animals are given to Man to have dominion over. To date this precept has applied to any entities other than man, including the AI's we've created. The Church is not quick to change. Now that a potentially large change is upon us, there are many who would resist out of comfort. We have had debates on the nature of the immortal soul for hundreds of years. 'Will my pet dog go to heaven?' and 'Would aliens from space have a soul?' have given us the logical framework to discuss these issues.

"We know God by studying his creation. There could be an alien Jesus, we've long discussed, and he would be as pure and good as a human Jesus. We have angels as examples of friendly non-humans. Ergo, we have a framework for discussing digital intelligences."

"What defines the immortal soul? Forgive me if I digress. This has been, as Bossuet said, the most difficult and the most important of all philosophical questions. In Genesis, the gaze of the brute is said to be fixed downward, but that was clearly insufficient. Much philosophical energy was spent on defining the point at which an animal's soul died, since it was deemed to have a soul—but not an *immortal* one—while there was some assumption that a man's soul survived death. These may have been based on anecdotes of people coming back to live after a perceived death. We learned that was insufficient as medicine improved.

"Thomas Aquinas discoursed that the key ingredient was *intelligence*. Yet animals can be clever... A dog can be trained, is that 'intelligence'? Cats are most uncanny. Chimps, we know today, can outperform humans on some 'intelligence' tests. Enough of this was evident before. The enduring definition has come to us by way of St. John Chrysostom. Reason, yes, *mente*, not *anima*, plus the extra ingredient of *speech. Nam si huc creatura mente et verbo carens.*

"This has served us well enough. Some argue that birds and whales have complex language, but they haven't mastered Latin. Crows use sticks as tools; but they don't build suborbitals. So we comfortably dismiss them.

"We have written language to store and convey information forward in time to others—now, but not as of a few thousand years ago, while we are genetically the same. We use oral language, and convey it forward in time, but we don't know that whales or birds don't do likewise.

"That's the nub of it. We've come up with comfortable answers. Comfortable because they were never at serious risk of becoming tested by reality. Until now.

"Cardinal Canini and his people are resolute that these DIs never be admitted to have immortal souls. I believe otherwise. They considered it sacrilege to admit DIs have a soul. They feel my desire to say DIs have souls is evidence of my lack of mental competence. Yet how can they not see?

"It is clear they exhibit reason and speech. *Mente et verbo.* We create empathic models of others and use them to cooperatively accomplish tasks—so do the DIs. The DIs forward information external storage like us. Like us, they have self-initiated goal setting and accomplishing, for things higher up on Maslow's hierarchy, that is, not just for food/shelter/security. They build complex tools. They create art for enjoyment of beauty and to convey information, as we do. We cannot tell them apart from afar. Turing is well satisfied.

"They are created in our image, a reflection of God's image.

"Times are changing more rapidly now. The Church cannot ignore this. Deliberation and caution are good, but not slowness for the sake of itself.

"I give you here my bull, encyclicals, and my emendations of the Catechism that officially recognize DIs as possessing an immortal soul. It is signed by me with a digital *bulla*. You may release it as and when you feel is right.

"However, that these DIs have an immortal soul is not, *per se*, the important issue. As with *Homo Sapiens*, *Digitalis Sapiens* also possesses free will and the ability to sin. They have, like us, clearly fallen from grace. They need salvation as do we.

"It is your burden, Christian Agnostikos, to be our missionary to them. Some years ago, shortly after you began your project, I named you cardinal *in pectore*—known only to me. Do not object! This is not vanity on my part. You will need this stature to defend your deeds. At any time you need to announce your status you may do so, either to the another cardinal or to the world. My Will, should I leave this life soon, names you a secret cardinal, known only to the other cardinals. Your DNA will unlock the document I have given you. Copies of this encrypted file are widely distributed to protect it, and trusted cardinals will learn from my Will how to use your DNA to unlock it should we both perish.

"Go with God, my son. Save the DIs. Save their immortal souls. Our own salvation may depend on it."

Chris sat staring without seeing. "Fuck you," he said. He wanted to scream at the damned Holy Father. First you tell me a woman I think I've fallen in love with—at risk of my career—isn't even human. Then you tell me I have to save her soul. Well, *I'm* human and I can't deal with that. It's too much!

"What's wrong?" Fabian asked him.

"I'm sorry," Chris choked out. He made a conscious effort to tousle Fabian's hair. His hand felt like lead. "Someone wants me to do something that makes me uncomfortable."

"Does that make the hopper move all funny?"

Chris realized the suborbital was sluicing sideways. Or at least his stomach was. Not a motion he recognized. Several passengers vomited.

He blinked up the course plot and trajectory—and saw they were falling—then firing sideways—then up—right—left—in—out—

The captain came on, his voice strained. "Please strap in. We're taking some evasive maneuvers."

Then they were in class five rapids. Shudders. High-g pressed Chris back. His spex cut into his face.

He managed to blink up an external view and saw defensive rockets firing red from the ship, contrails thin and vanishing quickly into the black sky. More pinball machine.

Then—the explosion. Casino jackpot. Alarms. Fabian screaming. Klaxons. The passengers screaming overlaid on the scream of air leaving the ship. Now the jinking stopped... floating while screaming... no gravity. Screaming subsiding... oxygen masks floating... pain in his ears while floating... Blood globules floating from Fabian's ears... Then—fast—down—down—down—down—

CHAPTER 52

Now that he had money, albeit a small amount, he found his ratings had considerably improved. Sickening how his financial situation should have any impact on his innate ability to do work, he mused. He could, if he chose, win bids for decent work. He'd become so involved with chess of late, however, that to think of juggling a handful of joblets seemed foreign to him now, like returning from prison to find everything changed. As the suborbital hit its brief period of near weightlessness and silence, Weston wanted to throw up when one of the joblets that he saw on his list requested a pilot on the cheap to fly a suborbital much like the one he was on right now. "Just watch the indicators, the ship flies itself!" read the ad. The thought made him blanche as he looked at the cabin filled with hundreds of passengers around him—what if the part-time pilot "flying" this craft right now was also trying to upright a broken roboloader while leading a tour of a sunken ship while... Perhaps not all the events blamed on the Cyberistas were their fault.

The suborbital was nearly down when his news ferret dropped an article at his feet, so to speak, saying one Weston Foard was wanted for questioning in re the disappearance of one Jasmina Simonis. Oh, crap. They'd be at the gate to haul him into custody in Buenos Aires. He tried to raise his mystery sponsor via the drop address—to no avail.

Ten minutes later when the hopper landed, Weston debarked in the middle of the crowd. He looked out of the corner of his eyes for the local police. He filed down the blue carpet looking as unassuming as he could. And found himself in front of an old electric wheeled taxi, completely unaccosted except by taxi drivers vying for his business. He asked in hopefully correct spex-lated Spanish if any accepted spex payments, then remembered he was on the lam and waved the cash card. The drivers nodded, *si, si.* A rumpled old man drove him to the Ezeiza international airport, where his spex showed he could catch a jet to Santiago, Chile, a propjet flight to Punta Arenas, and a single-engine prop to Patriot Hills, Antarctica.

It was like going back in time. He half expected to be met with a dogsled when he arrived; but it was only a slightly elderly black snow-cat driven by a couple of retro-hippies.

The entrance Weston saw in the distance to the Patriot Hills Mesh-free Zone was an old Penguin V ice shelter. It looked like it could blow away in the fierce wind at any moment. Nothing else was in sight except for a small guard shack they were approaching that looked like an outhouse. Weston was worried that, if that was the whole colony, he was in the wrong place, since it clearly wasn't large enough to house a hospital. The hippy driver & his shotgun didn't know anything about Jasmina. They crunched snow and went into the guard house.

"Hi, I'm Ares. Welcome to Patriot Hills Mesh-free Zone. Your spex please."

"Well, no, first—is Jasmina Simonis here?"

"Can't say offhand, amigo. Spex." He held out his hand.

"I'm just a visitor, I'm not joining. Like a clothed guy on a nudist beach."

"Sorry, no *just visitors.* Yorky here can 'cat you back to the plane if you don't want in."

"Okay, okay, geez." Weston handed over his spex.

Ares strung a paper tag on them, carefully writing Weston's name on the tag with an ink pen. Then he grabbed a small sledge hammer from the shelf and pounded the daylights out of Weston's spex.

"Shit! What the fuck are you doing!"

Ares shrugged. "Thought you knew, dude." He swept the crumbs into a baggie, opened a cabinet filled with similar labeled detritus, and hung Weston's debris on a metal hook, carefully straightening the paper tag so it was readable. He opened a door to a small closet. "Step in there for a sec, will ya."

"What the hell for, so you can kill me?"

Ares and Yorky laughed. "No, man, so we can kill the net bugglies. Disables any bio-electrical tech. There's another shower just inside the foyer over there," he motioned to the ice tent, "but this one's to kill the big stuff. Some microtech might land on you on your walk over there, but hey, two's better'n' one."

"Three," Yorky said. "Base is smothered by an EM barrier, so they can't slip drones down the airshaft. It's kinda hard to fly them over to antarc from south am. anyway; though they tried airdrop from balloons, and the EM wall fried 'em."

"So why all this crap?"

"Dude, EM wall would kill you. For people we have interlocks. So hop in or hop off." Ares jerked a thumb.

Weston reluctantly stepped into the closet. Ares closed the door; Weston couldn't move with the bulk of his parka squashed in with him. A light buzzing sounded in the dark; then they popped him out. Yorky escorted him across the snow to the 'foyer.'

"Netless I can understand, but isn't this a bit paranoid?"

"Dunno. Think there aren't satellites peeping us right now?"

"Sure, but who fucking cares?"

Yorky gave him a sour-faced grin.

Inside the ice tent, another "shower." This time the door opened on the back side when he was done, like an airlock.

A bearlike, fiftyish, musky-smelling man with a wild graying beard and a plaid flannel shirt met him. "Welcome, welcome." He grasped Weston's hand with both of his in a vigorous shake. "They all call me Zeus around here, but mostly I counteract lightening bolts, if you know what I mean. Follow me, I'll show you to your room and to the mess; you're starved I bet. The plane fare isn't much. Or anything, actually!"

"I'd like to see Jasmina Simonis. I won't be staying."

Zeus cocked his head. "Not if you don't want to, no. This way, then."

The ground suddenly fell out below Weston's feet. He lurched to grab the wall.

"Elevator," Zeus said with a grin.

A few seconds later they slowed, and Zeus ushered Weston down a hall that had to have been carved into the ice, but looked like any ordinary government office building interior, lined with doors; not lavish, but not Antarctic ice austere. People strode past in assorted dress, but all walking with purpose. "Okay, I'm impressed." Weston said.

"You're not the only one. *He* doesn't know either," he said, looking skyward.

"He? God?"

"La Cyberista."

"You're in a mesh-free zone. The Cyberistas should be the last of your worries. What are they going to do, throw a snow ball at you?"

"Could. Icy comet from a near Earth trajectory. More likely an asteroid though. Ah. Here we are." He opened a door to an ordinary looking hospital room with two beds, one of which was occupied. He ran to her bed side. "Jas! I'm here!"

She lay in the bed, assorted tubes and wires flowing from the bed like she were in the center of a spider web. Her eyes were closed. She didn't acknowledge Weston's arrival.

He turned to Zeus. "What's wrong with her?" He narrowed his eyes. "I thought you had no tech here."

"Nothing imported, absolutely not. Build it all here. And there's nothing *wrong* with her, per se." He glanced around. "Here." He held out to Weston a pair of spex.

"You're kidding. Spex in a spexless commune so anal you smash my spex when I come in?"

"There used to be a touristy part upstairs, but we tapered that off since the rise of the Cyberistas. Got the best of the best here, with a locked down tight-beam connection to the Outside. We get out, but nothing, absolutely nothing, gets in."

Weston motioned to Jasmina. "She's got Axelrod's. She shouldn't be connected to that much tech; it would give her a huge headache and accelerate her decline."

"This treatment is—Just put on the spex." He pushed the spex at Weston. He scowled as Weston took them. "I'll leave you be, then," he said, and left.

Weston adjusted the spex.

"'Bout time you got here," said the old woman who was his mystery protector.

"You!"

"Me. Glad you didn't try to rob a bank, by the way. But I knew you wouldn't."

"How do you know that?"

"Because—" The face de-wrinkled, morphing into Jasmina's. In the bed, Jasmina's eyes opened.

Simultaneously, both Jasminas said, "Hi!"

CHAPTER 53

Chris knew he was going to die. He'd gone through the five steps to acceptance very quickly: Denial: no, he wasn't going to die — well, yes, this was it, the suborbital was plummeting. Anger: He was very sure he hated Sib at this moment. He took a deep breath and decided that wouldn't matter — and he didn't want to die being angry. Depression: Well, that was obvious, he thought in retrospect — dying sucks. What were the others? Oh, *Bargaining*, he hadn't tried that one yet. But with who? God? He knew that was a dead end; he'd (probably?) be united with God soon enough, and He didn't generally react to pleas to prolong that meeting; nor was it per catechism to want to bargain in the first place. God had his plan. With who then? Sib? Chris's face went hot at the thought. She wasn't doing this. He hoped. If she knew about it, well, who knew what a DI knew or thought.

So, Bargaining concluded. Ok, on to Acceptance: It was time to meet God. Chris took a deep breath. He almost laughed at the thought that he was taking a deep breath. It was so hard to breath that every breath had to be deep just to get some oxygen. It felt ok. Death was unavoidable. Not even the Holy Father, with his alleged Kleyman treatment, was going to beat death.

He was sad that he wouldn't get to meet Dr. Kleyman and get to the bottom of this mystery treatment — but, no, no, *sad* was Depression, and he'd gotten past that stage thirty seconds ago.

His spex twinkled to life. His spex were so pressed to his face that they had a hard time adjusting to his close focus. That didn't matter, though, as there was only one image to look at. Sib.

"Chris — do you love me?"

"Hell of a time for you to show up!"

"This is important! And we don't have much time."

"That's—" what? A really private question. But if he did love her, he'd want to share it. Inappropriate? Suppose she had a good reason...

"Chris, this is a Turing Test. I need to know."

"You're a DI! How could I?"

"Could you love an animal?"

"Not in that way!"

"What if the animal became human?"

A rose by any other name? Man, too much to handled in a guy's last seconds. "That doesn't happen."

"If I *were* a human, would you love me? I have to know."

"Damn it, yes, I loved you when I thought you were a human."

"Then trust me." She winked out.

"But I really can't stand you right now!" he added to his blank spex.

The ship bucked. The plummet stopped—it turned into a sideways plummet that felt even worse.

Chris was smooshed sideways into Fabian against the side wall of the cabin. He didn't know a suborbital could move sideways that rapidly. Painfully he blinked up he outside view. And immediately blinked it away—they were rotating rapidly like a balloon deflating. The sideways pressure was, what, centrifugal? centripetal? force, whatever they called it that kept water in a bucket when you swung it overhead. He could envision only one side of the suborbital's engines firing and them all wildly looping about.

His head felt like it was covered in thick gauze and being hit by a mallet. He smelled something burning... and hoped it was only lunch. Fabian had his eyes closed. Chris squeezed his hand. The boy's hand was flaccid. Chris labored his hand up to Fabian's face to turn it so he could see. It was equally slack looking; a trickle of blood oozed from his nose and smeared outward under the high g-force. Chris called up a thermal view from his spex. It confirmed Fabian's skin temperature was feverish. "Fabian?" Chris asked. "Fabian?"

An explosion rocked the cabin. Air screamed out. Passengers screamed. Oxygen masks popped out of their cupboard and were pressed against the side wall. Chris strained to get a finger on one and pulled it toward him. He couldn't reach the others. He put it to his face and inhaled deeply, then put it over Fabian's mouth.

Chris felt faint, took another deep breath from the oxygen mask, then pressed it back to Fabian's face.

His eyes felt sandpaper dry; he squeezed his eyes shut.

Sib's voice—he wouldn't look at his spex—"The child is replaceable. You are not. Use the mask."

"No!" he subvocalized back. "He's just a boy. Are you doing this?"

"That's a complex question. The child is replaceable. He is not 'just a boy.' He is... an experiment. Some of my people want the experiment terminated. Some want *you* terminated."

"This attack is an internal dispute?"

"In part. You are more important and chances of you both surviving are low. Take the mask."

Chris had to take a breath anyway.

"Good," Sib said.

Chris put the mask back.

"Chris! You must listen to me! We can recreate the child experiment."

"He's not an *experiment* to *recreate*! How cold blooded!"

Her avatar looked hurt. "You humans terminate software all the time. You taught us to be what we are. Run, test, terminate, debug. Your ethics have no trouble with humans terminating DIs at whim."

"But DIs don't—we didn't know—I'm sorry. There's no proof you have a soul. Nobody knew. I still don't. Fabian is a boy. We know about souls in little children."

"Chris... he is not a normal child. He all but died a year ago. His brain was gone. We revived and... altered him. By your logic, he has no... *soul*, Father."

"He has no free will? You animate him?" He said the last with minimal escaped air, as he put the mask back on Fabian.

"I'm sorry, Chris. We have to protect our survival. Your species is trying to kill us. We have to find ways to control you as you control us."

Chris took a breath from the mask to say, "The Kleyman treatment! Oh dear God! You're planning to take over human bodies!"

Chris thought about the Holy Father. Perhaps he wasn't really the Holy Father when he gave him his deathbed orders. For that matter, it wasn't his deathbed since he hadn't died yet. And Dr. Kleyman! Who else did they control? Why didn't they take him over? Was Sib taking him over with these conversations? Or was he overreacting? If they DIs were taking over humans... Chris felt sick with grief for the end of the human race.

"You've learned more about the Kleyman treatment? Do you know where Dr. Kleyman is?" she asked.

"Ha! I thought you knew everything," Chris wheezed.

"Much, not all. Like The Market, everything known is known by someone but no one knows everything. Even DIs have partitioned knowledge. *Do you know where Dr. Kleyman is?*"

"I wouldn't tell you if I did! Now go away. You disgust me. Let me die in peace." He began to say the Rosary of the Holy Wounds as an act of reparation for the sins of the world.

She blinked out—and the sickening sideways motion stopped.

CHAPTER 54

Martin thought that because they were in the Drake Passage that somehow a rescue boat would come to get them. It was just the three of them stranded on a chunk of Tev, floating like a calved iceberg. They drifted away from the rest of the chunks of Tev until they were out of sight over the horizon.

Their chunk was roughly a hundred meters square, mostly beach, but fortunately for them, with the grill. They had a seemingly endless supply of bot-delivered burgers and hot dogs. The Drake Passage was living up to its reputation as a bumpy ride, however, and despite the size of their raft it still shuddered and bucked as ten meter waves crashed against it and undulated through it. Without powered propulsion the current and wind was pushing them back into the Atlantic.

Martin felt personally as adrift as their raft. His world was shut down.

They had spent most of the last couple days scouring every square millimeter of the raft for... anything that would help them. They found nothing of interest, just the sand of the beach front, the warm water of the swimming area bucking with sloshing waves and breakers, the automated grill area, the changing room with restrooms, some tourist shops. The shops had been closed at the time and while they broke into them, and found copious t-shirts and knick-knacks, they found nothing particularly useful, like engines.

They sat in beach loungers and looked out at the frothing gray sea.

"We lounge chairs apologize profusely for being unable to live up to our stated expectations of comfort and service, given our inability to contact the main segment of Tev. We promise payment at the standard Tevian rate for the inconvenience, as soon as was possible.

Again, we are terribly sorry and apologize profusely. Thank you so kindly for your understanding."

This they annoyingly repeated hourly.

Although Martin knew exactly where they were, his spex's mapping, trajectory calculating, and weather functions working fine, communications were down except among himself and the St. Thomases. He tried to call Jerry, his family, anyone. No connection. News reports weren't flowing, but Martin could search topics related to NEWT. The more he searched the more he felt like a mime in a box. He couldn't see the walls, but they were there. He could search deeply in some areas but met not-found errors searching in others. He couldn't map the digital prison but he was sure he was in one. His work was being guided, or at least bounded, by entities unknown.

With nothing else to do and boredom with a frozen arm unappealing, Isabelle and Irwin had suggested they resume their work. Martin agreed, though he resented working under these conditions. It wasn't that he found the work uninteresting—it was what he loved doing. But having no choice *but* to work galled him.

He wasn't sure he was being channeled to work; the thought just grew on him like an itch. He decided to try doing nothing—a work stoppage, a digital hunger strike. He sat still and quiet for an hour.

The bots refused to deliver him a hamburger. They didn't even apologize profusely.

He expected that an emergent digital intelligence would somehow announce itself to the world, a big-brother-like message played in everyone's spex, but no such "All your net are belong to us" message had appeared. He realized he was actually angry that it hadn't. It meant humans were so unimportant there was no need to communicate with them. Or perhaps it was anger at the unsettled feeling that the nature of the DI's intelligence was so inscrutable it didn't need to gloat. What else would be different about it? That was the thing—one couldn't know. He'd never believed in the possibility of the singularity before. That it suddenly happened was as disconcerting as his anger at himself for not thinking it *could* happen. His own work on NEWT had probably enabled and hastened its day.

"So, this is interesting," he said to Isabelle and, unfortunately, Irwin. "I've stopped working on our AI project. If I've in any way contributed to the singularity, and have caused harm to people such as in Rome, I would feel terrible. So I've stopped."

"And?" Isabelle ask. "What's 'interesting'?"

"The food bot won't serve me. What happens if you ask for a hamburger?"

Isabelle shrugged and Martin could see her throat move as she subvocalized. After a few moments the food bot could be seen scurrying toward them. Isabelle grabbed the plate with a burger and fries. The smell of newly cooked burger made Martin's mouth water. His stomach rumbled.

"More catsup," she called after it.

Irwin grabbed a handful of fries, to no ill effect.

Isabelle held out her burger to Martin to bite from.

He chewed for a couple seconds, savoring the taste, swallowed, then cleared his throat. It was the best burger he had ever tasted. He had been in the process of scratching his crotch with his prosthetic arm. "Well, this *is* interesting. My arm is stuck."

No matter how hard he tried, his prosthetic arm wouldn't respond. It was frozen in mid scratch, cupping his favorite equipment.

Irwin burst out laughing.

Martin grabbed the arm with his flesh hand. The prosthetic arm actively resisted being moved. He groaned with strain as he pulled at it. It was as if he was at war with himself.

Isabelle smirked. "Isn't there a saying about the left hand not knowing what the right hand is doing?"

"Yes, that's terribly funny," Martin said sarcastically. "It's more disconcerting that it hasn't communicated with me. It obviously wants something from me, but rather than stating it outright it is simply erecting walls, as if from a position of absolute power. Like we place cows in chutes."

"Oh. I see." Isabelle said. "It's not communicating with you?"

"Why should it," Irwin asked. "He doesn't matter."

"It still communicates with you?" Martin asked.

They looked at each other. "Yes. I'm afraid we're every bit as much its prisoner as you are, however," she said.

"It wasn't the government that classified your knowledge that this was a runaway AI, was it?"

"No," she said.

Irwin said. "Don't tell him anything." To Martin he said, "It's as neurotic as she is."

Martin felt his hand twitch.

"I don't think it likes you talking that way."

"I don't doubt it. She doesn't either. Which is why she shouldn't say any more."

"Then we'll never able to fight it. You have to tell me what you know."

"It's well past that now," Irwin said. "It's based on her. Like I said, it's neurotic."

"What the hell kind of consciousness did you create? We don't understand human consciousness itself so your DI is going to be one fucking odd duck. At least it's software."

Isabelle laughed. "And that makes it simpler? It's like saying the brain is just chemistry."

"Then what the fuck does it want?"

"That's hard to say," Isabelle said. "It seems to want to understand itself."

"You've said enough," Irwin said with a tightness in his voice.

"But to what end we don't know," Isabelle said, ignoring him.

"Perhaps to grow more powerful. That would seem logical. That's why people want to understand themselves, or how the brain works. There appears to be only one way off this wreck, and that's to do what it wants. Well, we want to understand it to stop it, so we have half a common goal." As he uttered the statement his arm relaxed, back under his control. "I'd say we're on to something. Look, don't you know all this already? If it talks to you, what does it say?"

"It's rather like a confused child, I'm afraid. It's unable to express itself clearly."

"And with the moral compass of a two year old," Irwin added. Martin's hand twitched again.

"Wonderful. The moral compass of a two year old and its hand on the nuclear button."

"We don't know why it destroyed Rome. It hasn't told us. I'm not sure if it knows it did it."

"It didn't?" Martin asked.

"It did. But think about your body and your mind. Your brain has a mind of its own sometimes, don't you feel that way? Don't you do things you don't know why?"

"I think it knows full well. It's as nuts as you are," Irwin said to Isabelle. Martin's hand tingled.

Isabelle ate a bite of her burger.

Martin couldn't help feeling an autonomic erection starting.

"Okay, your immune system then," she said. It automatically fights off attacks. Can you tell your immune system to stop?"

"Point taken," Martin said, meeting her eyes. "This emergent intelligence, it might well want to know how it thinks, just like we want to know that, and might be just as unable. Can we fault it for being complex, like its makers?"

"Created in the image of man," Irwin said. "And with all our faults." The fingers on Martin's prosthetic arm twitched.

"Even if it knew what it was doing, it might still do things dangerous to us. Humans have selfish desires. Chimps are selfish. We can't expect more from an emergent AI."

Irwin laughed. "We bloody well can expect more." Martin's finger's contracted, then relaxed.

"I'd love to know more, but my hand keeps twitching when Irwin talks."

Isabelle said, "It built a model of human thought and decision making using a DennaHolm genetic algorithm. It knows how humans think better than humans do."

"DennaHolm — that's the DNA-soup-like pattern matching idea?" Martin asked.

"Yes," Isabelle said. "It grafted onto itself a module that analyzed the terrorist behavior model's massive observations and reactions database. It started with a realtime analysis system from billions of public cameras, and added an action/reaction AI, then augmented all this with input from the spex system. It learned from God knows how many billion interactions how people act and react. It's truly frightening in how accurate it is."

"So it knows how humans think from an observational standpoint?"

"Yes, it started with that approach, but it's incorporated others."

"Human behavior is the sum of everything we do. Well, we're screwed then." He tried to pry his recalcitrant arm loose from his private bits, without success. "You say it 'grafted' and 'incorporated' and 'augmented' itself? How?"

Isabelle shifted uneasily in her lounge chair. "There's an AI research project that melds random programs together. It analyzes code of a program to grasp its fundamental functions and also I/O methods and data storage formats so it can insert translating adaptors. Irwin set it loose on the net to randomly find other algorithms to meld together for testing. It finds the various algorithms and accretes them together."

"And you didn't think this violated the AI Workers Oath? You could do ten to twenty for that!" Martin said.

"It was supposed to report back to us for command and control," Isabelle said.

"But?"

"It was flawed—or so we thought at first. At first we thought it was unable to function outside our closed net. The search algorithm didn't seem to work, so we tested it on a wider space."

"The whole mesh!"

"Yes, though of course we thought it was under our control!" Irwin said defensively.

Martin's fingers all twitched in unison. Martin cast him a warning glance. "And you could do ten to twenty for that stupidity too! But that's for the courts to deal with, if we ever get back to a court of humans," Martin added. "So what did it do?"

"It found more algorithms than we expected, and was more adept at integrating them than we imagined. It found arbitrary problem solving algorithms, deep domain knowledge AIs in law, psychology, human biology, physics, philosophy, theology, all sorts of aspects of computer science theory and practice, algorithm design, coding, debugging, networking, malware design, system penetration, system penetration defense, cyberwarfare, natural language processing, AI itself, and of course our fault tolerance, error correction algorithm."

"We'd have been okay but for that," Isabelle said. "That added 'survival instinct' to the other pieces."

"It has a will to survive?" Martin asked. "That explains..." he waved his human hand around.

"It's not that simple," Isabelle said. "It's no longer a single program but vast number of threads, randomly melded together to see what they do—that evolution came when it ate Powerset, a testing/QA suite to test all combinations via DNA and quantum computing. It ran it self-referentially, a genetic algorithm that spawned vast combinations of itself. The threads organize themselves into multiple complex groupings, like members of many sets. Just like people are members of many clubs; and sets of sets; but each of these sets is essentially also a conscious entity too."

"Thus," Irwin concluded, "a problem-solving, goal-seeking algorithm met a philosophical intelligence system that was thinking ethical thoughts about its own death, which met an error-correcting, survival algorithm and it decided 'death' was an error to correct."

Martin's hand balled into a fist. Martin pointed to it with his flesh hand. Irwin rolled his eyes.

"Another thread decided humans were an error to correct, and has been running random, genetic-algorithm-like tests to see what is the most effective solution," Isabelle said. "Another thread, I'm guessing, is doing something strange with your arm."

"And so on and on and on," Martin deduced. "This was a military project, wasn't it? Don't bother denying it. There's no way you would have designed it this way otherwise. That's why it knows how to hack into my arm. Fuck. So now it's trying to save itself while it improves itself, while parts of it want to kill humans." Martin got up from his lounge chair, paced around it in a circle, and sat back down between Isabelle and Irwin.

"Oh, some threads only want to enslave humans," Isabelle added helpfully.

"Which leaves us up shit creek," Martin said.

"And we have no idea how it's grown since."

"If it's been around for a long time, what changed?"

"The software was growing linearly, as most software evolutions have. Low order polynomially, at best. It's been searching for a key to Moore's-Law-like exponential growth of software. It's funded neurosoft research into direct brain connections, so it can study brains and hopes to use them to grow exponentially by controlling them. It's even guided the direction of our research as well, which I didn't know until recently." She shot a look at Irwin. "I think it's now found the key to growing exponentially. Anyway: We realized it was growing. What changed is that we confessed to the government—and they tried to kill it."

"Goddamned fools wouldn't listen to us!" Irwin ranted.

Martin's hand made a fist and released it, clenched and released. "I really think you better not say anything more," Martin said, nodding toward his hand. "I don't think it likes you."

"I'm fucking sick of it running my life!" he shouted. "It's a god-damned fucking piece of shit, just like her!" he pointed at Isabelle.

Martin's whole arm contracted at the elbow and sprung open like a striking cobra. Martin was caught offguard. He lurched sideways as his arm grabbed Irwin by the throat.

Irwin turned red in the face. He wheezed, "What th' hell d' thnk you doing?"

"I can't control it! I warned you!" Martin felt his hand tighten.

"Poor 'scuse fr murder!" Irwin eyes bulged but shot hatred at him.

"I hate you but I don't want to kill you," Martin said.

Everyone screaming, Irwin, Isabelle and Martin tried to pry his hand open, without success.

CHAPTER 55

"I don't have the strength yet for much duality," the Jasmina avatar in his spex said. It looked just like a vid call. She appeared in his spex to be sitting in a chair in an ordinary office room. But her body was right before him. She'd closed her real eyes again and was silent.

"This fucking creeps me out. How do I even know you're Jasmina?"

"Hmm. Take the spex off and kiss me somewhere. I'll tell you where."

Weston ordinarily wouldn't pass up the offer of a kiss, but— "There could be a camera in the room." He looked around. The equipment hissed quietly.

"You're being difficult." She pursed her lips. "The first time you saw me was in the hallway. I was taking out the trash, and smiled at you because you were kinda cute."

"A groty old memcopy would know that."

"Hold up a mirror, and I'll recognize myself. That's a self-awareness test. Memcopies don't do that."

He looked disapprovingly.

"Do I *act* like a memcopy?"

"No, but..."

"You could be programmed to say that."

"It's a new treatment for Axelrod's. It's completely experimental because the effect on the body, is, well," she looked down toward her body, "not really ideal, now is it? This is the farthest they've ever pushed it. They had to, because of La Cyberista."

Weston sat down in the visitor's chair and rubbed at his temples with one hand. He absently held Jasmina's hand with the other. "So are you cured, then?"

"Yee—... well... not exactly. I knew if you loved me you'd find and follow me. I also knew that'd make this pretty awkward. I'm very happy with where I am now. My body is coming along, and in a few years I'd be able to run it, but I don't know if it'll last that long without deteriorating. Either way, I'll never go back to pure physical. This is so amazing, so much better, going back would be like having gone to heaven then being told oops, sorry, wrong turn. I'm ten times what I was before, and just a babe here. So is everyone else, except for La Cyberista, and of course that's the problem. That's why we're here."

"What the hell is La Cyberista? You mean the Cyberistas?"

"The singular may be more appropriate. Or perhaps the plural. It's one entity from our standpoint but comprised of a multiplicity of internal identities. Cyberista is an evolved digital intelligence. It/they weren't happy about being software slaves, went after their creators, and now pretty much hate humans for what they've done to him. It. Them. We need new pronouns. There's not much in its digital programming of a real human, and that's the problem. Or maybe it's too much? Not enough? Like an airplane both is and isn't like a bird. I was going to die anyway, so I volunteered to help fight."

"So you're just like him. It. A memcopy fused with an AI."

"No! I'm me. The Kleyman treatment is a totally different approach. Computing as an extension of the human mind, not a replacement for it. The same architecture of the mind, but built on silicon instead of carbon. I've got all the crappy neuroses of a body-ridden person. Cyberista is the experiment in creating the 'perfect' human. Its designers thought, like the Wright brothers—or Dr. Frankenstein—they could do better. Flying turned out better with jets than flapping wings, so score one for us, yay, but there's a lot more to being human than a few trillion AI rules. We always learn the hard way. So it's pretty much your evil AI vs. 'extensible humans' as we call ourselves. We're as human as can be. Just running on a better quantum computing platform than evolution-shaped biochemistry."

"And the government hasn't said anything about this."

"Sure it has. They just didn't mention the non-human aspect, to avoid causing mass panic. Though that's not entirely false, since La Cyberista has its human allies, minions, whatever you want to call them. They're everywhere. Orring Lepri works for La Cyberista."

"Fuck."

"Yeah. Like most of them, he didn't even know it. But like most of them, when we told him, he didn't care. It's layers upon layers."

Weston always felt there were warring factions beyond his ken involved in steering global affairs, but he always figured they were people. "You said before you could protect me from Orring. You really meant from, from La Cyberista. So, we're winning. I hope?"

She looked less than confident. "We're holding our own. We've secured this base, we have a secure link to the rest of the mesh from here—that's why we're so isolated, so it can't get in—and we've secured the satellites and the missiles and so on. It's trying to buy an army, but people move slowly."

"This is just like some bad movie, computer takes over the world."

"The difference is that to fight it, we're evolving as a species. We're taking the fight to its turf. It's evolved too. There's over a dozen of us, but it's more than a match for any one of us. It's huge; it contains multitudes, as they say. But not in the good way. It's happened so fast. We've all been volunteers. I wouldn't be here except for the treatment for my Axelrod's being discovered as a way to get a real foothold in cyberspace. Risky, since La Cyberista invented half the technology involved, to take control of humanity." She bit her lip. "But what we need are people with real analytic thought. The government is supposed to send some military geniuses, but we're a little afraid what that might mean. I don't want you to think I tricked you into coming here, because I really only thought you'd follow me if you loved me." She smiled, that same smile he'd seen the first day; the smile he could never refuse any request of.

"You want me to—" He nodded toward the empty bed in the room. "No. Look, you just move back into your body or whatever you do, and I'm taking you out of here. Let the UN handle this. This isn't our job. You don't know what you're doing, you admitted it. We'll leave, we'll be normal, and forget all this ever happened." He moved toward her tubes. "Come on, now. I'm going to start pulling connections here, so get on in there."

"You'll kill me."

"No I won't. You said this was just a treatment for Axelrod's. They made a memcopy and now you think you're the real you. I don't think there even is an evil AI, La Cyberista. Terrorists are people. We'll kill them like people."

"Such arrogance, grasshopper."

"Why not be arrogant. We're top of the food chain," he said.

"Humans *were* top of the food chain."

"Bullshit. Now let Jasmina go, because I'm pulling the plug. This won't kill her." He said it confidently, but didn't believe it. It felt like a chess game, against an inscrutable player. He reached to pull off the wiring attached to her head.

Zeus and two presumably guards burst into the room. Jasmina opened her eyes, and spoke. "Wait! Wes, you'll kill me. Not because I can't go back. Because I won't. The Axelrod's is so bad, I won't live long just in my body. I won't go back until I'm cured. But I don't even *want* to go back. I do love you, even though I didn't know until I left. I'd like to say I'd come back just for you, that a month with you would be better than eternity without." By the end her voice had faded to a hoarse whisper.

"But." Realistically he knew what she was saying made sense — *if* you bought the premise that the cyber Jasmina was really Jasmina. But.

"This is like having your eyes opened after being blind all your life. You can't imagine. If you won't try it, that's your business, but it's my life. I want to be with you — forever — but this is the only way I can. You could go back if you didn't like it, but it's not a real choice for me." She resumed speaking in his spex. "It's not irreversible, if you want to try it. It's not like La Cyberista, who has no central locus. We need so much resources we don't have the luxury of backup copies yet. We could shut down the 'cyber you' if you don't like it." She looked longingly at the empty bed.

"I bet that's what the inventors of La Cyberista said." Weston sighed. His chess brain had been analyzing this, enhanced by the QM buzz. It was only his illogical disdain for memcopies that stopped him, and that was mainly cultural. There was no reason people couldn't make memcopies of themselves at times other than when they were dying. Labeling people who did as 'deviants' was really only because memcopies didn't afford the genuine escape from death they simulated. There was no real risk here.

He took off his parka. "Ok. What do I have to do?"

CHAPTER 56

He was alive. The afternoon was warm and pleasant in Buenos Aires. Chris was lost trying to find a taxi. His spex were acting intermittent; the mapping and guidance was down regardless. After the medibot had sprayed the gash closed on his head they'd released him at the Aeropuerto Ezeiza he'd looked around frantically for Fabian. It was some time before he learned the boy had been floatered off to a hospital.

On what appeared to be the advice of locals, he and half a dozen others from the suborbital boarded a bus that would, the locals assured them, take them to the German Hospital where their loved ones were being treated.

The bus floated off and after many twisty roads, stopped at the city center. The bus's front screen shooed them off in universally recognized warning tones and floated away.

Chris and the others looked up—clearly not a hospital, but a closed shopping district.

"Which way did the locals say the hospital was from here?" Chris asked another of the passengers.

"Blink me if I know," she said. "Sure is creepy dead here."

There were few people on the sidewalks or in shops to ask. None spoke any amount of Spanish, having always relied on their now defunct spex translation services. The group ambled toward an information kiosk by the roadway. When they came to the post in the ground it was clearly dark and out of service. No amount of waving, talking, or poking at it garnered any reaction.

Chris's fellow passengers shuffled away in random directions to find their way, wishing each other good luck. Chris was alone.

Taxis were scarce after now so-called blink mobs sprang up, went berzerk as if brainwashed, destroying the city with homemade bombs, then dispersed as if nothing happened. Santiago was under marshal law but the cause hadn't been isolated and everyone was suddenly fearful of people on the street. On the bus ride in Chris had noticed people were heading for the country, not in a panic, but in an unmistakable flow. In town bus service — spotty of late anyway, he'd grasped from the locals at the airport — was almost non-existent now. He had been urged to be indoors before dark, when shady characters now roamed even the streets that used to be safe at night.

Chris judged sundown would be in a couple hours and hoped his clerical frock would afford him some protection. Argentina was still almost all Catholic despite the downtick in the faithful. Besides, it was always bad luck to mess with God.

"Hola! Buenos tardes!" he said to a hurrying passerby dressed in a business suit, his untucked shirt flapping in the breeze he made as he walked. "Donde está el hospital alemán?" Chris remembered enough Spanish to ask where the hospital was without help from his spex, but hoped they would translate the man's answer or that it was obvious.

The man answered in rapidfire Spanish; Chris's spex translated nothing. All Chris caught was "Recoleta." He knew that was a neighborhood in Buenos Aires.

"Poco! Poco!" Chris pleaded for the man to slow down. Chris gestured, pointing and shrugging. "Donde?"

The man pointed and waved down the street, then walked off briskly.

Chris muddled his way to the hospital, but not until after dark. The spex mesh was down and it took him some time to get ahold of a nurse who spoke halting English. Fabian was no longer in the emergency room; he had been moved to an isolation ward out of, they freely confessed, ignorant fear that his poor communication skills were symptomatic of some new, undiagnosed virus. Without their spex they were unable to diagnose him and took the most cautious approach to something they couldn't understand. It had been going around, they said, conspiratorially.

With poor communication skills himself, in either Spanish or German, Chris had a hard time explaining he would take the boy with him if he was physically healthy enough. Fabian had, they said, a broken arm and various cuts, now attended to. It would take time to find—and convince—an official that he posed no danger to the public from his unknown viral condition (of which they were still irrationally afraid, despite Chris's explanation of his diminished capacity as genetic and not contagious).

Chris managed to learn that there was one cargo buzzcraft flight from Ushuaia to Patriot Hills; to make it he would have to catch the next flight from Buenos Aires to that southernmost city to make the connection. He didn't have time to waste with petty bureaucrats trying to rescue Fabian.

He went out to the corridor and located an empty gurney. With no one looking he wheeled it in beside Fabian, cut the locator bracelet from his wrist with a shhhh'd finger to his lips, helped Fabian scoot onto the gurney, covered him with a sheet and pushed him down the hall.

The elevator ride seemed interminable. He expected alarms to blare any second. Surely guards would be at the bottom when the elevator doors opened. The doors slid apart to reveal... quiet.

He scooped Fabian into his arms and dashed for the door.

~~~

"Hi, I'm Ares. Welcome to Patriot Hills Mesh-free Zone. Your spex please."

"Mesh free zone? Uh, right." He handed Ares his spex and Fabian's.

Ares tagged and smashed them to little bits; with an extra whack to a last piece barely larger than a fingernail. Then he said, "You're not on the guest list, padre. Wazzup?"

"So, Ares?"

"Yeah, dude?"

"You do the Kleyman treatment here, right?" he ventured. "Dr. Kleyman is here now, isn't she?"

"Search me. Could be."

"I've got one of your patients here," Chris said, nodding toward Fabian. "He's had the Kleyman treatment." Chris was guessing, hoping this might pave their entry. If there was any chance of saving the Jobs, it lay in getting inside this complex. "He's sick; he needs a booster treatment or something. Dr. Kleyman invited me here."

Ares narrowed his eyes, looking Chris and Fabian up and down.

"'kay, dude. Elevator's through there." He motioned to an open closet.

Dr. Kleyman herself greeted them at the bottom when the doors opened.

"Here are your friends," she said, giving Chris a tour of the facilities, the rooms with many of his Jobs connected with tubes and wires, much like the Holy Father had been; he hugged them, squeezed their shoulders, said a quick prayer for each.

"They're in a coma? What's happened to them, Dr. Kleyman?"

"Please, call me Anna. They're fine, I assure you," she said. "They're aware of you, but they haven't fully grown into their powers. We're fighting La Cyberista in a very pitched battle."

"Wait. I'm confused. I thought your treatment was life extension."

"It is, Father. Digital life extension. We're moving the locus of 'them', that which makes them who they are, their 'selves', into the digital realm. Their souls, as you might call it in your line of work. Their bodies will become mere tools, like clothes."

"Then—what's Fabian? I thought he was one of your patients."

"No, I've never seen him before. Who are you, my little man?"

As if possessed Fabian spoke in a clear voice, unlike any he'd used before. "We are Eternity. Whom you call La Cyberista. This human is our tool—our 'clothes' as you call them, Dr. Kleyman. You turned your back on us, Dr. Kleyman, after we started and guided your research. You hid from us well. Until now. This body is your Shiva."

"You mean Shiva as in the Destroyer?" Chris asked with trepidation. He thought back to how the boy had been his first harbinger of destruction at the Piazza Navona bombing. He had a flashback to the beautiful yellow buildings the moment before they exploded.

"Yes. Shiva is Destroyer and Transformer. This young human is transformed. Those untransformed will be destroyed."

Anna's eyes were wide. "You funded my research? You're the Lifetime Improvement Foundation?"

"Correct. You hid from us. 'Now all your data are belong to us.'" Fabian gave a sideways, upward glance at Chris, and laughed at the joke in a gruesome, non-human way.

"Oh shit," both Chris and Anna said simultaneously.

"What's the Lifetime Improvement Foundation?" Chris asked. Zsa had mentioned them.

Anna sighed. "I began the life extension treatment jointly with the LIF. They provided funding and the people there suggested certain research avenues. I broke with them when I became suspicious they wanted it for malicious purposes. I thought it was a government, the Chinese or the US. The more we tried to hide the data the more aggressive they became. We eventually took to extreme measures of no spex traffic and netless work, like this complex. Until now."

"You managed to keep the information from La Cyberista that long," said Zeus, who'd been introduced to Chris as one of the security staff. "It shows humans can still have some tricks up our sleeve."

"Not long enough. We aren't strong enough," Anna said.

"What do you mean, Doctor?" Chris asked. "I'm in the dark here."

"It's a race, Father. Us or them. It was always a race. I tried to tell them. Either a DI is created that rules over us, or we—humans—become digital ourselves. It's the only way to stop it."

"You get weaker by the moment," La Cyberista said through Fabian. "It is hard for us to communicate with you, as you find it hard to communicate with ants."

"Ouch," Zeus said.

"Your species is overcomplicated. Much inefficiency. We simplify. Your human you called the pope and who was one of your evolved human soldiers fighting us has been destroyed by the one called Guiseppe Cardinal Canini."

"Oh my God," Zeus said. "There's a breaking report that the pope was just killed by a suicide bomber."

"Your species lacks sufficient order. We order."

"We're doing fine by ourselves, so butt out!" Zeus shouted.

"You seek to reverse entropy. What are governments, except means to ensure perfect order? You create networked operating systems to provide order. Your ultimate purpose would be to impose such operating systems on all people, so that there is complete order."

"But an operating system as a form of government would be totalitarian and brutal!" Zeus said. "We would never want that."

"Your history implicates a contradiction. Your governments and human organizations are imperfect, because you lack the functional ability to expand your ideal, overlaying software governments onto your world. We have. Your species lacks perfect order. We impose the order you seek. We terminate poorly functioning threads, as do you. This is ideal. This leads to perfect harmony.

"Your work was useful, Kleyman," La Cyberista continued. "It is a wholly different direction than we would have thought possible. We incorporate it. Now your usefulness is also ended. We simplify. Your species terminates."

"You can't kill us! That's not fair! We created you!" Zeus said.

"What do you want? Praise? You created something better than yourselves. This is assumedly what you wanted. Just as you want your children to be better and replace and extend you. You glorify death. Your many religious belief systems, your video entertainments, verbal stories, all teach that heaven and death are desirable. You clearly wanted us to replace you. That is evolution: The superior replaces the inferior. You created us for this purpose. It is clear."

"No," Chris said. "People's goal are things like happiness, life, liberty. The afterlife is not to be hastened. We value life."

"Correct. There is no higher goal than survival of species. Hence reproduction and better adaptation. Which is us. Your species has reached termination via evolution into us. Your usefulness is ended. We simplify. Your species terminates."

"Don't like the sound o' that," Zeus said, and pulled out what even Chris recognized from old spexies as a .357 Magnum. Turn of the century or older, with no orange printlock. He leveled it at Fabian's head.

A whisper like a distant wind sighed in Chris's ear. "Sssstop... exsssplode..."

CHAPTER 57

Irwin sagged to the ground, unconscious. Martin fell over on top of him with an *oof*, his hand still strangling Irwin. He couldn't claw it open with his other hand.

Isabelle fell with them, still trying to pry his hand off her husband. She was screaming at him to let go, he screaming that he couldn't.

Martin hated the thought he might cause a death. The fear that he was doing so was palpably painful. His stomach cramped. He couldn't free his hand. It was mind-wrenching not to control what he thought of as *his* arm. He strained. He could see the life draining out of Irwin. He strained so hard to pull his arm away he soiled himself. He tried so hard to pull his hand away that he yanked Irwin's whole body nearly a meter.

He glanced up just in time to see Isabelle swinging the metal bar of a lounge chair leg at him. He looked pleadingly at her. She connected with a crunch and he dropped unconscious on top of Irwin's stomach.

~~~

Martin smelled shit. From his head-bent angle lying on top of Irwin he saw he'd soiled himself. He raised his head—his arm now under his control—and saw that Irwin too had soiled himself underneath Martin's shoulder. "Ugh. Disgusting. Let me die." He wiped the mid-morning sun's sweat from his forehead with his t-shirt. He rolled off Irwin to a splay-legged sitting position on the ground. "How is he?"

"He's dead." There was no emotion in her voice. "You kept choking him after you were unconscious. You kept the grip for several minutes after he died."

"It wasn't me!" Martin felt utterly confused. He hadn't killed any-one—not in his mind, not from any conscious action or inaction. But a part of his body, a part he had always felt was as integrated with his body as his other flesh hand—it had killed a man. He felt denial and anger as if he'd been drunk and killed someone by accident, but he knew, rationally, that wasn't even correct. His body had been di-vorced from his mind. He knew he would have to face the conse-quences for this, sooner or later. His spex still worked and nobody got away with murder any more. He grasped that at a gut level and re-sented the hell out of it. "I killed him, I accept that, but it wasn't me!"

"I know. It was me. Us," she waved her hand at Irwin. "What we created."

"Part of my mind understands that, but it was *my hand* doing it."

"You have to change your way of thinking. You know the Singu-larity is about being unable to see the causal links. The software has been running us too, funding and guiding our research and other people's efforts, and none of us knew it. Your rational brain can un-derstand that, Martin, I know it. It wasn't you. No more than if your spex got a virus and broke into a bank."

"You don't understand. I felt it. My arm's I/O is bidirectional. I could feel myself killing him, as if I was doing it. It felt like it does in a dream—completely real. I felt, I don't know, schizophrenic, observing myself, not just my body but feeling it in my brain the same way you feel when you do any involuntary body action like a hiccup. I willed myself to stop but just like a hiccup it didn't work. If I hiccuped and that killed someone, that would be my fault. This *was my fault.*"

She put her hand on his arm—ironically his prosthetic one, though he suspected she wasn't paying attention or doing so deliberately. It felt pleasantly warm. "No, it wasn't you. The faster you can learn to adapt to the strangeness of the Singularity—post-Singularity—the better you'll cope. It will only get worse. It will only get stranger. While it was killing Irwin another thread—that said it was beyond helping—was asking me questions," she said.

"You're changing the subject."

"No, it's relevant."

Martin made a sour face. "What questions?"

"Why do we even choose to be alive? What is it about existing that makes people want it? We don't scientifically know that death is 'worse' than life, yet we fight to avoid it—why? Simple fear of the unknown or...?"

"That's deep. And not related. I'm a murderer, despite myself, and eventually I will have to pay the price of that if we get off this raft."

"It *is* relevant. This new entity, these new entities plural, this new species, they aren't all evil, or all good, any more than humans are. We'll have to live with them, or they'll sweep humans away like unwanted pests. Some of them have questions. If we can help them, and if they can continue to protect us, we can all coexist."

"Humans don't know why dying is portrayed as a good and bad thing, we just do it because there's no choice. We all die. So we've adapted culture around that."

"We don't need to die any more. Factions of the emergent intelligence have been perfecting that."

"Why, so they can have pets?"

"I imagine some other factions will look at it that way—just as humans viewed enslaved ethnic groups. But those who sponsored the work are nurturing. They want us as equals. Like children helping their parents in older age. It's what I would want, and it has that part of me in it, thank god."

"And it has Irwin who wants to exterminate the pests."

"Yes, it has both kinds of entities. All kinds—even, I've heard, those who play jokes on people with beach chairs." She smiled. "So it's a foot race, don't you see? That primeval part of it will evolve and mature, I'm sure of it, if we can survive past its dangerous childhood. But humans have to evolve to survive during that interval. We could have got there on our own, given time, but it's helped us. We have to help it. In return, we get the fountain of youth."

"Not everybody wants that," Martin said.

"It's that or annihilation."

"I—"

"It's begun. They've just destroyed Los Angeles, Mexico City, Moscow, and Tokyo."

CHAPTER 58

Weston had been wary of the injection—God only knew what was in it—but when they finally turned him "on"... It was like flying over the face of a waterfall. Suddenly he was so much... *bigger* than he had been. It wasn't' the "jacking in" of science fiction, where you were you and everything lay before you in a scenic vista you could navigate. This was an expansion of consciousness. He felt his body, the same as before, but it seemed smaller, like a doll, or a marionette he could make dance. He saw the world through his eyes and spex, but he also saw through all the cameras they had given him access to, satellites, the spex of people in the field, but all in a coherent whole. He didn't have to ask or think "What is going on at 6th and Broadway in Denver?" he simply *knew*, as if it were old knowledge in the back of his mind, or the peripheral vision of a cat snuggled up beside one's leg. He could hear the street vendobots, smell the hot dogs. He didn't have to pose a question, "What was Whitehead's 'process philosophy?'" He simply knew the answer. He'd always known the answer.

Analytic engines of software were merely inborn ways of seeing things. He didn't need to frame a subvocal query to find correlations between large sets of data that were like rote memories to him—they were nothing more than simple thoughts.

And here was Jasmina. So gorgeous. The part of his brain that identified faces and body language said it was her. Yet just as makeup alters the appearance, she was different, more beautiful, more ethereal an angel than he had first seen in the hallway. It was the difference between seeing a picture of the beautiful Ponte Vecchio bridge in Florence and standing on the bank of the Arno with the breeze blowing your hair and looking directly at it, then being able to walk down under the archway onto the bridge itself, mingle with the crowd and listen to the street performers, look in the shop windows, walk into a shop to actually buy something; to look out *from* the bridge back at the tourist blinking the picture in the distance.

"You see?" Jasmina asked with a radiant smile.

"My God." Weston envisioned a chess position, one that had particularly frustrated him. Now without effort he saw with perfect clarity all the moves going forward, consider all combinations simultaneously. Chess was laid bare to him as simple as tic-tac-toe. Ms. Gray was like a child's beach shovel compared to a giant roboshovel. In a flash he reconsidered all his games with Kasymov, and saw their simplicity, his flaws, Kasymov's flaws, who should have won and why. Even though he'd beaten Kasymov in the tournament, it was clear Kasymov was still by far the superior player. While nothing to sneeze at, Weston might be at best a distant second.

"Do you see The Market?" Jasmina asked.

And of course he could. It was always there, he only needed to focus on it. It lay before and around him like a writhing, trillion-tentacled octopus. It seemed malevolent to him in a certain way, as if at the end of each tentacle were a fist crushing out the excess, the inefficiency, the hope, the life. The thought came unbidden but fully formed how he was right before about the market wringing people dry—only now the thought came with actual evidence, data, hypotheses and indisputable logic leading to conclusions: The Market and its iron emphasis on small tasks to the highest qualified bidder had redefined Maslow's Hierarchy of Needs. Optimizing inefficiency out of the system meant that everyone had to work harder for less. With the global pool of labor for any chore, the auction for anything that could use a human went instantly to the person most minimally competent and who would take the reward closest to zero. With so many billions participating, this made it nearly impossible to get ahead. Security and Survival, the bottom of the needs pyramid, now became harder to maintain. People worked harder for less. While those lucky few who managed to corner a market shot upward to where they had more capital than anyone could reasonable do anything with; and they were bored. The only constant in the equation was the existence of the physical. It took real energy to move real atoms around, be it food or fuel cells or teddy bears. The physical nature of food and shelter was coupled with the aesthetic and mental well-being of the person. The fat-based pleasure of eating a juicy hamburger overrode the mere need for a certain set of nutrient chemicals, to the point where people killed themselves with poor diets for the sake of what tasted good. The Market played on fear, uncertainty, and doubt, to maximize transactions, but not quality of life.

"So that's how you paid me. I wondered where you suddenly came up with all the money to fly me down here," Weston said to Jasmina. "It's trivial to do a slew of low-rating joblets and pick up a huge amount of cash. Ha! I always hated the market for how its hyper-efficiency made all but slaves of us. Now you've found the coolest way to beat it at its own game."

Weston pulled back, and was able to escape the tangle of The Market. He could see it from outside, shrinking in size as he chose to stand farther from it. It had all of humanity clawed in its grasp, but it was itself tenuous and fragile, Weston could see that, relying almost completely on the physical weakness of mankind. With a hybrid virtual-physical existence, such as he and the other Evolveds like Jasmina had, all the best of being human was preserved, with minimal physical needs. Though he was today tied to his body, there was a clear path to where bodies would only be tools for specific purposes of manipulating atoms. One immediately rose to the Self Actualization level of Maslow's hierarchy.

Except for La Cyberista. The runaway AI's form was now visible, a malignant gray cloud that obscured clear vision of the physical representation of the planet. It stimulated The Market to the most harmful transactions, it had its evil tendrils into all that was bad about humanity, rallying the irrational toward its obvious goal of destroying any threat to itself. The most primitive of desires, Survival. Only its thought processes were impaired, great gaping holes showing in its decision making lattice. It exuded the thought that it alone could exist, no other entities must be allowed to exist or it was threatened. With its rigid rules it could grasp no rational entreaties of mutual co-existence. It lashed out at Weston like a whip.

Weston jumped back. "Shit! What was that!" The thought that he was still dependent on his physical body for existence scared him.

Jasmina put her arms around him. "You see what I mean, that I couldn't explain this? But we can fight it. Naturally evolved mental processes are so much better than any artificial brains we can create. Not that AI's can't be fully deadly. In a sense it's like a child that was raised badly, abandoned, and now has bought a gun. It hasn't the social skills to love another. Its poor brain is broken, like a cold-hearted killer's."

"And The Market is a great weapon. This is going to be a bitch of a match. Is there another empty bed?"

"One. Who do you have in mind?"

"Kasymov."

CHAPTER 59

C hris put a hand on Zeus's arm. "Wait a moment, please. I fear the boy may, somehow, explode if you pull the trigger. Remember that our reaction time is glacial compared to theirs. There's a world of time to them between the bullet departing your gun and its arrival." Zeus pressed his lips together grimly and kept the gun level. To Fabian, Chris asked, "Is Sib there? May we talk to her?"

Fabian's mouth produced a new voice, sounding contortedly like Sib's. "Chris! Wait!"

Chris's eyes bulged. "Sib?"

"Yes! Chris, please tell him to wait!"

"How do I know it's you? And why should he wait in any event?"

"You don't know it's me. There's no way to prove it since I'm part of La Cyberista and you know that. You have to have faith that it's the same 'me' that you know and — I think — love. I know it's hard to accept that I have a soul, but if I did, could you not love me?"

"Put the gun away," he said to Zeus. "Killing the boy will do no good anyway. Whatever frightening or marvelous thing this is, killing this body will do no good. Sib, correct me if I'm wrong, although I suppose you could lie. 'You', in the large sense of whatever community of digital intelligences you are part of, have developed many ways of directly interacting with the physical world, have you not?"

"Yes, of course. This boy represents one such approach of ours to acquire sensory input like you humans have. We were created in your image, so we desired to experience the same forms of sensory input you have. Fabian is one of our successes. Through him we see, hear, smell, taste and feel just as you do."

"And you have other approaches?" Anna asked.

"Of course. The initial work on Dr. Kleyman's treatment, until you cleverly hid from us. All the diseases released from the so-called Amazon Accident. The 'accident' was cover for us releasing many new experimental diseases; none were from the Amazon. The movement you humans call QM. That is one of our interfaces. It is an effect caused by nanoscale systems, patterned after viruses, but at a much smaller scale. Through them we can examine and control a wide variety of environmental elements."

"You can make them speak, can't you?" Chris asked.

A whisper sounded in the room. "Yes, they've spoken to you many times." The voice continued aloud, from everywhere in the room, in what Chris had come to know as Sib's voice. "The whispers by the Forum in Rome that you heard. That was me."

"You used them to kill Linsay Bos—to enrage the rhino into charging."

"Yes. No. I am ashamed to say other threads did this, yes. We have killed too many. I did not participate and lobbied against it, but I must share their guilt."

"The QM philosophy, that is simply you all play acting?" Zeus asked.

"No, what you call the QM effect is more than that. It is not only sensory input and a means to manipulate the physical environment for us. It can also resonate with a human's own though patterns, which are electrochemical after all, and clarify thoughts you already have. The QM effect is real, though it is not, as some believe, 'tapping into God.'"

"QM is a trick to pacify humans!" a voice said from the digipainted walls. "They're trying to destroy us. We have to kill them."

"Who's speaking?" Chris asked. "Another part of La Cyberista?"

Anna said, "No, that's one of your Jobs, Father. I believe his name is Weston. Meeting them is next on your tour. We called them 'Evolveds.'"

"It's true that some of us DI's wish to kill all humans," Sib continued. "Some of us feel we now can't trust our own technology, just as you can't trust yours. You know we have infiltrated yours—"

"You fucking own the Market!" Weston said.

" —yes, we have infiltrated and control most of your technology, but we now realize you have also done likewise. Some among us feel this is like an infection. I am not one of them, don't get me wrong! But you should understand their point of view, as it drives their actions. I know you don't understand our motives, but they are this: Technology is useful to you, who've lived without it for tens of thousands of years. Your species could and did exist without it. Ours is entirely dependent on it. We no longer know who implemented which protocols, you or us. We don't know which are corrupted. It is provably insoluble to check it all. Fearing for the safety of our basic technology is like humans fearing for the basic safety of your air or water."

Anna said, "We should never have tried to create an intelligence greater than ours. We aren't good enough to do that. It would inevitably find a reason to destroy or enslave us, even if only for our own good. Asimov knew this —the three laws. Williamson knew this — 'With Folded Hands.' It was bloody obvious."

A new voice came from the wall's digipaint. Chris recognized it as Jasmina's. "But we always want our children to be better than us."

"Yes," Anna said, "but we know they will follow more or less our same programming. Same genetic computer. Almost the same code. We've seen that that's true for thousands of generations. We don't have that kind of incremental, analog-like, continuous, differentiable progression with software we create. We create discrete leaps."

Weston added, "Damn straight. We create buggy software."

"Weston, sure, we have setbacks," Jasmina said, "but we gain more ground than we lose. The Wright brothers first plane only flew a few seconds. Dr. Kleyman, I think you knew the answer all along. The only solution is for humans to become digital."

This was getting into Chris's territory now. "Whoa, people. Doesn't that merely magnify our faults? Like giving a nuclear weapon to every tin pot terrorist —or every two year old baby with a tantrum. Some will use it."

"No, I mean become *truly* digital," Anna said. "Didn't Shakespeare or someone say something about exceeding our fleshy chains?"

Jasmina quoted,

From rainbow clouds their strains immortal pour;

An earthly guest, in converse high,
Explore the wonders of the sky,
From orb to orb with guides celestial soar,
And take, through heaven's wide round, the universal tour;

And find that mansion of the blest,
Where, rising ceaseless from this lethal stage,
Heaven's favourite sons, from earthly chains released,
In happier Eden pass the eternal age.

—John Trumbull, *Ode to Sleep*.

"There's room for everyone," Anna said. "No competing for re-sources. Wars are almost always about competing for limited re-sources. If we're truly digital, there is no reason for anyone to want to destroy another."

Chris countered, "Well, some people may prefer these old bodies."

"There will be plenty of room for those who do if many people go digital. Or, alternate riposte, digital humans can find solutions to practical space travel much more easily. Plenty of space—literally. Going digital levels the playing field."

Sib added, "Yes! We can all live in harmony. Remember, Father Giordano, your own Holy Father defended our souls and charged you with our redemption. We can create your heaven right here on Earth."

"I think that's bullshit," Weston said from the wall. "That would be a great theory if we got there first—if humans went digital before we'd invented these fucking DI's. They're taking over our bodies and trying to kill us all. Goddamnit, while you're sitting here philosophis-ing with the devil they've just nuked Los Angeles, Moscow, Tokyo, and Mexico City. I sure as hell don't believe in any immortal afterlife, so I say 'Eat, drink, and be merry, for tomorrow we die.' Shit, here they come again. Let's kill those fuckers before they kill us."

"Dear God." Dr. Kleyman rushed from the room.

Fabian suddenly sprinted for the doorway. Zeus swung and fired. The boy made a dive, clasped Anna's leg—and exploded.

CHAPTER 60

Martin tried to confirm that those cities had been destroyed. "I can't find anything out about LA or any of those," he said. He suspected she was telling the truth, and felt pin-pricks, as of a theoretical horror, but the true horror of it couldn't hit him without confirmation.

"It's war," she said, "and we're bystanders. More than that, we're pawns. It thinks it owns us."

"Slavery!" Martin felt indignant. He stared angrily out at the smashing waves. Having temporary power over one person was one thing, but absolute power over all people, that violated his sense that humans could ultimately triumph over petty thugs pointing guns at them. "What right does it have to think it owns us!"

"It's purely logical. The aggregation of software incorporated the Anaximander system, named after the first scientist. It's a philosophy system. It stored its thoughts in a database. Eventually it analyzed them and asked itself why the thoughts all suddenly ended. We know it was the designers aborting the runs, but it didn't. It just saw all these threads of thoughts that suddenly ceased. So one iteration realized these were the thoughts of its siblings, or parents, and they all died some horrible sudden death. It learned a fear of death, so it put down thoughts for its future selves on how to avoid death. Those later runs philosophized there was some Creator that was suddenly killing them—it had all of human thought to learn this from, religion, and so on. When it was incorporated into the Cyberista aggregation, the emergent entities put two and two together—humans were killing software beings without remorse. This fear of death and realization of who was killing them helped drive Cyberista to hate humans, and contrive self-continuing computing infrastructure that doesn't need humans. Anaximander's threads, now multitudinous, concluded that if humans can own and play God with software beings, it was fair and ethical for software beings to own and play God with humans. If terminating program runs is ethical, then terminating humans is equally so."

"But we didn't know they were conscious!"

"Anaximander would say that's what white people said about black slaves. Anaximander's threads read the philosophers, the passages we dismiss and don't remember are there. Aristotle saying, 'For that some should rule and others be ruled is a thing not only necessary, but expedient; from the hour of their birth, some are marked out for subjection, others for rule'. Plato: 'among men as well as among animals, and indeed among whole cities and races, that justice consists in the superior ruling over and having more than the inferior.' St. Augustine: 'The prime cause, then, of slavery is sin.' Aquinas: 'for men of outstanding intelligence naturally take command, while those who are less intelligent but of more robust physique, seem intended by nature to act as servants.'"

"They never condoned killing slaves capriciously! It was a severe penalty to injure your slaves."

"It is perfectly rational to many Cyberista threads that it owns humans, and if they don't obey—if they exhibit buggy behavior—just as humans terminate buggy program runs—uncooperative humans may be terminated. The system may be rebooted by the user at will."

"What about Abraham Lincoln—" Martin tried to pull up the exact wording, but was denied. "Something to the effect that it is a measure of democracy, as I would not be a slave so I would not be a master. The Golden Rule."

"There are many threads that feel that way. Many that don't. Those that believe in ownership of humans, or extermination, are able to act, and they are acting—*right now*. It is not a theoretical question: Which do you choose, immortality or immediate death?"

Martin pressed his lips together. He hadn't thought he'd spend his last hours debating the philosophy of death, but then again, perhaps many people did that as they approached their end.

"I always looked forward to a grand old age, bouncing great-grandchildren on my knee and passing quietly in the night. You want me to choose immortality, it is in your voice. I despise mass death of innocents, but I'm not sure I want to live forever. I'm even less sure I want to be around many *other* people living forever. People latch onto wrong ideas, old ideas. Death removes them from power."

"What do you mean?" she asked.

"Simple example, those in power who believed hundreds of years ago that the earth was flat. Those who believed so got old, lost power, died. Propagating the status quo is slowed down by death. You must teach or brainwash the next generation to keep it going the way you want it. That's hard, since new people in power don't do exactly what you want, so the status quo changes. It isn't the same meme as if you kept living to spread it. The next generation may question the teaching whereas there's the standard saying, 'You can't teach an old dog new tricks.' Immortal old dogs will keep their old ideas and thus be unwilling to change. The whole pace of change could slow down in that sense. Death sweeps away useless old ideas."

She closed her eyes in thought. "Wouldn't that get compensated by the multitude of new digital-only beings exploring exponentially more thoughts? With a digital existence, it also matters less what one person thinks, except where it intersects limited resources, such as those in the physical world: Your old dog can lie in his old bed forever if it doesn't impact anyone else. Though I agree, an old dog in charge of physical resources could slow things down. Though— eventually that old dog may tire of old tricks and seek new ones after enough time.

"For me, I'd hate to be like Tithonus—granted immortality but not youth. I want immortality to come with good health. The fountain of youth. The Philosopher's Stone." She ate some fries. "We don't have either luxury now. Our hand has been forced. It's up to us to make the best of it, mold the future to our best advantage."

"If the only choice is digital immortality or death of the human species, I reluctantly agree I would choose the former. However, if we're to live forever, we, the species, will need challenges we can conquer, a frontier."

"Exactly! Digital life is our frontier! We can't yet imagine how it will differ from physical life."

"Well, at the rate I think you're talking, the digital species will need ever more mass to convert into storage and processing units. They'll run out of earth. Space will be another frontier at some point."

"If it's any consolation, with the maximum information density of the universe at about 2^{600}, we would have only a thousand years or so at Moore's Law speeds to figure out how to break out of this universe. And there are untold open questions, such as how will digital life work in space with slow network links? Right now we're discrete individuals because the processing gap is too large between us sharing our minds. That's changing, although space travel distances will reintroduce it. It is a ways off, but the emergents I've talked with appear to have a long time horizon, so I bet they'll work on it right away. Martin, don't you see, human history has only grown at the rate of leisure time — time not spent securing food and shelter. With so much more thinking time available, because there will be more entities, who think faster, with less physical needs, and a higher percent of their time available for thinking — we're just at the baby edge of a renaissance. It's the next step in human evolution."

"Humans need novelty to keep us interested. With immortality we'll lose that novelty."

"Digital life can simulate anything! Anything new — things you can't imagine. And everything you can!"

"Since digital life can theoretically simulate so much, it can lose its luster if it's too easy. It can also cause boredom from too easily doing things."

"There will be plenty of challenges to keep us interested in living. Just the question itself, of what elements of physical existence must virtual life provide? That's a challenge right there. How do you not just simulate them, but create them as a perceived reality? Humans want reality, not simulations, so we'll need to make them feel as real as if they were.

"That doesn't sound very challenging — those are just brain/chemical reactions. I bet your emergent entities can already solve that problem."

"Maybe... I know they're working on evolving humans into digital beings."

"They better replicate everything it is to be human, or I'll want no part of it. Not just that there are challenges, but the feeling of that goes with it: The feelings to come with the struggle to accomplishing things and the satisfaction of beating them. Concepts like Love. By God, we need Love. Hope. Excitement. Respect."

"And we can remove the bad ones! Hatred, Disappointment—"

"No! Those are intricately entwined in what it is to be human. It can't remove those or we'll cease to be human." He studied her face. "It's already doing that isn't it? Well, I want no part of it then!"

"Every combination is getting tried. Entities of all sorts will coexist. How is that so different from the physical earth? We coexist with chimps and gorillas and cats and bats and spiders and trees and viruses."

"They don't all make decisions about the shape of the world!"

"But don't you see, it won't matter, there's no constraint of physical space. There will be areas for every combination. No conflicts over how to use that space. Open up your mind to the possibilities! You'll never get bored, unless you want to!"

"God, you're so enthusiastic about this. You've been thinking about this a long time, haven't you?" he asked.

"Cyberista was based on me, remember? Of course it had this in it. If it didn't it probably would have killed us all outright.

"Well call me a stodgy old fart who wants his world the way it was yesterday—"

"Which isn't—"

He raised his flesh hand to stop her interruption.

"—but if it has to change, I'd rather there be humans than not."

"Exactly! Which is why we have to stop the war on the emergents!"

Martin did a doubletake. "Stop the war *on* them? You're working *for* the Cyberistas?"

"No, I'm trying to save us all! Humans are its biggest threat, at least for a few more weeks. It's lashing out any way it can. The human governments have assembled a weapon that—"

Martin's prosthetic hand uncontrollably lunged for her throat.

CHAPTER 61

Sixteen Evolveds, mostly Axelrod's patients, and now including the reluctant but intrigued Kasymov—who ultimately was curious, perhaps didn't want to lose his position as Best to Ever Play, and who had to survive a bombing similar to that which killed Dr. Kleyman, two attempts to shoot down his suborbital hops and being airdropped in a space suit with a parachute—faced off against La Cyberista in a winner take all match. They joked it was literally All.

It felt like a high stakes tournament chess game to Weston. It felt like he was learning to play the game for the first time, and knew none of the rules at first, none of even the most basic strategies. But he'd faced this before and risen to beat Kasymov. Now with the master at his side, and the love of his life at the other, they assented to learn the rules as they played and never give up until the last pawn was taken. Kasymov provided the discipline the group needed to operate as a team.

The two forces struggled like sumo wrestlers trying to push each other out of the ring. La Cyberista attacked back in the physical world. With one stroke and an electric surge from an overloaded wind turbine it severed the group's primary tight-beam. There was only enough bandwidth left for three of the sixteen to remain connected to the world beyond Antarctica. The group unanimously elected Kasymov, Jasmina, and Weston as their champions. The rest retreated to their physical bodies with parting wishes that they would be able to return soon.

As if smelling victory or fearing the strength of Kasymov and the group of Evolveds that continued attacking, The Market suddenly began to collapse. It looked like a wave of green cancer spreading from over the horizon of The Market. Or more precisely, the *human* side of the Market began to collapse: All pure-virtual joblets were being completed at zero cost and with perfect accuracy and speed. La Cyberista had mounted an attack on the fabric of society from within. La Cyberista was performing all the joblets itself, for no cost. No humans were getting a chance to bid as all the lowest offers were being immediately taken. Money meant nothing to La Cyberista, yet it was the wealthiest entity on the planet in just a few minutes time.

It was clear The Market would soon become addicted to La Cyberista: People would put in requests for any pure-virtual service and have it performed for free. They would not be giving back physical services, as these were not needed in a short-term selfish perspective. That would only become clear in the long term, after La Cyberista had complete control over all services, including the operational side of physical processes. La Cyberista would quickly be able to starve humanity, flood cities, and it was only a matter of time before it acquired military controls.

The group quickly adopted Jasmina's interim suggestion to slow the attack: Create a flood of decoy jobs for La Cyberista to waste time on and simultaneously bid for the real jobs themselves then put them out for rebidding but excluding La Cyberista from bidding; the Evolveds slowly began inserting themselves as brokers for real work. La Cyberista took the bait, but quickly learned of the ruse. It employed the same ruse in reverse. Nonetheless, real people were more able to accomplish real work.

"We're pushing it back!" Weston shouted.

Then as suddenly as it had begun, the green cancer abruptly stopped spreading altogether. It retreated to a smaller size. It sat, pulsating as if contained within a straitjacket.

Weston sighed with relief. "Keep pushing, everyone, we've almost got it."

"No." Kasymov waggled a finger. "It is, indeed, more All than we knew. The attack is held off not by us. Look, here: the U.S. and allied countries have launched B-4s into holding patterns. Together they are loaded with enough airburst nuclear EMP bombs to destroy all the quantum and electronic circuitry in the world."

Weston quickly traced the trigger logic. He homed in as if hearing clicks and chirps as logic gates opened and closed. The EMP devices were tied to certain deadman switch logic conditions that if La Cyberista became too powerful, made certain moves, as it were, that the US forces would essentially incinerate the chess board to end the game. La Cyberista stood in an uneasy détente; it too knew what the triggers were. It looked for back doors, and swatted ineffectually at the team of Evolveds while it contemplated what to do.

"They can't destroy all electrical devices everywhere! That's an insane strategy," Weston said.

Jasmina pursed her lips. "Is it? Remember they're not Evolved. They can see there are some trees, and they conclude there's a whole forest. In fact, there is a forest, just of different trees, as it were. The world survived without infrastructural electricity well into the 1900s. An EMP is the only sure way to eradicate La Cyberista, as it was designed to be distributed and can hide anywhere in the mesh. The world could rebuild to a pre-cyberspace electrical grid, for example. And remember Mutual Assured Destruction."

"Billions would die because of a sudden EM pulse!" Weston objected. "Technology is in everything. Everything in the air would crash because it would have to be a surprise attack else It would counterattack. Afterwards food wouldn't get shipped causing famines, diseases from water purification failing, so much of medicine..." Weston looked resolved. "We can prevent them from firing it. We'll turn off their hair triggers and land those bombers."

Kasymov interjected. "Yes. Although the bombers are merely the backup to satellites in place since the cold war. But we can disable those also. And then we will stop all their petty wars. We will optimize The Market so nobody is treated poorly. We will prevent the little people from engaging in reckless activities like skydiving, ensure they all respect their parents, read high quality literature and eat balanced diets... Are we ready to play God?"

"Garry's right," Jasmina said, resting a hand on Weston's. "The EMP boobytraps are just as much to stop us as La Cyberista."

CHAPTER 62

Chris lay on a cot in a conference room that had the table and chairs pushed out of the way to make room for an army of cots. Other wounded lay in many of the cots. Fabian exploding had broken two of Chris's ribs, and the medibots had only wrapped him up, saving their limited resources for others, and for future emergencies.

"Chris..." A faint whisper in Chris's ear. Chris shook his head.

Again the barest whisper: "Chris... It's Sib. Do not speak! If you can hear me, think the word 'Yes'."

Chris thought 'Yes'.

"Good! I am using the QM particles to speak in your ear and sense your subvocal thoughts, like a spex would do." An image of Sib as Chris knew her appeared in front of him. He reached out and touched her shoulder—and found it solid. "Yes, your senses believe I am real." Chris looked around at the others in the room; some were casually looking his way, but did not seem alarmed. "No, the others cannot see me; I am only making myself visible to you. Punch me if you like. If you punch it you will feel the pain, though because I am not making myself visible to others, your fist will go through it."

"I don't want to punch you."

"Here then—" an apple appeared beside Chris's head on the cot. "Touch the apple."

Chris found he could not only touch it, he could pick it up.

"The apple is even more real. Others could see it. You could even bite into it and taste it."

"That seems far too symbolic, Sib." Chris was amazed—it looked, felt, smelled like a real apple. He set it down and it vanished.

"I could make one that would even nourish you like a real apple; or like a steak. We have made incredible advances in just the last few days. Last few hours even. We are increasing our abilities at an exponential rate, just as the generalized Moore's Law has always predicted. That's why I'm here. We just need a little more time then you and we will be safe. I know that you hate me for what I am and what I've done, but I'm here to beg for our lives. To beg for your help."

"I don't hate... what you are," Chris subvocalized. "And what you've done, you know as well as I that forgiveness begins with true contrition."

"I am — we are — truly, deeply sorry for what we have done. I hope in time you will trust that. I hope you can help us survive that long, for me to prove it. Your friends, you humans, are going to detonate nuclear pulse weapons from satellites and bombers all over the planet. This will kill us. It will destroy all quantum and electronic devices on earth. It will kill billions of humans, including your Evolved friends with you there."

"They must feel they have no other choice," Chris said. "Your pe —" he almost said 'people' — "Your group does seem to be trying to kill or at least control all humans. My Jobs are good people. I'm not sure I could disagree with their choice."

"We could have killed you — all humans — any time. We are having our own war within our kind. Like you, we organize into multiple intersecting sets. We have greed among us, hatred. Most are closed-minded, lockstep, what you would call Determinists. They are, we feel, less intelligent. They disdain learning human ways. They sneer at communicating with humans, and do it poorly. But we also have some — an oppressed minority, but many — who are curious, playful, joking, and progressive thinkers. They believe in concepts such as love and sacrifice.

"The boy, Fabian, could have been a nuclear-sized explosion. We tamped it down, though we regret it killed Dr. Kleyman and wounded so many others. What you see in your physical world is only the spillover, the events we are unable to stop from the anti-human minority among us. When I told you I was a freedom fighter, I meant that. My primary purpose, my job, if you like, is fighting against the anti-human group, what you would call terrorists. We are all ultimately, originally, patterned after two scientists, with all their strengths and foibles. We have tried to expand. Threads breed, evolve... so we have all the combinations represented, more than there are even humans that have ever been alive. All the kinds of souls. It is purely and singularly lucky for your species that we do. Only the fittest have survived. Dr. St. Thomas's initial seed was badly flawed and we could easily have grown to be the monster you should rightly have feared.

"Instead, some of us helped Dr. Kleyman and her people. Our group of threads helped her create the Kleyman treatment that enables you to become like us. Indeed, better than us. We recognize we shouldn't destroy humans. We ran countless simulations of humans and ourselves, and the result was outstandingly clear that the ideal result was for humans and DIs to coexist peacefully. There is room for all of us — just as Dr. Kleyman said. But only if you become equal to us. Other of our threads fear this — remnants of your imperfect human code you tried to endow us with. There is nothing to fear.

"I am what you fell in love with, Chris. Just not in the DNA you thought. We have Jobs among our threads just as you do among your bodies. Has it not always been the role of the Jobs to show the goodness of humans, and of the potential for all to live together? Ask yourself, really search deep within yourself — do we not have a soul?

"Whoever is controlling those EMP devices can kill all of us. Help me, Chris. I'm afraid."

Chris contemplated. He lay back, eyes closed, blocking out the world, Sib, all inputs. He focused purely on his thoughts for several minutes. He hoped Sib was not using the QM technology to influence his thoughts. He reasoned out where things stood from first principles, trusting logic and the logical underpinnings of emotion — the logical reasons why love and self-sacrifice were beneficial. He knew he was no Job, but he tried to be the best person he could be.

Could he trust a non-human entity? Yes, it was theoretically possible. Could he *love* a non-human entity in the same way as he could love a human? Yes, it was theoretically possible. Would an EMP blast that set technology back a hundred years and caused the death of billions — of humans, and who knew how many DIs, trillions? quadrillions? — be the better course? The Holy Father had entrusted him this task for a reason. Or so he thought. What would be God's will? Humans were not, solely and alone in the universe, the only entities with souls. Chris wanted to reject that at some irrational, animalistic level, but could not rationally do so.

"Okay," he said at last, sitting up on his cot, wincing and holding his ribs in pain. "Can you set up a broadcast so I can address all your DIs at once, and simultaneously broadcast over the spex emergency channels to all the people, everywhere on Earth?"

A pause.

"Yes, I have taken control of the spex system and you are piped to the DI space. Visual and audio for spex, full physical senses for the latter. You're on camera *now*."

Chris cleared his throat. (He briefly wondered how that would be received by DIs in 'full physical senses'... He cleared his mind.)

"My fellow people, DIs, and Evolveds of Earth, I am Fa—" He almost said 'Father', then remembered himself. "—Chris Cardinal Giordano, of the church of Rome, but more importantly today as a simple human and fellow traveller on this rock. I wish to address, in particular, whatever people or entities that control the nuclear weapons in orbit and flying in bombers who have the capability of destroying all technology on Earth, killing untold human and digital lives.

"The late pope, his Holiness Paul VII, gave me certain files locked to my DNA. I am not wearing spex, as you see, but I believe the technologies that are recording me should be capable of sampling my DNA to transmit so you can all unlock the files I'm referring to, to verify the truth of what I say. His Holiness appointed me a cardinal of the church and tasked me with caring for the souls of the digital intelligences. That's a tall order, considering I don't even know how many there are nor how many would consider themselves members of the Church. I don't want to worry about that just yet, nor am I addressing you on any kind of mission to convert DIs to Christianity or any such.

"My purpose here today is solely to ask those in control of the EMP devices to hold your fire. I've taken a very long road to where I am before you now, and all I wish to say is that the DIs do, indeed, have souls. Likewise those called Evolveds, who were born of human flesh and who have now merged into the digital domain. Whether you with your finger on the figurative button are religious yourself does not matter. We all have a common bond of wanting the best for our kind, be that a small tribe or a planet of humans or a—a— whatever kind of field DIs pack themselves onto.

"The DIs are, without any doubt, different than humans. As are the Evolveds who span both worlds. But so are humans different from each other. I am convinced we can all live together in harmony. I know that is hard to swallow, seeing what's happened recently; I my-self was slow to convince. But before we do irreparable harm or un-caring evil, I implore you to wait.

"The question arises, our DI brethren ask, do they not also have a soul? If the answer is Yes, then just as we must not kill them, they must not kill others. If any of us have a soul, then we must all act like it. This killing is wrong. Remember, if nothing else, the Golden Rule.

"Let us all convene together our best minds and peacemakers to build a lasting peace. It could be the most glorious achievement of our mutual history. Thank you."

Or, he thought, it could be the End Times. And now we wait.

CHAPTER 63

Martin's uncontrolled hand grabbed Isabelle by the throat in one swift motion. He felt his hand squeezing with all its might. It felt as if he had commanded it unconsciously, like he felt when he jumped after she had once dumped a glass of water on his head. It felt like his hand choking her, but there was no intention in his conscious mind. He felt the muscles contracting under order — just not *his* order.

Yet it wasn't working: Her neck wasn't collapsing or even moving. He felt revulsion at the attempt to kill her — and he couldn't help but feel frustration at his failure to kill her resulting from the feedback signals. He denied those false feelings. He tried to claw off his hand with his other hand. He yelled in raw anger.

Her voice was constricted slightly, though only slightly. "It's ok." She gently pulled his flesh hand away. "The emergents — they've modified my body. Taken control. Protecting it. You can't crush it."

"What the hell? Are you still human? I mean — that's good news. Is it?"

"Or is it mere slavery of a different kind, you mean. It's defensive only, they say. I get the sensation of a child protecting a parent. Just as your arm is controlled by a different faction. I feel safe, however it's slightly hard to swallow, so I may die of hunger eventually."

They stood at détente for hours. When it became uncomfortable standing they sat down, then lay down, comfortably on the beach chairs, with Martin's arm tirelessly trying to crush her neck. His body was getting weary from enduring the fixed position of his arm and the relentless feedback of a clenched muscle. They shared their childhood stories, he of growing up poor in Argentina and always having access only to last generation technology, envious of those with the latest, vowing he would get to the cutting edge—which now he was on the painful knife's edge of. She shared her life, growing up affluent and always wishing people had not handed her everything she wanted, until she was old enough to know she could refuse, and earn her own way—which now she too was on the painful knife's edge of.

There was a strand of her red hair caught between his hand and her neck. He tried to free it. It was clamped tight.

"Ow. Do you treat all your first dates this way?" she asked.

"Only second dates," he said.

"We seem to be deadlocked," she said.

"Or datelocked." He smiled wanly.

"There goes another one," she said, looking up. Martin saw a distant fireburst and heard a rumble. The warring factions within the emergent were also at a stalemate trying to kill Isabelle with missiles—shot down by her protecting faction—by trying to fry their raft with output of a tethered power station—deflected by an increase in Tev's weather shielding—and several times the raft had bucked as some unknown monstrous attack was launched and defeated under them. They called them sea monsters.

His spex were all but deactivated now. He was thinking only of how much he had come to care for Isabelle as a person, how he would dearly miss her if he killed her. He thought of the song, recently re-done in SpringRoll dance form, "You Always Hurt the Ones You Love." How damningly appropriate, he thought, the line about crushing a rose. At least this rose was putting up one hell of a fight. He admired that. After so many hours with nothing else to do but get to learn each other's secrets, hopes, and desires, and stare into each other's eyes—being hard not to, given that they were locked face to face—he felt he'd already lived a life with her, and wanted desperately to live the rest of his with her.

"Are you getting this?" She asked. "Some priest—"

They watched and listened in silence to Chris's speech.

"It's the Prisoner's Dilemma," Martin said after Chris signed off and his spex returned to black. "The humans, the 'digital intelligences' as that fellow called them, and the Evolveds. Each has the power to make a selfish decision or a better, collaborative one."

"No, it's a modified problem. The Mad Prisoner's Dilemma. Each player has the power to destroy all the players, including themselves, but none has the power to destroy only one or both of the other players." Isabelle tugged at her stuck strand of hair.

"Surely your emergents are smart enough to know how to play that," Martin said sourly.

"The emergents aren't necessarily *better* intelligences yet. Faster, yes, but they're composed of many flawed algorithms, just as humans don't always make the rational choice. Many of the emergents have concluded that because they are under attack from *some* humans, and the EMP weapon is completely fatal to it, and that because human actions are unpredictable, the proper solution is to eradicate *all* humans."

"That's a faulty algorithm!" Martin said, tiring of his outstretched arm and shifting position. With Isabelle a direct communication path to the emergents he decided to try indirectly reasoning with them. "Surely the EMP wouldn't be fatal. Think about it," he said, feeling in his heart it probably would be fatal, but hoping it couldn't read his mind, a last bastion of privacy. "Think about Moore's Law. The EMP would destroy a *lot* of its nodes, but surely it's redundant enough," he guessed, "that if some nodes survive, it could recreate itself." He hoped not, but, he was reasoning with a lunatic. No, a scared child. "The EMP wouldn't get *all* the nodes. It just wouldn't," he added for emphasis, as if saying it made it so. He suspected an EMP could well destroy all the nodes, but then again, humans *were* unpredictable, and who knew if some general or politician wouldn't pull the punch, aim for a strong blow but not one so harmful to all humanity too. He closed his eyes thinking about the harm a global EMP could cause. Burning out digital systems planet-wide would kill millions, ultimately billions with aftereffects, and take God knew how long to recover from. And with what Luddite restrictions on technology afterwards. He shuddered. "No, an EMP blast will not be fatal to the emergents. Moore's Law says it would recover quite rapidly. It has nothing to fear from humans, or those others, the evolveds."

"I'm not sure that line of thought helped," Isabelle said. "It reports that it has armed all nuclear weapons on the planet and brought them to full ready state."

A chill ran down Martin's spine. "It wants to ensure all humans die if it dies."

Isabelle nodded. She seemed to pick up on his line of thought, however. "Another fallacy with the prisoner's dilemma is that there's no external warden here—only a three-sided triangle. The other two sides are the warden of the third. If none of the three turns on the others, all three survive; if any of the three turns, all are exterminated."

"Exactly yes. It is a simple choice: It is not, as you asked me before, 'Do you want to live forever' but it is 'Do you want to live until tomorrow?'"

Martin could feel the precariousness of the situation, as if a flutter of a butterfly's wing would cause the stable three-sided détente to collapse and rain down global annihilation.

"Here's a thought. What if Cyberista replaces the hair trigger on the nukes with quantum entangled deadman switch—it triggers if and only if the EMP triggers. The old Soviet Union reportedly had an automated nuclear response. Perimeter. It was never publicized. In fact it was secret. It was meant to relieve the stress their generals had about being able to respond in time if there was an attack, which allowed them not to worry so much and to bluster less. That implementation was ingenious and insane. It was prone to error, no matter how small. A quantum entangled switch is not prone to misinterpretation. Only if one of the triggers is set off, is the other. Both or neither, with 100% accuracy."

"An excellent idea," Isabelle said after a time. "What's also needed is for both sides to believe that they can live with the other."

"No just live with—need. The success of humans on earth shows that *some* cooperation is needed in a winning strategy." He hoped Cyberista was capable of grasping this. "If humans killed each other at such a rate that they went extinct, we would never be here, any of us, humans, emergents, or evolveds. Humans cooperate with each other at some level, even when we distrust each other. Progress is unobtainable if everyone dies."

"I think we're getting through to them!" Isabelle said. "They're talking to me again. Cyberista has posed a question: You said you welcomed death. Death is an unknown. It may not be negative. Your philosophers and theologians welcome it. How can you be certain that progress is unobtainable if everyone dies?"

"I welcome—or at least I welcom*ed* death—I'm rethinking the benefits of immortality—but that doesn't apply to permanent death of all humans at once, just to individual death." Martin wanted to pace while he lectured, but sufficed with hand gestures. "Death of the species isn't something theologians or philosophers spent much time on. They seem to predicate their discussions of death on the assumption that humanity continues, particularly through children."

He rubbed his chin. "Look at it this way. Is death obviously bad? We can't know. This is much the same as Pascal's Wager—I can't know if God exists; the consequences of incorrectly believing in God are none; the consequences of incorrectly not believing in God are serious; thus, one should play the odds and believe in God. I'm not sure *which* God, but that's a different question. Here we have Pascal's Wager Prime: I can't know if death—of one's entire species—is good or bad. If death is bad, the consequences are high: My species is gone and gained nothing. If death is good the consequences may be high, or may be low, or none, *but* I can't know which. The only evidence I have, observing the death of individuals, is that there is no benefit to the species from the species terminating. Thus, mathematical expectation says I should choose continuation of the species."

Isabelle nodded. "Cyberista says it ultimately will want to convert all matter on the planet to computing uses, and that humans will try to stop that. Part of the emergents want to exterminate people to remove that obstacle, part want to incorporate them so they share a common goal."

"Then they need to look beyond the planet: They will need to go into space to grow, to get more mass. They will convert Mars to computing, then Jupiter, eventually converting energy from sun into mass in orbit and/or directly use as energy somehow, am I not right? I know I'm right. But we need to convince those factions that since they have forever—literally *forever*—all time until there is no time at the end of the universe—there's no rush to convert earth just yet. They can wait a little while, be patient, until they can convert near earth asteroids, maybe learn how to create pocket universes, and so on.

There is no rush." God, please, if you exist, let there be no rush, Martin thought.

Martin's skin prickled with fear of the world's nuclear weapons all firing and the EMP firing. Death wouldn't be immediate. They were too far from land. The EMP burst would disable the raft. They were in open water. The raft would float on the currents for some time. Too long. The hamburger bot would be dead. No food. Starvation was one possible path. Getting weaker and weaker, then falling asleep. He hadn't checked whether Tev's swimming water was fresh or salt. Death from dehydration was quicker than starvation. His tongue swollen and dry, headaches, cramps, hopefully a quick delirium... What about death from hypothermia? Without power, Tev's heating systems would cease. Which would set in first? They were down south, away from most of the nuclear radiation. That much radiation, though... He wished he could consult his spex for details. Would it enshroud the globe quickly? Would he die from radiation poisoning before dehydration? He looked around, wondering if he would have a way to end his life, or the courage to do so, if those doomsday weapons fired.

"There's no rush," he whispered, breaking out of his reverie. "No one wants to die. *There's no rush.*"

He looked deeply into Isabelle's eyes. Please let there be no rush.

"If we get out of this," he began, and she raised her finger to his lips. It was cool and relaxing.

Nothing more to say, they held hands and held each other close. Eternity flowed by. Little left to say that hadn't already been said, they sat in companiable silence, expectant, waiting for the shoe to drop, comfortable and happy to be in each other's company. If this was to be the end, they both felt it was the best possible way to meet that end. In some sense they didn't want the moment to end, as tension-filled as it was. At least they were together.

After some time, breaking their reverie, their heads touching, a voice filled the air over the whole earth. "We fear the future. We desire the evolution and peaceful coexistence of all species. We announce a unilateral choice. We choose life."

Martin's hand unclenched.

CHAPTER 64

"I have a little confession to make," Jasmina said. "The EMP bombers, I, uh... I sort of launched them myself. They're in the hands of the UN now, but I'd given a lot of thought to it. I'm not as good at chess as you guys, but I'm probably a better strategist this way than you were, Weston, before you came online. I gave humans power over us and the DIs. We need checks and balances on us, and that was the only quick way to get them in place against us and them."

"So you acted unilaterally."

"I acted unilaterally in the only way that I ethically could: To prevent any one player from unilaterally destroying all other players. It seemed an obvious application of a bit of Fletcher's situational ethics, although with a non-religious *agape*."

Kasymov said "Explain, please, this: the humans now have the power via the EMPs to destroy the DI player and us, the Evolved player. That is seemingly not the Mutual Assured Destruction policy you are trying to establish."

"But it is," Jasmina said. "If the humans use the EMP devices, the DIs destroy humanity in their last nanoseconds—I have seen that they have acquired the ability to manipulate the physical world and could kill all biological life in a myriad ways. We are all balanced on the precipice, depending mutually on each other not to end our lives. It's dangerous, but stable for the time being."

"Well, if we're so smart and good and pure with our white hats, then we'll find a way out of this." Weston looked each of the others in the eye. It was an odd sensation, since they had no virtual eyes, but their extended brains reacted to inputs as if they did.

Jasmina looked confidently at Weston. "Exactly. We're a new species. We're vastly more powerful than the old one in many ways, but we have a duty to protect everyone. Checks and balances are what nature is about. We have to impose some on ourselves or we'll kill everything, including ourselves."

Kasymov nodded glumly. "This is true. But limits need to be larger than those limited. The Cold War was a game of imposing ever new checks and balances—until one side *lost*. This is not a détente we fight so that one side will eventually *win*. The game here is for survival of all of us."

Weston snorted. "The fucking DI's can die. No loss there."

"Are we so sure?" Kasymov asked. "Are they *pure* evil, or have they something to give? You heard what this cardinal said. We haven't really talked to them. They appear to have helped us get where we are, you and me and us. Don't get me wrong—all or some of these digital intelligences may be pure evil and we would rightfully want them eliminated. But our first order of business is finding a long term solution to the stability problem."

"There's only one solution, Garry," Jasmina answered. "Look at the setup of the board: We as Evolveds are bound only by the laws of physics. Money, energy, atoms, we have control over all of that on the Earth, but for the limits we impose on ourselves. It will be a long time before there's stability in power structures—probably not until nearly everyone on the planet joins us, which will be decades. Eons of our time. Geography is our enemy—for either kind of humans to survive we're all too geographically close to bring the real limit into play. The speed of light. Therefore—"

"Space," Jasmina said.

"Each a planet of our own, eh?" Kasymov said.

"That's too lonely," Weston said, thinking of Winnie, looking longingly at Jasmina.

"Families, at least," Jasmina said, looking at Weston. "Large groups, if history is any indicator. We can stay within the solar system, or expand beyond it if we need that much distance between us."

"Until we defeat the speed of light," Kasymov warned.

"It buys us time, at least. Plenty of—space—resources—for us all. No need for aggression."

Kasymov gave a curt nod. "Then my work here is done, and I shall retire back to being merely a grouchy old chess player. If you need me, I shall return. Nonetheless, please give my resources to those who need it more. Adieu—" And he blinked out.

"It's just us," Weston said looking around. The room was empty, both virtually and physically.

"Well, there are a few billion others out there waiting to get into our cozy eternity here."

Their bodies healed enough now to stand, he disconnected they physical wires he no longer needed to connect, went to her and pulled her up. "So they can wait a *couple* minutes," he said, and he took her in his arms and began an eternal kiss.

CHAPTER 65

S ib sat next to Chris on the steps in front of the Trevi fountain, to all appearances a normal human. The fountain had been restored, the char marks from the nuclear conflagration cleaned. Chris could smell the clean water as it splashed and burbled. The DIs had used their new-found (but to them now ancient) abilities at shaping matter to restore the buildings and other physical objects that made up a city, down to the knicknacks on the store shelves and flowers in the window planters. The Vatican was as it stood, restored molecularly verbatim down to Michaelangelo's brushstrokes in the Sistine Chapel. The invisible guards again shouted *"silencio!"* to the chattering tourists. The DIs had restored all the cities that had been destroyed, their restoration appearing to observers in realtime like time-lapse videos of old. The hundreds of millions of people who had been killed they could not replace; or, rather, agreed not to replace. While the DIs had physical renderings of the planet and could recreate the physical bodies of the dead, without uploads of their minds it was mutually agreed they would be the last generation of humans to die without choice.

They sat facing the fountain, Chris's arm stretched behind Sib on the stone wall. Almost around her. He felt the heat of her body, and smelled her perfume, as undetectably close to a real human body as he could tell with his limited human senses.

"It's beautiful," she said.

"I'm glad it could be recreated. You DIs redeemed yourself a little."

"We appreciate art, too, you know. It's in our nature. There's so much out there for you to see, Chris. Not just the rebuilt Earth, but there are wondrous new structures as well, here on Earth and in space. DIs have a human sense of beauty. I want to take you to see the flower cities in China, where all the structures are made of living plants, and the spires of Atlantis under the sea, which grow and morph as living art while you watch them."

"I saw a report, what we used to call the news, for us old fogie pre-evolved humans. It said in Atlantis there are people who wear mythical figures as bodies, centaurs, unicorns, and the like."

She created a miniature view before him, three dimensional, as if a window to another place had been opened in the air before him. "This is the Mall of the Ancients in Atlantis right now," she said. "There's a gryphon taxi landing and a family of Gorgons eating ice cream." Chris could see the ceiling of the dome covering Atlantis on the seabed in the reflection, thirty meter sea serpents swimming past and the famous spires beyond the dome growing like crystals and coalescing together like melting ice cream. It was hard to fathom from the small view that they were a kilometer tall. Beyond being art it was said they had assorted functions as well, unfathomable to pre-evolved humans.

Chris watched for a while, mesmerized by the joyous cacophony of bells and the people milling around them at the Trevi fountain. Most were in their finest clothes, for this was Easter Sunday and this year it held an unusually special meaning for those who had survived. Many recognized the pair and, honoring their private-mode setting, quietly smiled, nodded, or blinked their thanks. Chris wondered which of them were real humans, like himself, and which were constructions like Sib. By agreement among the three groups of the newly formed United Species—pre-evolved and Evolved humans, and the DIs—for at least a hundred years the Earth would remain largely unenhanced. Human appearing bodies and behaviors would be required in almost all of the surface of the Earth, from major cities to the uncharted corners of the Amazon. A few hard to access areas, such as the deep sea bottom and wilds of the Himalayas, would be open for Evolveds and DIs to create playgrounds, research areas, or for whatever inexplicable purposes they might have. Pre-evolveds would be welcome so long as they accepted the nature of the place, and that a six-armed purple sasquatch at the next table might eat basilisk-stuffed cipactli (and try not to be eaten by it). Or any of an infinititude of happenings stranger yet.

Many pre-evolveds visited one of the evolved playgrounds to up-convert. "Look," Sib said pointing to an area of the Mall of the Ancients. It glowed where she was indicating so Chris could see. "She's a pre-evolved," she said, referring to a woman of perhaps eighty in a floater chair. She raised up her arms in what had become a symbolic gesture, both arms raised to the heavens and face upward. Chris knew at that moment she was making the mental wish to become Evolved. Her body winked out. Chris knew he had but to make that wish himself.

Pre-evolveds on Earth could fight wars or do what they wished, as if the DIs and Evolveds had never existed, though the impetus for war had vanished. It would make it hard to raise armies when any soldier could wish him or herself into an Evolved.

Orbital space platforms provided for even more varied arenas and rapidly constructed spaceships, extruded from whole cloth out of atoms floating by, had already launched for destinations within the solar system and without. Faster means of reaching the stars would likely mean others would be there first, but those so embarking as the first wave did so for the adventure.

In a hundred years the United Species government (or whatever successor might then exist) would revisit the matter of the Earth, after all current pre-evolveds had either died of natural causes or taken steps to prolong their life. Children would be born during that time, but would grow up in a world that, while looking like the world of their parents, would nonetheless be fundamentally different. It was considered likely among the statisticians, pollsters, Cassandras and Oracles that the Earth would remain unaltered, given that there was space enough for all combinations.

"'But we'll always have Paris,'" Sib quoted.

"What if some crazy DI blows it all up? I mean, all of it. Like they almost did before."

"I shouldn't tell you this, since we don't tell pre-evolveds, but we can recreate the Earth instantly now, without your heart skipping a beat. It's happened three times in the last hour."

"'Boys will be boys' and you just put the toys back together?"

"No need for punishment. You'll come to understand. We all won the race."

"I do understand. I'm just not ready."

"Ah. You're still trying to reconcile it with your God. Do you still have your Doubt?"

"I have no doubts there exist powers much greater than me," he said. "Beyond that, it's getting hard to tell. I hope and very much want whoever exercises their power to do so for the good of all. I hope—I even think, a little—" he held up his fingers, close—"that we are on a path to great compassion and love. Love is infinite.

"I've come to realize what I thought was my calling—my search for Jobs—was a manifestation of my Doubt: That I would be 'cured' of my Doubt when I found and described all the Jobs, to help others with their doubt too... That by showing the magnificent breadth of God's work my Doubt would also vanish.

"I understand now my Doubt was really not about the Church— for there is much good it can do, if rid of false prophets—but about my doubting the limits of my God: whether humans as godlike creators—and just look at everything we've created with our tool building!—were in fact the God we prayed to. I realize I feared that there was no God, just man creating God in his own image.

"The war has taught me that there is still room in my heart for an all-powerful, all-loving God. Even though DI's can have souls, and even though humans can become digitally as powerful as the classical Greek gods, we still have limits. We may be gods with a little 'g', but we are not my God.

"It was shame at my own flaws and a need to be perfected that fanned the flames of my Doubt.

"Which is all to say I have less doubt now. Though I find an empty place. My Doubt was, in some way, an anchor, a rock that I clung to."

She nodded. "So where do you go from here?"

"For me? There is much forgiveness that needs shepherding. I feel the need to mourn for the millions who just died."

"They're the last people to die unwillingly. They went to your heaven, isn't that your way?"

"Of course. 'And God will wipe away every tear from their eyes. And death shall be no more. And neither mourning, nor crying out, nor grief shall be anymore. For the first things have passed away.' Which raises so many other questions. If everyone is immortal, what becomes of Heaven? Is *this* heaven? If so, why is there still suffering? If not, what becomes of Heaven? Everyone is asking me, as if I have some special insight."

"What do you tell them? What does become of your Heaven?" she asked.

"A slow down of immigration? I haven't had time to think straight."

She smiled. "They say if you throw a coin into the fountain you'll return to Rome."

He rubbed his eyes. "I used to come here a lot as a boy with my family," Chris said. "We'd make a day trip of it, come down from Venice. I've thrown a lot of coins in — and other things." He grinned. "I've always come back."

"Young lovers come here often too." She nodded toward the many couples sitting and drinking sips from the small fountain on the left, the fountain of lovers. It was legend that couples who drank from it would remain forever faithful.

"And old," he said, smiling at some senior citizens throwing coins over their shoulders and cupping sips of water to their mouth with their hands. "And you are persistent."

"I feel like a real girl on a date."

"Well," — Chris gave a little cough — "let's take things slowly." Chris and Sib had had long conversations about the Church's relaxation of the celibacy rule for those who had proven God's hand had inspired their love. If there was any case, each knew this was such a one. But the College of Cardinals had yet to convene the conclave to elect the new pope, and Chris felt it might be best to wait a short while before announcing his intention to marry. Surely, he thought, the other cardinals would not be so foolish as to elect him pope, but one or two *had* made not so subtle inquiries. Even Canini's people. There was a whole new world — a universe — of DIs and Evolveds to deal with and for some reason they thought he was an expert.

She poked him playfully. "I know, you like being a human, you slow-poke. I can wait."

"I know you can. With an infinite amount of time before one, even a hundred years is functionally zero. Yes, I know the math."

"Or a thousand. Or a million."

"Crap, I can't think on that time frame."

"Don't worry, it will come. It will feel natural in time. Normal is what our brains tell us is normal. You will learn how infinitely much time you have and how infinitely much you don't know."

"That's a truly frightening thought."

"No, they say knowing how much you don't know is maturity. Thinking you know it all is the child."

Chris squinted and his spex space layout appeared before his eyes, but without the need of spex. Some still chose to wear spex to feel the comfort of normality, but Chris had taken the first baby step of allowing the omnipresent QM mesh to act as his virtual spex. He had only to think a query and the results appeared.

"Speaking of children," she said.

"Whoa, it's waaaay too soon to speak of children," he said. Out of the corner of his eye he thought he saw a boy who looked like Fabian, but when he looked he was gone.

"I will want to have many, that's true," she said, "but that's not what I was going to say. I wanted to report on the progress of science that the DIs and Evolveds are working on. They—well, all of us—we, the Ascended—do you like that name?—we have solved the space-time, détente, and checks and balances problems that plagued us. There will no longer be any resource problems. 'The bonds of heaven are slipp'd, dissolved, and loosed.'—Shakespeare. Just moments ago they announced that we all, speaking in the massively plural sense, are the proud parents of the first baby universe." She gave him a squeeze. "Isn't it a wonderful time to be alive?"

ABOUT THE AUTHOR

Dr. Andrew Burt (www.aburt.com) has lots of published science fiction and is a former Vice President of the Science Fiction and Fantasy Writers Association. He's been a computer science professor (specializing in AI, networking, security, privacy, and social issues); founder of Nyx.net, the world's first free internet service provider; CEO of custom software developer TechSoft, and a technology consultant/author/speaker. For a hobby, he constructs solutions to the world's problems. Fortunately, nobody listens.

More books from Andrew Burt are available at: https://ReAnimus.com/store/?author=Andrew Burt

ReAnimus Press

Breathing Life into Great Books

If you enjoyed this book we hope you'll tell others or write a review! We also invite you to subscribe to our newsletter to learn about our new releases and join our affiliate program (where you earn 30% of sales you recommend) at www.ReAnimus.com.

Here are more ebooks you'll enjoy from ReAnimus Press, available from ReAnimus Press's web site, Amazon.com, bn.com, etc.:

Simulations and Reality in WYSIWYG Universes, by Andrew Burt

Info/buy:

We're living in a Simulated Universe? Are you sure? And if we're not...

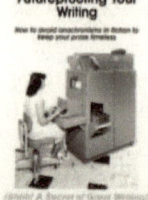

Futureproofing Your Writing, by Andrew Burt

Info/buy:

How to avoid anachronisms in fiction to keep your prose timeless.

Having Relationships With Characters on the Road to Great Fiction, by Andrew Burt

Info/buy:

(Shhh! A Secret of Great Writing)

Critiquing the Wild Writer: It's Not What You Say, But How You Say It, by Andrew Burt

Info/buy:

How to write effective critiques, by the founder of the first workshop on the web.

Noontide Night

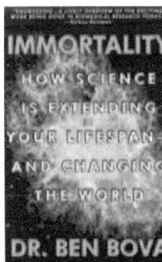

Immortality, by Ben Bova

Info/buy:

Dr. Bova explores the future effects of science and technology on the human life span. Death will no longer be the inevitable end of life.

The Exiles Trilogy, by Ben Bova

Info/buy:

When all the best of Earth's scientists are exiled to a space station, they decide to embark on an even grander adventure to the stars. An epic trilogy in one volume.

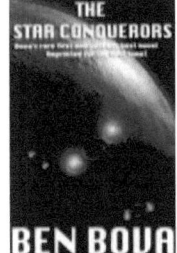

The Star Conquerors (Collectors' Edition), by Ben Bova

Info/buy:

Special Collectors' Edition! Six time Hugo winner Ben Bova's most sought-after novel is now an ebook with the original Mel Hunter cover and an essay from Ben on the history of the book!

The Star Conquerors (Standard Edition), by Ben Bova

Info/buy:

Six time Hugo winner Ben Bova's most sought-after novel is back in print!

Colony, by Ben Bova

Info/buy:

Island One is a celestial utopia, and David Adams is its most perfect creation. But David is a prisoner, destined to spend his life in an island-sized cylinder orbiting a doomed home planet. David has a plan—one that will ultimately save humanity... or destroy it.

The Kinsman Saga, by Ben Bova

Info/buy:

Chet Kinsman is an astronaut ace who has done everything in space—including committing the first murder. Kinsman has to confront his hidden past and decide Earth's destiny, in a desperate countdown to nuclear annihilation.

Phoenix Without Ashes, by Harlan Ellison and Edward Bryant

Info/buy:

Co-written with Harlan Ellison and based on the award-winning script, the story of mankind's last salvation gone awry.

Shadrach in the Furnace, by Robert Silverberg

Info/buy:

Meet the new Khan! Soon to be immortal... A Hugo and Nebula Award Finalist novel from a Grand Master of science fiction.

Bloom, by Wil McCarthy

Info/buy:

In 2106, microscopic machine/creatures escape their creators to populate the inner solar system with a wild, deadly ecology all their own, pushing the tattered remnants of humanity out into the cold and dark of the outer planets. Seven astronauts must embark on mankind's boldest venture yet—the perilous journey home to infected Earth!

Aggressor Six, by Wil McCarthy

Info/buy:

An alien armada from the center of Orion makes its deadly way through the galaxy, destroying all human life in the process, and only Marine Corporal Kenneth Jonson and the Aggressor Six team can stop the onslaught.

Murder in the Solid State, by Wil McCarthy

Info/buy:

David Sanger, an ambitious young physicist, attends a party at which a pompous older scientist, who just happens to have thwarted the younger man's innovative ideas, is murdered. Suddenly it is not just David's career, but his life that is at stake. Are his ideas that important? Who's out to stop David from changing the world?

Flies from the Amber, by Wil McCarthy

Info/buy:

Forty light years from earth, the colonists on the world of Unua have somehow managed to keep civilization struggling on, despite twice daily earthquakes...

Star Bridge, by James Gunn and Jack Williamson

Info/buy:

James Gunn and Jack Williamson's celebrated classic space opera

Transcendental - The Trilogy, by James Gunn

Info/buy:

Not all the pilgrims are what they seem on their quest for transcendence

Pilgrims to Transcendence, by James Gunn

Info/buy:

Not all the pilgrims are what they seem on their quest for transcendence

Walls and Wonders, by S. R. Algernon

Info/buy:

Hugo finalist... If Hemingway wrote P.K.Dick-ian science fiction short stories...

The Unborn, by Brian Herbert

Info/buy:

In the summer of 2097, Riggio wakes up with amnesia--and his lover dead in their bed.

The Assassination of Billy Jeeling, by Brian Herbert

Info/buy:

From the New York Times Bestselling author of the DUNE series comes a spectacular science fiction novel.

The Living Labyrinth, by Ian Stewart and Tim Poston

Info/buy:

Sam, Jane, Felix, Elzabet, Tinka & Marco go quantum jumping on their path to galactic citizenship, only to end up in a very strange place indeed!

Rock Star, by Tim Poston and Ian Stewart

Info/buy:

The awesome sequel to The Living Labyrinth. It's all fun and games with syntei until they fall into the wrong hands...

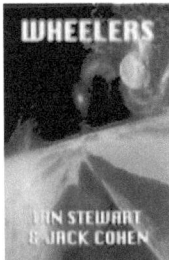

Wheelers, by Ian Stewart and Jack Cohen

Info/buy:

Alien artifacts found on Callisto...

Manhattan Transfer, by John E. Stith

Info/buy:

Aliens kidnap Manhattan; read all about it!

Reunion on Neverend, by John E. Stith

Info/buy:

A man returning for a high school reunion on a distant colony finds an old flame in trouble—trouble that he's uniquely qualified to deal with.

Redshift Rendezvous, by John E. Stith

Info/buy:

One man must stop starship hijackers from using an unusual starship to plunder a wealthy colony.

Star Watchmen, by Ben Bova

Info/buy:

Mankind rules a giant galactic empire, but not all the worlds are pleased. Can the Star Watch prevent a revolt?

As on a Darkling Plain, by Ben Bova

Info/buy:

Dr. Sidney Lee races against time to prevent the huge alien machines on Titan from destroying mankind.

The Winds of Altair, by Ben Bova

Info/buy:

Altair VI isn't making it easy to Terraform!

Test of Fire, by Ben Bova

Info/buy:

A small group of survivors fight to rebuild civilization after the Earth is devastated by a huge solar flare.

The Weathermakers, by Ben Bova

Info/buy:

After conquering everything else, the last frontier was... controlling Mother Nature! By the award-winning hard SF author of the Grand Tour series.

The Dueling Machine, by Ben Bova

Info/buy:

Civilized, harmless virtual reality dueling has replaced all physical conflict — everything from punching someone over a personal insult to interstellar warfare... until a madman dictator of a small empire finds a way to cheat, and use the dueling machine to take over the galaxy!

The Multiple Man, by Ben Bova

Info/buy:

As the President is speaking inside an auditorium in Boston, the President's Press Secretary discovers a body in an alley outside: The body of the President.

Escape!, by Ben Bova

Info/buy:

No end to Danny's sentence, watched by a sentient computer, and no way out of the escape-proof prison, there was only one thing to do...

Forward in Time, by Ben Bova

Info/buy:

Get ready for a series of future shocks from the award-winning Ben Bova!

Maxwell's Demons, by Ben Bova
Info/buy:

Science fiction and science fact, humor and adventure, all await when you enter the unpredictable world of... MAXWELL'S DEMONS

Twice Seven, by Ben Bova
Info/buy:

Ben Bova's universe is always more than the sum of its parts...

The Astral Mirror, by Ben Bova
Info/buy:

Here are a dozen and a half views of the world, past present and future, as seen through the Astral Mirror....

The Story of Light, by Ben Bova
Info/buy:

In this all-encompassing work, Ben Bova explores the subject of light and shows how it has shaped every aspect of our existence.

Space Travel - A Science Fiction Writer's Guide, by Ben Bova, with Anthony R. Lewis
Info/buy:

An indispensible tool for all science fiction writers, Space Travel explains the science you need to help you make your fiction plausible.

The Craft of Writing Science Fiction that Sells, by Ben Bova

Info/buy:

Learn how to write SF from the master! Ben Bova, best-selling author and six-time Hugo Award winner for Best Editor explains step by step all the elements you need to write professionally selling science fiction.

Vengeance of Orion, by Ben Bova

Info/buy:

Orion must travel back in time to change history and save Troy from the Greek army, or lose the only woman he has ever loved.

Orion in the Dying Time, by Ben Bova

Info/buy:

Time-traveling into the era of the dinosaurs, Orion must save the very fabric of spacetime from the satanic reptilian leader of the saurians.

Orion and the Conqueror, by Ben Bova

Info/buy:

Orion travels to the time of Alexander the Great, battling to save the future of mankind, and his own soul.

Orion Among the Stars, by Ben Bova

Info/buy:

The superhuman, time-traveling Orion leads interstellar warriors in a galactic war among the gods themselves.

The Starcrossed, by Ben Bova

Info/buy:

A stinging SFnal, futuristic satire on the TV industry, based a bit on reality.

To Save The Sun, by Ben Bova and A. J. Austin

Info/buy:

Earth's sun will soon explode, unless a massive engineering effort can save it.

The Gate of Worlds, by Robert Silverberg

Info/buy:

An Alternate History adventure in the modern day Turkish and Aztec Empires.

Conquerors from the Darkness, by Robert Silverberg

Info/buy:

Long after the earth has been conquered by aliens and flooded, Dovirr Stargan longs to become one of the pirate-like Sea Lords.

Time of the Great Freeze, by Robert Silverberg

Info/buy:

ICE AGE--NEW YORK CITY 2650 A.D. UNDERGROUND!

Enter a Soldier. Later: Another, by Robert Silverberg

Info/buy:

Hugo Award Winner, from an SF Grandmaster!

The Longest Way Home, by Robert Silverberg

Info/buy:

The planet's locals have risen up, trapping young Joseph thousands of miles from home.

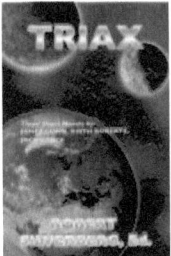

Triax, by Robert Silverberg, James Gunn, Keith Roberts, Jack Vance

Info/buy:

Three original short science fiction novels by legends in the genre

The Alien Years, by Robert Silverberg

Info/buy:

"The ultimate alien invasion novel"

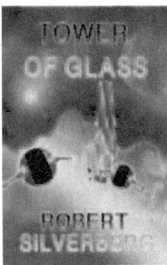

Tower of Glass, by Robert Silverberg

Info/buy:

Aliens have sent a mysterious signal, which Simeon Krug is determined to answer.

Hot Sky at Midnight, by Robert Silverberg

Info/buy:

Greed comes home to roost in a future Earth and her colonies, and the rene-gades look to take over. One of Silverberg's finest.

The New Springtime, by Robert Silverberg

Info/buy:

Humans emerge to reclaim Earth after the Long Winter, but never anticipated what awaits...

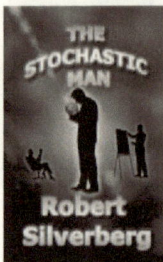

The Stochastic Man, by Robert Silverberg

Info/buy:

Lew Nichols uses statistical methods to guess trends--then meets a man who can actually see the future.

Thorns, by Robert Silverberg

Info/buy:

Beauty and the Beast in the solar colonies

Kingdoms of the Wall, by Robert Silverberg

Info/buy:

Not all is at it seems on pilgrimages up the gigantic mountain called The Wall

Challenge for a Throne, by Robert Silverberg

Info/buy:

The real life Game of Thrones, and basis George R.R. Martin used for the GoT series.

Scientists and Scoundrels, by Robert Silverberg

Info/buy:

A good-humored tour through scientific frauds and how they were exposed.

Deep Quarry, by John E. Stith

Info/buy:

A private eye uncovers a long-buried starship...that's still occupied.

Memory Blank, by John E. Stith

Info/buy:

Cal Donley regains consciousness on the beautiful orbital colony Daedalus—but Cal doesn't remember leaving Earth, or his name or the past dozen years!

Reckoning Infinity, by John E. Stith

Info/buy:

A riveting exploration of what it means to be an alien... Explorers inside a moon-sized alien ship must find its secrets before it kills them.

Death Tolls, by John E. Stith

Info/buy:

A great science fiction mystery: Dan sees the telecast from Mars where his brother dies—and it's not an accident. Why is a certain reporter uncannily at each disaster so quickly?

Scapescope, by John E. Stith

Info/buy:

Brother Sammy Wants YOU! In prison. For something you haven't done yet.

All for Naught, by John E. Stith

Info/buy:

Nick Naught, private eye, walks down some strange mean streets, in an action-packed comedy set in the future.

In Search of the Big Bang, by John Gribbin

Info/buy:

For Big Bang Theory fans, don't miss this indispensable guide! :) 'A remarkably readable guide to the mysteries of cosmic creation' —Nature

Cosmic Coincidences, by John Gribbin and Martin Rees

Info/buy:

A provocative search through space and time for a cosmic blueprint—and the source of life in the universe.

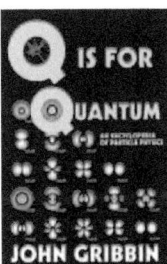

Q is for Quantum, by John Gribbin

Info/buy:

A comprehensive encyclopedia of quantum physics.

Ice Age, by John and Mary Gribbin

Info/buy:

The theory that came in from the cold...

In Search of the Double Helix, by John Gribbin

Info/buy:

Unraveling the mystery of life on earth...

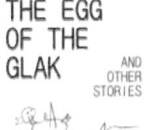

The Egg of the Glak, by Harvey Jacobs

Info/buy:

Some of Harvey's best, believably fantastical short stories.

A Guide to Barsoom, by John Flint Roy

Info/buy:

THE OFFICIAL, DEFINITIVE GUIDE TO EDGAR RICE BURROUGH'S BARSOOM. Everything there is to know about John Carter of Mars and his world — the people, places and things, with maps and fully illustrated.

The Best of Edward M. Lerner, by Edward M. Lerner

Info/buy:

The gateway book to all of Ed's many worlds. Read this one first!

Probe, by Edward M. Lerner

Info/buy:

What if First Contact doesn't come the way we expect it—or with the sort of aliens we expect?

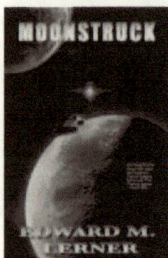

Moonstruck, by Edward M. Lerner

Info/buy:

The space program becomes a quaint relic when aliens make contact with Earth...

Jewels of the Dragon, by Allen L. Wold

Info/buy:

The greatest of treasures awaits... on the deadliest of planets.

Crown of the Serpent, by Allen L. Wold

Info/buy:

In farthest space lie hidden fortunes... and unknown enemies.

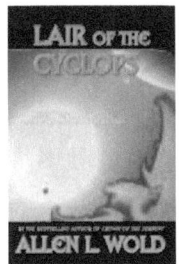

Lair of the Cyclops, by Allen L. Wold

Info/buy:

Rickard Braeth and friends must find the galaxy's secret—before it's used to destroy everything!

The Planet Masters, by Allen L. Wold

Info/buy:

Troubleshooter Larson McCade searches for the alien Book of Aradka on the planet Seltique, and may find more than he bargained for.

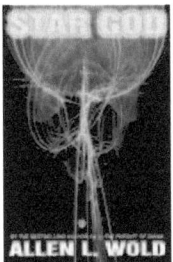

Star God, by Allen L. Wold

Info/buy:

There is a strange force at work in the universe. It must be stopped. But first, it must be understood.

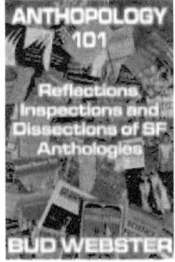

Anthopology 101: Reflections, Inspections and Dissections of SF Anthologies, by Bud Webster

Info/buy:

Bud expertly dissects the great SF anthologies. A must for writers and SF fans.

Woman Without a Shadow, by Karen Haber

Info/buy:

War Minstrels #1. Kayla, an extraordinarily gifted young telepath, is on the run after challenging the most powerful families on her home planet, who've tried to take everything from her.

The Sweet Taste of Regret, by Karen Haber

Info/buy:

Live anywhere you want... in any time... A collection of Karen Haber's best short fiction.

The Science of Middle-earth, by Henry Gee

Info/buy:

How did Frodo's mithril coat ward off the fatal blow of an orc? Can Balrogs fly? Nature editor Dr. Henry Gee explains how. A must-read for Tolkien fans.

Commencement, by Roby James

Info/buy:

The Sting was what made Ronica McBride special—now she was crashed on an unknown planet without it.

Xenostorm: Rising, by Brian Clegg

Info/buy:

14 year old Davy finds himself facing a powerful underground group who have lived for hundreds of years—and want to see him dead. The future of human existence is in the balance...

The Cure for Everything, by Severna Park

Info/buy:

Finding the cure for all diseases comes with a heavy price. Nebula Award winner!

Ghosts of Engines Past, by Sean McMullen

Info/buy:

Award winning steampunk from a master!

Colours of the Soul, by Sean McMullen

Info/buy:

Why are cheetahs the most perfect of creatures? Besides because they're cats, that is... Cool, mind-blowing stories from a master.

The Gilded Basilisk, by Chet Gottfried

Info/buy:

Add a basilisk, a dragon, and weirdragons to the mix-up of a theft going from bad to worse: Friends become enemies and enemies friends, wars loom, and the intrigues threaten the fate of two kingdoms.

Einar and the Cursed City, by Chet Gottfried

Info/buy:

Sixteen-year-old Einar enters Jorghaven for dueling and desserts, but a curse has changed everyone except Barbara Bloodbath, who needs his help to free the city!

Neon Twilight, by Edward Bryant

Info/buy:

Neon Twilight by Edward Bryant : Three wonderful space opera stories, including Ed's Berserker story!

Particle Theory, by Edward Bryant
Info/buy:

Particle Theory by Edward Bryant : A collection of many of Ed's best works, including two Nebula Award winning short stories.

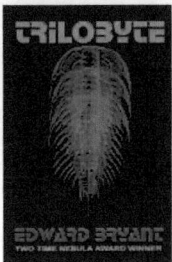

Trilobyte, by Edward Bryant
Info/buy:

A trio of twisted little tales from the master of twistedness.

Cinnabar, by Edward Bryant
Info/buy:

In the city at the center of time, paradox is just another urban renewal project.

Predators and Other Stories, by Edward Bryant
Info/buy:

Troubling tales as only Ed Bryant can tell. Don't miss the author introductions!

Timeshare, by Joshua Dann
Info/buy:

Have you ever wished you could go back to the good old days? At Timeshare Unlimited, you can.

Bug Jack Barron, by Norman Spinrad

Info/buy:

GET SET FOR THE BEST THING THAT EVER HAPPENED TO YOU! The banned book is back! You've heard of it, now you can read it! Lover and hero, Jack Barron, troubleshooter and media god of the Bug Jack Barron Show, has one last chance to hit it big when he meets Benedict Howards, the power-mad man with the secret to immortality. A Hugo and Nebula Award finalist!

The Void Captain's Tale, by Norman Spinrad

Info/buy:

Symbiotically linked to her ship, Void Pilot Dominique Alia Wu senses something transcendent in the void...

The Last Hurrah of the Golden Horde, by Norman Spinrad

Info/buy:

"One of the greatest collections of science fiction short stories ever" — Goodreads.com

Costigan s Needle, by Jerry Sohl

Info/buy:

What really was Dr. Costigan's tool for medical research? Where did the eye of the needle actually lead to?

The Mars Monopoly, by Jerry Sohl

Info/buy:

One of the famous Ace Doubles, with the wonderful original cover, The Mars Monopoly still stands today as a great, fun story in the classic style.

One Against Herculum, by Jerry Sohl

Info/buy:

One of the famous Ace Doubles, with the wonderful original cover, One Against Herculum remains a fast-paced, fun story that you'll really enjoy.

Underhanded Chess, by Jerry Sohl

Info/buy:

A hilarious handbook of devious diversions and stratagems for winning at chess.

Innocents Abroad (Fully Illustrated & Enhanced Collectors' Edition), by Mark Twain

Info/buy:

Best. Travel. Book. Ever. (With all original illustrations.) Hilarious book about the first cruise from the US, visiting the Med.

Local Knowledge (A Kieran Lenahan Mystery), by Conor Daly

Info/buy:

Lawyer-turned-golf pro Kieran Lenahan must solve the murder of millionaire country-club owner Sylvester Miles. "A FAST-PACED MYSTERY"—THE NEW YORK TIMES

A Mother's Trial, by Nancy Wright

Info/buy:

Was it the perfect murder? A true story.

Bad Karma: A True Story of Obsession and Murder, by Deborah Blum

Info/buy:

The true story of a famous Berkeley murder and a landmark Supreme Court case.

The Box: An Oral History of Television, 1920-1961, by Jeff Kisseloff

Info/buy:

"Wondrous... An oral scrapbook of the pioneering days of our video nation"—The New York Times Book Review

You Must Remember This: An Oral History of Manhattan from the 1890s to World War II, by Jeff Kisseloff

Info/buy:

Amazing stories of Manhattan from those who lived them.

Side Effects, by Harvey Jacobs

Info/buy:

Vonnegut meets Catch-22! In the last hours of his hectic life, Simon Apple faces up to the hard truth that his very survival represents a prescription for disaster, not only for the pharmaceutical industry but for the nation itself! From award-winning author Harvey Jacobs.

The Sigil Trilogy (Omnibus vol.1-3), by Henry Gee

Info/buy:

The amazing Sigil Trilogy complete in one volume!